Sabrina Jeffries is the *N_____ _____ling* author of more than 50 novels and wor_____ the pseudonyms Deb_____

Whatever time not s_____ country or writing in_____ith her husband and a_____r passions – jigsaw puzz___, _____

With over 9 million books in print in more than 20 languages, the North Carolina author never regrets tossing aside a budding career in academics (she has a Ph.D. in English literature) for the sheer joy of writing fun fiction, and hopes that one day a book of hers will end up saving the world. She always dreams big.

For more information, visit her at **www.sabrinajeffries.com**, on Facebook at **/SabrinaJeffriesAuthor**, on Instagram **@authorsabrinajeffries**, or on X **@SabrinaJeffries**.

Praise for Sabrina Jeffries, queen of the sexy regency romance:

'Complex, intense characters heat up the pages with scintillating love scenes amid the intrigue. Jeffries continues to impress' *Publishers Weekly*

'Quick wit, lively repartee, and delicious sensuality drive the elaborate plot of this sinfully delightful addition to Jeffries's latest series' *Library Journal* (starred review)

'The women she writes are spirited, intelligent, devilish, brave, independent and politically and culturally savvy. They are true heroines' *Bookpage*

'Another exemplary Regency-set historical brilliantly sourced from her seemingly endless authorial supply of fascinating characters and compelling storylines' *Booklist*

'Sabrina Jeffries is an absolute artist with Regency romance' *Fresh Fiction*

'Sparkling banter, unique hero and heroine, and intriguing mystery make it irresistible' *Austenprose* (5 star review)

'Master storyteller Jeffries is at the top of her game' *RT Book Reviews*

ACCIDENTALLY HIS

Sabrina Jeffries

HEADLINE
ETERNAL

Published by arrangement with Zebra Books,
an imprint of Kensington Publishing Corp.

First published in Great Britain in 2024
by HEADLINE ETERNAL
An imprint of HEADLINE PUBLISHING GROUP

1

Cataloguing in Publication Data is available from the British Library

ISBN 978 1 4722 8865 3

Offset in 11.33/12.98 pt Times New Roman PS Pro by Jouve (UK), Milton Keynes

Printed and bound in Great Britain by Clays Ltd, Elcograf S.p.A.

Headline's policy is to use papers that are natural, renewable and recyclable
products and made from wood grown in well-managed forests and other
controlled sources. The logging and manufacturing processes are expected
to conform to the environmental regulations of the country of origin.

HEADLINE PUBLISHING GROUP
An Hachette UK Company
Carmelite House
50 Victoria Embankment
London EC4Y 0DZ

www.headlineeternal.com
www.headline.co.uk
www.hachette.co.uk

*For Wendell Williams and Julie Brennan,
and all of my autistic son's many other caregivers
through the years. Thank you for your hard work,
dedication, and loving care. I know Nick appreciates it,
and his parents definitely appreciate it! Y'all are the best!*

Chapter 1

London
August 1812

Colonel Raphael Wolfford nodded a greeting as Sir Lucius Fitzgerald settled into the carriage seat opposite him. While the carriage rumbled on, the spymaster surveyed Rafe with a keen eye.

Rafe arched an eyebrow. "Perhaps I should have worn my uniform."

"Why start now? On the Peninsula, you were always some Spanish peasant or Irish mercenary or whoever you needed to be to unearth French secrets. You're the only soldier I've ever known to dress as a Jack in the Green to gain intelligence. So tonight, you're better off playing who you actually are for once: heir presumptive to a viscount."

Rafe gave a rueful chuckle. "I've always heard that ladies prefer a man in uniform."

"Not these ladies. If they see a uniform, they'll assume you're the spare, not the heir, and that wouldn't suit the purposes of your plan, now, would it?"

"Probably not."

"Besides, we don't want anyone knowing you're still a commissioned officer. Or that you've been in England over a year and a half." Sir Lucius removed his pocket watch to check the time. "So, are you absolutely sure about attending this event as your true self?"

"Yes." Even if he still wasn't sure who his *true self* might be. "I see no other way to continue this investigation."

"You understand that your proposed scheme is uncertain at best and dangerous at worst."

Rafe shrugged. "Uncle Constantine risked his life to uncover the truth, so the least I can do is risk mine." Instinctively, he smoothed a hand over the secret pocket in his breeches that held the blade he carried everywhere. "Though I don't see the danger in it, honestly. My uncle was using an alias when he was shot, so it's not as if the damned spy for the French knows who Uncle Constantine is, and thus who I am to him."

"We can't be certain of that. Constantine can't tell us if he was recognized as General Wolfford . . . or even if he was forced to reveal his identity in order to make headway in his investigation. Hence, my worry about the danger."

A pistol shot to the head of Rafe's uncle a year and a half ago had put an end to Constantine's inquiries, leaving the old general a bedridden prisoner to demented ravings. That would not be Rafe, damn it.

"Yes, well, after the most recent information we received, I have to do *something* more," Rafe said. "Going about incognito hasn't worked. I need to infiltrate that nest of vipers to find and unmask the culprit."

Sir Lucius eyed him askance. "Is that what you consider the Harper sisters and Elegant Occasions to be—a nest of vipers?"

"Not them," Rafe said irritably. "Their involvement in treasonous activity is tangential at best, although I still haven't ruled out Lady Foxstead's new husband. But their father, his servants, and possibly even their mother and her new husband undoubtedly have a hand in it."

"That's what your uncle believed, at any rate."

"And no one could ever say he lacked for good instincts in intelligence work. He taught me everything I know."

Just not enough. Rafe gazed out the window at the passing oil lamps, which shed about as much light as his spying on the Harper family from afar had done. Rafe hadn't before encountered a wilier enemy than Osgood Harper, the Earl of Holtbury. The bastard never took a step wrong, as evidenced by his successful divorce from his first wife and marriage to another Society woman. Both spoke to Holtbury's devious ability to use rules, power, and money to his advantage.

It grated on Rafe. "But I still don't know for certain who the spy is. Or where Uncle Constantine hid his notes and most recent reports about it. Or who attacked him when he got too close."

"These things require patience. And you've already succeeded in eliminating people in the Harper family's outer circle as suspects: several of their close friends, the Elegant Occasions butler, a handful of other servants. . . ."

"Yes, but time grows short. Wellington has already suffered setbacks because of this spy. And with Napoleon invading Russia, Wellington must strike hard in the Peninsula while he can."

Sir Lucius tensed. "What did that new Edinburgh physician you consulted say about Constantine's memory?"

"He confirmed what I'd begun to suspect. The old general will never recover his mind. And he may not live much longer, either." Uncle Constantine's work had always consumed him, even after his retirement from the army, so before he died, Rafe wanted him to know his mission had been completed, even if Rafe had to say the words to a man only half-aware of their meaning.

The sudden ache in Rafe's chest made him clench his teeth. As his uncle always said, *Letting your heart rule your head / Is the surest way to end up dead.* Uncle was fond of rhyming rules.

Rafe fought for calm. "That's why I must get inside their inner circle."

"Hence, my concern about the danger."

"It will be worth it if I learn something of value. Taking increasingly greater risks with no result—like at that May Day affair—frustrates me." Especially when his investigation into his late mother wasn't progressing, either.

"You got closer to the earl than ever before at that event."

"For all the good it did me." Rafe huffed out a breath. "Masquerading as a Jack in the Green didn't exactly make it easy to cozy up to the man. Besides which, I was nearly unmasked." By the man's daughter, Lady Verity Harper. The vixen was sometimes too inquisitive for her own good.

"Given your reputation, I find it highly unlikely they would have guessed who you were. Why, you even fooled Beaufort, and their chef knows you well."

"Oh, I took care of the matter, never fear. But it was a near thing," Rafe said. "*You* try slipping onto the grounds of a hunting lodge when the guests are all family and friends, and the only servants or performers are thoroughly inspected by the very people I wish to deceive. It's nothing like entering a ball in the city where I can blend in and people don't all know each other."

Sir Lucius arched an eyebrow. "Are you saying the Chameleon is no longer capable of insinuating himself anywhere he chooses?"

The familiar nickname irked Rafe. Perhaps he'd deserved the moniker on the Peninsula. Or, more likely, that was what happened when bored soldiers amused themselves—their stories of his various exploits grew more legendary with every retelling. Especially since he'd managed to do his work without his true identity being known by anyone but a select few. Wellington. Sir Lucius. His uncle.

Rafe stiffened. "War requires different strategies. Abroad, I was gathering intelligence on the enemy and not on my own countrymen. Even you must admit that any further spying I do on that family will gain me naught until I can become a trusted friend to them."

"By courting Lady Verity."

"Why not? Someone needs to. The woman has been running amok for far too long."

Sir Lucius smirked at him. "Do I detect a trace of irritability in your tone?"

"Not a bit."

Liar. Of course Rafe was irritable. He had a mission, and Lady Verity Harper had been thwarting it. Every bloody time he'd veered close to uncovering some important bit of information, she'd shown up, forcing him to retreat before he could be caught or recognized. It was time he regained control of the situation.

"You think to turn her up sweet," Sir Lucius said, "so she'll tell you whatever you wish to know."

He shrugged. "Every woman in Society wants a husband."

"I wouldn't be too sure about that. Although if you have to court a lady to unmask our quarry, it might as well be a pretty one."

"Her looks have naught to do with it." Granted, he was attracted to the woman. Who wouldn't be? The green-eyed, gamine beauty with golden skin and hair of dark honey kept every fellow guessing . . . and wanting to know more.

Still, her substantial charms notwithstanding, she was his best way in. Particularly since the other two sisters were already married, and happily, from what he'd seen.

Sir Lucius cleared his throat. "Once you enter Society as yourself, it will become considerably more difficult to return to being incognito. You'll lose any advantage you gained from subterfuge, and you'll have to see this to the end, even if it means ruining your reputation as the future Lord Wolfford."

"I don't care." Besides, he'd never really wanted *that* role. When he'd left for the army as an ensign, he'd merely been a general's heir, since Uncle Constantine hadn't yet been given the viscountcy he'd later gained in service to his country. Few of Rafe's fellow soldiers had known him as anyone but an officer with military connections. "I'll have to reveal myself once Uncle Constantine dies, anyway. At least I can get some use out of the revelation."

A sigh escaped Sir Lucius. "I'll admit your timing is impeccable. That upcoming Elegant Occasions event at the seaside gives you the perfect opportunity to examine the family up close."

"I was told even Holtbury's former wife will be there."

"Lady Rumridge."

"Yes," Rafe said. "Talking to her will be my first priority, given her new husband's army rank. *She* could even be the one passing on information. I couldn't ask for a better situation in which to question her than a two-week-long house party spent with her and the other subjects of my investigation."

"Assuming you succeed at getting invited."

Rafe crossed his arms over his chest. "Elegant Occasions wants to introduce some female clients to marriageable gentlemen, and I am eminently marriageable. I'll do what I must to wrangle that invitation. Better still, Exmouth is within a day's journey of Lord Holtbury's estate, so if the courtship progresses well, I can travel there as a friend of the family, possibly even as Lady Verity's fiancé."

Sir Lucius's face darkened. "You don't actually intend to make an offer to Lady Verity, knowing you don't mean to honor it. That would be a level of deception even your uncle would disapprove of."

"True." Although if it came to that . . . No, he knew better than to admit to his superior that he would go so far. Sir Lucius was a gentleman at heart, after all.

But Rafe was a soldier who couldn't bear the thought of his compatriots dying because some aristocrat had decided to sell information about troop movements to England's enemies. "I should hope I know how to flirt with a woman without ending up leg-shackled."

"Do you, now?" Sir Lucius snorted. "If I have any doubts about your plan, it centers around your ability to court a woman of rank. You've rarely encountered them in your profession, and you've never had a mother or sisters to learn from, so where is all this vast knowledge of flirtation coming from?"

Rafe drew himself up stiffly. "I've been around women enough to realize they're no different from men. Show some interest in them and their affairs, and they will tell you whatever you need to know."

His superior laughed outright. "That statement makes my point. Women can be vastly different from men. Most men underestimate them. This isn't some poorly educated servant girl in rural Devonshire or even a wide-eyed eighteen-year-old in the throes of her first Season. This is an earl's daughter with experience running a business. Wooing a clever, sophisticated woman like Lady Verity might take skills you've never needed to develop."

"Perhaps. But she hasn't had a suitor since Lord Minton scandalously rejected her years ago. She'll be happy to be courted at all."

"Or his behavior has made her suspicious of men. You may find her more immune to male attention than you assume."

Rafe scoffed at that. How hard could it be to charm a

woman whose only experience of the world was in the rarefied atmosphere of Society? "Even so, her family will be interested in me *for* her. Surely, they will welcome any respectable suitor and attempt to influence her choice. That alone might gain me an invitation to their house party." He narrowed his gaze on Sir Lucius. "Unless you're concerned they might recognize me from my previous forays."

Sir Lucius waved that off. "There's no chance they even know you exist. I realize playing 'the Chameleon' in polite society has been difficult, but you've managed it successfully thus far, or I would have heard otherwise."

Rafe threw himself back against the squabs. "Well then, unless you have a better plan, this seems my best opportunity for worming my way into their circle."

The spymaster gave him a long, assessing look. "One more thing—rumor has it that Minton has been talking of pursuing Lady Verity again. I gather he's changed his tune now that her sisters have married so well, so you may find yourself competing for her attention."

"Rumors abound in Society—that doesn't make them true. And even if they are, I can handle Minton." In preparing for this, Rafe had made a point of observing the baron, only to find him unworthy of Lady Verity or any other respectable female. "The man's an arse."

"You'll get no argument on that from me." Sir Lucius looked thoughtful. "But she still might have feelings for him. If you run him off, what happens to Lady Verity after you find the spy and end your courtship of her?"

"Whatever happens, she'll be better off than with Minton. Besides, by then, her family will have far more to be concerned about than my failed courtship of her. She might not even *want* to marry me once she learns why I was wooing her."

"We'll see." The man rubbed his chin. "And you still

intend to retire from the army once you find your uncle's attacker?"

"Someone has to look after Uncle Constantine and the Castle Wolfford estate. I'm the only one who can."

Sir Lucius glanced away. "If he lasts until then."

Rafe bit back an oath. The man who'd been the only father Rafe had ever known deserved better. So, Rafe meant to make sure that the villain who'd shot Uncle Constantine paid for it with his—or her—life.

The carriage shuddered to a halt in front of an imposing manor house he'd visited before, although never as himself. Situated across from Hyde Park, it lay upon land belonging to the Duke of Grenwood. Who just happened to be the new husband of the former Lady Diana Harper.

"Are all the Harper sisters attending this charity auction?" Rafe asked.

"I would hope so, given the Grenwoods' hosting of it. Have you come prepared to bid? You must make your attendance appear believable."

"Don't worry," Rafe murmured as his footman opened the door. "I can play the bored, rich lord in search of amusement well enough."

Sir Lucius chuckled. "Not *too* bored or Lady Verity will find you dull. No doubt she and her sisters spend half their days dealing with such fellows."

"I'll see what works and go from there."

After that, there was no more discussion—neither of them dared risk being overheard. But Rafe had his plan laid out. He would use Lady Verity's native curiosity to draw her in, and then would charm her into giving up her family's secrets . . . or at least showing him where to look for them.

What could be easier?

Chapter 2

Lady Verity Harper surveyed the tables for any items that marred her perfect setup: a tartlet abandoned on the white linen, a spill of sauce staining the shine of a silver epergne, a plate of biscuits placed with the savories and not the sweets. This was the best time to do it, since most of the guests were in the ballroom examining goods to be auctioned off to benefit the Foundling Hospital.

As the second—and last—event Elegant Occasions was hosting for the charity this year, they needed to impress Society and raise a great deal of money. Because in October, when she and her sisters held an auction to benefit their other big charity—The Fallen Females of Filmore Farm—they wanted people to be so excited about the possible offerings that they would bid higher for items than they might otherwise.

It was always harder to raise money for charities that helped women of ill repute than ones that helped babies. Much as that annoyed her, she had to acknowledge the difficulty and act accordingly. Hence, her determination to make this auction go extremely well.

"Where do I put the little soufflés, my lady?" one of her brother-in-law's footmen asked.

"One tray should go over by the turkey skewers, and the

other by the marzipan. People are beginning to enter from the auction room."

Once the dining room filled with people, the staff would be in charge of replenishing the tables, and she could get some fresh air. It was rather warm in here.

"All is in readiness, madam. These are the last of the food." The footman set the one tray down where she'd ordered, then paused with the other in his hand. "And there's a Sir Lucius Fitzgerald looking for you. Shall I send him over?"

"Sir Lucius . . . Sir Lucius . . ." She tapped her chin. "Oh! I met him last week." The engaging fellow was a bit older than her other brother-in-law, Lord Foxstead, and an eligible bachelor besides, which would normally put her on her guard.

But as undersecretary to the war minister, Sir Lucius was mainly an important connection she dared not ignore. "Yes, I can speak to him now for a few minutes."

As best she could recall, Sir Lucius was rather good-looking—with black hair cut severely, a firm chin, and incongruously warm blue eyes. Still, she resisted the urge to pat her hair and make sure her curls weren't drooping. A man in government like him would expect a perfect wife. She could never be that. She never *wanted* to be that. She wasn't sure she even wanted to marry anyone, for pity's sake.

So, she kept her hands down and pivoted toward the door, only to find *two* gentlemen approaching. One was Sir Lucius, of course, but it was the other who captured her attention. Something in his gait or the shape of his face seemed familiar. His olive skin and hair of darkest ebony didn't remind her of anyone, but his hooded eyes and longish nose made her think of a certain Jack in the Green—

Her pulse faltered. For a moment, she was almost certain . . .

But no, how could it be? His skin and hair were too dark. The few glimpses she'd had previously of the man she'd dubbed the Phantom were of a white-skinned, blond fellow. Then again, when Eliza had seen him once, she'd said his blond hair looked odd, "like a wig." And he could have lightened his skin, she supposed, although that seemed unlikely.

Besides, surely even the Phantom wouldn't be so bold as to approach her in Society. Not after all the Elegant Occasions events he had sneaked into wearing various disguises. And in the past few months he seemed to have disappeared, anyway. Either that or he'd been too well-disguised for her to notice him of late.

Nonsense. She would always notice *him*, the devious devil, even if the rest of her sisters thought she was mad to be spotting him everywhere. She never forgot a face. So, this could not be him. It made no sense.

"Lady Verity," Sir Lucius said as he approached. "How good to see you."

"My sisters and I are honored you came," she told the undersecretary as she offered him her hand to press. "When we invited you, we weren't certain if you could fit it into your schedule. I know you're very busy running the war."

He laughed. "I'm not exactly running it, but I do handle matters the war minister cannot." When she raised a brow, he added, "Like introducing a friend of ours to you and your family. This is Mr. Raphael Wolfford, nephew to Viscount Wolfford of Wiltshire. Rafe, this is my new acquaintance— and dare I say 'friend'?—Lady Verity Harper. Lady Verity and her sisters run Elegant Occasions, which is hosting this affair, I believe."

"We're doing our best." Verity turned to Mr. Wolfford.

"How nice to meet you, sir." She tried to examine his features furtively, but she'd never been this close to anyone she thought might be the Phantom, so she wasn't sure what she was looking for.

What she saw was a well-dressed man about thirtyish, with eyes as icy-gray as a winter sky beneath thick eyebrows the color of strong coffee. Unlike that of every other man in the room, his straight hair looked as if he'd done no more than run a brush through it. No wax, no fancy curls . . . no nonsense.

He was taller than she was, too, which was a nice change since she towered over many men. His Mazarine blue tail coat with gold buttons and his cream-colored breeches also showed a form as well-shaped as any discerning woman could ask for. And he had a very simply tied cravat.

It *might* be another Phantom costume, but it appealed to her even so. She tried to hide her reaction. "I suppose Sir Lucius tempted you here with tales of our exotic auction offerings."

His sudden smile caught her off guard with its blazing beauty, which sent a delicious shiver along her skin. "Actually," he said, "I came because of the charity being supported. I have a soft spot for orphans."

"Rafe's parents died when he was a babe," Sir Lucius added, "so his uncle raised him. He's the viscount's only heir."

Mr. Wolfford cocked his head in a way that caught her attention. She would swear she'd seen the Phantom do the same. But it made no sense. If this was him, what had he been looking for at so many of their events? Why would he reveal—or rather appear, yet not reveal—himself now? What had changed?

Lord, this uncertainty was vexing. She gazed steadily at

the man. "Well, we all know what being an heir means. You are also now in search of a wife."

Sir Lucius seemed taken aback by her forthright remark, but Mr. Wolfford merely tipped his head. "A very astute observation, madam."

"Not as astute as you'd think. That's part of what my sisters and I do: arrange the meeting of eligible parties in congenial surroundings that encourage courtship."

"Ah." Mr. Wolfford's eyes gleamed at her, making them appear more silver than gray. "Then I have come to the right place."

"You have, indeed." She narrowed her gaze on him and decided to be bolder. "Have we met before, sir?"

Did his strong chin tighten a fraction in response or was she just reading things into his every gesture? "I daresay I would remember meeting a lady as lovely as you."

The husky words seemed genuine and not those of a practiced seducer. Then again, she sometimes had trouble picking out falseness in a man, which was evidenced by how easily Lord Minton had snared her attention years ago.

Either way, Mr. Wolfford had a beautifully resonant baritone voice that warmed her blood, which was a trifle annoying under the circumstances, to say the least.

"My friend is also a newly retired colonel just returned from the Peninsula," Sir Lucius offered, "so unless you were there, Lady Verity . . ."

"Of course not," she said with a laugh. "I could hardly have helped to run Elegant Occasions from Spain or Portugal." She returned her attention to the colonel. "How long ago did you return, sir?"

"It's been a month. But I've spent the past three weeks at my uncle's estate, seeing to matters there. He's getting too old to manage things alone, I'm afraid."

"I see." Should she believe him? If he'd only been in England a month—and in town a week—he couldn't possibly be the Phantom. And surely Sir Lucius wouldn't lie to her about Mr. Wolfford's identity. Sir Lucius was with the government, after all.

Unless he was unaware of his friend's other life? But that would be unlikely, wouldn't it?

She forced a smile. "Well then, Mr. Wolfford, we're pleased you took the time to join us. Forgive my impertinence, but I do hope you've come prepared to bid on an item or two."

"Of course. In fact, I hope you can take a few moments to show me the items in person . . . and perhaps guide me toward ones I should bid on?"

Another sign he might not be the Phantom. Surely he wouldn't risk being alone with her if he thought she might have recognized him from previous affairs.

She tipped her head toward him. "I'd be delighted. Although I warn you—I will be trying to sway you toward the costliest ones at every turn."

He chuckled. "I would expect nothing less."

Half turning toward Sir Lucius, she said, "Do you wish to join us, too, sir? I'm sure I can find you a jeweled watch fob or silk hat to tickle your fancy."

"I'm sure you could," Sir Lucius said. "Which is precisely why I shall let you use your charms on Mr. Wolfford. He has more of a fortune than I do."

"And I know exactly where he should spend it," she said lightly, then led Mr. Wolfford toward the room where the auction items were laid out. As soon as they were alone and strolling about, she said, "So, should I call you 'colonel'? Is that what you would prefer?"

"I've sold my commission, so no. 'Mr. Wolfford' is fine. Or . . . Rafe, if you prefer."

That took her by surprise. "We just met."

He shrugged. "Everyone calls me Rafe, including my uncle. I see no reason you shouldn't."

"How very unusual." And a bit suspicious, although she wasn't sure why. Had Lord Minton corrupted her opinions of men so much that she couldn't trust *anyone* the least bit friendly?

Then again, in this case, suspicion might be warranted.

As they wound through the tables, she pondered how and what to ask to confirm whether he was the Phantom. But he kept drawing her attention to the various objects for sale, wanting more information about each one.

He started to walk past a sewing kit, then looked at it again. "Is that made of seashells?"

"Almost entirely, yes, of shell and mother-of-pearl. It's also gilded with the purest gold."

"And someone *donated* such an item?"

"A very rich someone."

He surveyed the rest of the table. "I see you have many shell items. Did this rich person donate all of them?"

"Actually, no. Mary Parminter, a spinster not quite as rich, donated about half the shell art. The pieces belonged to her cousin Jane, who lived with her until she died last year. The cousins had traveled together all over the world and gathered shells wherever they visited, then created objects from them. They even built a house decorated liberally with shells of all sorts."

"Have you seen it?"

"Briefly. My sister and brother-in-law purchased a seaside home in Exmouth, where the Parminter house is also situated, so we all toured A La Ronde when first visiting the town."

"I shall have to make a trip there. I can't imagine a house decorated in seashells. It sounds rather . . ."

"Odd? Beautiful? Vulgar?"

"Interesting," he said, with a smooth smile. He examined the sewing kit. "I assume you're trying to take my measure, madam, by gauging my opinions."

"How else can I figure out the sort of wife you're seeking?" *And whether you are who you say you are?*

His gaze shot to her. "Have you decided to make finding me a wife your mission?"

"I told you, that's what my sisters and I do."

"For your clients. Not just for any gentleman you meet, I would imagine."

She shrugged. "Our clients are generally women, so we need *respectable* gentlemen to marry them. Besides, I don't mind giving out free advice when it suits me."

He lifted an eyebrow. "And I don't mind taking it when it suits me. As long as I'm sure it does." He eyed her intently. "What did you think of the shell house?"

The abrupt return to their previous subject threw her off. "I think . . . well . . . it's beautiful. One wouldn't expect it to be, but I loved it. Why?"

"You're not the only person who can take someone's measure. And based on your answer, I'd venture to call you an artistic sort, Lady Verity."

"You could say that." An idea shot into her head. "I enjoy all kinds of art, especially when they're joined with nature. I have a passion for Green Man renderings, for example, as well as Jacks in the Green."

Not so much as a twitch of a silky dark eyebrow betrayed

him. "Aren't Jacks in the Green those sooty fellows who dress up as trees for holidays?"

"And bushes," she said. "Really, any kind of foliage they can stick on their wicker framework."

He eyed her skeptically. "Doesn't sound all that artistic to me. On the other hand, the Green Man has been illustrated in cultures around the world. I saw one on a church in Lisbon."

"Between battles, I assume?" she said a bit tartly.

He chuckled. "You'd be surprised how much architecture a soldier encounters while marching from town to town. There are great swathes of time spent loitering in camp while the senior officers decide where and when to strike."

"I shall have to ask my other brother-in-law, Lord Foxstead, about that. He was a captain in the infantry."

"Was he?" Mr. Wolfford continued moving down the aisle between two sets of tables. "Interesting."

"You said that before. 'Interesting' seems to be a word you use to avoid speaking your true opinion."

He laughed. "A direct hit, madam. I congratulate you."

Verity caught sight of her sister strolling down their aisle ahead of them, which gave her an idea. "You would like my brother-in-law, you know. He thinks in terms of battles and wars, too. In fact, there goes his wife now. Eliza can tell you more about whom he served under and such."

That way Verity might learn if Mr. Wolfford actually did serve in the army, although surely the undersecretary wouldn't lie about *that*.

Even better, Eliza had seen the face of the Phantom full-on. Perhaps *she* would be able to recognize "Rafe." Assuming that Mr. Wolfford was indeed the Phantom, which Verity still couldn't be entirely definite about.

"I'm always eager to meet other soldiers and their

wives," he said, which gave her pause, since he would have to know if he'd encountered Eliza before.

Still, Verity was determined to make certain. "Eliza, wait! I have someone to introduce to you!"

As her sister halted and turned to greet them, Verity watched Eliza's face, but nothing in her expression indicated recognition. Quickly, Verity performed the introductions, with Eliza making the same appropriate replies as she would with any stranger.

Verity sighed. "Eliza is the one who arranges—and sometimes performs—the music for our events," Verity explained. "One must always have good music, don't you agree, Mr. Wolfford?"

He smiled. "Of course, since 'music has charms to soothe the savage breast.'"

Eliza blinked. "You read Congreve, sir?"

"Doesn't everyone?"

"Not everyone *we* meet," Verity said. And certainly, no officer she'd ever met, despite their gentlemanly education.

"I spent a great deal of my childhood alone," he said. "And my uncle had an extensive library. I read as many of his books as I could manage."

"As it happens," Eliza remarked, "we have books in our auction, too, some of them very old and valuable."

"I don't care about the value of a book," he said, "just the content."

"Easy not to care when you can afford any book you want," Verity muttered.

"Verity, don't be rude," her sister chided her. "Mr. Wolfford was just stating his opinion."

"Yes, Lady Verity," he said, humor glinting in his gaze. "My *true* opinion."

Was he laughing at her?

"Besides," he went on, "I thought having a fortune was preferred by women seeking suitors."

Definitely laughing.

She tipped up her chin. "Yes, all other things being equal—age, character, general amiability . . . honesty." Then realizing that neither he nor Eliza seemed to realize why she sounded so sour, she added, "Forgive me, I'm always a bit . . . testy on our auction nights. I want everything to go well."

Eliza patted her arm. "And it will, my dear. It always does."

"I'll do my best to help," he said.

Still laughing at her.

He *had* to be the Phantom. He just had to. He had a certain understated arrogance she found most annoying. And his eyes were too pretty a silvery gray.

Oh, her sisters would laugh uproariously at *that* observation.

Perhaps you just want *the handsome, witty fellow to be the Phantom to justify spending more time with him.*

Perhaps. Given the dearth of interesting men in Society, that would hardly be surprising.

He looked down at the nearest table, which held an elaborate place setting, then read the long description on the placard beside it. "I see that Elegant Occasions donated an item to the auction, too."

Lifting his gaze to them, he added, "That reminds me of something I wanted to ask. How did you three end up running your business? Sir Lucius told me you're earl's daughters. I may not have been in Society very long, but even I know it's frowned upon for a gentleman's daughters to be in trade."

"Sir Lucius didn't tell you of our parents' scandalous divorce?" Eliza asked. "I thought everyone talked about *that*."

Verity fought a burst of temper. Why had Eliza mentioned

that to *him*, of all people? "It's been six years, Eliza. Surely the gossip has died down some by now."

Eliza chuckled. "A tiny bit, I suppose. But I'm sure he will hear about it somewhere eventually. Might as well tell him ourselves. That way he'll get the truthful version. But I'll keep it short."

She turned to Mr. Wolfford. "First, our mother ran off with her prominent lover, a major general in the army. Then our father divorced her publicly, and my two sisters, who weren't yet married, were considered pariahs as a result, through no fault of their own. We call it, 'The Incident.'"

"Quite an understatement," he drawled.

"I can't imagine why you'd think so," Verity said, her voice dripping with sarcasm.

Eliza's gaze darted between them. "Anyway, my husband at the time ran off to fight in the war, leaving me alone in a London town house. So, when someone asked our help with arranging a ball and offered to pay us, it seemed a good idea for us to combine forces and set up a business."

"To be honest," Verity said, "we were tired of being gossiped about for what we had *not* done and decided to do something that would get us gossiped about for what we had always done but not been paid for."

"Especially since we were good at it," Eliza said. "After my husband was killed in the war, leaving me with nothing, we all needed the money, anyway, and it allowed us to support ourselves without relying on our unreliable parents."

"I see," he said in a bland tone that belied the interest in his eyes. "And now you're so successful that you can give some of that money to charity."

"Exactly," Verity said. "Now that our services are valued, people even bid on them."

He glanced back at the placard that described their bid. "What exactly does it mean that the winner of this gets a costly dinner prepared to your 'meticulous specifications' by Monsieur Beaufort, Head Cook for Elegant Occasions? Is he preparing the meal, Lady Verity, or are you?"

"I decide the menu after speaking to the winner and determining what their ideal meal might be."

He lifted one supercilious brow. "Couldn't they just tell the head cook what meal they want?"

"They could. Or they could tell me their favorite dishes and let me figure out what they truly crave."

"You're claiming to be able to read a person's thoughts," he said skeptically.

Eliza smiled. "She can do it, believe it or not."

"Don't be absurd, Eliza. I can't 'read a person's thoughts.'" She stared him down. "But I do have a particular skill at knowing how to arrange ambrosia for people who don't even know what sort of ambrosia they desire."

He dropped his gaze ever so fleetingly to her mouth. "Guessing what another person desires. *That* would be a neat trick indeed."

"It's not a guess. It's more of a . . . speculation, if you will, based on questions I ask." She flashed him a coy look. Or what she hoped was a coy look, since she was woefully out of practice at such things. "And if you wish to watch me succeed at it, sir, you should bid on the item later."

"I assure you," Eliza put in, "Verity's meals are sought after at these affairs. She really does know how to figure out a person's tastes and then translate that into dishes that Monsieur Beaufort can prepare impeccably."

A half smile crossed his lips. "Ah. You've both baited the hook well, I see. Perhaps I *will* bid on that, if only to see how Lady Verity pulls it off."

Verity nodded. "Please do. We hope to make a great deal of money at this auction." And in the meantime, she might corner her Phantom at last.

At that moment, the bandleader came over to murmur in Eliza's ear, and with apologies to them both, her sister hurried off with him, no doubt to deal with one of those musical emergencies that came up from time to time at events.

Verity was on the verge of making another teasing remark when she caught sight of a gentleman entering the room whom she did *not* wish to encounter. The very fellow who'd once broken her silly, girlish heart—Lord Silas Minton.

What the devil was he doing here? He'd spent the past years avoiding her and her family, and *now* he showed up at one of their affairs? How dare he?

Well, she wasn't staying around to find out why. If the scoundrel so much as tried to speak to her, she was liable to brain him with the nearest ice bucket. Better to prevent that from happening.

So, determining whether Mr. Wolfford was the Phantom would have to wait.

Chapter 3

Rafe couldn't help noticing Lady Verity's stricken expression. He followed the direction of her gaze and stifled a groan. Minton. And Rafe had to pretend not to know the fellow, or have her wonder how he could have met the baron when Rafe had only been in town a week.

"Is something wrong?" he asked.

Her gaze flew to him, overly bright. "Forgive me, but I-I need to go. It's stuffy in here, and far too warm."

She started for the French doors that led out onto the terrace, and he followed swiftly. "That's an excellent idea. Do you mind if I join you? I could use some fresh air myself."

That seemed to startle her. Then she nodded. "Why not? The gardens are lovely right now with the lamps lit."

"No doubt." Rafe offered her his arm, relieved when she took it. It showed that she trusted him.

It showed she hadn't recognized him.

He hadn't expected her to, since he'd never before been close enough for her to register his features and had always been disguised, besides. But for a moment there, when she'd mentioned Jacks in the Green . . .

No, that was purely coincidental. She'd also let him lead her into the subject of the Grenwood's new seaside house, and surely if she had suspected he might be angling for an invitation to their house party, she wouldn't have done so.

As they reached the doors, he stepped forward to open them for her, and she breathed in deeply of the air before passing through. In that moment, he was given a nice view of the rise and fall of her breasts. It caught his attention the same way her playful teasing and searching glances had.

She might not be as buxom as her sisters, but she had a damned pretty bosom all the same, especially in a gown that showed it to good effect—cut low and tight enough to tempt a man's gaze downward. One might even call her gown daring, intended purely to attract attention from men.

Damn it all. He jerked his gaze away as an unfamiliar emotion assailed him. Guilt.

That was the trouble with spying on one's own countrymen. Because a true gentleman didn't do so. A true gentleman certainly didn't deceive a woman or take advantage of her trust.

Or lust after her bosom.

He forced himself to ignore the guilt. He'd never been a true gentleman, so it hardly signified. His uncle had raised him to be a soldier, and he was always that above all. Whether people called him Mr. Wolfford or heir presumptive to Viscount Wolfford, in his heart he was Colonel Wolfford on a mission, nothing more, nothing less.

Clearly distracted, she didn't take his arm a second time, and he rather regretted that. He liked the feel of her hand on his arm. It was . . . different.

"Better now?" he asked as they walked in the night air.

"Hmm?" she said, darting a quick glance behind them, no doubt looking for Minton. "Oh. Yes." She relaxed a fraction. "Much better, don't you think? August in the city is always so soggy."

"I wouldn't know. I've only been here a week." Saying

it helped to remind him of his plan. Of the lies he had to
tell to support his story. And to allay her suspicions, if she
had any.

Uncle Constantine's voice sounded in his head. *When
playing a role, always stay as close to the facts as possible.
Remembering lies is harder than remembering the truth. But
don't give too many details. Keep things vague, unverifiable.*

Easier said than done.

She gazed up at him, her eyes gleaming with interest in
the lamps of the lit terrace. "You were never in the city before
you became an officer?"

"I might have been, briefly. I don't remember." Now,
that was true. When she looked surprised, he added, "I was
sixteen when I joined the army." Also true.

"So young?"

The thread of sympathy in her voice discomfited him.
But at least he'd taken her attention off Minton.

Rafe shrugged. "For an orphan like me, it made sense."

"How old were you when your parents died?"

"Only a baby, actually. They were in a carriage accident
while traveling abroad. I was somehow spared, along with
the coachman. He wrote to my uncle, who went to South
America to fetch me to England."

"Thank heaven or who knows where you would have
ended up?"

Who knows, indeed? Rafe never had, since Uncle Constantine had always been vague on the subject of his parents' deaths and how Rafe had survived. All he knew was
his father had been a mapmaker and thus had gone to Brazil
to map part of it. There he'd met the woman he married, a
Brazilian merchant's daughter named Julieta. Rafe didn't
even know his mother's maiden name or where she'd been
living in Brazil when she'd met his father.

Indeed, it had begun to occur to him that perhaps his

uncle's reticence was by design. Rafe hadn't been able to discover much about his parents since his return to England, no matter how much he'd investigated. That struck him as odd.

Then again, perhaps their having spent their lives traveling had made it impossible for his uncle to learn anything without retracing his brother's steps in Brazil to find Julieta's family. That would have been difficult in his uncle's situation. He'd been serving in the army half a world away when he'd left to fetch Rafe. He'd been understandably less concerned with investigating his brother's wife than with carrying his nephew to England, where Rafe could be looked after.

But recently, Rafe had begun to question the story more, particularly after his own time on the Peninsula. There were inconsistencies he couldn't ignore. They could be explained away, but still . . .

"So," she asked as he took her down some steps into the gardens, "your uncle raised you?"

"Not exactly. Being an active army officer with no wife, he had the servants at his Wiltshire estate look after me. Later, I had tutors, and—once old enough to join Uncle—a commission as his aide-de-camp. I served under him until he retired after being wounded at the Battle of Alexandria. Then I was a Hussar in the King's German Legion before finally serving under Wellington on the Peninsula. I've been in the army half of my life."

"Good Lord. That's . . . The army takes boys that young?"

"I was lucky. If I'd joined the navy, I would have been younger still."

She shook her head. "I'm sorry. I didn't know. We don't have brothers, and all the officers I've met are older."

"It's not so bad, you know, being in the army young. It makes a man out of you right quick."

"Whether you want to be one or not, apparently." She gazed up at him, a trace of pity in her face. "Did you even *wish* to go into the army?"

No one had ever asked him that, not even his uncle. Her doing so made him oddly uncomfortable. And defensive. "I got to see the world, didn't I? Besides, I preferred being with my uncle—the closest thing I had to a father—to reading all the time or roaming an estate with no one but a few servants around, and certainly no one my age."

"It sounds lonely."

The soft timbre of her voice didn't sit well. "A bit, I suppose." Eager to change the subject, he smiled at her. "Of course, if I'd had someone as lovely as you to keep me company—"

Her startled laugh caught him off guard. "If you insist upon being a flatterer, sir, you should at least learn to vary your compliments."

"What do you mean?" he asked warily.

"You've called me 'lovely' twice already. I assure you, once per evening is quite enough. But feel free to call me 'clever' frequently. I do so like that particular compliment."

Damn. Who knew that turning a woman up sweet had rules? "I'm afraid I'm not used to being around lovely . . . *clever* women. It turns me into a babbler."

She raised an eyebrow, even as a teasing smile lit her face. "I somehow doubt that. I'll wager you've never said a word wrong in your whole life, to a woman or anyone else."

"You'd lose that wager. My tutors regularly rapped my knuckles for saying words wrong."

She chuckled. "So did my governess. Not that it helped. I tend to speak my mind regardless."

"I've noticed."

Her expression turned belligerent. "You disapprove?"

"Not at all. I prefer a blunt woman to a devious one any day."

"Funny," she shot back. "I feel the same about men."

Hmm. "So, if I were to tell you that your pearl bandeau is hanging loose, you would be grateful, not embarrassed?"

Her mouth dropped open, and her hand went right to her bandeau. When she found it intact, she said acidly, "If you'd been truthful, I'd be grateful. As it is, I'm merely annoyed. I do hope you don't mean to make a habit of speaking falsely of a lady's coiffure."

He laughed. Then hearing a crunch of gravel on the path behind them, probably someone else seeking cooler air, he lowered his voice. "It depends on whether you'll make a habit of accepting my visits."

He congratulated himself on having caught her off guard, for she halted on the path to flash him a considering look. "I'm not yet sure, sir. Let's see how the evening goes."

"I'm amenable to that, if it means spending more time in your company."

The footfalls had halted on the path, and he looked back to find Lord Minton frozen, his gaze fixed on the two of them.

Hell and thunder. Well, there was one good way to determine whether she still had feelings for the man. "You there," he said as Minton started to turn. "Are you following us? Listening in on our conversation?"

Lady Verity looked back and groaned audibly. "Pay him no mind," she muttered, though her eyes flashed at Minton.

Minton drew himself up in an offended stance. "I am merely making sure that the lady isn't being taken advantage of by some scoundrel new to Society."

"As if you care," Lady Verity bit out. "And this is no scoundrel, Lord Minton. This is Colonel Wolfford of the

Wiltshire Wolffords. He also just happens to be the Viscount of Wolfford's heir."

When Minton looked taken aback, Rafe said, "So, you know this fellow, my lady?"

"I did. Once." She stared Minton down. "But it has been some years since I've had the misfortune to encounter him."

Rafe couldn't help but take an inordinate pleasure in her haughtiness toward the baron.

"I just want to talk to you, Verity," Minton said. "That's all. A moment of your time." He glared at Rafe. "In private."

For some reason, those words raised Rafe's hackles. Knowing that Minton had rejected her in the past, Rafe wasn't inclined to be tolerant. "First of all, sir, it's *Lady* Verity. And I don't think she wishes to talk to *you*."

"I can speak for myself," Verity said, though she edged closer to Rafe. "But Mr. Wolfford is right. You are the last person in the world I wish to bestow a moment of my time upon. You said quite enough to me six years ago, Lord Minton."

Minton took a step forward and said in a placating tone, "I didn't know what I was doing at the time."

She stared him down. "Then let me tell you what you were doing—saving your own skin from scandal. Sadly, I couldn't do the same. But I managed to rise above it, and you had naught to do with that, so forgive me if I don't believe a word you're saying." She slipped her hand around Rafe's arm. "Now, if you'll excuse us, sir, Mr. Wolfford and I were just returning to the house for the auction. We don't want to miss it."

Rafe nodded curtly at Minton, then took her down a different path that led toward the terrace, circumventing Minton, who stood staring after them like a wounded puppy.

As soon as they were out of earshot, Rafe murmured, "Now that I've witnessed your enmity toward that wretched fellow, you must tell me what he did to you." Since he'd been told only the barest bones of the scandal with Minton, he wanted to hear the full story told in her own words anyway.

"Why?" she snapped, clearly still unsettled by their encounter with the baron.

"So I don't make the same mistakes he did, of course."

She blinked, then gazed up at him, her throat working convulsively. "You couldn't possibly, sir, since my parents aren't likely to divorce their current spouses."

"His behavior was part of 'The Incident,' was it?"

"What else?" She halted just short of the terrace doors and sighed. "I might as well tell you. All of London Society knows what happened, and so will you once you've been around long enough. Lord Minton certainly didn't keep it a secret."

Her eyes, glittering golden green in the light spilling out onto the terrace, narrowed on him. "And since you seem bent on defending me—for what purpose, I'm not entirely sure—I should at least warn you I am still not accepted by the highest sticklers in Society. Not that I care one whit, mind you, but you should probably know."

"I stand duly warned. Although I should still like to know what he did."

Facing him, she squared her shoulders. "Lord Minton had just made an offer of marriage to me privately when Mother ran off with Major General Tobias Ord. Once his lordship learned of her indiscretion, he suggested we not announce our betrothal until the scandal blew over. Except it never did. My mother refused to come home, all of Society was gossiping about it, and Lord Minton's family was aghast."

She stared down at her hands. "So, he proceeded to court Bertha, my supposed friend. Up until then, it had been widely known he was considering offering for me, but his courtship of Bertha became so public that people started gossiping about it. By the time he got around to informing me he had 'feelings for another,' after having left me in limbo for weeks, Society had made up its own story for why he had transferred his affections from me to Bertha."

His anger at Minton, which had been building as she told the story, got the better of him. "Don't tell me—they somehow found a way to blame it on *you*."

"Isn't that always the way?" she said with an edge in her voice. "The gossips said he had surely refused to align himself with me because I was a licentious jade like my mother."

He caught his breath. It was worse even than he'd thought.

She lifted a hard gaze to his. "It went downhill from there."

"How much more downhill could it go?"

"Well, for one thing, after Father decided to divorce Mother . . ." She muttered an unladylike oath. "Like the coward Minton is, he let people believe the stories making the rounds about me rather than admit why he suddenly didn't want me."

"And he deems *me* a scoundrel." He paused. "But he didn't marry Bertha, I take it."

"That's actually the amusing part," she said bitterly. "She caught a bigger fish while Lord Minton was dithering over her, and he suddenly found himself without either heiress in his pocket." As if realizing what she'd just said, her defiant gaze snapped to him. "Yes, it appeared that his interest in both of us had more to do with our dowries than our persons. Which just made everything worse."

"I can well imagine."

"No, you cannot. Men are not bought and sold in the marriage market the way women are. What's more, a man like you would have to murder someone to endure the level of scandal and rumor-mongering that my sisters and I did. That we occasionally still do."

She lifted her chin in a defensive gesture he'd begun to recognize. "Before the scandal, I had my pick of suitors, you know, but like a silly, blinded-by-love schoolgirl, I chose Lord Minton. And every one of those suitors vanished with the wind after Mama eloped with the major general."

He eyed her steadily. "I seem to have struck a nerve."

Chagrin crossed her face. "Forgive me, but speaking of Lord Minton makes me irritable. Still, you did ask, you know."

"I did. And I'm glad you told me. Now I know how to act the next time we encounter him publicly."

"What do you mean?" she asked warily.

"Although I'd prefer planting him a facer or calling him out, those would probably only embroil you in more scandal. But giving him the cut direct would be appropriate, don't you think?"

She broke into a smile. "Most appropriate." Her tone turned cynical. "Still, my sisters and I give him the cut direct on the rare occasions we see him, and he doesn't seem to notice."

"I'll make sure he notices from now on."

"Will you?" She flashed him a considering glance. "Are you absolutely sure we've never met before?"

He searched her face, looking again for signs that she recognized him from their previous, mostly distant, encounters. But her expression was hard to read, and he didn't see how she could possibly have done so, anyway.

"I'm sure." Remembering their earlier conversation, he added, "I always take note of the clever women I meet."

Her lips twitched, her fit of temper over Lord Minton apparently finally over. "Don't forget 'lovely,'" she teased him.

"That, too," he said. "Now, don't you have an auction to oversee?"

"I do. Thank you for reminding me. If you'll excuse me, my lord . . ."

And with a slight bow, she hurried off, leaving him to admire her no-nonsense walk, her swan-like neck, and the way the neckline of her white gown dipped to expose a nice portion of her supple back. A very pretty back to go with a very pretty front.

He wondered if her beautifully sculpted figure continued beneath the gown and layers of underthings. Did she have a small waist, too? A slightly curvy derriere to match her slightly curvy bosom?

When he stiffened inside his breeches, he muttered a curse under his breath. He wouldn't get to see either of those, and it was just as well. Although her stimulating and sometimes prickly conversation would make this endeavor more entertaining than he'd expected, he must take care not to be so caught up in flirting with her that he forgot his purpose.

He had a mission, after all.

Chapter 4

Verity and her sisters watched from beyond one doorway as the bidding began. There, they could chat, too, without bothering the bidders.

"Five pounds says that Lady Sinclair will not only bid on that ruby bracelet but win," Verity said in a lowered voice.

"I'll take that wager," her brother-in-law Geoffrey said.

Diana poked him with her elbow. "You will not. You know you never win against Verity. She has an instinct for these things, and you do not."

"Of course I do," Geoffrey retorted.

"You are not a gambler, and you know it," Nathaniel, the Earl of Foxstead, put in. "The only place you ever take risks is in investments. Besides, Verity always keeps her ear to the ground at these events, so she usually has knowledge the rest of us don't."

"But perhaps not so much tonight," Eliza mused aloud. "She's been a bit distracted by a certain gentleman."

Diana scowled. "Oh, yes, I saw that Lord Minton is here, the scoundrel."

"Not him," Eliza said, smirking at Verity. "The handsome fellow Sir Lucius introduced her to. A colonel *and* a viscount's heir."

Verity rolled her eyes.

"I met him while you three were preparing to get the auction started," Geoffrey said. "Fascinating fellow. He served on the Peninsula. And other places before that, from very young."

"Under whom?" Nathaniel asked, perking up at mention of the war.

"General Wolfford for part of the time, I believe. That's his uncle, and he's ill, I gather."

Nathaniel frowned. "General Wolfford was instrumental in winning the Battle of Alexandria. But I haven't heard much about the nephew."

"Didn't General Wolfford get his viscountcy as a result of that battle?" Eliza asked.

"If so, his nephew can't inherit it," Nathaniel pointed out.

"Wait, I remember reading about that," Diana said. "They gave the general a special remainder when they offered him the title, so his nephew could inherit. Like what they did with Admiral Nelson, so his older brother could inherit. Otherwise, it would die with the general, since he has no children."

"Clearly, you know more about it than us. I shall have to introduce you." Eliza got a certain glint in her eyes. "He and Verity spark fires off each other."

"What?" Verity cried. "Nonsense. You're making that up." Although when he'd stood up for her against Lord Minton, it had been hard not to swoon. Well, if she *ever* swooned.

She mustn't swoon over Mr. Wolfford, for pity's sake. He might very well be the Phantom. Indeed, it was on the tip of her tongue to ask if they recognized him, but if they had, they would have said so, and bringing that up was likely to expose her to endless ridicule.

Especially if she proved to be wrong. But perhaps there was another way to broach the subject. "So, you haven't met him yet, Diana?" she asked.

"I don't think so. I haven't even encountered Sir Lucius yet this evening." Diana looked far too smug. "Speaking of Sir Lucius, he's unmarried, too, you know. I found that out when we were introduced to him last week."

Eliza waved her hand dismissively. "He's too old for Verity. At least ten years her senior."

"She might prefer an older fellow," Diana remarked. "Especially after her disastrous engagement to Lord Minton."

"I was never engaged to Lord Minton," Verity bit out. "Not formally, anyway."

"Oh, pish, who cares about formalities?" Eliza said. "He made an offer, and you accepted."

"Before I knew he was an arse," Verity grumbled.

"Why can Verity say 'arse' and I can't?" Geoffrey complained.

"Because *she* can't, either," Diana told him. "She just does. It's not the same."

"That's hardly fair," Geoffrey said.

Diana sighed. "I tell you what. Whenever you two are with us, you may both say 'arse' as much as you please, so long as no one else is around to hear it."

"Is that the rule?" Geoffrey said. "Excellent. Does that mean I can also say 'damn' and 'hell' and 'bloody' with impunity?" As a newly minted duke who'd previously been a civil engineer, Geoffrey had a rather colorful vocabulary that Diana and Eliza had been trying to divest him of. And sometimes Verity, too, though she rather liked his colorful vocabulary.

Diana scowled at him. "You can only say the words Verity says. We don't want you blistering our own ears."

This entire conversation annoyed Verity. "Damn. Hell. Bloody. There you go, Geoffrey. Now you can say them all."

"Look what you started, Diana," said Eliza, who never

spoke a vulgar word. "Geoffrey will surely forget himself and 'say them all' while others are around."

"I will not," Geoffrey protested. "I'm a gentleman."

"You could have fooled me," Verity muttered.

"Do not insult my husband," Diana said. "Only I am allowed to do that."

"By the way, was I right about Lady Sinclair? Did I win my wager against Geoffrey? I wasn't paying attention."

"You lost," Geoffrey said, smiling to himself.

"Liar," Verity said. "You weren't paying attention, either."

"And he didn't wager," Diana said.

Eliza shushed them. "I'm trying to hear who bids what."

They fell dutifully silent as other items continued to come up for bid. Mr. Wolfford and even Sir Lucius, despite his crying poor, made bids, some of which they won. When she tallied the funds up in her head, Mr. Wolfford's bids mounted to thirty pounds, a very nice sum indeed.

She couldn't help noticing that Lord Minton bid on nothing, although she could see him standing near the front. She wasn't sure if his miserliness showed he didn't care about charity or was simply lacking for funds. That would explain why he was coming around her again. The foolish fellow must think Papa still had a dowry for her.

Little did Lord Minton know that once she'd defied Papa by moving into Eliza's house, her father had cut her off, saying he would reinstate her dowry only if she returned home. Thankfully, she wasn't that desperate, and Nathaniel and Eliza had said she could stay as long as she pleased. Being there did make it easier for her and Eliza to run Elegant Occasions, together with Geoffrey's sister and Diana.

Verity got more nervous as the auction went on. Hers was the last item. What if no one was interested in it? Although surely Mr. Wolfford would make at least a token bid.

"Verity's item is coming up."

"I hope she breaks the bank this time," Diana said.

"Shall I bid against whomever else bids, to send it higher?" Nathaniel asked.

"I don't need your help, you know," Verity said.

"Would you lot please be quiet?" Eliza said. "I want to hear who bids."

The bidding started low, of course, as it always did. But after a healthy smattering of bids, she heard a familiar voice call out, "Thirty pounds." Considering that the whole meal would cost them seven pounds, two shillings to produce, that was impressive, which sent a little frisson of satisfaction through her.

"Mr. Wolfford is bidding," Eliza said smugly. "I told you he and Verity were *simpatico,* as my half-Italian husband would say."

"Thirty-two pounds!" called out another familiar voice.

Verity groaned. "It's a good thing I don't have to *eat* the meal with the bidder. That's Lord Minton."

Geoffrey looked at Diana. "Shall I bid over—"

"No!" the three women said in unison.

"Only if Mr. Wolfford looks as if he'll lose," Eliza said, ever practical.

"Forty pounds!" cried Mr. Wolfford.

Verity caught her breath. Then grinned.

"Take *that*, Lord Minton!" Eliza said to their little group. "That's what you get for toying with our baby sister's affections."

"Hear, hear," Diana said, sotto voce.

But it was only the beginning. Lord Minton bid over him. Then, to her shock—and intense gratification—Mr. Wolfford kept bidding until Lord Minton got the message and stopped . . . at two hundred pounds! It was a princely sum.

They all stood stunned as the auctioneer said, "Going once, going twice . . . sold to . . . er. . ."

"Raphael Wolfford!" her new advocate called out.

She wanted to kiss him, even though this would mean the beginning of gossip about the two of them. Though, if he did happen to be her Phantom . . .

Wait, he was not *hers* in any way. But he obviously wanted something from her. Why else bid so high? And how had Lord Minton even managed to keep up with the bidding for so long? She couldn't believe he could afford it.

She scanned the room, but Lord Minton seemed to have left. Good riddance, if so. Perhaps Mr. Wolfford's aggressive bidding had made him leave. Although Mr. Wolfford seemed to have mysteriously vanished himself.

"Well, after that dramatic display," Eliza said, "we should invite Mr. Wolfford to the house party."

"But we've already settled the guest list," Diana said.

Eliza sniffed. "It's *our* house party—we can invite whomever we want. I say we should invite him. He's eligible, he's just proven himself a friend to Elegant Occasions, and he's obviously smitten by Verity."

"Right," Verity muttered. Mr. Wolfford struck her as the sort of man who didn't allow himself to be smitten by anyone.

Her sisters turned to her. "You shall have to break the tie. What do you think? I mean, if you dislike the fellow or are worried he's pursuing you too aggressively . . ."

"First, he's not pursuing me at all. Second . . ." Verity trailed off before she could make any other protest. Inviting him wasn't a bad idea. It would give her a chance to get to know him and thus figure out once and for all whether he'd been the one skulking about at their previous affairs.

Of course, that meant he'd be skulking about at another

one. If he accepted. And if he was even the Phantom, which she still wasn't entirely certain of.

That was another reason to do it, actually. At a house party, she might be able to trap him into admitting the truth, *whatever* the truth was. If she didn't continue the association, she'd never know who he really was and why he'd been sneaking into their events.

"I think we should invite him," Verity announced. "It's the least we can do when he's giving two hundred pounds to the Foundling Hospital. Why, that's more than we made at our first auction entirely."

"Then it's settled," Eliza said. "We invite him."

"Wait a moment, Eliza," Geoffrey told her, a frown spreading over his brow. "You don't even know who the fellow is. He might be some swindler out to . . . well . . . swindle you and your guests."

"Sir Lucius introduced him to me," Verity pointed out. "Do you really think someone from the government would do such a thing?"

Geoffrey looked over at his wife. "Perhaps not, but I still say we should exercise caution."

"How about this?" Nathaniel put in. "I'll see what I can learn about Wolfford through my friends in the army. Someone must know if he's who he says he is."

"And we'll look him up in Debrett's, too," Diana said. "A viscount's heir presumptive would appear there."

"The general was just made a viscount three years ago," Nathaniel said.

Verity sighed. "That may not have made it into Debrett's, then. Debrett hasn't released a new edition since 1808."

Eliza tapped her chin. "I know someone else I can ask about the general and his family—our cousin, Major Quinn. He was in the army long before Nathaniel."

Her husband grimaced. "Must we? I thought he'd gone abroad again."

"No, he's still on leave," Eliza said. "I'm not sure why."

"For some nefarious reason, no doubt," Nathaniel grumbled.

The earl was none too fond of Major Quinn, probably because their distant cousin had been planning to propose to Eliza before Nathaniel had. Or that was the rumor, anyway. Eliza had never known if it was true, and apparently hadn't really cared, either.

Their discussion was interrupted by the approach of Mr. Wolfford himself from down the hall. Oh, dear, she hoped he hadn't overheard what they'd said. That would be awkward in the extreme. Although he didn't look as if he had. He looked flushed with success.

In any case, it was time to see if either Diana or Nathaniel recognized him from any of their events, particularly the May Day one.

Verity introduced him to them, and to her chagrin, neither showed even a hint that they remembered him. Were they blind?

Or was *she*?

No matter. She would get to the bottom of it somehow. Just see if she didn't.

Mr. Wolfford participated in some polite small talk with her family and endured a few questions, but as soon as conversation stalled, he asked her if he could have a few private words with her.

"Of course," she said, ignoring her sisters' raised eyebrows. "We need to discuss when you wish to have your special meal."

"Exactly." He smiled faintly. "And you need to ask me all your special questions in preparation. No time like the present to talk that over."

"Feel free to have your discussion in the breakfast room," Diana said. "We're not using it for anything this evening."

But both Diana and Eliza gave her a warning look that said, *Be sure to leave the door open.* She resisted an urge to stick out her tongue at them. The audacity of those two! They'd both been guilty of enjoying tête-à-têtes with their husbands before marrying, and now they thought to deny *her* one? Of course, Eliza had been a widow, so most people overlooked any such behavior, but Diana . . .

It didn't matter what her sisters and their suitors had done. She wasn't them. So, when he offered her his arm, Verity took it with a defiant look at her sisters. She could take care of herself. Why, if Mr. Wolfford did anything untoward, she would simply scream her head off, high auction bid or not.

Years ago, after enduring initial attempts by supposed gentlemen to see if she was the licentious lady they'd heard, she'd learned that a loud, protesting feminine voice in the hearing of others would send rogues fleeing faster than anything else. Either that, or not going anywhere alone with them in the first place.

Sadly, or perhaps not so sadly, her caution had also given her a reputation for being prickly and dangerous to court. She didn't care. Besides, she'd already been alone with Mr. Wolfford and nothing had happened, so she ought to be safe. And if she knew anything about her sisters and their husbands, one or another of them would come strolling by from time to time, anyway.

"Thank you for your bids," she told him as they left her nosy family behind. "I know that the Foundling Hospital can well use the funds."

"I'm glad to hear it. Before I came to this affair, I looked into what they do and how. They seem a very noble cause."

"They are."

An uncomfortable silence fell over them. Feeling his intent gaze on her, she took a deep breath. "And thank you for bidding so high in particular on my dinner."

"I told you, I'm curious to see how you manage it."

"Two hundred pounds worth of curious?" she asked skeptically.

She looked up at him to find him staring ahead now. "I could not allow that . . . blackguard Minton to gain such close access to you. He's proven himself untrustworthy."

He sounded sincere. It rather surprised her.

"Yes, he has." She halted outside the door to the drawing room. *And now* you *get to prove yourself trustworthy, at least in this.* "Here we are."

They walked inside, and she noticed he made no attempt to close the door. That was a good sign. But neither did he take a seat or even lead her to one. Instead, he went to stand staring at her in the mirror. How very odd.

Suddenly, he turned to fix her with an assessing look. "There is one other thing I am even more curious about than whether you can succeed at creating a meal of ambrosia for me."

"Oh?" she said, truly perplexed.

He came closer. "I wish to know what it would be like to kiss you."

Normally, that would send all her protective instincts on high alert. But he said the words so emotionlessly, as if he were bent on attempting an experiment, that she had to tamp down an urge to laugh.

Then the finances of the situation struck home, and a chill came over her. Oh, why must he be like every other man in her world?

She forced lightness into her voice. "I see you expect a great deal for your high bid, sir: a lavish meal *and* a kiss. Or did you assume more—that your bid earned you the right to do as you please with me? Because I assure you, my favors are not for sale, so if—"

"No!" he cut in, looking genuinely chagrined by how she'd taken his words. "No. Forgive me, that's not what I meant at all. Obviously, I'm not explaining this very well."

"Clearly." She crossed her arms over her chest. "So, what *did* you mean?"

He steadied his shoulders. "Look here. I don't really care about the meal. God knows, I'm not known for my refined palate. Indeed, I would gladly give the same monies to the Foundling Hospital for no other reason than that it's a good cause, and tell you to keep whatever funds you need to create the dinner. No offense."

"A-All right." This had to be the oddest conversation she'd ever had with a man.

A muscle worked in his jaw. "But you are the first woman I've met in Society whom I find interesting." He edged nearer. "The first I have ever considered kissing. Most are predictably snobbish, and I'm . . . well . . ."

When he trailed off, she understood. "An orphan at heart," she said softly.

His gaze shot to her and he stiffened. "I was going to say 'a soldier,' but I suppose 'an orphan' will do."

He looked uncomfortable and proud all at the same time. It was rather endearing. If she could trust it. "I see."

Now he looked agitated. "Forget I said anything. I'll pay the money for the dinner to the Foundling Hospital, and to make up for insulting you, I'll not expect you to create it. Because I really didn't mean to imply—"

"Here's the thing." She searched his face, but it was clear he had ventured into an area he wasn't sure of, and wished to retreat. Which entirely changed how she felt about his request. "You want a kiss, and I want not to be treated like a . . . lady of the evening, giving out my favors for money. So, how about this?"

She ventured closer. "I will still give you what you paid for—the meal—since it is, after all, what you bid on, and I have just enough pride in what I do to want to prove my abilities to you. But since I, too, am a bit curious about how you kiss, we will both kiss as something utterly unrelated to your bid. Will that suit?"

"Any arrangement that ends with us kissing is amenable to me." When she started to bristle, he said hastily, "I don't mean 'arrangement.' Damn, what a poor choice of words. Great, now I have cursed before a lady." He groaned. "I am very bad at this, aren't I?"

She raised an eyebrow. "At what?"

"Flirtation. Courtship." He waved his hand into the air between them. "Whatever *this* is. Sir Lucius warned me that I was, and I scoffed at him."

He'd talked with Sir Lucius about courting her? How very intriguing.

"But apparently, he was right," Rafe said testily, "and I am a dunderheaded fool."

"You are, indeed." Trying not to laugh, she walked up to kiss him lightly on the lips. "But that needn't keep us from kissing," she said with a smile. "Now it's done, and neither of us need be curious about it."

"Done?" he said, a sudden glint in his eyes. "Hardly."

Before she could even think, he settled his hands on her waist, pulled her close, and pressed his mouth to hers again. Her heart flipped over. This was a better kiss than her own and masterfully done. He toyed with her lips, his breath mingling with hers, warm and fragrant with the smell of cloves.

"You taste good," he murmured against her mouth, and

as if to emphasize that, he tugged lightly on her lower lip with his teeth.

"You smell good," she whispered before he covered her lips with his again, more forcefully this time.

He smelled heavenly, to be honest, his scent some heady, masculine mix of bay rum and cinnamon that made her light-headed. Or perhaps that was the kiss, now fierce and tender by turns. Never had anyone given her such a kiss.

Basking in the pleasure of it, she slid her arms about his waist, her eyes sliding closed all by themselves. He ran the tip of his tongue over the seam of her lips and coaxed them apart, then plunged his tongue inside her mouth.

Oh, help. That was very wicked. Lovely. Different. Intoxicating. Her cheeks were aflame, and her blood was, too. Especially once he began to slide his tongue in and out, as if to possess her. She wasn't used to that sort of . . . bold behavior. It made her want to be bold, too, to slide her fingers through his silken, wavy hair and feel his hands on her in unacceptable places . . .

The sound of talking in the hall made her pull away from him, a bit regretfully. It was Diana and Geoffrey, conversing more loudly than normal and not so subtly warning them to behave.

He didn't alter his stance an inch, though his hands did fall to his sides. But his eyes—those glorious silvery eyes—bore into her and then fixed on her mouth, which still tingled from their kisses.

She shook off her reaction. Realizing that her sister and brother-in-law would think it odd if Mr. Wolfford and she remained quiet, Verity said in a carrying voice, "So, you see, sir, even if you don't prefer sweets, we find that a little sugar works well in the sauce."

He looked at her, uncomprehending, and she poked him. Then it apparently sank in. The beginnings of a smile on

48 *Sabrina Jeffries*

his lips, he drawled, "I find that a little sugar works well in just about anything." He had the audacity to reach out and trace her lips with his finger.

Naughty man. Removing his hand from her mouth, she flashed him a chastening look. "*Anyway,* I have a list of questions you can answer, as I mentioned before. If you'll give me your direction, I'll send them to you, and you can write out your answers at your leisure."

"Of course. At present, I'm at the Albany."

That caught her off guard. Only the best of Society's bachelors had taken rooms at the Albany since it had opened nearly ten years ago. Poets, politicians, and playwrights had all graced its halls, and so had a duke's son or two. She could hardly imagine the Phantom there.

Unless he was staying in someone else's rooms as a guest, which was certainly possible.

"I see." She listened a moment, but it sounded as if Diana and Geoffrey had moved on. "They'll be back soon," she said in a low voice. "So, why don't we decide when the meal should take place, and I can return to my family before you're . . . *we're* tempted to do any more . . . er . . . experiments in flirtation."

"I like the experiments."

"So do I," she conceded, "unwise though they may be."

"They didn't feel unwise." His eyes gleamed at her. "Surely, one more won't hurt."

Her heart began to pound so loudly in her chest that she feared he might hear it. Not once in their courtship had Lord Minton *ever* made her want like *this.*

All the more reason she should refuse. Which was why she groaned when she heard herself say, "Very well. One *short* one."

Without even answering, he stepped forward and took her in his arms. And just before his mouth came down hard on hers, she saw the hunger in his expression, felt that same hunger course through her own body, and knew at once she was in trouble.

Because gluttony was a sin, and she was about to sin most grievously.

Chapter 5

Rafe knew he was playing a risky game—one he could lose if it scared Verity off entirely. But how better to strengthen his connection to her?

It had nothing whatsoever to do with his urgent need to plunder her mouth again.

Closing his eyes against that thought, he deepened their kiss, exulting when she parted her lips to let him in. The heat of her mouth when he tangled his tongue with hers made his breath quicken and blood rush to his head. No matter how he struggled to ignore her attractions, kissing her proved a revelation, showing that Lady Verity could turn from thorny into rose petal soft in his arms.

It made him ache for her. He wanted to taste more, touch more . . . feel more.

Damn.

Her hands grasped his lapels as if to hold him close, and he indulged in the urge to nuzzle her cheek and scatter kisses to her ear. "You taste like sunshine," he whispered.

She chuckled, not the effect he'd intended. "And what does sunshine taste like?"

He tugged on her earlobe with his teeth. "Oranges."

Her breathing stuttered. "That must be . . . the orange oil in my perfume."

Wisps of her hair tickled his nose. "I'd love to see you with your hair down."

Hell and thunder. Had he actually said that aloud?

She stiffened. "That's not likely to happen, Mr. Wolfford," she said, and started to pull away.

"Rafe," he said, correcting her. "Call me Rafe, Verity."

"I did not give you leave to use—"

He cut her off with another kiss, this one long and deep and thorough, eliciting a moan from her that fired his blood. Then he pulled back to murmur, "You were saying?"

She gazed up at him, her eyes the green of forests in afternoon light. "You're an impertinent fellow, aren't you . . . Rafe?"

"Sometimes. But then, you're an impertinent woman, Verity."

"How can you possibly know that when we just met?" she said in a light tone, though something in her words sounded a warning.

He ignored it. He'd obviously spent so long as a spy, he saw danger everywhere. "You were impertinent from the moment you said an heir must need a wife."

A reluctant smile crossed her lips. "True. Although do please refrain from calling me Verity around my sisters. They'll think we're doing naughty things."

"We *are* doing naughty things," he said, punctuating that with a nibble on her lower lip. *Just not naughty enough for me.*

He noticed how her throat moved convulsively. Nothing aroused him more than seeing a woman aroused. Especially one who didn't bother to hide it.

"I-I don't want them to know what we're doing," she whispered, "or I'll never hear the end of it. And they'll become annoyingly overprotective."

He smiled. "As you wish, my lady."

Lifting an eyebrow, she left his arms. Clearly, the kissing was over. Not that he minded. He really didn't.

Right.

Not meeting his gaze, she touched a hand to her hair as if to make sure every curl was in its proper place. "Now, we really must discuss when and where to meet for your meal."

She probably did *not* mean the kind of meal he was wanting at present.

"I don't suppose we could do it in my rooms at the Albany." Where he could quite literally have his cake and eat it, too.

"Not unless you have a full kitchen hiding inside them."

He chuckled. "Good point. Unfortunately, although I hope to look for a house to lease once the Season starts in the spring, I don't yet know exactly how long I'll be in London, so I'm not sure what day to tell you."

"My family and I will be leaving town for a month next week, so it should happen before then."

"Ah. Where are you going?" he asked, though he already knew.

"To a house party."

You could invite me, he thought. *You could ask me now.*

But no, she was still too cautious to do something that rash without her sisters' approval. And he'd heard enough of their conversation after the auction to know that they weren't quite ready to do so, thanks to their meddling husbands.

You know perfectly well you'd be just as cautious if you were in their shoes.

Yes, he would.

"We could always do it after you return," he said. "Assuming I am still in town. No doubt, you have much to prepare before your trip."

"It's fine," she said with a wave of her gloved hand. "Let

me consult with my chef and see if he can manage it before
we leave town."

Rafe forced a smile, though inside he was wincing. Monsieur Beaufort, of course. Beaufort wasn't going to be happy
with Rafe for winning the bid on the dinner, but there
wasn't anything Rafe could do about it now. He'd made a
tactical decision to bid, and he didn't regret it. To be fair, he
had tried to get out of claiming the meal, but that wouldn't
assuage Beaufort's temper. "Leave word at the Albany for
me, and I'll try to arrange my schedule to meet his and
yours."

"Thank you for being so accommodating," Verity said
brightly.

He caught her hand. "I could be more accommodating,
if you wished."

She narrowed her gaze on him. "In what way?"

"Why don't we go into the garden to discuss it?" Where
he could kiss her senseless without worrying about her
chaperones, to ensure she went back to her sisters and insisted he be invited to the party.

"That would be unwise," she said smoothly, disappointing
him. Until she added, "We should return to our companions."

Our companions? That was a good sign. She was already
thinking of him as part of the circle. "Very well. Another
time then."

They were leaving the room when a footman approached
with a message for him, a terse note from Sir Lucius that
read, *We must speak privately. Meet me in the stone garden
building. You know the one.*

Something dire must have happened or Sir Lucius would
never have contacted him in the middle of this affair.

He looked at Verity. "Forgive me, but Sir Lucius requires

my help. He rode here in my carriage, and I . . . er . . . need to help him back into it."

To his surprise, she laughed. "Had a bit too much champagne, did he?" she said.

"Exactly," he said, hoping that Sir Lucius wouldn't take offense.

"Well, I cannot complain. He bid at the auction respectably, and he introduced me to *you*, who bid more than respectably. So, if I don't see you later, I will understand. I'll send word to you at the Albany once I know when we can fulfill your auction item."

"Thank you." He thought of something as they entered the ballroom. "Is Lord Minton still here?"

Her face hardened. "I don't think so. But I'll make sure not to wander alone in the garden."

"Good." For more reasons than one. "Or if you choose to do so, take the duke or Lord Foxstead with you."

Her expression gentling, she placed her hand on his arm. "Thank you for your concern. I won't be caught off guard by him again, I assure you. Now, go take care of your friend."

With a nod, he hurried to a door leading into the gardens. When last he'd been at Grenwood House—in disguise, of course—he'd explored the entire property and found an abandoned laboratory building at the back of the garden. Sir Lucius must have remembered that from his report.

The moment Rafe strode inside, Sir Lucius emerged from the shadows. "We've received intelligence from the Secret Office that Napoleon has crossed over into Russia."

The Secret Office was appropriately named, since it was literally the best-kept secret of the British government. A clandestine branch of the Government Post Office for nearly three centuries, it read every piece of mail sent to— and from—England and any foreign country. Every day, a small group of clerks and translators combed those letters for anything significant to England's well-being before sending the mail on its way.

During wartime, the Secret Office was essential. The public didn't know of its existence. Even many in government didn't know. And spymasters like Sir Lucius wanted to keep it that way.

The very fact that the spy they sought avoided using the mails meant the person had friends in very high places. Which is why Rafe and Sir Lucius had resorted to their current investigation.

"If Napoleon wins in Russia," Sir Lucius went on, "we'll be hard-pressed to beat him at all. And if he wins on the Peninsula . . ." With a shake of his head, he lowered his voice. "We also received word of a battle where the British advance guard was taken by surprise. *Someone* knew we were coming."

"Damn it all to hell."

"Wellington is marching on to Madrid. He needs to hold the city if we are to have any chance of fighting Napoleon after Boney subdues Russia."

"Assuming Boney *succeeds* at subduing Russia," Rafe said. "They're coming into winter there, and Russian winters are brutal."

"All the same, I would feel better—the War Office would feel better—if we could root out the spy who's sharing our troop information. So how goes it with Lady Verity? Any luck there?"

"It's coming along well," he said evasively.

"It ought to be, given your bid at the auction. I doubt the War Office will reimburse you for that two hundred pounds you're spending on a mere dinner."

"I don't expect reimbursement. Consider it part of my revenge on behalf of my uncle."

"Your family coffers contain so much?"

"They contain enough," Rafe said. "I had to get Lady Verity's attention somehow, you know. And it seems to have worked, too. I overheard her and her sister's discussion about inviting me to the house party."

Sir Lucius let out a breath. "Excellent."

"But I also overheard Grenwood and Foxstead express alarm that the ladies might not know enough about me. The gentlemen insisted on finding out more before inviting me."

His superior nodded. "We anticipated that, and it's already handled. We even went so far as to 'sell' your commission to an officer, so he could take your place in Spain. Because you didn't wish to go back to the war with your uncle at death's door, your status as an active duty soldier has been kept entirely secret. Nor does anyone know the true state of your uncle's 'illness' but me, you, and the war minister."

And two or three servants at Castle Wolfford, whom Rafe could trust to keep quiet. "Good. Because I think the Harper sisters are leaning toward inviting me. Of course, if Foxstead or Grenwood talk them out of it, it might indicate one of *them* is the spy."

"I can't see it being either of those two. You should make sure of that, of course, but Grenwood hasn't been in Society long enough, and Foxstead was a damned war hero, for God's sake."

"True."

Sir Lucius took out a cigar and lit it off the candle he'd apparently brought. "I noticed you got Lady Verity to go off with you alone after the auction. Was that wise?"

Wise? No. But enormously enjoyable. Not that he would tell Sir Lucius that.

The spymaster went on. "At least recognize that if you take this 'courtship' too far, you could tip your hand. Or worse yet, find yourself facing the same danger your uncle did. I don't want *two* wounded Wolffords on my conscience."

"I'll be careful." Now, if only Verity hadn't shown herself capable of laying waste to his defenses when he least expected it. "I couldn't just leave without letting my 'friendship' with her blossom, so to speak. Not after hearing them speak of searching my past to make sure I'm suitable for their jaunt to the seaside."

Hearing the bitter tinge in his voice, he wasn't surprised when Sir Lucius said, "I suppose I shouldn't have told her right off that you were an orphan. But you're the one who spoke of having a soft spot for orphans in the first place."

"She would have found out eventually." The truth was, he hadn't meant to mention orphans at all. It had just come out, the minute he saw her in the flesh, so close, so beautiful, so . . .

Unpredictable. That was it—Verity was at her core unpredictable. He'd spent his entire military career using predictability to manage his missions—to assess enemy soldiers and their commanders, foreign civilians in politics, certain servants in high places and low. But there was no using predictability against Verity, and he found that downright irritating.

And fascinating, too.

Nonsense. He wasn't fascinated in the least. Not when she was succeeding at throwing him off his game. "Besides, she and I had to arrange when and where to fulfill my auction-winning bid."

"Ah, yes."

"She does seem to like me, which works in our favor."

The undersecretary puffed a moment. "Does she? How could you tell?"

Some part of Rafe was loath to reveal that he and Verity

had kissed, more than once. "Let's just say we flirted quite a bit while we talked about kitchens and when to meet."

Apparently, Sir Lucius didn't realize that the word "flirted" could cover many sins, for he smiled. "Thank God you've moved so far forward in such a short amount of time. I will make sure the road is cleared for you to proceed. Whomever Foxstead and Grenwood find in my office to report on you for their invitation will be told only the most attractive information about you."

"Thanks," Rafe said dryly. "I didn't realize there was *un*attractive information circulating about me."

Sir Lucius shrugged. "You're a spy. And our countrymen don't like the idea of being spied on by their own government. Which is precisely why we've kept the Secret Office secret all these centuries." He clapped Rafe on the shoulder. "Don't worry. I'll make sure they don't hear a word about your spying, or even that you were one of Wellington's Exploring Officers."

"You do that. Perhaps I will get to the seaside yet."

"You'll be on your own there, you realize."

"As I was whenever I went out as an Exploring Officer."

"This is different. If you need me, send a note by messenger. I'll bring help. Assuming you succeed in getting yourself invited."

"I will, I swear." He'd better, no matter what it took. He'd been preparing his whole life to do this sort of work, thanks to his uncle. So, he'd always known what he was getting into every time he went out on a mission—a shadowy world where nobody trusted anybody. That was why he trusted no one but his uncle and a handful of men like Sir Lucius. Best to keep it that way.

Although sometimes the lies and secrecy wore on him, to say the least. Having any kind of normal life was difficult when one couldn't trust. So, Sir Lucius was right about one thing—getting involved with Lady Verity in a romantic way had its dangers, especially if her family proved as treacherous as he feared.

Whatever happened in the next few weeks, Rafe must keep his wits about him with her. Or he could end up like his uncle—with his wits stolen from him.

And possibly his life.

Chapter 6

Two days after the auction, Verity sat bent over the table in the breakfast room at Foxstead Place, where she could get some privacy now that breakfast was over. Between Nathaniel, Eliza, and Jimmy, she sometimes found that difficult.

But living with her sister was better than living with their second cousin Winston and his new wife, Rosy, in her sister's old town house. Rosy was now doing a great deal of the fashion work for Elegant Occasions, and Winston was helping with an assortment of tasks—including consulting on men's fashion and etiquette—so they had needed somewhere to live in London, and Eliza's small town house had been perfect for a young couple.

That certainly made things easier on her and Eliza. But Verity had flat-out refused to live with them, knowing that the newlywed couple needed privacy. It wasn't quite the same with Eliza and Nathaniel. There was far more space at Foxstead Place, for one thing. Besides, Eliza had been married before, and little Jimmy was there, too, so it felt less . . . intimate.

Eliza and Nathaniel were taking care of Jimmy, the illegitimate son of Eliza's late husband, while the lad's mother and Hussar stepfather were on the Peninsula. Verity thought both couples were quite unconventional in their arrangement, but little Jimmy *was* a dear, and it would have been unconscionable to take the two-year-old to the war as well.

Good Lord, they certainly had a lot of officers in the family, didn't they? Mr. Wolfford should feel right at home with this lot, assuming they decided to invite him to the house party. She hoped they did. She wanted to know once and for all if he was the Phantom.

Verity took a sip from her cup of chocolate, only to discover it had gone cold. Ugh. Setting it down, she focused on the task at hand—making a list of everything she'd noticed about the Phantom. She had to do *something* to keep from dwelling on why it was taking Nathaniel and Geoffrey so long to uncover the truth about Mr. Wolfford. Unfortunately, her list wasn't helping her get any closer to determining whether the Phantom was Rafe.

She groaned. *Mr. Wolfford*, not *Rafe*, for pity's sake. If she wasn't careful, she'd call him by his Christian name in front of everyone, and she'd never hear the end of it from her family.

"What are you doing?" Eliza asked from behind her, making her jump.

"Good Lord," Verity muttered as she shut her notebook. "Were you *trying* to give me heart failure?"

"I don't have to try," her sister said blithely. "You regularly claim to suffer heart failure over badly arranged salads and sour milk in the white soup. I'm not sure how to avoid the process."

"I'm not as dramatic as all that, for pity's sake," Verity grumbled. "What are you doing here, anyway? I thought you and Diana had gone shopping."

"We did. Three hours ago. We're done."

"Oh. I guess the time slipped away from me."

Eliza looked over at Verity's closed notebook. "Were you working on the menus for the house party?"

"No. Those are already done." She thrust her notebook in her apron pocket. "And stop being nosy."

Curiosity leapt in Eliza's face, but she didn't pry. Eliza never did. But Diana would. Verity would have to find a very good place to hide her notebook.

"Fine," Eliza said. "Can I see the menus?"

"Not until I've gone over them with Monsieur Beaufort. Because you know how particular he is about meals being seasonal. Anyway, I have the meals covered. Have you heard back from the guests we invited? Have we decided for certain to ask Mama to come?"

"I don't think we should, but she's eager to see the baby, so Diana wants to have her."

"Some of the mothers and chaperones won't want their charges exposed to someone who's persona non grata in Society."

"Diana has arranged a compromise," Eliza said. "She convinced Mama to come the first two days only. Diana will explain the situation to the chaperones so that if they prefer to arrive after Mama leaves, they can. Some may not care, but at least they can choose whether to expose their charges to the scandalous Lady Rumridge. Later they can truthfully say to rumormongers that Mama wasn't there."

"If you can get her to leave. You know how she likes sea bathing." Verity made a face. "*I* don't have to bathe in the sea, do I? The tiny creatures in there get up under my bathing gown and sting. It's most unsettling."

"Not to mention the jellyfish. We know how you feel about *those*." Eliza gazed kindly at her. "You needn't set one foot near the ocean if you don't wish."

"Good." Verity smiled at Eliza. "I prefer to walk on the beach and pick up shells." She clapped her hands. "Oh, and we must plan a jaunt to A La Ronde. I didn't get to see everything last time."

"We'll do whatever all the ladies wish." Eliza winked at her. "And whatever all the gentlemen agree to accompany the ladies to. That is the point, after all."

"I know Isolde and her mother are coming to the house party, but I can't remember who else."

Diana walked up just then. "Lady Robina and her brother, Lord Ambridge, with his wife. Major Quinn."

Eliza groaned. "Must we?"

"He's our cousin. And he could use a wife."

"Nathaniel will complain," Eliza grumbled.

"He's married to you now, dear," Diana said. "He won't care anymore."

Eliza looked skeptical.

"Besides," Diana continued, "I think the major and Isolde might be enamored of each other, so we should encourage that. Oh, we also have Lord Henry and his twin, Lady Harriet."

"Both?" Verity said. "She's not our client."

"No, but he's quite eligible and won't come without her."

"That's because she makes trouble wherever she goes," Verity muttered. "Oh, blast, and they both go by Harry. It gets confusing when they're together."

"Well, not *very* confusing, surely," Diana said. "One's a woman and one's a man. If I say 'Harry is trying on a gown,' we all know who that is."

"Yes, but if you say, 'please pass the sauce to Harry—'"

"For pity's sake, call them Lord Harry or Lady Harry, and no one will be confused," Diana said irritably. "That's what you should be doing anyway."

"I suppose." Verity leaned on the table. "And who else?"

"Just the chaperones. Oh! And the American chap with the shy sister."

"Mr. Nigel Chetley and Miss Ophelia Chetley," Verity supplied. "She's come out of her shell a bit since Eliza and I have been working with her. They both made quite a splash at Devonshire's ball. I think Mr. Chetley is intent on gaining her a titled Englishman for a husband since they're filthy rich."

Diana sighed. "Can you please *try* not to be so forthright at the house party? We want to help Miss Chetley, not hinder her."

Verity drew herself up. "I would *never* say that to anyone but you two. And perhaps Geoffrey. He doesn't seem to mind how forthright I am."

"Because you and my husband are alike in that," Diana said.

"Yet you love us both for it," Verity pointed out. "Admit it."

"I love him in spite of it. And I love *you* because you're my sister. Who doesn't love their sisters?"

"*Someone* must dislike their sisters," Eliza said dryly. "Probably several someones."

Diana sniffed. "Well, I don't dislike either of you, although you do tromp on my nerves from time to time." Looking suddenly concerned, she sat down next to Eliza. "I should probably tell you I invited Sarah and the boys."

Verity jumped up. "Have you lost your mind? If Sarah and Papa come and so does Mama, our parents will fight the entire time!"

"I'm not daft enough to invite Papa," Diana said. "Just our stepmother and her sons. Besides, she's not coming while Mama is there, although I honestly don't think Mama gives two farthings that Papa married Sarah after the divorce."

After all, Mama had her new husband, Major General Tobias Ord, now also Viscount Rumridge, who was serving his country in Portugal. Mama saw him rarely these days.

"How did you invite Sarah without having to invite Papa, too?" Eliza asked.

"I merely implied it's a women-only sort of party where we discuss fashions and children and all the topics men generally find dull," Diana said. "Once Sarah finds out otherwise, we can say we changed the scope of the event. She won't mind."

"She never seems to mind anything," Verity said. "How she manages to stand up to Papa is anyone's guess."

"She doesn't, as far as I can see," Diana said. "Papa probably wouldn't come, anyway, even if I did invite him. Besides, it will be nice to see Sarah's little ones. It's been a long while."

Verity sank back into her chair. "Since you have your own 'little one' now, I'm surprised you'd be eager to see our stepbrothers."

"Actually," Eliza put in, "I'd like to see them, too. Jimmy could use someone to play with, especially at the seaside."

They heard a sudden commotion down the hall. "The men are here," Eliza said cheerily.

She'd been married less than a month, so she still apparently missed her husband when he was gone. Although, now that Verity came to think of it, that was true of Diana, too, and she'd been married over a year.

Verity wondered sourly if the men felt the same. From what she'd seen, most other men were incapable of missing their spouses. Certainly, Papa was that way—with both his wives.

At that moment, Geoffrey and Nathaniel strolled into the breakfast room to take seats at the table. Geoffrey poured himself some chocolate from the pitcher beside Verity.

"That's fairly cold by now," Verity warned him.

The big ox shrugged. "It's hot outside. I wouldn't mind a bit of cold coffee."

"It isn't coffee—it's chocolate."

"Even better!" He took a sip, then licked his lips. The man did love his sweets. "Besides, we told the butler to bring tea and coffee and cake. Gathering up important gossip makes me hungry."

That certainly got everyone's attention.

"You learned more about Mr. Wolfford?" Verity asked, hardly able to contain her excitement.

"Was he really a colonel?" Eliza asked.

"More importantly," Diana put in, "is he really a viscount's heir? Who cares what his army rank was? Or for that matter, which regiment he was in?"

"I already know that, anyway," Verity said. "He was in the King's German Legion. At least until he served on the Peninsula."

They all stared at her.

"What? We did converse while we were together at the auction. I found out all sorts of things about him. Unfortunately, none of them would help us confirm that he's who he says he is."

"He is who he says he is," Nathaniel said blithely.

At that moment, a maid and a footman walked in with large trays and began to set out a coffee urn, a teapot with cups, sugar, cream, and a plate of cakes.

"Oh, good," Nathaniel said as he jumped up to go pour himself a cup of tea. "Cook *did* still have some almond and seed cakes left. And she's also put a bit of marzipan on here for you, Geoffrey."

When Geoffrey rose to join him, Verity snapped, "For goodness' sake, can you two stop thinking with your bellies for once and tell us what you found out?"

Geoffrey turned to Nathaniel. "Methinks the lady is overly interested in a certain viscount's heir."

Nathaniel placed two cakes on his plate. "Methinks the lady is also overly interested in a certain retired colonel.

Oh, wait, perhaps they're one and the same." He winked at his wife. "Might we soon be sending your sister off to live elsewhere?"

"You would never do that, admit it," Verity said with a roll of her eyes. "You need *me* to keep Jimmy entertained on the nursemaid's day off."

"She has a point," Eliza said smugly as Nathaniel brought her a cup of coffee. "And it's not as if this house doesn't have plenty of room for her."

Diana let out an impatient breath. "Oh, come now, tell *me* what you learned. I'm dying to know."

"If you insist," Geoffrey said, plopping down beside his wife and handing her a cup of tea. "He was indeed a colonel—a decorated one, in fact—who served on the Peninsula and sold his commission when his retired uncle fell ill."

Nathaniel took up the tale. "His uncle is quite famous in military circles—he won many a battle against the French. Of course, that was long before my time in the army, but I gather that Mr. Wolfford served—"

"Under his uncle at that time," Verity said. "Yes, he told me that."

Nathaniel gaped at her. "Then why were we even sent to check up on him?"

"We didn't send you," Eliza said. "You two sent yourselves. We just went along with it."

"And anyway, he could have been inventing the whole thing," Verity said. "We had to know if it was the truth."

"Besides," Diana said, "we're far more interested in the viscountcy. Is he as eligible as he seems, given his outrageous bid at the auction?"

"From what we learned, yes," Geoffrey said. "Even before his uncle was made viscount, they both were from the prominent and very rich Wolfford family in Wiltshire. Mr. Wolfford is the son of the general's younger brother, who—"

"Died abroad. He told me."

"He told you a great deal, didn't he?" Geoffrey said. "Did he tell you that his family owns Castle Wolfford?"

"Wait, isn't that one of those country houses built to *look* like a Gothic castle?" Diana asked. "Like Strawberry Hill?"

Geoffrey blinked. "You *do* listen when I wax on about architecture and buildings."

"Sometimes." Diana reached over to pat his hand. "Who wouldn't find a pretend castle fascinating? It's like . . . like . . ."

"A fairy tale," Verity said, a little in awe. "No, he didn't tell me *that,* to be sure. Imagine actually living in such a castle. One would feel like a princess. And I do adore Strawberry Hill."

"Just to be clear," Nathaniel said, "you're not worried that we couldn't find out exactly what Mr. Wolfford did on the Peninsula to get his colonelcy and such."

"I don't even know exactly what *you* did on the Peninsula," Verity said. When Nathaniel opened his mouth as if to explain, she added hastily, "And I don't care to, either. So, no, I'm not worried. He served his country. That's good enough for me."

Although it still didn't explain the Phantom. Had she gone awry in thinking it was him?

"The only reason they didn't say what he did," Nathaniel went on as if she hadn't spoken, "is everyone is being secretive about what's going on there, since the war for Britain is primarily being fought on the Peninsula. It's a matter of our country's security, we were told."

"Thank you for that explanation," Verity said. *Which I decidedly did not ask for.*

Men. Did they ever listen to women?

"Well then, that's settled," Eliza said. "We invite Mr.

Wolfford. And it will even up the numbers of single men to single women, which is always better."

"They're already even," Verity pointed out.

"You're forgetting to count yourself, my dear," Diana said. "Until now, there was one more unmarried lady than there were unmarried men. But not if Mr. Wolfford comes."

Verity hadn't considered that. "But you shouldn't include me in the . . . I mean, this house party wasn't intended to . . ." She scowled at Diana. "This party is supposed to be about securing husbands for Isolde, Miss Chetley, and Lady Robina. You two had better not have planned this with the idea of finding *me* a husband."

"Not planned, exactly," Eliza said. "But why *shouldn't* you find a husband, too? Lord Minton has been routed, thanks to a certain viscount's heir, and you did just remark that Mr. Wolfford's castle sounds like something from a fairy tale."

"I know, but . . . Well, I'm not even sure that I . . ." She should tell them she suspected him of being the Phantom. But they would laugh endlessly at her for such an idea now, given his and his uncle's history. "Oh, very well, then. Invite him. Just be aware that one night's conversation between us doesn't necessarily mean we would suit."

And a couple of very nice kisses didn't either. Although if she mentioned the kisses, her sisters would be even *more* likely to play matchmaker.

"Of course not," Diana said in a suspiciously soothing tone. "No one's saying that."

Verity knew that tone. It meant Diana was matchmaking.

But before she could protest, Diana added, "Now, we merely have to make sure he accepts." She smiled at Verity. "You should use your feminine wiles on him."

"I don't think I have any," Verity said truthfully, then paused. "What the devil *is* a 'wile,' anyway?"

"I believe it's a playful trick or something like that," Eliza offered. "I could look it up in the dictionary to be sure."

Verity eyed her askance. "That was a rhetorical question, Eliza."

"If you say so."

"I, for one, think you have plenty of feminine wiles, Verity," Geoffrey said. "Not as many as Diana, of course, but you did get Mr. Wolfford to bid quite high on your dinner. He must have had a reason for that."

That *was* odd, wasn't it? She'd like to believe he was impressed with her speech about the dinner, but she doubted it.

Wait, he *had* given her a reason for bidding so high. "He did it to help our charity, he said, because he's an orphan himself."

"Then why bid on your dinner in particular?" Nathaniel pointed out. "Why not bid on one of the other items of high value?"

Why not, indeed? He'd also said he'd wanted to protect her from Lord Minton, but she wasn't quite sure she believed him. They'd just met, after all. Why would he have cared?

Then again, the way he'd kissed her . . .

"I told you, dearest," Eliza said. "He's clearly smitten with Verity."

Perhaps. Although if he was, she wished she knew why.

Well, there was only one way to find out. They'd have to invite him to the house party, and she'd have to spend more time with him.

But Lord have mercy on his soul if she discovered he had some devious purpose. To quote the Bard, she would "eat his heart in the market-place."

Just see if she didn't.

Chapter 7

Two days after the auction, upon being shown into the drawing room at Foxstead Place, Rafe was surprised to find the Earl of Foxstead awaiting him rather than the man's wife and Verity.

Foxstead, whose military manner and trim form reminded him that the man had once been an army captain, rose to greet him with a firm handshake. "Nice to see you again, sir. The ladies will be down shortly—some issue with a missing glove, I believe. I was sent to entertain you in the meantime."

To interrogate him, more like, but that was fine by Rafe. Perhaps he could find out a few things about Foxstead in the process.

When the earl gestured to a seat, Rafe took it, not surprised when Foxstead took one nearer the door. Definitely the tactic of a soldier who wanted to position himself where he could head off "the ladies" if Rafe's responses displeased him.

"Have you come to pay a call on Lady Verity?" Foxstead asked.

Odd that the earl wasn't mentioning the invitation Rafe had received yesterday. "Yes. I wished to give her the answers to the questions she sent to me at the Albany." When Foxstead looked blank, Rafe added, "For the meal I bid on."

"I forgot about that. I suppose you wish to set up the time, et cetera." Foxstead stared him down until something Rafe had said seemed to register. "You're staying at the Albany?"

"For now." Rafe could see the wheels turning in the man's head. No doubt, Foxstead would send someone to find out about Rafe's sojourn at the famous lodgings for bachelors. Foxstead's "spy" wouldn't learn much. Rafe had only stayed there as his real self for a week and a half. Before that, he'd had rooms under an assumed name in a seedier part of town, where he wouldn't risk being recognized by anyone.

"You could have just sent the answers over," Foxstead pointed out.

"They were too complicated to relegate to paper. I needed to explain myself." And this was getting them nowhere. So, rather than wait for Foxstead to interrogate him, Rafe decided to take the battle to Foxstead. "I understand you were in the army and on the Peninsula."

That gave Foxstead a start. "You know my history, do you?" he said, a hint of suspicion in his voice.

"Who doesn't? You're a war hero. Sir Lucius told me that much at the auction."

Foxstead's face cleared. "Of course. He would know of my time in the war."

"He certainly knows all about mine."

"Speaking of that, what exactly did *you* do on the Peninsula?"

Rafe couldn't say much. Foxstead might know that an Exploring Officer specifically did intelligence for Wellington, who'd personally recruited Rafe. "I was in the Corps of

Mounted Guides." Which was the official name of the elite group.

Foxstead frowned. "I've never heard of it."

"I'm not surprised. We acted as guides in Portugal for British generals and their staff." Until Wellington took hold of it and turned it into a reconnaissance unit. "I was recruited because of my facility with languages."

"What languages do you speak?"

"French, Spanish, Portuguese, and German. I also have a reading knowledge of Italian, Latin, and Greek."

Foxstead blinked. "That is indeed a facility for languages. I do speak French, of course. And a little Portuguese."

Rafe rattled off a question in Portuguese about how long Foxstead had served on the Peninsula.

Wincing, Foxstead said, "Not *that* much Portuguese and certainly not that fluently." Then, in halting Portuguese, he answered the question and added a remark of his own in English. "I understand you were one of the few British soldiers in the King's German Legion."

"I served with them until I joined the Corps of Mounted Guides."

"Was the corps at Talavera?"

"Tangentially." If one could call it that. "You were there, I understand. I heard of your exploits. We all did."

Foxstead waved his hand dismissively. "I left the army not long after."

"Because your father died." When Foxstead gave a start, Rafe smiled thinly.

That seemed to take the man aback. It afforded Rafe some satisfaction to watch Foxstead registering that Rafe, too, could delve into someone's army life.

"Any more questions?" Rafe asked.

Foxstead cast him a considering look. "Let me put my cards on the table. You've probably heard gossip about

Verity and her former fiancé. But no matter what people say, she's a respectable woman who deserves to be treated—"

"I assure you, I have no ill intentions toward Lady Verity and certainly wouldn't heed any gossip about her. From the moment I met her, she struck me as a woman of principle. What's more, I'm sure that a man like you, a fellow soldier, would never tell me she's respectable if that were not the case."

Foxstead's expression cleared. "Precisely. It's just that some people . . . well, make assumptions because she's also a bit . . . outspoken."

Rafe couldn't prevent a rueful smile. "I noticed."

Foxstead unbent a little. "Frankly, she's the bluntest female I know, and the other two sisters aren't exactly wilting flowers. But Verity has a big heart and feels more deeply than she lets on. So, be careful with her, if you take my meaning."

The warning unsettled him. The idea of being responsible for Verity's *heart* made him squirm. "Thank you for the information. I will be as gentlemanly as you undoubtedly were with your wife."

Instead of reassuring Foxstead, that seemed to bring the man up short. "Yes, of course." He shifted in his chair. "As long as we understand each other."

"We do." But that wouldn't stop Rafe from courting Verity. From finishing his mission.

The door opened to reveal the two ladies, and both gentlemen jumped to their feet. A maid bustled in, too, and set about placing tea and coffee things on the table in front of the settee.

"I hope we haven't kept you gentlemen waiting too long," Verity said with an unreadable look at Rafe.

Her very entrance threw him off guard. He hadn't been prepared for how seeing her again might affect him. For how instantly it would remind him of kissing her soft mouth, nuzzling her silky cheek . . . drowning in her fragrant scent.

Today, in her white, artfully draped gown, with her hair swept up into a circlet of woven ribbons, she looked like a Greek beauty of legend. Aphrodite. Helen of Troy. Certainly, a woman whose face could launch a thousand ships.

He must have been staring particularly hard, for she faltered. "What? Do I have something in my teeth?" Her pretty eyes gleamed. "Or perhaps my bandeau is hanging loose again."

"Forgive me," he said hastily. "I wasn't prepared for such a vision of beauty this morning." When she looked skeptical of the compliment, he added, "A very *clever* vision of beauty, to be sure."

The Foxsteads exchanged bewildered glances, but Verity apparently remembered their previous conversation and gave a musical laugh. "Your flatteries are improving, I see. Although you should probably refrain from continuing in that vein, sir, or my head will grow too large for my bandeau, loose or otherwise. Flattery begets vanity, a vice I'd rather not acquire."

"You assume my compliments are insincere," he said. "I assure you, they are not. I'm simply unaccustomed to being around ladies of your caliber."

"Caliber?" Verity echoed. "Now you compare me to a bullet?"

Rafe eyed her closely. "I meant the word figuratively, as you well know."

Foxstead muttered to his wife, "Either that, or he compliments like a soldier."

"You have no room to criticize, Nathaniel," Lady Foxstead said. "You haven't shed all your soldier trappings, either." She smiled at Rafe. "I assume you received the invitation to the Grenwoods' house party in Exmouth?"

"I did." Rafe said, finding the byplay between the couple fascinating. It occurred to him that he knew no married couples socially beyond officers and their wives. Certainly, none like them.

Foxstead murmured something in his wife's ear, and she told him, "I wasn't going to wait for you to do all that. I sent it yesterday."

With a roll of his eyes, Foxstead wandered over to pour himself some coffee.

Meanwhile, his wife approached Rafe. "I gather you mean to accept our invitation?"

"How did you guess?" Rafe asked.

"Well, if you'd meant to refuse, I can't imagine you'd take the trouble of coming here in person to do so."

"Actually," he said, with a side glance at Verity, "I wanted to learn a bit about what's expected of me. I've never attended a house party. As your husband probably remembers, we didn't have them on the Peninsula."

Lady Foxstead's eyes twinkled. "I suppose not. Although judging from your perfect manners, I suspect you know more about Society than you let on."

"I suspect so, too." Verity narrowed her gaze on him. "No house parties? Going to war must be dull indeed."

When Foxstead snorted, Rafe stifled a smile. "'Dull' isn't the word I would use. There are periods of dullness, of course, but periods of insanity as well. Like marching up a hill, only to be ordered to run back the way one came."

"Sounds like the work of ineffective officers," Foxstead drawled.

"Or enemies behaving unexpectedly. As you well know, war is never how you anticipate." Rather like Verity. One had to learn to adapt to the unpredictable.

"Well, Mr. Wolfford," Verity said, "you should expect

only entertainment at our house party. Good conversation, fun activities, and excellent food."

"Are you in charge of the food?" Rafe asked.

"For the most part. Along with my sister's kitchen staff, of course."

Foxstead set his cup in its saucer. "Then you'd best have prawlongs for my wife, and plenty of food of all types for Geoffrey. That man eats more than an elephant, I swear. What about you, Wolfford? Any preferences?"

"I'm not particular about food. Everything Lady Verity served at the auction was delicious. I can't imagine her putting anything on a menu that wasn't tasty."

Lady Foxstead laughed. "As I said, a man with good manners."

"Or . . ." Verity said, strolling up to him. "A man who is testing my ability to surmise what to give him for his auction dinner. Did you answer my questions?"

"That's why I'm here," Rafe said evasively. "To discuss my answers in person. And to ask for advice on appropriate attire for a house party at the seaside." At present, his wardrobe was minimal, and he needed to expand it before he left, which was only a little over a week away. "Speaking of that, Lord Foxstead, do you have a tailor to recommend, who can provide clothing quickly? I plan to meet with one today, but I confess he doesn't inspire confidence."

"I do have one I trust," Foxstead said. "Here, I'll write down his name and address for you."

He had just finished jotting it down on a piece of paper when a lightning bolt in the form of a child barreled through the door and right at Lady Foxstead's legs. "Missis Pears! Missis Pears! Help, help!" he cried, tears streaming down his cheeks. "My soldier fall in fire! My soldier burn!"

"Oh, dear," Lady Foxstead said. "Don't you worry— we'll take care of it."

This must be Jimmy March, the towheaded ward of the earl Rafe had seen from time to time while observing the family from afar. Rafe had wondered about the strange situation, speculating that perhaps the earl was keeping the child to blackmail Mrs. March and her husband into helping him pass on information.

But somehow, he couldn't see it. Especially when Lord Foxstead hefted the boy in his arms to say soothingly, "Her ladyship and I will fish him out if we can, and if he's too burnt, we'll give him a proper burial and buy you a new one."

Sir Lucius might be right that Lord Foxstead was exactly what he seemed, a war hero who protected his own.

"We'll return directly, Mr. Wolfford," Lady Foxstead said as she rushed out with her husband, who still held the lad in his arms. "Why don't you and Verity start your meal discussion?"

The three of them disappeared through the door.

"Why don't we, indeed?" Verity said. "But do you mind if we go out into the garden to do it? I must see what's available in the way of herbs. I was so busy with the auction, I hadn't had time to do so."

"Shouldn't the servants be gathering your herbs?" he asked as he followed her out and down a hall until they reached a door leading out to a well-manicured garden.

"I prefer doing it myself," she said as she strolled outside, pausing only to pick up a basket and clipping shears, which had apparently been left waiting for her by the garden door. "It inspires me to think of new food combinations."

He took the basket from her, and she let him, walking languidly down the path with the shears in her hand.

"Should I be worried that you're holding on to the

shears?" he drawled. "Those would make a formidable weapon."

She shot him a coy look. "Why, yes, they would. So don't try anything naughty, sir, or—" She snipped the air. "I may just clip your . . . cravat."

"It's not my cravat I'm worried about," he muttered.

Ignoring him, she stopped by a fragrant bush. She bent slightly to cut several long stalks, and a scent of rosemary wafted to him.

"Have you ever had rosemary in a salad?" she asked.

"No."

"It's quite interesting. Also, with a bit of garlic, lemon, salad oil, vinegar, and lavender, it is quite good for dressing salads, too."

"It would have to be good indeed to make a salad palatable."

"Don't you like salad?" she asked lightly.

"I'd sooner eat lawn clippings." When a merry laugh escaped her, he added, "Wasn't one of the questions on your auction meal list about greens I'd prefer?"

She continued down the path, stopping occasionally to clip things and add them to her basket. "It was. I'll wager I could make a salad that would change your mind about them. But I'd have to try a few ingredients on you first."

"I'd prefer that we skip the lesson in salads. I'm rather firm in my dislike of them. Come to think of it, I'm not all that fond of oysters, either. Or mushrooms—they taste like mud."

"Not when properly cooked." She paused to wave the shears at him. "I thought you said you weren't particular about food."

"I'm not. Aside from disliking oysters, mushrooms, salads, calves liver, whelks, that nasty meat jelly cooks pour over perfectly good foods . . ." He caught her looking at him with a raised eyebrow. "All right, so I'm a *little* particular. But if I'm hungry, I'll eat whatever is placed in front of me. I just might not enjoy it."

"Hmm, that won't work for me. I aim to provide you with a pleasurable meal, not mere satisfaction of hunger. I should add that I also have a long list of foods I hate—sweetbreads being one—but if I couldn't eat salad, I would die."

"*Die*?" he said incredulously.

"A slight exaggeration. Very slight." She grinned. "So, now that I know the ingredients you hate, are there any particular *dishes* you dislike?" When he opened his mouth, she added, "And don't just say, 'anything with the foods I just listed.'"

He couldn't help laughing. Not only had she mimicked him very well, but he'd been about to say that very thing. Wait, was *he* predictable?

"I'm serious." She continued down the path. "I'm sure there are dishes you dislike that nonetheless contain foods you enjoy. For example, I despise plain boiled chicken. I love chicken generally, if it's roasted or fried or fricasseed or covered in a delicate sauce, but plain boiled chicken makes me shiver."

"Ah. I take your meaning now." Rafe followed her in bemusement. He'd never met a person so . . . involved with all the nuances of food. Indeed, he'd never thought food had nuances. But he did know what he liked and disliked. He said the first thing that came to mind. "I dislike anything with a creamy sauce that entirely hides the item . . . um . . . being sauced."

"That's common, actually. Some people hate not being able to see what's underneath." She halted to look at him.

"You did write these down, didn't you? In answer to my questions?"

He winced. "I thought it would be easier just to explain in person."

"For you, perhaps. Not so easy for me." Abruptly, she turned and headed for the house. "Now we'll have to go back inside so I can take notes. I didn't bring any writing implements or paper with me."

"You're annoyed," he said as he strode beside her.

"I'm not annoyed," she bit out, which just proved that she was. "Although I *did* say at the auction that you would have to answer a list of questions, and you *did* agree to do so."

"I know," he said irritably, "but in all fairness, I didn't realize when I bid I'd have to put effort as well as money into this 'special meal.'"

She halted to glare at him. "I'll return your money, if you prefer."

"Please don't. As I told you before, I'm perfectly happy just giving the funds to the Foundling Hospital as a donation. You need not create an elaborate dinner for me." He lowered his voice. "Indeed, when I came here today, I was hoping to gain a moment or two alone to do something *other* than talk about food. Like continuing our 'discussion' in the drawing room a couple of nights ago."

"What discu—" She blushed as it hit her, then shot him a chilly look. "Sorry to disappoint."

He suppressed a curse. He was handling this badly. "I'm not disappointed. I just—"

"There you are, mademoiselle!" boomed a familiar voice from the door leading into the garden.

Damn it all to hell. Monsieur Beaufort was coming down the path. Why in God's name must he show up now?

Rafe cast the man a warning look just as the dusky-skinned Frenchman recognized him.

Fortunately, Beaufort hesitated only a moment and covered his surprise well. "Oh, mademoiselle," he told Verity, "I did not know you had a guest, or I would not have interrupted."

"It isn't a problem," Verity said blandly. "He wasn't expected. If I'd known he was planning to pay a call, I would have told you." She turned to Rafe with an odd glint in her eyes. "Mr. Wolfford, may I introduce Monsieur Beaufort, chef de cuisine extraordinaire?"

"I'm delighted to meet the famous monsieur," Rafe said, holding out his hand to shake Beaufort's. "I hear that your syllabub is exceptional."

"So I am told by those who eat it," the man said archly. Beaufort was well aware of his own worth. After all, he'd been the head cook at the Society of Eccentrics, a London gentlemen's club, for nearly twenty years.

Then he paused as if to reconsider his answer and added, "It is the Devonshire clotted cream on the top. I make Devonshire Syllabub."

"Ah," Rafe murmured. "I do like clotted cream." And Beaufort knew it, too.

"But do you like *syllabub*, Mr. Wolfford?" Verity asked.

"Yes, actually," Rafe told her.

She lifted her gaze to the skies. "Thank heaven. I began to think you didn't like anything."

"I have a fondness for sweets, I confess," he said, resisting the urge to give her a meaningful glance.

Apparently, even that didn't protect him from Beaufort's sharp, dark eyes, because questions shone in his expression. Rafe would have to visit Beaufort later to explain.

Verity flashed Beaufort a tight smile. "Mr. Wolfford won the bid at the auction for the Elegant Occasions meal. But there's some question of whether he actually means to eat it."

Rafe stifled a groan. Obviously, he'd insulted her. "Of course I mean to eat it. I merely didn't wish to put you to any trouble."

"It sounded as if you felt I'm the one giving *you* trouble."

"I should not have implied that," he said. "I am merely too lazy to answer your questions. But I am also genuinely curious to see how you use my answers, so of course, I will do so."

Beaufort looked at Verity. "I can ask the questions of Mr. Wolfford myself if you wish, so he won't trouble you any longer. That way, I will also know his preferences, and we can consult on his answers."

Rafe bit back a protest. He hadn't wanted to have the discussion with Beaufort here and now, but it looked as if he would have to. If Beaufort so chose, he could reveal Rafe's plans to Verity in a heartbeat.

She seemed to find Beaufort's offer surprising, but finally said, "Very well. I must fetch my notebook and pencil anyway. Why don't you two chat a moment while I do that?"

They both nodded agreeably, then watched as she hurried into the house.

"Let's move to the foot of the garden, so we won't be overheard," Rafe said.

"Very well," Beaufort answered, "but we do not have much time. Lady Verity can be swift when she wishes."

"I know."

"Do you?" Beaufort halted by the gate. "Why are you here? I told you when you began this investigation last year that the Harper ladies had nothing to do with spying for the French. If I had thought they did, I would have helped you myself, but I know them to be only good, kind—"

"I trust your judgment," Rafe said hastily. "I do. But we

now have reason to believe the spy is among their friends or family, so I can only root the bastard out by becoming one of their friends."

Beaufort hissed a French curse between his teeth. "You are certain the spy is one of their friends or family?"

"I am, thanks to some information we gained recently. And as you might realize, I can say no more than that, but you know me. I wouldn't pursue a line of investigation if I didn't have something to go on."

"Why did you not tell me this sooner?" Beaufort asked.

"Would it have changed your mind about spying on the Harper ladies?"

"I do not know," he said sullenly. "They have been very good to me. No one wants an old chef, no matter his reputation, but they've promised to hire me for as long as I wish to keep cooking. And they pay very well." He fixed Rafe with a wary look. "But you should have told me before about your decision to step in personally. Do you now suspect *me* of being a spy?"

"For the French? Don't be absurd. I, of all people, know you fled France for a good reason."

Because as a free black caught up in the revolution, Beaufort didn't feel certain of being kept safe from the mob. And given that Napoleon had recently reinstated slavery, Beaufort had probably made a wise decision.

Beaufort relaxed a fraction. "I did, indeed." He gave Rafe a considering look. "Still, you seem to be trying to sneak into the good graces of the Elegant Occasions ladies by befriending Lady Verity." His brow clouded over. "I do hope that is all you are attempting with her."

Damn. Beaufort could be entirely too perceptive. "Of course." Except for the occasional kiss.

"Because if you mean to do more, I must tell you she has

already had one man court and discard her. She deserves better than to have you do the same."

"I know about Minton, and I don't intend that. Besides, I don't think she likes me all that much right now. So, for the moment, I am merely trying to get my auction prize and stay close to her and her family." He cocked his head. "Why are you so determined to protect her in particular?"

Beaufort sighed. "To be honest, she is like a daughter to me." He fixed Rafe with a warning look. "Which is why I will not stand by idly while you play with the lady's emotions. So step carefully, sir, or I will be forced to act. I owe her and her family that much."

"I will do my best." Rafe looked over toward the house and grimaced. "Here she comes now. Just watch what you say. And don't let on that you know me. She thinks me merely a viscount's heir." A sudden thought occurred to him. "Damn, we didn't discuss that bloody meal of hers."

Beaufort dismissed that concern with a wave. "Do not worry. I know what you like. Not for nothing did I cook for you and your uncle all those years ago."

Rafe cast him a rueful smile. "And very well, too. Just don't tell her about that."

"*Merde, mon ami.* Do you think me a fool?" He narrowed his gaze on Rafe. "If I were you, I would not insult the man who also knows all your dislikes. Do you remember the mulligatawny incident?"

"Lentil soup." Rafe shuddered. "Don't remind me."

"I will gladly serve it to you if you are not careful. Besides, I assure you that few are aware of my life before I started as head cook for the Society of Eccentric. She is not one."

That was all they could say before she was upon them.

Chapter 8

As Verity approached, she couldn't help noticing that the two gentlemen seemed rather comfortable together for people who'd just met. Could they have known each other before?

No. If they had, Monsieur Beaufort would have told her. She would trust the man with her very life, and there were few people she could say that about.

Certainly not Rafe. She didn't know what to think of him. For instance, why had they gone down to the other end of the garden for their conversation?

Then again, Monsieur Beaufort tended to watch out for her. Perhaps he'd been lecturing Rafe on how to behave toward her. The way her brother-in-law apparently had, according to what Eliza had just told her.

"You were gone awhile," Rafe observed as she reached them. "You must have had trouble finding your pencil and paper."

Might as well be honest. "Actually, I was waylaid by my brother-in-law who was eager to tell me about your 'facility with languages,' among other things."

"Why?" Rafe asked, looking truly perplexed.

"Probably because the only other language any of us

speak is French, and I'm sure Monsieur Beaufort can attest it's not very good French."

"Mademoiselle!" Monsieur Beaufort cried. "You speak the most elegant French I've ever heard."

"Is that good?" she teased him. "I'm not sure how elegance translates to 'facility' with a language. Besides, you're just trying to make me feel better about my inability to speak three other languages and read and write three, like Mr. Wolfford."

"Not a bit," Monsieur Beaufort said with a twinkle in his eyes. "I speak the same three languages you do."

"Three?" she asked.

"You forget the language Monsieur Wolfford does not speak—the language of the kitchen. I daresay he would not know a griddle pan from a stew pan from a saucepan. Or what use is made of a pastry jigger or a peel."

Rafe chuckled. "I freely admit to knowing none of that."

"And probably don't wish to know, either," she shot back. "Given how you feel about your auction prize."

When his face froze, she almost regretted provoking him. But before he could offer some pointless flattery to soothe her feelings, she turned to Monsieur Beaufort. "So, have you worked out what sorts of foods and dishes Mr. Wolfford likes?" she asked lightly.

"Yes, mademoiselle." Her chef de cuisine tapped his head. "It is all up here. I will tell you after Monsieur Wolfford leaves. We can have tea and a nice chat."

Her stomach sank as she turned to Rafe. "You're leaving? Now?"

"Apparently so." He smiled thinly. "I have to consult with my tailor about my attire."

She fought to hide her disappointment. "Be sure to have him make you a bathing costume for the seaside."

Monsieur Beaufort glowered at Rafe. "You are going to Exmouth with us?"

"I am, indeed," Rafe said, continuing to stare at her. "I accepted my invitation when I first arrived this morning."

Time to nip in the bud Monsieur Beaufort's new over-protective attitude toward her. "It won't be a problem, will it, Monsieur Beaufort?"

The Frenchman stiffened. "Of course not, mademoiselle. No trouble at all."

"If it makes things easier, we could arrange to have Mr. Wolfford's special dinner take place then as well."

"An excellent idea," the Frenchman said, though he clearly didn't like the thought of Rafe spending so much time—possibly alone—with Verity.

It was rather sweet, although she did tire of these over-conscientious men hovering about her.

"You two can work that out," Rafe said. "I don't want to be any trouble."

"It is nothing." Monsieur Beaufort made a typically Gallic gesture. "One more meal, one more person."

Blast. She hadn't informed him yet. "Actually, it will be five more. Sarah and the boys are going, too. I intended to tell you today."

"*Sacre bleu*," Monsieur Beaufort complained, then went on in French about children underfoot and Lord Holtbury in attendance.

She soothed him in French, insisting that her father wasn't coming, and she was already adding kitchen staff to make the entire affair go well.

Rafe stared at her. "Now I see what Monsieur Beaufort means. Your French is indeed elegant, madam. You must use it often."

"Of course. The monsieur and I generally speak French when we're together." She lowered her voice as if to con-fide a secret. "It's a great advantage when the kitchen staff is around, too, since they rarely know French."

His face cleared. "Right. Of course."

"Don't you have to go to your tailor, sir?" the Frenchman said coldly.

"First, I need a word with Lady Verity in private. Do you mind, monsieur?" His firm tone implied that he didn't care if Monsieur Beaufort *did* mind. That Rafe would do as he pleased.

Her heart hammered in her chest. Now that the moment was upon her, she wasn't sure how she felt about a tête-à-tête with him. Not after his curt words earlier about his auction win.

"It is not for me to mind," Monsieur Beaufort said. "If Lady Verity wishes it, I have no reason to object."

They both looked at her, and her hands got clammy, which they hadn't done in years. "I . . . I can spare a few moments, I suppose. Why don't you go inside, monsieur? Cook has some questions for you regarding spices you might need at the seaside. I'm sure we won't be very long, will we, Mr. Wolfford?"

"Not very," Rafe repeated in a decidedly noncommittal tone.

Monsieur Beaufort gave a civil nod to them both. But then he flashed Rafe a rather dire look before heading to the house.

"He doesn't seem to like you," Verity said. "What did you say earlier?"

"Nothing that ought to anger him. But as you know I can be blunt sometimes and entirely unaware of it."

As could she, but she had her sisters to correct her. Rafe had no one but a sick, elderly uncle and an undersecretary in the War Office who seemed more like an employer than a friend.

Trying not to let that soften her toward him, she folded

her arms over her waist. "Well? What did you wish to tell me in private?"

"I wanted to apologize for another blunt remark." He sighed. "I fear I insulted you earlier by refusing your special meal, and I never intended that."

She fought to ignore the thrill coursing down her spine. "I took no offense."

Stepping closer, he said in a low voice, "Liar. I know that you did."

"So, you apologize for one insult and follow it with another? I'm not a liar, sir. Indeed, I'm used to much worse insults from men. At least you apologized, which is quite unusual. Most never do. For anything, honestly."

He winced. If ever a man looked contrite, it was him, and that unsettled her. Nor did it look feigned. Rafe was certainly no Lord Minton.

Unless he really is the Phantom.

She pushed that suspicion from her brain.

"All the same," he said, "I will answer your questions. I'll bring the whole list here tomorrow, so we can discuss 'my special meal' to your heart's content."

"You can't," she said simply.

His face fell. "Why not?"

"I won't be here. The entire family is leaving tomorrow. We're traveling to the seaside early to prepare for the house party."

That seemed to catch him by surprise. Then his gaze narrowed. "In that case . . ." Glancing around the garden, he pulled her behind the big oak near the wooden gate and kissed her.

Lord, could he kiss. He knew how to make it soft and firm, lazy and hungry by turns until he had her craving more and more. But before she could get the merest bit of her cravings satisfied, he drew back.

"What was that for?" she asked, feeling her cheeks heat up.

"To sustain me until I can see you again," he said hoarsely.

It was the sort of blunt remark she liked from him. "Are you in need of such sustenance?" she asked, trying not to read too much into his words.

"So dire a need I'm not sure one kiss will prove enough."

The promises glinting in his eyes made her breath catch in her throat. Good heavens, she must be careful around the daring fellow. "It will have to do." Turning away, she said, "Now go on, so I can—"

"Sweetheart," he said, tugging her back against him, "stay another moment."

The endearment softened her some, and his embrace melted her more. She could feel every inch of his taut, lean body against her back and derriere. No man had ever held her so intimately. So scandalously. Could he feel her knees wobble? Hear the thundering of her heart?

She couldn't let him. She must stay firm, hide from him her weakness for strong arms and hot kisses. "What about your appointment with the tailor?" she asked, sounding breathier than she liked.

"It's not a fixed one." He bent to whisper in her ear. "But I'm afraid I cannot have him make me a bathing costume."

He tugged on her ear lobe with his teeth, an oddly sensual maneuver that sent her pulse into a wild throbbing.

She stifled a shuddery breath. "Why not?"

"Men at the seaside bathe au naturel, which is why the bathing areas are separate for the sexes. So, wearing a bathing costume would subject me to ridicule by the other chaps. Surely, you wouldn't inflict that upon me."

She didn't answer at first, caught up by a sudden image of him au naturel. She'd never seen a man in such a state, except for a Greek statue or two. Would he look like that, firm and chiseled and impossibly handsome?

No doubt he would.

The very thought made her mouth water. Swallowing hard, she whispered, "You shouldn't mention such things to me, you know."

"Why not?" He nuzzled the nape of her neck in a sensual gesture that sent her reeling.

"Because . . . Because . . ." Because why not, indeed? She couldn't think how to answer. His heated breath on her cheek matched the strange fires engulfing her at the thought of him entirely nude, his sun-drenched skin gleaming like antique gold.

Not that she would get to see that when they bathed. Separately. Unfortunately.

She groaned. And her groan only deepened when he stroked her belly through her gown.

"I've heard it said that some *women* bathe au naturel," he murmured, like the serpent tempting Eve.

But he wasn't lying. Her sisters had said so, too, and made it clear none of their female clients must be allowed to do such a thing. At the time, Verity had wanted to ask, "Might I do so?" knowing full well they would chide her for even considering it around their guests.

He moved aside her fichu to kiss her bare shoulder, and her blood jumped to triple time. "*I* shall have to wear a bathing gown," she managed, "if only to set a good example for the younger ladies." Not that she intended to do much bathing, but he needn't know that.

"If you didn't have to set an example, would you bathe au naturel?"

"E-Even if I did such a thing, I'd be at a separate beach," she choked out, "so you wouldn't see me anyway. You might as well . . . stop suggesting it."

"A man has to try," he said, a bit of humor in his tone

as he kissed along her neck, leaving little bursts of heat everywhere his lips touched.

Lord, why was he so good at this? "You clearly enjoy trying . . . all varieties of wickedness." Such *delicious* wickedness.

"How would you like to try some wickedness yourself?"

She tensed. "Don't believe the rumors about me. I have never done half the things the gossips accuse me of, and certainly not—"

"No, my prickly rose, I wasn't saying you had." He turned her to face him, pressing her up against the trunk of the oak before giving a rueful laugh. "Indeed, anyone who's ever spent five minutes in your company can tell that you have your defenses so high it's damned near impossible to climb over them."

Leaning one arm against the tree, he bent toward her. "I know why, too. Remember, I met the arse who put those walls there." He caught her chin in his hand, his eyes seeming to see right through to her soul. "But surely you wish to relax your vigilance sometimes and let a little pleasure creep in. Just for yourself."

"Perhaps." She stared at him. "There are times, I admit, I wouldn't mind experiencing a *little* pleasure."

She lifted her hand to stroke his jaw, the way he was stroking hers now. His hand dropped lower, down her neck to the dip between her breasts, then traced a line lightly along the top of her bodice as if seeking a way inside.

Her breath halted as she waited, wondering what he might do next. And if she would let him, would even welcome it.

Then a door slammed nearby, and it yanked her right out of the sensual haze he'd wrapped her in.

"But not here where my family might see," she whispered, and slid from between him and the tree, relieved that he let her. At least he was that much of a gentleman. "I must go in," she said, though her breath came so heavy she feared the whole world would hear it.

"Not before you tell me one thing." He snagged her hand. "Am I forgiven?"

"F-For what?" *Kissing me senseless? Speaking wickedly? Touching me so deliciously I want more?*

"For insulting you earlier," he replied in bewilderment. "You never said."

"Oh. *That.*" She let him hold her hand, since she felt incapable of letting go of his. "How about this? Send me your answers to my questions whenever you wish, and Eliza's butler will see that I get them before everyone starts to arrive in Exmouth. Then I will forgive all."

"Very well. And I shall see you in Exmouth sometime next week, sweetheart." He lifted her hand to kiss it, and she felt the kiss even through her glove. But when he passed the edge of her glove and kissed along the bare skin of her forearm up to the crook of her elbow, she thought she'd melt right there.

That would not do. "Y-Yes," she murmured, then withdrew her hand. "It should be most . . . entertaining."

Then she hurried off, cursing herself for such an insipid answer. Entertaining? It would be maddening. Even as she feared he might not be who he said he was, she would always be wondering when they could be alone again.

She was a fool. A silly, infatuated schoolgirl.

A flirt. And the worst part was she enjoyed flirting with *him* most of all.

Chapter 9

With lightning in his blood and thunder in his heart, Rafe stared after Verity, unable even to follow her because of his prominent arousal. He prayed she hadn't felt it against her.

Feeling like a fool, he banged his head against the oak. Now he'd put her on her guard again, and just as they were to part for a while, too. It wasn't wise or strategic or anything but his damned body wanting her.

Yet how could he have kept from being aroused? Her skin had been pure silk against his lips, and her citrus scent had inflamed his passions. Not to mention that her eager responses . . .

Good God, he would swear his hadn't been the only passions inflamed. Still, he shouldn't have reacted like a stallion to a mare in heat. He'd stood there pawing her where anyone could see them from upstairs if they'd looked out.

Clearly, he'd lost his head. What if she convinced her family to disinvite him to their house party? That would make any future attempts to investigate them even trickier. He simply must be more cautious.

Realizing he was standing there witless, like a servant boy yearning after a princess, he cursed, then headed for the house. In a matter of moments, Rafe was out the door, hurrying down the steps to his curricle.

As he pulled away, he wondered why she inspired such reckless desire in him. Why did she make him yearn to hear her cry out her pleasure beneath him? He'd never experienced such all-encompassing need. Mildly pleasurable encounters with occasional camp followers, lusty married women, or, once in a great while, ladies of the evening were all he knew.

This went far beyond that. Nothing had prepared him for the power of his wanting. He could hardly bear to watch her walk away and do nothing to bring her back.

Thank God, he wouldn't see her for a week. It would give him a chance to marshal his defenses, to remind himself he had work to do and she was naught more than a distraction.

Besides, he could use the time to go home and see his uncle, assess his condition, and try once more to get something intelligible out of him. Since it would be two weeks or more before Rafe could return, he could also make sure Castle Wolfford was secure, perhaps add a couple soldiers on half pay to watch the place. If anyone ever connected Uncle Constantine to the man asking questions in Minehead under an alias, he and his uncle would both be at risk. While he didn't think it likely after so many months, it was possible.

But first, he must attend to one item in particular: Minton. Rafe needed to know how dangerous the man might be to Rafe's mission.

It took Rafe the rest of the day to investigate. Rafe learned Minton was dangerous, all right, but mostly to Verity. He was in debt to everyone and badly in need of the funds marrying Verity would provide.

Damn the bloody arse. Rafe would need to keep an eye on the man when Verity was nearby. It was the least he could do for her, right? It wasn't connected at all to Rafe's visceral impulse to protect her from harm.

Fortunately, Minton had *not* been invited to the house party and couldn't even afford to live in Exmouth while the family was there, so she ought to be safe for at least the next few weeks.

Between visits to Foxstead's tailor, a final meeting with Sir Lucius, and settling certain business affairs, it took Rafe another day to get out of London. By the time he set off for Castle Wolfford, he was dreading the visit. Uncle Constantine seemed worse every time Rafe saw him, and the thought of him dying before Rafe could find the man who shot him . . .

That must not happen.

It was a long day's journey, but fortunately, Castle Wolfford lay only ten miles off the road from London to Exmouth. Once he finished at home, he would have only one more slightly longer trip to Exmouth. That left him a few days at Castle Wolfford to handle estate matters.

As his traveling coach passed through the gatehouse, Mrs. Pennyfeather, their housekeeper, met it. She'd begun as his nursemaid, so she'd always been like a mother to him.

At fifty-two, Pen was still as spry and affectionate as ever, if a bit grayer. "Colonel Wolfford!" she cried as he climbed down from the coach. "I'm so glad you've come. Everyone will be delighted to see you."

"Including my uncle?"

Her face fell. "If he's having a good day."

"Ah," he said past the lump in his throat. "So, he's much the same as before."

"Except his rants have grown more urgent in tone." He followed her as she entered the house and went to the kitchen. "I was about to bring him his tea, so how about I add some for you, and we bring it up together?"

"I should bring it to him alone this first time. It's less likely to confuse him." When she looked disappointed, he added, "But come up in an hour, Pen, and we'll catch up."

She brightened. "That will be perfect, sir." Pen handed him the tea tray. "Dr. Leith will be here later, as you requested, to report on the general's progress."

"Thanks."

Bracing himself for anything, Rafe climbed the stairs with the tray and headed for the master bedchamber, where his uncle had been since he'd become bedridden. When Rafe entered, his hoary-headed uncle sat in bed with his back against a pillow, staring out at the waning afternoon. The place above his ear where the pistol ball had entered had left a round scar where no hair grew.

Thinner than before and fragile now, the powerful figure who'd guided Rafe's entire life was gone, and all that was left was a shadow passing time until death. Rafe felt suddenly rootless. What would he do without Uncle Constantine?

Then his uncle saw him. "Is that tea? Thank you, good man. I'm parched." He waggled a thin finger at the bedside table. "Set it here, if you please."

His uncle's lack of recognition was a punch to Rafe's gut. Choking down his pain, he walked over to put the tray down. "Uncle, it's me. Rafe."

"Raphael? Good, good, you're here! Have you any honeybees for the tea?"

"I brought the honey, yes." One peculiarity of his uncle's condition was that he'd ask for items inexactly. *Honeybees* when he meant *honey*. *Cow* when he meant *beef*. They could usually figure it out, but not always.

"The clouds have been bright lately," his uncle said.

"That's a good sign."

Uncle Constantine shook his head. "I don't know. They

should be black." He frowned suddenly. "Pray, do something for me."

"Anything." Rafe poured the tea and added the honey.

Uncle Constantine caught his wrist, nearly oversetting the cup and saucer as Rafe held it out. "You must let the boy out. You must!"

Oh, God, this again. "Uncle, what boy? Where is he?"

"You know. The boy with all the keys." Then, as usual, confusion caught him in its grip, and he faded off into muttering. "Keys. Has them all. The boy." He suddenly fixed a hopeful gaze on Rafe. "Did you let him out?"

"No, but I will." *If I can ever figure out who the bloody hell he is.*

His uncle relaxed then and took the cup, lifting it shakily to his lips. "Yes. Good." He drank deeply. "I-I'm not well, you know. My head hurts."

For the hundredth time in the past eighteen months, Rafe cursed the spy who'd fired the shot. "Shall I call for Pen? See if it's time for your laudanum?"

That got him agitated again. "No laudanum. Makes me sleepy." He set down the cup. "Must let the boy out!" He tried to struggle from the bed, but Rafe knew he'd fall if he stood, so Rafe held him in place, which was pitifully easy to do.

"Stay in bed, Uncle, and have your tea. There's some good brown bread with butter here, just how you like it." When his uncle went limp, Rafe released him and put the food in front of him.

The general picked at the bread like a bird choosing seeds. "You'll . . . let the boy out?"

Rafe stifled a sigh. "If he has the keys, why can't he let himself out?" Using logic was pointless, but he had to do something, didn't he?

"He can't get out! You must help him." He slumped

against his pillow, then a vague look came over his face, and he returned to staring out the window.

Rafe sat down with his own cup of tea to ponder again the "let the boy out" phrase. A common theme in his uncle's ravings, it made no sense. His uncle had never married or had children. Rafe had been the closest to him and had never been locked up anywhere.

Could Uncle Constantine be thinking of Rafe's father, Titus, the handsome young man depicted in a portrait downstairs, who'd died so tragically young? It seemed unlikely. Besides, Uncle Constantine had disliked talking about his brother before the gunshot, so why would he rant about him after?

"She'll be angry," his uncle said in a singsong voice. That was part of the rant, too.

"Once I let the boy out, you mean."

"Yes." He grinned. "The old bitch will be vexed."

"Who is the old bitch again?" Rafe asked.

"You know."

"I wish I did," Rafe muttered. "I hope you're not referring to Pen."

His uncle looked confused. "Who?"

"Is he talking about the boy and the old bitch again?" Pen said as she bustled in and started putting things to rights, straightening a cushion here, rubbing at a spot on a table with her apron there.

"Yes." Rafe poured himself some tea. "And the keys."

"He never talks about the keys around me. Just you. Probably because you're the man of the house now."

"You have all the keys, though. So, none of it makes sense."

She came over to touch his uncle's head with the back

of her hand. "He's a bit warm. Perhaps I should fetch a cold cloth."

"Not yet. I need to ask you—he says his head hurts, but I noticed no laudanum around to give him."

A sigh escaped her. "Dr. Leith says the laudanum is bad for him. Increases the confusion. I think he's wrong, but . . ."

Rafe swallowed hard. "I don't want him to suffer," he said in a ragged voice.

She offered him a kind smile. "He doesn't seem to. Never cries out except to rave. I give him rum, since it helps calm him. Dr. Leith has no problem with rum."

"Who does?" Rafe murmured, garnering a laugh from Pen.

His uncle had fallen into a doze, so Rafe and Pen exchanged the latest news. Then he decided to ask about the one thing he'd been unable to find information on. His foreign mother. "When I was a boy, Uncle Constantine would sometimes speak Portuguese to me. Do you remember?"

"Oh, yes. Him and that wet nurse of yours."

That caught Rafe off guard. "You mean, there was someone looking after me before you?"

"Certainly. When the general brought you here from South America, after your parents died, he brought a wet nurse with him. He said she'd cared for you while your parents were alive. I think her name was Ana. Poor lady didn't speak a word of English. Just Portuguese. He was the only one who could talk to her, and I gather his Portuguese wasn't all that good."

He frowned. "I don't remember any of that."

She laughed. "Of course not. You were only three when she died of consumption. That's when they made me nursemaid."

"Where was she from?" he pressed.

"South America, I assume, like your mother. Your uncle

never said otherwise. You know how he is. Keeps his cards close to his chest."

"To say the least." The man had been uncommunicative *before* he'd been shot, but now, he was damned near impenetrable.

"Did he ever tell you anything about my mother? Who her family was? The town she was from?"

"Not a word."

"Is it possible that . . ." He paused before he spoke. *Is it possible my mother was my father's mistress, not his wife? That I'm not legitimately my uncle's heir?*

It was his greatest fear. Once his uncle died, the College of Arms would trace Rafe's line to ensure he was legitimate, and Rafe wanted to know beforehand what they'd find. The lack of documents at Castle Wolfford for Rafe's mother—and Uncle Constantine's reluctance to talk about her—worried him. But once Rafe asked the question and got people thinking about it, he couldn't go back.

He sighed. He wasn't ready for that yet.

"Is it possible that what?" Pen asked.

"Nothing."

They chatted until his uncle roused again. "Let the boy out" was the first thing he said.

Rafe rose to leave. He could only take so much of this.

Then his uncle said, as usual, "He's got all the keys."

"The keys to what?" Rafe snapped, knowing the question was pointless. Uncle Constantine never answered it.

"You know. The pistol."

Rafe gaped at him, then looked at Pen. "Has he ever mentioned a pistol?"

"No. But he *was* shot by one."

"Exactly. I daresay he's trying to say who did it."

But although Rafe mentioned the pistol more than once over the next few days, his uncle said naught about it again.

Rafe also did another search of the house, looking for the man's later notes and reports, but it was no use. He found none.

Besides, it was time for Rafe to leave. The house party was his only hope now for getting information, and arriving late wouldn't endear him to anyone. So, although it pained him, he left his uncle in the capable hands of Dr. Leith and Pen.

As he set off for Exmouth, his mind inexplicably wandered to Verity. He wished he could tell her about his uncle. He wondered what she would make of it, if she'd have some insight into his uncle's ravings. But he dared not tell her a bloody thing, not now, not ever.

Why would she even be interested, anyway? She was too busy planning his "special meal." Had she received his answers to her damned questions yet? What would she make of them? At this point, he was so tired of thinking about his uncle and the seemingly endless investigation he didn't care. Or so he told himself.

Soon, the rhythm of the horses' hooves and the sun warming the carriage lulled him to sleep. Sometime later, while dreaming of joints of veal served to him by a scantily clad Verity, he was suddenly jolted awake.

Still drowsy, he looked out to find that the carriage had halted in the middle of nowhere. Then he realized why. Another equipage had broken down on the road ahead. The coachman was trying to repair a wheel, and the passenger—a finely dressed, middle-aged woman—was railing at him as he did so.

Just then, the servant said something to her and she looked his way. Rafe recognized her at once. It was Lady Rumridge, of all people. He had occasionally seen the Harper ladies' mother on his spying jaunts, but had never actually met her.

Now, it took all his effort to tamp down his jubilation.

If he played this carefully, the situation could give him the perfect opportunity to question her in a setting he could control. So, when she started toward his carriage, he climbed out and went to greet her.

"Please, sir, would you be so good as to help my coachman?" With one hand working a fan and the other fluttering over her bosom, she was the very picture of a damsel in distress. "He's taking an abominably long time to fix the carriage, and I am expected in Exmouth for dinner."

"I wouldn't be much help in the matter of fixing carriages, madam," he lied, "but as it happens, I too am expected in Exmouth for dinner, at the Duke of Grenwood's house there. Perhaps I could offer you a ride, instead."

She brightened. "How wonderful! The duke is my son-in-law. That's precisely where *I'm* going, accompanied by my maid."

"Then allow me to introduce myself." He doffed his hat. "I am Mr. Raphael Wolfford of the Wiltshire Wolffords. Perhaps you've heard of my family?"

Turning coy, she looked him over more thoroughly. "I certainly have. Isn't your uncle now a viscount?"

"And a retired general." He smiled cordially. "Why don't I go speak to your coachman about removing your belongings for the trip? Then we can get on our way. I see no reason we can't reach Exmouth in time for dinner."

"Oh, sir, that is *very* good of you." She fluttered her long brown lashes at him. "One so rarely meets gallant gentlemen anymore. You are clearly the exception."

"I try to be." *Except when I'm with your daughter, and I become some creature I don't recognize.*

Undoubtedly, she would *not* approve.

He strode over to consult with her coachman, who was more than happy to have the Rumridge footmen transfer her ladyship's luggage to Rafe's carriage. After promising to send someone back from the next town to help Rumridge's coachman fix the wheel, Rafe ushered Lady Rumridge and her maid into his carriage and took a seat across from them.

As they set off, he examined her up close for the first time. Although he knew her to be forty-five years of age, she looked ten years younger, with light brown hair that bore no hint of gray and very few lines etching her pretty face. Clearly, she was the source of her daughters' good looks. Her hazel eyes matched Verity's in shape if not in color, although her form was more the buxom shape of her eldest daughter's.

Her maid seemed the sort who pretended not to notice anything while trying to make herself as unobtrusive as possible. But her employer was quite the opposite, sizing him up the way an unattached maiden might. Damn. He'd heard that the viscountess was a flirt, but this went beyond the pale, since she was married *and* a good bit older than he.

He cleared his throat. "I understand your husband is a major general on the Peninsula," he said in an attempt to remind her of her marital state.

Undeterred, she made a face. "He is, indeed. You're fortunate your uncle retired. I cannot convince my dear Tobias to do so himself."

An odd comment for a flirtatious female. "Forgive me, madam, but we are at war, after all. My uncle only retired himself because he was wounded."

"I suppose that's a different situation, since my Tobias is hale and hearty. Still, it's rather trying on a wife."

"So I've been told. Not having a wife myself, I wouldn't know firsthand."

The glint in her eyes gave him pause. "I assume you're hoping to remedy that, or you wouldn't be attending my daughters' house party."

Uh oh. Perhaps he had misread this situation. "You assume correctly."

She made an elaborate show of settling her skirts. "Were you aware that my youngest daughter is not yet married, Mr. Wolfford?"

It took all his skill not to laugh. He should have known. She wasn't sizing him up for herself but for her remaining unmarried daughter.

"I was aware, yes. We met a week or so ago."

Lady Rumridge tilted her head. "You have to admit she's pretty."

"I will admit no such thing." When she blinked, he added, "Lady Verity is nothing less than beautiful."

That made her cast him a more appreciative look. "As I said before, you are gallant, indeed. Of course, Verity is not as full-figured as my other two daughters, and she's a bit too tall for a woman, but—"

"To me, she's perfect in all her proportions," he said, growing uncomfortable discussing her daughter as if they were rating a horse at auction. "And intelligent, too."

Lady Rumridge gave a dismissive wave of her hand. "Not that any man cares about that."

"You'd be surprised," he muttered, eliciting a startled smile from the maid.

The viscountess smoothed her skirts. "I suppose you've heard that I will only be at the house party for two days."

"I hadn't, actually." All the more reason he should question her now, while he had the chance.

She thrust out her powdered chin. "There's so much demand for my attendance at various affairs that I couldn't spare more than that. Although, honestly, I don't know how entertaining this party will be. Some of the others won't even arrive until after I'm gone. So, it may be dull." She broke into a smile. "But not for you. I'm sure my daughter will make it very entertaining for *you*, no matter how many are in attendance."

"I'm sure all of your daughters will. And there's the seaside to enjoy, too."

"Quite true. I do like sea bathing."

"As do I." This small talk wasn't getting him anywhere. He needed to steer the countess toward the subject of her knowledge of her husband's movements.

"I'll wager your husband wishes he could enjoy it with you." A clumsy segue, to say the least, but somehow he didn't think Lady Rumridge would notice. "He's posted on the Peninsula, is he not?"

"Oh, yes," she said a bit dismissively. "He was briefly here for Eliza's wedding but had to rush off on a transport to Spain. Some boring mountain pass or other. Near Madrid, perhaps?"

"My lady," the maid whispered, "you're not supposed to say where. His lordship said it's unwise."

"Oh, pish," Lady Rumridge remarked. "Who cares about that around here? It's not as if we have Frenchmen lurking on every corner. Besides, Mr. Wolfford's uncle was in the British army, too, so Mr. Wolfford could hardly be a Frenchman. And even if he were, who would he tell?"

Who, indeed? Rafe thought wryly. He began to feel sorry for the major general. "Actually, madam, I was an army colonel myself, so my fellow soldiers would consider my being a Frenchman bad form."

She laughed, as he'd intended. "You are too gallant a man to be French."

"I daresay there are plenty of gallant Frenchmen."

"Not according to my husband," she said with a sniff. "He says they are dirty scoundrels, all of them."

That did sound like something the major general might say, given his reputation for being high-in-the-instep.

Except, of course, for eloping with another man's wife. And possibly being involved with a French spy, although that seemed less likely by the moment.

Rafe flashed her his most congenial smile. "I suppose your husband told you a great deal about his adventures on the Peninsula when he was here."

"He did, indeed," she said, almost confidentially. "He described an officer who actually married a Spanish woman and took her about with him on a little donkey. Can you imagine?"

He bit back an oath. "I can. That sort of thing has happened more than once . . . minus the donkey." He leaned forward. "Did he tell you of his association with the famous Wellington?"

"Of course. The man sounds pompous, if you ask me." She lowered her voice. "Do you know that his wife is such a dull thing he hardly ever stays at home with her? How he decided to marry her, I can't imagine."

How Lord Rumridge decided to marry the woman before him, *Rafe* could not imagine. "You heard that from your husband?"

"Oh, yes. He related all manner of gossip about the officers and their wives. Why, one has a wife who prefers wearing trousers on their marches. Trousers! I can hardly countenance it. Even Verity knows better than to do that, and she is very single-minded in her attire."

The comment arrested him. Single-minded? What might that mean? Could she be persuaded to wear trousers? He would love to see that. Or her in a lower-cut gown for the house party. Might she even go sea bathing nude? He could envision her floating on her back in the ocean, her hair like a nimbus of gold floating out around her and—

God, he had to stop imagining such things before he embarrassed himself. Besides, he had a job to do.

Banishing the thought of a naked Verity from his mind, he said, "I suppose your husband tells you all about where he and his men are marching to and what they mean to do and such. In his letters, I mean."

Her maid shot him a sharp look, which he ignored.

"No, indeed," Lady Rumridge said. "I don't care which dusty Spanish town they are heading to, for pity's sake." She tapped her chin. "Or is it Portugal he's in at present? I can't remember. I'm not sure if it was Madrid or Lisbon he was headed for when he left. One of those." She turned to her maid. "You're the one who posts my letters. Do you know?"

The maid stiffened. "I-I can't remember, my lady."

At least *she* had taken the general's warnings to heart.

"Anyway," the viscountess said, "he knows better than to speak to me of *that*. I couldn't care less. He's gallant, like you. He writes of how much he misses my bouncing curls falling on his shoulder at night . . . sweet things of that sort."

"I see," Rafe said.

He really did. Because one thing was rapidly becoming clear. Either Lady Rumridge was the cleverest French spy ever to operate in England, or, which seemed more likely, she had no sense whatsoever of when to hold her tongue. Because if the major general had been sharing information with his wife that he intended for a French spy, Lady Rumridge seemed entirely unaware of it. Rafe would have to look elsewhere for the spy.

Chapter 10

Verity was up to her ears in mussels, since the fish market had brought a wheelbarrow full for her and Monsieur Beaufort to pick through. She wanted the finest to make a dish of mussels and onion stew, apparently Rafe's favorite.

Even though she still thought the two men seemed to know each other better than they let on, Monsieur Beaufort scoffed at the idea. She did wonder how it could be possible when—*if*—Rafe had only recently returned to England.

If Rafe truly *was* the Phantom, he'd have been in England far longer. And that would have given him a chance to have met Monsieur Beaufort. But Rafe would also have to have hidden his identity well until now, and she couldn't see how a viscount's heir could have returned to England without a soul knowing of it. Even if he'd managed it, why suddenly decide not to hide his identity anymore? The whole thing was a conundrum.

She'd thought many times about presenting Monsieur Beaufort with her theory about the Phantom, but she feared she wouldn't get a straight answer. Because if he knew Rafe was the Phantom, he would deny it to protect his friend. And if he *didn't* know, he would deny it because he didn't know. The first would break her heart, and the second would merely raise his suspicions about Rafe, which she wasn't ready to let him do. She couldn't win either way.

Besides, at the moment she had more important questions for Monsieur Beaufort. "Are you sure the mussel and onion stew is Mr. Wolfford's favorite?"

"That is what he said. He grew up eating it in the west country, and hoped he would get to have it while he is here." He shot her an injured glance. "I would not lie to you about that, mademoiselle."

"You *might* . . . if you thought it would benefit me. You know, you might tell me he enjoys something you know he doesn't, so making it will insult him. But that won't work with me. If he hates the stew, I'll tell him what you told me, and he'll blame it on *you*. So, if you're taking this convoluted path to make sure the man doesn't cozy up to me . . ."

"I do not know this word 'convoluted.'"

"Yes, you do," she snapped. "It comes from the French *convoluté.*"

The rascal smirked at her. "I do not know it in French, either." When she raised an eyebrow, he laughed. "Ah, *mon amie*, you are so much fun to tease."

"You're trying to change the subject. You don't like Mr. Wolfford, and you especially don't like me and Mr. Wolfford associating with each other."

Monsieur Beaufort sighed. "You may associate with whomever you please. I would not presume to say otherwise."

"Hmm." She didn't believe him. Nor did she mean to let him act like her brothers-in-law, who'd been trying her patience ever since Mr. Wolfford had first met them. She understood only too well that women needed protecting sometimes, but if men kept wrapping her up in cotton wool, she would stifle!

"In any case," he said, "I do not dislike Mr. Wolfford. I

merely think you should be cautious. He is the sort to sweep a *jeune femme* off her feet with his charm and attractions."

"Well, you'll simply have to believe me when I say my feet are firmly planted on the ground. I'm a full-grown woman, not a schoolgirl mooning over some handsome fellow."

What a lie. Spending a week away from him had only heightened her mad infatuation. By day, she could put him out of her mind for hours at a time. But at night, she relived every moment they'd spent in the garden. The kisses. The caresses. His fingers stroking along the top of her bodice . . .

Damn him!

Realizing Monsieur Beaufort was eyeing her skeptically, she added, "I'm perfectly capable of making my own choices regarding men, you know."

"Of course. But perhaps we should turn our attention to the mussels. Do you truly wish to buy enough to make stew for the entire county?"

She looked down and winced at the huge pile she'd amassed. "Perhaps I did get a bit carried away."

"It is of no matter," he said gently. "I will pickle some and make mussel pie with the remainder. One should always eat seafood at the ocean, after all."

"*Some* seafood, at any rate."

"You should go dress. People will start arriving soon. I will take care of the mussels."

"Thank you." She removed her heavy gloves and shoved them in her smock pocket before squeezing his arm. "You know I couldn't do any of this without you."

He flashed her one of his rare, winsome smiles. "No, you could not. Now go. You have guests coming, and I have much to do."

Taking his advice, she left the back garden behind, then skirted the manor house to look out over the ocean. She might not want crabs nibbling on her toes or salt waves drenching her skirts, but she did love how the sea looked from here—with the sun frosting the dark waters, the fishing boats bobbing on the waves, and the seagulls dipping in their dance.

Then the sound of carriage wheels crunching on gravel caught her attention. Someone was arriving early. One of the gentlemen? Mama?

She should probably run and change clothes, yet she stood immobile as she watched the equipage approach, her heart suddenly pounding. Was it Rafe's?

Blast, why did she care? She shouldn't indulge this dangerous infatuation.

Still, even knowing how she looked, she decided to meet the carriage. She'd just reached the front of the house when the carriage door opened and Rafe stepped down to look around, clapping his hat on his head.

Like rushing water seeking a path, he fixed his gaze on her, and in an instant, she was back in the garden with his hands on her, hearing him say, *"How would you like to try some wickedness yourself?"*

The two of them froze—him in the act of smiling, her in the act of staring.

Heavens, but he looked delicious in his summer beach travel attire—an ocean-blue coat, a figured, shell-white waistcoat, and a sand-colored pair of nankeen trousers with polished Hessians. Even his military stance reminded her of how dashing he must have looked as a cavalry officer.

But before she could do more than venture a smile, he turned to help someone else out. Mama? Her heart sank. How the devil had her mother ended up in Rafe's coach?

While Rafe remained at the carriage door to help her mother's maid down, Mama spotted Verity. Blast it, Verity should have fled while she had the chance.

"My dear girl!" her mother cried.

As Rafe consulted with his coachman and Geoffrey's grooms, Mama headed toward her. "I'm so glad to be here at last," she gushed as she walked. "It's been a most vexing afternoon. My carriage lost a wheel! Can you believe it? If not for Mr. Wolfford coming along, I swear we should have been roasted alive on the road while John Coachman tried to fix it. Even now, the colonel—Mr. Wolfford was a *colonel*, you know—is arranging for my carriage to be fetched here from some town. He's quite a fellow."

Yes, he was. This dance between him and her would be so much easier if he wasn't. "I'm glad he could rescue you, Mama."

Her mother reached her and kissed Verity's cheeks before drawing back to examine her as always. "So, this is what you wear to greet your mother—a horrible smock over a dismal gown? Why, you don't even have a pair of gloves on!"

"I wasn't yet dressed for company. I've spent the day preparing for the house party, as have we all. I didn't expect anyone to arrive this soon."

With a sly glance back at Rafe, her mother leaned close to murmur, "You don't give Mr. Wolfford enough credit. He was clearly eager to arrive."

Wonderful—now her mother was playing matchmaker. "Mama—"

"He asked me all sorts of questions about you, my dear."

Verity didn't know whether to be thrilled or alarmed by that, especially given her past experience with men. "I'm sure he meant nothing by it."

"I'm sure he did. He even asked about my dear Tobias and what he does on the Peninsula. Clearly, he wants to know all about your family."

That arrested her. The major general? Why on earth

would Lord Rumridge matter to Rafe? Could this have something to do with the Phantom? But what?

Oblivious to Verity's distraction, her mother added, "I must say I like your young man. Strong, handsome, well-mannered. You could do worse."

That made her bristle. "He's not my young man. And remember that you also liked Lord Minton. Look how he turned out as a suitor." That should be a reminder to herself as well. Mama wasn't the most reliable judge of character.

Her mother busied herself repairing her coiffure. "I confess Lord Minton disappointed me greatly. But when I ran away from your father, I didn't expect it to ruin *your* prospects, dear. You know that."

Verity gaped at her. Good Lord, Mama could be so utterly oblivious sometimes. "I did *not* know it. We three girls realized it would be a huge scandal from the moment it happened—how could you possibly have been unaware of it?"

Her mother shrugged. "I was in love. And truly, to my mind, you and Eliza were already settled—Eliza with her husband and you with Lord Minton. I suppose I should have waited for Diana to find someone, too, but I feared she would never attract a man with that dreadful red hair of hers. So I did as Tobias wanted and ran away with him."

"And the rest is history," Verity said coolly. "But why are you bringing this up *now,* after years have passed?"

Mama avoided her gaze. "Well . . . you see . . . before I came here, Diana wrote me a letter warning me not to ruin your chances with this new beau. She insisted I should not stay past the day after tomorrow, so as not to scandalize the mothers of your guests and thus give Mr. Wolfford pause about courting you."

Ah. That made sense. Diana was very good at using guilt

to get Mama to behave as she *ought* toward her daughters. And Elegant Occasions.

Her mother sniffed. "She said it was the least I could do after ruining your future by running off with Tobias. But how could I have known a fellow like Lord Minton would be so ridiculous as to give up the daughter of an earl for the likes of that simpering little heiress Bertha? I could hardly countenance it." Looking toward the carriage, she hissed, "Shh, Mr. Wolfford is coming. Straighten up! And be nice. You can be quite pleasant when you want."

Before Verity could even say something cutting, Rafe reached them. "I'm sure you weren't ready for us yet. Please forgive me for arriving much too early." He sounded truly apologetic.

Verity smiled. "It's fine. Though I'm sure I look a fright."

"Nonsense." His gaze ran over her so warmly she felt it like a kiss. "You simply look as if you've been busy."

Her mother was watching them and flicking her fan madly. "Forgive me, sir, but my daughter speaks the truth. I assure you she normally looks much more attractive."

"Thank you, Mama," Verity said dryly. "I don't know how I survive in London without your constant encouragement."

Rafe appeared to be fighting a laugh, but as usual, her mother completely missed Verity's sarcasm. "I don't know how you do, either. Your sisters are neglecting you even more than usual now that they're married."

"I am certainly not blaming—" Verity began.

"Oh, no!" her mother cried, and ran back toward the carriage. "You there!" she shouted to one of the grooms about to hand down a valise to a footman. "Stop that, this minute! That contains several delicate items, and they must be handled with great care. None of your throwing them about will do!"

Verity released a long sigh.

Rafe stepped nearer and lowered his voice. "I assume you and your mother are not close."

"I try. But she can be . . ."

"Overwhelming?"

She shook her head. "Hard to take for more than an hour." Forcing the irritation from her voice, she added, "However did you endure her for longer?"

"I quite enjoyed myself, actually." Eyes twinkling, he murmured, "I interrogated her about her daughter."

To her vast annoyance, her pulse sped up at those words. "Which one?" she asked lightly.

His brow quirked up. "You know which one," he said in his lovely deep voice. "The only one who interests me."

She was about to smile when the rest of his words sank in. "Oh, Lord, she didn't actually *tell* you anything about me, did she?" She shuddered to think of the tales her mother could relate.

He grinned at her devilishly. "A few things."

"Wonderful." Lifting her skirts, she headed for the side door so she could get to her bedroom and change without having to deal with her mother anymore.

He followed her. "Shall I repeat what she said?"

"I don't know. How bad was it?"

"Not too awful. She did relate a story of the time a jellyfish stung you, and how that made you hate bathing in the sea."

"Nonsense," she said, perversely not wanting him to glimpse her weakness on that score. "You should know Mama says a lot of things, not all of them true."

"I'm glad. I was disappointed to hear you might dislike sea bathing."

"Why?" she asked, then remembered what he'd said that day in the garden about her bathing naked, and added hastily, "Never mind. I know why. I see that a week has not dulled your naughty nature." *Or your potent appeal.*

He chuckled. "I'm not naughty with anyone but you."

"A likely story," she said, though his claim pleased her shamefully.

"Did you receive my answers to your questions?"

The abrupt change of subject brought her right back to her discussion with Monsieur Beaufort. "I did. Although they perplexed me."

Instantly, he stiffened. "How so?"

She slanted a glance at him. "For one thing, there was no mention of mussel and onion stew anywhere, even though I was told it's been your favorite since boyhood, apparently."

He blinked. "How did you . . . ah, of course. Monsieur Beaufort. I suppose he revealed all my secrets."

"So, it's true, then? That you told him you like mussel and onion stew?"

He paused a moment, then smiled. "I did, indeed, when he and I talked that day in your garden."

"I see. So why not include it on your list of favorite dishes?"

He shrugged. "I didn't wish to trouble you. All that work taking the mussels out of the shells, et cetera."

"I have kitchen staff for that. Surely you don't think either I *or* Monsieur Beaufort do that sort of work."

"I have no idea." He bent to whisper, "Indeed, I'm looking forward to watching what sort of work you *do* perform. And how you perform it."

She paused outside the door to cast him a chastening look. "That had better not be another veiled reference to something wicked."

"'Veiled'? Never." His grin proved that quite well. "I am always direct about anything wicked." He narrowed his gaze on her. "And you enjoy that, I daresay, since you're fairly forthright yourself."

As heat spread through her, she realized she'd best get

inside before she made a fool of herself. "True." She opened the door, but when he reached to hold it for her, she said, "Do *not* follow me, sir. I'm going to my bedchamber to change clothes before the arrival of our guests, and you cannot observe *that*. Unless you wish to ruin me."

That seemed to give him pause. Then he said in a surprisingly serious tone, "Very well. But am I allowed to *imagine* how you might look while changing clothes? If I could be there, I mean?"

She blushed furiously, and she rarely blushed. "I can hardly force you to behave as a gentleman in your thoughts, sir. Just know I will be behaving as a lady in mine."

"Will you?" he asked, his voice a rough whisper. *How would you like to try some wickedness yourself?*

In her head, she said, *Yes, please.* Then she swiftly squelched the idea.

But it was too late. He knew. Somehow, he *knew*. He held her gaze a long moment as if seeing into her very unladylike mind. Then, without waiting for an answer, he tipped his hat and returned to his carriage, leaving her shaken.

Hastily, she went inside, then paused to lean back against the door. She had to compose herself. But it was hard to do when her blood ran high and her knees shook beneath her gown. He'd smelled of fresh air and sunshine, and the way he'd looked at her—as if he could see through her very clothes—still sent her heart into a most inconvenient fluttering.

Her sisters had long ago explained how lovemaking worked, so she knew the mechanics of the thing. But they hadn't sufficiently told her how a man could make a woman lose her good sense to the point where she actually contemplated doing it outside the confines of marriage.

Verity had never lost her good sense around Lord Minton.

Meanwhile, Rafe turned her into a quivering mess whenever he made a provocative statement.

Lord help her. How would she endure the next two weeks? Because with Rafe around, flirting and teasing and making her want to throw herself into his arms at every moment, this would surely be a monumental test of her restraint.

She could only hope that between helping her sisters and their charges and trying to make sure the meals ran smoothly, she would have no time for flirtation. Because her restraint flew right out the window whenever he smiled at her.

Chapter 11

The drawing room was crowded that evening, so Rafe found a spot from which to observe and take stock. In addition to the Duke of Grenwood, the Earl and Countess of Foxstead, and Lady Rumridge, about nine guests had agreed to attend the house party despite Lady Rumridge's presence.

It hadn't taken long to learn why some guests wouldn't arrive until she left. Unsurprisingly, Lord Holtbury's second wife, Sarah, was one. But she'd be here eventually, so he could question her then. He doubted the new Lady Holtbury knew much, but as the earl's current wife, she might say things she didn't realize were important.

When would Verity join the group? She was probably dealing with the kitchen staff—but knowing that made him no less impatient to see her.

He shouldn't care so much about a woman he was only investigating. Yet this afternoon, when she'd had her defenses up, he'd wanted nothing more than to haul her into some empty room and kiss her senseless. It wasn't gentlemanly of him. Or wise. That ought to make him cautious.

It didn't, especially after a week of trying to drive her from his mind, then having her dangled so tantalizingly out

of his reach this afternoon. Damn, the things he'd said to
her. Clearly, he'd been travel-weary or distracted or . . .

Too besotted with her to be circumspect.

He stiffened. Nonsense. He was always circumspect.
The truth was, he needn't even continue to court her. The
important thing had been getting invited *here*. It's not as if
they'd toss him out now. If he pulled back from Verity, she
wouldn't have expectations he couldn't fulfill, and he
wouldn't have to worry about breaking her heart.

Then why did the very thought of putting distance between them rankle? He told himself he still needed a reason
to hang about because her family would only trust him if
they thought he was courting Verity. But that was a lie.

And he didn't care. So what if he had this primeval
craving to bed her? He had it under control, wouldn't let it
affect anything. He could keep this just a flirtation.

Right.

"Stubble it," he muttered to himself.

"Sir?" a nearby footman asked him.

Bloody hell, when had he started talking to himself?
Probably after he'd officially met *her*. "Yes?" he asked the
servant.

"Can I fetch you something, Mr. Wolfford?" the man
asked, looking perplexed. "A glass of wine, perhaps?"

"Um, yes. Sherry, if you have it." Sherry was perfect for
sipping without fogging one's brain. Especially when one's
brain was already buffeted by dangerous thoughts of a
certain desirable woman.

After Rafe got his sherry, he set about actually doing his
job. Methodically, he reviewed who was who in the room.
Earlier, he'd been introduced to them all and had memorized the names and faces. He hadn't needed to do it for
everyone. Some guests he'd already reported on from

previous Elegant Occasions affairs, despite not having actually met them.

"So, you've staked out your field of battle," murmured a familiar voice.

Ah. At last, *she* was here.

Taking a large swallow of his sherry, he turned to where Verity stood just behind him with a glass of champagne in her gloved hand. Then he caught his breath.

Tonight she wore something other than the typical white—a gown of bronze-green silk that made her similarly colored eyes sparkle and lent her hair the sheen of honey. The low cut of her bodice displayed the tops of her breasts, between which sat a pendant on a gold chain—a golden scallop shell with a pretty piece of coral at its center.

He wanted nothing more than to lean in and place a kiss right where that pendant was nestled so cozily. God save him.

"I see that Botticelli's Venus has joined us," he said hoarsely, not bothering to hide his appreciation as he slowly scanned her attire. "Rising from the sea in all her perfection."

She quirked up one honeyed brow. "I shan't chide you for that flattery since it was rather poetic." She bent close to whisper, "But you should keep it between us, since everyone knows Botticelli's Venus rises *undressed* from the sea."

"Perhaps I could persuade you to enact that scenario sometime," he whispered back. "I'd be happy to play the god Zephyr and blow you to shore."

She shook her head. "That seems in keeping with your naughty bent."

"What can I tell you? You bring out the naughty in me." Sadly, it was true. "Hope springs eternal that I also bring out the naughty in you."

"I shan't dignify that with an answer," she said although a self-satisfied smile graced her lips.

"Because you know the answer would be 'yes.'"

Her smile faded, replaced by an intense stare. "You certainly are sure of yourself."

He met her gaze and lowered his voice even further. "I know when I want a woman. And I know when she wants me, too."

She swallowed, then looked away, the tips of her ears pinkening. He couldn't remember the last time a woman had made him this reckless. Probably because it had never happened. Apparently, she also brought out the recklessness in him.

The Duchess of Grenwood entered, cradling her new infant, and all the female guests surrounded her with assorted exclamations and coos. The men headed over to the wine bottles to replenish their glasses. That left him and Verity virtually alone at the other end of the room.

"I take it you aren't fond of babies?" he asked.

With a determined air, she sipped some champagne. "I'm fond of my niece. But I spent all afternoon with her yesterday, so I'm willing to let others have the chance to admire her chubby cheeks and sweet little mouth."

"Does she favor your sister? Or your brother-in-law?"

"Both, actually. A veritable blend of the two. Her red hair; his blue eyes. And she's clearly going to be tall like them both since she's quite a *long* baby."

He shook his head. "I'm afraid I know naught about babies. I've never been around one."

"Suzette is the first *I've* been around. It almost makes me wish for one of my own." She seemed to realize what she was saying because she forced a smile. "But then she starts wailing for her dinner, and I am more than happy to hand her back."

"Can't say I blame you." He took a sip of his sherry. "If not for needing an heir, I wouldn't try to sire a child, myself."

Then realizing what she could deduce from that, he mentally kicked himself. What a bloody stupid thing to say to a woman one was supposed to be courting.

After a strained moment, she said, "Well, the others seem to feel differently. Look there, even Lord Harry is taking a peek."

"Good for him," Rafe muttered. This was going badly, indeed.

Just then, Grenwood strolled over to join his wife, and she gazed up at him with such blatant adoration that Rafe was envious. No woman had ever looked at him like that. He could see how a man might get used to having a beautiful woman look at him so softly.

He stifled an oath. Damn, he was letting these Harper ladies get under his skin, and that wasn't wise, not until he was absolutely certain they'd had nothing to do with their father's activities.

Still, he had to admit that from what he'd seen so far, it seemed dubious that they might be involved. Rafe *wanted* it to be dubious. Because he liked the family and their friendly relationships with each other. He could see himself being part of it.

Part of it? What a daft thought. He could never be a part of anything that all-encompassing, that warm and enveloping. Surely, he would find such closeness cloying after a few days. It wasn't in his nature to be that happy.

Verity cleared her throat. "No doubt you're having trouble keeping up with who's who. Especially now that they're all bunched into a knot around my sister and my niece."

"Not at all." He named everyone in the room, both their given names and titles.

She eyed him with surprise. "How did you do that? You just met them this afternoon and didn't even have a chance to talk to them."

"Didn't need one. I already knew certain people—your family, Major Quinn—"

"How do you know *him*?" she asked, her gaze narrowing. "You were in different regiments and undoubtedly different postings."

"I met him at the auction, of course."

That seemed to satisfy her. "I forgot he was there. But you couldn't have talked to him long."

"I didn't have to. For one thing, he was wearing his uniform, as he is tonight. For another, Quinn is the typical infantry officer of a certain age, sure of his control of soldiers but weary of dealing with unruly civilians. It shows in every word he speaks."

She laughed. "You have captured his character exactly."

"To be honest, I can sympathize. After years in the army, I myself have the tendency to want to order people about."

"I hadn't noticed," she said, her lips quivering with an obvious attempt not to smile.

While her defenses were down, he tried extracting some information from her. "But don't you find it odd that Major Quinn is still hanging about in Society? His regiment is on the Peninsula. So why is the fellow here with all of you, away from his command?"

She shrugged. "He's on leave."

"They don't generally give officers leave for no reason and certainly not for as often as he seems to have had it."

"And as a former officer, you would know," she said, her gaze sharpening on him. "Why, do you have some theories about him?"

"No. I simply thought you might know the answer." Rafe still found it suspicious. Which was precisely why he was already planning to write a letter to Sir Lucius asking for more information on Quinn's leave of absence.

"Well, I don't." She set down her empty champagne

glass, avoiding his gaze for some reason. "Anyway, I suppose you already know the Crowders, too, from the auction."

The remark brought him up short. He couldn't remember if the Crowders had been there—he'd been too focused on Verity and her family to notice. "Were the Crowders at the auction?" he hedged. "I don't remember meeting them before today."

"Oh, right. I forgot." Her face cleared, and she once more met his gaze. "Isolde had a fever, so none of the family attended."

Was he imagining it or did she look relieved? Could she have been trying to trick him into misspeaking? No, that made no sense. What reason would she have to pick the Crowders over anyone else to test him with?

Except that he'd attended the Crowders' exclusive May Day party in disguise. And if Verity had recognized him from there . . .

A chill passed over him that he shook off. For God's sake, he'd been dressed as a Jack in the Green. Not even Sir Lucius would have recognized him.

"Then again," she went on, "if you didn't meet the Crowders at the auction, how did you fix them in your head so quickly? Or the others, for that matter?"

He wondered if he should tell her. Why not? What could it hurt? "Whenever I meet people, I use a mnemonic device for remembering them." When she looked at him expectantly, he added, "That's a method for—"

"I know what a mnemonic device is, Rafe. Although I don't need one. I never forget a face. If ever I encounter a person, I recognize them again later."

That caught him off guard. "Always?"

"Always. Ask Diana and Eliza. They're terrible with faces, so they look to me for that. They know I will pick that person out of a crowded room and tell them at once where we met her. Or him."

She stared at him hard, once again giving him pause. Was she hinting that *she* had recognized *his* face from before? That she knew he'd been at their affairs?

No, how could she? No one ever had. Although if she had . . .

Suddenly, she smiled and gave a dismissive wave of her hand. "Of course, if the person is masked or changes their hair too much or something, I'm at a loss. And I'm not as good at attaching names to the faces, so it doesn't help me much to be able to recognize them, does it? Perhaps I *could* use your mnemonic device. How does it work?"

His pulse calmed. Of course she hadn't recognized him. What was he thinking? None of her family had, and the one time he'd eavesdropped on them when they were discussing him, none had spoken of his looking familiar. Surely at least *she* would have said something if she had thought so.

"Rafe? Your mnemonic device?"

God, every time he turned around, she managed to rattle him. It was damned unsettling. "It's simple, really. I merely find something in their physical makeup and features to connect with their name." He grinned. "For example, when I met you, I dubbed you Verity Venus."

"A likely story," she said, clearly hiding a smile. "And what would you dub any other woman you found attractive? Anne Aphrodite? Mary Minerva? That hardly distinguishes them."

"I confess that, in this room, you are the only woman I'd associate with a goddess." When she arched one eyebrow, he said, "I take that back. I could have renamed Miss Mudford as Minerva, since she wears spectacles and has a goddess of wisdom look about her. Although I didn't. The chaperone's grayish brown hair is sadly the color of mud, so that was what I fixed on."

"And the Crowders?"

What had he used for them? That had been months ago. "Lady Crowder is 'Lady Powder Crowder.'"

A laugh sputtered out of Verity. "You're too awful. Although she does have a fondness for face powder."

"And her hair resembles black powder."

"That's because she dyes it to cover the gray. But don't tell anyone—it's a secret."

"Apparently, a badly kept one."

She flashed him a saucy grin. "Indeed. What about my friend Isolde, though? She doesn't powder her face. Or have hair the color of black powder."

"No, but when we met, I wanted to ask her to speak louder. So, she's 'Louder, please, Crowder.'" When Verity rolled her eyes, he said, "I know, it's a stretch, and more of a phrase than a nickname. But some names are harder than others."

"Well, she *is* very soft-spoken, especially when she's nervous." A sudden glee lit Verity's face. "Ooh, ooh, do the Chetleys!"

"That one's easy. Mr. Chetley is clearly barrel-chested, so he's Chestley, but without the *s*. His mother is rather well-endowed in that area, so it fits her, too, and links them."

With a suddenly chilly look, Verity raised an eyebrow. "And *Miss* Chetley? Who just happens to be the opposite of her mother and brother? Please don't tell me you've dubbed her 'Chest-less.'"

Why was she annoyed? Oh, yes. Verity wasn't like her large-breasted sisters. But then, their sort of figure had never appealed to him. "No, I did not. She is named 'Miss *Ophelia* Chetley.' Have you not noticed how her eyes are the light, almost clear, blue of water? Ophelia, who drowned herself?"

Verity looked skeptical. "Yes, but you're not supposed to call her Ophelia."

"Ah, but her brother and mother do, and since she seems not to say a word for herself, I think knowing her first name will suffice to remind me."

"I'm not sure about that one. Tomorrow, she'll speak to you, and you won't remember who she is, I daresay."

"I'll have them all memorized by tomorrow," he said offhandedly. "I only need one evening to fix their characters in my head."

"Very well." She ran a finger around the rim of her glass where it sat on the table. "What about the Harrys?"

"The man is Scary Harry, because of his 'frightened owl' hairstyle."

She nodded. "I don't know who came up with that ridiculous name for a man's coiffure, but it describes his most vividly. What about his twin? Are you using Harriet for her? Or 'Something Else Harry'?"

"The latter. She's 'Mary Harry,' only because she resembles a 'Mary' I kissed many, many times."

Her eyes widened. "Do tell."

Damn. He couldn't believe he'd admitted that to *her,* of all people.

He shrugged. "Not much to say. She was an actress I fancied when I was six or seven."

"You were around actresses as a child?" she said, clearly shocked. "Was your uncle friendly with—"

"Hardly." He gave a rueful chuckle. "But her image was in a book in his library. It seems she also wrote poetry. At seven, I thought her the most beautiful woman in the world. I kissed her author's picture probably a hundred times. I told myself when I grew up, I would find her and ask her to be my wife. But I never got the chance. She died when I was ten."

"Oh, *Mary*! You must be speaking of Mary Robinson, Prinny's mistress at one time." Verity sighed. "She was pretty, indeed. When *I* was seven, I saw a portrait of her in her costume for the role of Perdita, which made me wish to become an actress. She looked so dramatic in the painting."

"Seems fairly scandalous of you."

"That's why my wish proved brief. Mama made it quite clear I couldn't be an actress and remain respectable."

"I'm sure she did," he said, trying to imagine Verity on the stage, perhaps as Cleopatra or some other scantily clad figure.

God, he had to stop imagining her naked.

"I've never read Mary Robinson's poetry," Verity said. "Is it good?"

"I'm not the best judge. You may borrow my book when we return to London and see for yourself. But I warn you— her picture is faded from all the kissing." He clapped his hand over his heart. "She was my one true love." He lowered his voice. "Don't tell the other gentlemen. They'll laugh me out of countenance."

"It will be our secret."

"How reassuring," he said sarcastically. "We both know you can't keep one. You just told me Lady Crowder's."

She tipped up her chin. "I beg your pardon. I can keep important secrets perfectly well."

"If you say so."

"You're right about one thing, though—Lady Harry does resemble Mary Robinson, although she's far too shallow to be that august woman."

"And not nearly as attractive. 'Resemble' is about as

close as she gets." He captured Verity's hand. "She's not as beautiful as you, to be sure."

Clearly fighting a smile, she tugged her hand from his, with a furtive glance about the room. "Ah, but 'Lady Mary' . . . I mean, Lady *Harry*—" Verity scowled at him. "Now I'm going to want to call her Mary instead of Harry. I don't think I can use your mnemonic device, after all."

"Sorry," he said with a laugh.

"No, you're not." She tapped his arm with her fan. "You probably told me of it just to see if it tripped me up." She sniffed. "Fortunately, I already know everyone's names. And faces, too."

"Good," he murmured, "because three of the ladies are headed our way."

She turned just as Lady Harry, Miss Crowder, and Miss Chetley reached them.

"Is it true we're going sea bathing tomorrow?" Lady Harry asked in a girlishly breathless voice.

"We are, indeed," Verity said.

Lady Harry batted her eyes at Rafe. "Do you enjoy bathing in the sea, Mr. Wolfford?"

Uh oh. He kept forgetting that this affair was intended to help young ladies find husbands. And apparently, he was on the menu. "I do, actually."

"Did you do a great deal of swimming in Portugal?" Miss Crowder asked.

He'd have to be vague about that answer. "I . . . er . . . wasn't near the coast very long. I spent most of my time in Spain's interior."

"Have you ever been to America?" the meek Miss Chetley surprised him by asking.

"Not yet, no."

"So, do you know how to swim?" Lady Harry asked.

God, he couldn't keep up. These three were voracious. "I swim, yes." Hoping to move the conversation away from him, he turned to the one woman who could help. "What about you, Lady Verity? Do you know how to swim?"

She was obviously having trouble not laughing at his predicament. "Relatively well, actually. Our family has come to the seaside for years. But I prefer not to."

"Because she hates the ocean," her friend Miss Crowder offered.

So Verity's mother *had* been telling the truth. How interesting.

Lady Harry whirled on Verity. "Hate the ocean! How could that be? Everyone likes the ocean."

"I don't dislike the ocean per se," Verity said, with a frown for Miss Crowder. "I love to look at it, sail upon it, enjoy its breezes, and walk on its sands. I just . . . don't like to immerse myself in the water. So, there's really no reason I should swim."

Miss Chetley ventured a comment. "Mama made my brother and I take lessons. She says you never know when you might fall into a river or lake or . . . any body of water, really."

Lady Harry dismissed that with a sniff. "That's because you Americans live in such wild, untamed country. I assure you I've never had to worry I might accidentally fall into any body of water. Even if I did, I wouldn't drown. I have footmen to fish me out."

When Miss Chetley blushed, clearly embarrassed, Rafe said in a cutting tone, "Are you sure your *footmen* know how to swim?"

Lady Harry blinked at him. Obviously, she'd never considered that possibility. "Of course they do. They're supposed to protect me."

"Perhaps you should ask them if they can," Rafe said. "Just to be sure."

"An ability to swim will certainly come in handy tomorrow," Miss Crowder told Lady Harry coldly. "Perhaps you should take Miss Chetley with you when you enter the water."

"No one need rely on anyone for that," Verity said firmly. "There are ladies called 'dippers' there to assist you, all of whom *do* know how to swim. They will carry you into the water from the bathing machines and will even stay around to look after you, if you prefer."

Lady Harry flashed Rafe a provocative look. "I would prefer that the gentlemen help me."

I'm sure you would, Rafe thought, beginning to get a good idea of the sort of female Lady Harry was—one with enough rank and consequence to say and do just about anything if she thought it would get her an eligible match.

Verity looked fit to be tied. "It's a pity then, *Lady* Harry, that the gentlemen will be swimming at a separate beach a short distance away. Ours is for women only. No mixed bathing is allowed."

"I forgot about that," Lady Harry said. "Mr. Wolfford, is it true that the gentlemen who sea bathe do not wear—"

"Lady Harry!" Verity snapped. "Could I see you alone for a moment?"

"No need," she said, smiling like a cat in the cream. "I see that Major Quinn is here. I'll just go ask *him.*"

When she flounced off, Verity muttered something under her breath that sounded decidedly vulgar. He had to struggle not to laugh.

"She's been like that since she arrived," Miss Crowder said, a woeful expression crossing her face as she saw Major Quinn greet Lady Harry. "I do hope she settles down as the week goes on."

Meanwhile, Lord Harry was spinning some yarn across the room, to the vast entertainment of Mrs. Chetley, her son, Lady Foxstead, Lady Rumridge, and Miss Mudford.

Rafe suspected Lord Harry was already drunk. He might be eligible, but in Rafe's opinion, he wasn't any great catch. And the fellow ought to pay closer attention to his sister. For that matter, Miss Mudford ought to rein in her charge.

As Miss Crowder and Miss Chetley followed Lady Harry, leaving him and Verity alone again, Rafe murmured, "If Lady Harry is your client, I hope her family is paying you enough to put up with her."

"She's not ours, unfortunately." Verity sighed. "Because if she were, I could threaten to end our association with her if she didn't behave. But her brother is supposedly looking for a wife, so we thought it might be fine if he brought her. Unfortunately, even the strict Miss Mudford can't control her sometimes, and you're seeing an example of that."

"It looks to me as if no one can control him, either."

Verity shrugged. "They're both high-spirited and occasionally indiscreet. With their parents dead, they're feeling their way in the world. In such a case, I would rather err on the side of overkindness than overcaution."

He stared at her, once again faced with the unexpected. "That's very generous of you. Most would wash their hands of them both."

She cocked up one eyebrow. "Most have not endured what my sisters and I have. It makes us more tolerant sometimes, I suppose." She glanced over to where Major Quinn had apparently rebuffed Lady Harry and gravitated to Miss Crowder instead. "Although she's taxing my patience today."

"I could tell," he drawled.

"But *you* gave her quite the little set down when she picked on Miss Chetley."

He grimaced. "I don't like people with inflated opinions of themselves."

She was staring at him oddly now. "Oh, trust me, if she tries to ruin things for our clients, we will pack her and her brother off to London at a moment's notice. No eligible gentleman is worth that much trouble."

Lady Harry looked around, saw that Rafe was still standing there, and headed in his direction.

"Hide me, quick," he muttered under his breath.

The dinner gong sounded suddenly.

Verity grinned at him. "A timely intervention for you, sir. Because thanks to the rules of precedence, you will not be taking her in to dinner."

"Thank God." He bent close. "I'd rather be taking *you*."

Her grin faded. "You know that's not allowed either, unfortunately. Lord Harry is mine for tonight. Besides, I would be a boring companion at any meal. I'm liable to go on and on about the food, you know—explaining how it's made, asking what you think of it, having you taste things and then describe them . . ."

"I'm happy to do all that whenever you please."

She scoffed. "You didn't even want to answer my food questions at your leisure. I can't see you answering them ad nauseam throughout a meal."

Clearly, she was still smarting over his reluctance to play her meal game last week. "I tell you what—after dinner, I'll describe every single morsel for you and what I thought of it."

She stretched up to whisper in his ear, "After dinner, I'll be discussing tomorrow's menu with Monsieur Beaufort." Her gaze darted to where Lord Harry was bearing down on them. "But do feel free to describe them all to Miss Chetley."

When she laughed gaily, he groaned. He'd forgotten he'd be taking the tongue-tied American chit in to dinner.

He would much rather be continuing his flirtation with Verity this evening.

But it was probably just as well he wasn't. After dinner, he would join the gentlemen for port and would need to keep his wits about him if he wanted to get some sense of who had come to the party for reasons other than making a match. Exmouth had its share of smugglers, and any one of the guests might be bringing information from London to pass on to a fellow conspirator here.

After port, he'd have to slip away and visit a few taverns to get information on local smugglers. There'd be little sleep for him tonight, and lots to do.

So he must stay sharp and stop dangling after Verity like some obsessed suitor. Time enough for that in the coming days.

Chapter 12

The next morning, Verity stifled a groan as she and several ladies headed down the drive toward the road to the beach. Her head pounded like the surf, and she could only blame herself for it. That's what came of too much champagne and a night spent tossing and turning, thanks to Rafe.

Verity Venus, indeed. She snorted. She ought to call him Rogue Rafe because that was just what he was, with his smooth compliments. He was driving her mad. All his naughty insinuations and the hungry way he looked at her, as if he could eat her for breakfast.

Was it any wonder she'd had trouble sleeping? He'd . . . he'd made her *feel* things she'd never felt before in places she'd never felt much of anything before . . . and she didn't appreciate it. Not. One. Whit.

Especially since he'd disappeared with the other men after dinner last night, leaving her to soothe the young ladies, who were vastly annoyed that the eligible gentlemen seemed to have abandoned them for the evening. She and Geoffrey were going to have a discussion about that as soon as possible.

Isolde fell into step beside her. "I'm glad you decided to come swimming."

It wasn't as if she'd had a choice. She forced a cheery

smile. "Someone had to accompany all of you besides Lady Chetley and Eliza."

"Especially since Eliza has her hands full with Jimmy."

"But Molly is here, too, thank heaven." Indeed, the nurse-maid was carrying Jimmy, who wore an old baby dress, but Verity suspected that once they reached the water, that would vanish.

Miss Chetley and Lady Harry walked up to flank them. "Why couldn't we at least walk to the beaches with the gentlemen?"

Verity sighed. "Because you were all still dressing when the men were ready to leave."

"That wasn't *our* fault," Lady Harry grumbled. "Miss Mudford slept late, so we had to wait for her, and then she didn't even want to go! And it was Isolde's mother who complained of a headache, starting the whole discussion of who should stay behind with whom."

A troubled frown crossed Isolde's brow. "I still feel bad that Diana had to do so. I should have been the one to stay with Mama. Her headaches can be truly awful sometimes."

"I know," Verity said gently, "but your mother wanted you to enjoy yourself and not spend your time worrying about her. To be honest, Diana was loath to leave the baby, anyway, so playing hostess to the other three gave her the perfect excuse for staying home."

"*My* mama was ready at the correct time," Miss Chetley said, a bit bolder today than last night.

"*Your* mama has been chafing to swim since you arrived," Verity said. "Look at her up ahead—she's marching to the sea as if she means to swim the harbor."

"She could probably do it, too," Miss Chetley said proudly. "At home, she regularly swims across the small lake near our house."

"Good Lord," Verity grumbled. "Let's hope she doesn't

attempt to swim the deep waters here. That could get dangerous fast." Which probably meant Verity would have to go in the water just to make sure the American woman didn't drown. Blast.

Lady Harry scowled. "Why did *your* mama stay behind, Lady Verity? She said last night she enjoys sea bathing."

"She does, but never this early. Mama waits until the sun is high and the water a bit warmer. Don't worry—she'll be out here eventually."

They came to the pebbled path leading down to the women's beach, and the group descended toward the three bathing machines Elegant Occasions had leased. Lady Harry tried to see if she could spy the men's beach, but a large hill sat between the two, covered with rocks, prickly vegetation, and sand.

"Do you think the gentlemen are really wearing nothing at all?" she asked.

Verity didn't want to think about it. Every time she did, she also wanted to see it, especially if Rafe was doing so. "Probably. According to my brothers-in-law, most men do."

"I wonder what not wearing a bathing costume is like," Isolde said wistfully.

"Sticky, sandy, and itchy, I imagine." Verity broadened her gaze to include the group. "Even if you see a woman swimming naked, don't copy her. No respectable lady does it. Don't force me to chase you and throw a bathing costume over you."

The three ladies laughed.

"I swear I will," Verity warned.

"Oh, la," Lady Harry said, "you would not." She grabbed Miss Chetley's arm. "Come, we must hurry if we're to share your mother's bathing machine."

As the two women sped up to join Mrs. Chetley, Verity nudged Isolde. "Imagine what the gossips would say if they heard any of us were out here naked. Elegant Occasions would be ruined."

Isolde looked away. "I suppose. But Lady Harry won't do it, anyway. She doesn't even like sand in her hair. She said so loudly last night, and Major Quinn remarked upon it later. He did *not* approve of her squeamishness."

In Verity's opinion, Major Quinn was a stick-in-the-mud. "He probably wants a hardy wife, who can endure the privations of an army camp, assuming he means to take a woman back with him." Verity eyed her friend closely. "I couldn't help noticing that you and the major seemed quite cozy last night."

Isolde blushed. "He's certainly attentive. But he's done nothing to make me think he'd actually offer marriage."

Verity sighed. "He's cautious, that's all." And he'd been badly hurt when Eliza had chosen Foxstead over him. Or so they suspected. "Give him time to get to know you. That's why we invited him, after all."

They were passing a fancy bathing machine now, chained to a gnarled tree a good distance from the others. "Why is that one up here?" Isolde asked.

"A high-ranking lady in town, who bathes for medicinal reasons, owns it. She comes much later than this, when the water is warmer."

Lady Harry and Miss Chetley burst into laughter ahead of them.

"What has happened with those two?" Isolde hissed. "Last night, Lady Harry embarrassed Miss Chetley, and now they're thick as thieves."

Verity shrugged. "You know how mercurial young ladies are."

"Schoolgirls, perhaps, but they're not so young as all that." Isolde frowned. "They're up to something."

"I'll keep an eye on them. And I'll mention it to Eliza."

They'd finally reached the boxlike bathing machines. Resembling covered wagons on wheels, they were designed with steps that could be placed at beachside for entering the conveyance. While ladies changed inside, horses dragged the machines into the ocean. Then the horses were unhitched and brought back to the other ends to wait until they were needed again, and the steps were moved to the seaside, allowing the bathers to walk down into the ocean. The dippers, large and strong women, stood nearby to help bathers needing assistance.

After changing, their party descended into the water. Verity had hoped to get away with sitting on the little porch and looking out, but the others weren't having it. So, removing her mob cap, she walked in and let her hair drop into the sea.

The cool water didn't seem *too* bad today. At least she had bathing sandals this time to keep from stepping on anything spiny, and the long-sleeved, shapeless linen gown seemed to keep the little swimming creatures that she called "sea bugs" at bay enough to keep her comfortable. It helped that she only went waist-deep.

Plus, it was hard to be anxious about jellyfish showing up when she was watching Jimmy play. Naked as Adam in Eden, he was having a wonderful time, splashing around in the shallower spot where Eliza had asked the bathing machine operator to stop so he could actually walk in the water. Eliza and Molly hovered nearby, ready to snatch him up if he went under for any reason.

Of course, being Jimmy, he protested their attempts to stay close. "Jimmy big boy!" he cried. "Jimmy swim!" Never mind that his idea of swimming consisted of batting at the small waves eddying up to his waist, then leaving the water to go running back and forth on the sand like a landlocked Cupid.

Lady Harry had the dippers carry her into the water, and

for a while seemed content to view the scene like a queen carted about by loyal subjects. But she soon apparently tired of that and ordered the dippers to carry her deeper. Moments later, a wave hit her full in the face and the chit screamed. That was the end of bathing for her. She made the dippers bring her back to the bathing machine, then flounced inside to change.

Miss Chetley had been swimming happily about until then, but like a dog coming to heel, she returned to join Lady Harry. Her mother paid the two young ladies no mind. She simply swam about in great circles, pausing periodically to adjust her bathing gown more comfortably.

Suddenly, Jimmy started screaming. "Hurt, hurt!" he cried and tried to hold his foot up to show Eliza, which caught him off-balance and sent him vaulting backward into the water. By the time Verity reached them, her heart pounding, he was crying into Eliza's shoulder as Molly examined his foot.

"Is it a sting?" Verity asked. "Was it a jellyfish?"

"Oh, dear," Molly said, picking a small crab off his little toe. "It seems you've got a hanger-on, Master James."

"*Now* will you lot listen to me when I say the ocean is dangerous?" Verity snapped, but before she could snatch the crab, Molly put it on her own bare arm and showed Jimmy how it walked. Soon she had him giggling and wiggling to reach it.

"You see, Verity?" Eliza said, bouncing Jimmy in her arms. "Not everything is a jellyfish, my dear."

"I *realize* that," Verity said. "But when he screamed . . ."

She watched as Eliza set Jimmy down and he went right back to batting at the water, even laughing when Molly held his arm out so the crab could walk along it, too.

Tears suddenly stung Verity's eyes. She rarely admitted it to herself, but the one disadvantage to not marrying was that she'd never have children. Yes, Jimmy could be a handful, and Verity had seen her new niece send her doting father into a panic when she cried for her mother's milk.

But at times like these . . .

Dashing the tears away, she stiffened her resolve. She liked her independence, her freedom. So, Jimmy and little Suzette would be her children, along with the others her sisters would probably bear, but she would be able to hand them back whenever she pleased. And that was what she wanted.

It truly was.

"Are you all right?" Eliza asked.

"I'm fine." Except for the unexpected hole in her chest.

Eliza glanced around. "Where have the other ladies gone off to?"

Gritting her teeth, Verity scanned their surroundings. "I don't know what's happened to Isolde, but Lady Harry and Miss Chetley are probably sitting in the bathing machine, gossiping."

"Perhaps you should check," Eliza said. "It's been a while since they went in there to change."

"Right. Of course." She climbed up into theirs, but to her horror, no one was inside, and three sets of the gingham linen gowns lay discarded on the bench. In a moment of panic, she feared the foolish ladies were trying to swim naked after all, but their regular clothes were gone.

Had they headed for the house? Surely, they wouldn't without telling anyone. She hurried back to Eliza and explained the situation, relieved that Mrs. Chetley was still swimming in circles and hadn't noticed the girls' disappearance.

One of the dippers overheard them. "Begging your pardon, my lady, but I saw the young misses head off together down the beach a short while ago."

"Which way?" Verity asked.

The dipper pointed toward the men's beach.

Verity's heart dropped into her stomach as she exchanged a glance with her sister. "You don't think they . . ."

Eliza sighed. "I wouldn't put anything past Lady Harry." She nodded in that direction. "You'd best go after them. When you find them, take them home. Obviously, we'll have to go over the rules before we bring them out here again. If Mrs. Chetley comes looking for them, I'll tell her they returned to the house. I'll buy you as much time as I can to get them back there before us."

Swallowing her concern—and her guilt for not paying better attention—Verity went around to the beachside end of the bathing machine. Sure enough, she found three sets of shoeprints in the sand where they'd left the water and headed off to the hill. Verity followed the tracks briskly.

Thankfully, she came across the ladies only minutes later. Lying on the sand, they peeked over the edge of the hill to where the gentlemen stood about in the water, oblivious to the females spying upon them, just as those selfsame females were oblivious to her own approach.

Verity sank onto her knees behind them and gazed out at the sea, mesmerized by the sight of so much bared male flesh. The men were all shirtless, but she couldn't see below their waists. They were standing in the water discussing something, although they were too far away for her to make out any words.

Her gaze went right to Rafe. His olive skin, no doubt from his Portuguese mother, made him stand out. His back seemed sculpted of bronze, glimmering in the bright sun as if he'd just risen from the water and still had droplets all over him. How she wished she could view him more closely through a spyglass. Or see below the surface of the water.

Her cheeks heated, reminding her of what she was supposed to be doing now. "Ladies!" she hissed as she sank further into the rocky sand, determined not to be seen from the water. "You should not be here!"

Somehow, she'd managed to startle them, because their heads whipped around as fast as globes on swivels.

"We didn't mean—" Isolde began. "We were just—"

"We're so sorry, Lady Verity," Miss Chetley said, her expression as panicked as Isolde's.

"Don't apologize to *her*." Lady Harry sniffed. "She can't be much older than us."

"So, you're nearly twenty-six, are you?" Verity said, knowing full well that Lady Harry was barely nineteen.

Lady Harry frowned. "Good heavens, you *are* old."

"And you, madam, are treading on thin ice." Verity fixed her with a cold gaze. "I'll overlook this transgression if you three come with me right now. We'll return to the house and say no more about—"

Voices drifted to them from close by. A group of younger men were coming down the slope adjacent to theirs, and taking their sweet time about it as they joked and jostled and called up the hill to someone behind them.

Verity groaned. She and the others would be seen if they moved an inch. Fortunately, none of the men seemed to have noticed them. Yet.

Pressing a finger to her lips, she flattened herself against the sand, praying that no one veered in their direction. At least the men's bathing machines were grouped at the bottom of the other slope and not theirs.

But unless she and the other ladies wanted to slither down the stony hill on this side on their bellies, all they could do now was wait for the gentlemen to enter the bathing machines below and leave her and the other ladies free to escape.

Chapter 13

So far, this house party of Grenwood's was serving Rafe well. Last night in town, Rafe had learned things that might finally move his investigation forward. He'd long ago heard rumors concerning Holtbury's gang of smugglers, who sneaked French prisoners on parole—and possibly intelligence—to France and carried brandy back to England, but Rafe hadn't yet figured out how.

His investigation over the past year in the ports on the Somerset and Devonshire north coasts had turned up no such group. But last night at a tavern where he'd sat drinking with the locals, he heard of smugglers coming down the River Exe to use the port in Exmouth.

If that was how Holtbury's men had been traveling, it might explain how they'd managed not to be caught thus far. The south coast of Devon had far more traffic from smugglers than the north, with far more success. Tonight, he intended to return to the tavern and see what else he could learn.

But today Rafe had to focus on Grenwood. If he could just get the duke alone, he could discreetly question him about the Harper family. Fortunately, Lord Harry, Mr. Chetley, and the major had decided to swim a race against some young men who'd just arrived at the men's beach.

Grenwood and Foxstead said they'd rather watch than swim, so figuring this was his best chance to talk with the duke, Rafe stayed behind with the two gentlemen.

After a few moments of watching a very dull race, Grenwood obliged him by bringing up the topic of the Harper family himself. "I wanted to thank you, Wolfford, for rescuing Diana's mother on the road yesterday. I hope Lady Rumridge didn't bend your ear the entire way to Exmouth."

"She wasn't so bad," Rafe said. "Waxed eloquent about her new husband. I gather that her marriage to her old one wasn't the happiest."

"It certainly was not," Grenwood said. "Have you ever met Holtbury?"

"I haven't had the pleasure, no," Rafe said, trying not to grit his teeth.

"Wouldn't be much pleasure to it, I assure you," Foxstead groused. "Holtbury is a nasty fellow. The sort who believes women—even his daughters—are only here on earth to do his bidding."

"And his wives, too, I take it," Rafe said. "Did I hear earlier that the present Lady Holtbury is planning on attending the house party as well?"

"Sarah?" the duke said. "Yes. *After* our mother-in-law leaves, thank God. It would be quite unpleasant having the two under the same roof at the same time."

"I can well imagine," Rafe said.

Foxstead snorted. "I confess I still find it odd how the sisters have accepted their stepmother so easily. She's only a few years older than they are."

"Does she lord it over them?" Rafe asked.

"Not Sarah," Foxstead said, making circles in the water. "No doubt Holtbury picked her for her easy compliance."

"And her boys." Grenwood looked at Rafe. "Sarah has three sons by her first husband, who died in the war, I believe. We all think Holtbury probably picked Sarah because he saw that string of lads and figured she'd give him a son, too."

"Ah," Rafe said, "the everlasting quest for an heir."

"I don't mind the quest, myself," Grenwood said with a grin. "I find the process enjoyable. Don't you, Foxstead?"

"It never gets old," Foxstead agreed, and the two men laughed heartily.

Then Grenwood looked over at Rafe. "I assume *you* need an heir."

"Someday," he said cautiously. "I'm in no hurry to acquire one. My uncle is still alive, after all, and I have my hands full dealing with him."

"But you're looking for a wife all the same, aren't you?" Grenwood said, eyes narrowing. "That's why Elegant Occasions invited you here."

Damn. A bit of a blunder there.

"Of course," Rafe said as a small wave washed past him. "But I want to take my time to find the right one for me."

"The right one is the one you fall in love with," Foxstead said quietly. "Make no mistake—there's no point of marrying otherwise."

Rafe eyed him with skepticism. "I wouldn't have taken you for the fairy-tale sort, Foxstead."

"Don't bother arguing with him about it, Nathaniel," Grenwood said, shoving some wet curls out of his eyes. "Until our friend here *finds* the right one, he will scoff at love. Many unmarried men do."

Rafe thought of his uncle's warning about not letting one's heart rule one's head. Until now, it had never occurred to him to wonder why his uncle felt so strongly about hearts and heads when he'd been a bachelor all his life. Had he once fallen in love? Had it put him in danger?

Or had he merely been afraid that having a heart meant risking it being broken? Rafe would sympathize if he had a heart himself. Which he did not. The war had beaten it out of him. The closest thing to a heart he had was a healthy desire for the pretty woman who'd kept him tossing and turning last night, imagining her as Venus rising from the shell.

No, he would *not* think about Verity. "So, do you agree with Foxstead about love?" Rafe asked Grenwood, hoping to encourage him to talk more about the Harper family.

"Of course. I found love and have a wonderful marriage. Our father-in-law married the first time to start his dynasty, and as you can see, things went badly."

"And the second time?" Rafe asked, trying to bring the subject back to Sarah.

"That seems to be going fine so far, but only because Sarah lets him walk all over her," Foxstead said. "What if she never gives him a son? What if she can't have more children at all? I shudder to think what he'll make life like for her then. Siring an heir shouldn't be the only reason to marry. If things go wrong, you still have to live with each other."

"Unless you circumvent all the rules by divorcing your wife as Holtbury did," Rafe pointed out.

Grenwood turned sideways so a wave didn't hit him full-on. "That didn't exactly turn out well, either, did it? His daughters barely talk to him. They like his new wife and stepchildren better than they like him."

How interesting. "Even Lady Verity?"

Foxstead and Grenwood exchanged a knowing glance.

"She doesn't talk about him much, to be honest," Foxstead offered. "I assume you know what happened between her and Lord Minton."

"She told me a bit, yes," Rafe admitted.

Grenwood stared at him. "So *that's* why you bid so outrageously against him at the auction."

Rafe couldn't suppress a smile of satisfaction. "Among other reasons, yes."

"Good show, Wolfford," the duke said. "I approve."

"Glad to hear it," Rafe said, not sure how else to respond.

Foxstead rolled his eyes. "Anyway, after Minton played her for a fool, neither she nor Diana was eager to stay home and become Holtbury's hostess—doing his bidding and running his household and not having any sort of life. So they moved in with Eliza and started Elegant Occasions. In return, he cut them off."

Rafe stiffened. He'd known Holtbury was an arse, but . . . cutting off his own daughters? "What do you mean? He refused to see them?"

Grenwood cleared his throat. "Holtbury denied them their allowances, said he wouldn't give them a penny unless they moved back in with him. And that included their dowries."

"Wait, I didn't know that last part," Foxstead said. "Diana had no dowry when you married?"

"Not a penny. And I didn't care." Grenwood's eyes shone. "Still don't." He looked over at Foxstead. "That shouldn't surprise you, Nathaniel. You knew Holtbury refused to give Eliza's dowry to her first husband when she chose to marry the arse."

"Yes, but he thought Samuel was a fortune hunter, so Holtbury's disapproval was understandable."

Both men turned their gazes on Rafe.

Rafe could guess why. It was probably best to admit it. "I suppose this is your none-too-subtle way of telling me Lady Verity has no dowry."

"Do you care?" Foxstead asked.

"Why should I? I have plenty of my own money." *And once this is over, she'll never marry me. Not once she realizes what I've been doing.* "Does Minton know she has no dowry? Because he didn't act like it at the auction."

"True." Geoffrey shrugged. "He may not. I don't know

how he would have found out. It isn't generally known. The ladies are loath to mention it, as you might guess."

Even after all Rafe's investigation of the family, this was the first he'd heard of it. "Perhaps Minton is truly in love with her and regrets his previous actions."

"I doubt it," Foxstead said. "He's not the type. I was still in London when all that was happening, and he was known as a fortune hunter among us gentlemen. His behavior then was unconscionable. People don't change that much."

"Even if he professed his love on bended knee, she wouldn't have him." Grenwood gazed at Rafe. "You have a better chance of marrying her than Minton."

Rafe forced a smile. "I doubt she'd marry me if I asked. Lady Verity could have her pick of the gentlemen here. She wouldn't want an old warhorse like me."

The two fellows burst into laughter.

"Yes, you'd really be robbing the cradle," Grenwood said jovially.

Foxstead shook his head. "I'm just trying to imagine Verity picking Chetley or Harry. Neither is a match for her rapier wit."

"And can you see her with Quinn?" Grenwood asked. "He's older than Wolfford by a few years."

Which made the major older than *Verity* by at least ten. The very idea of Quinn with Verity made Rafe grit his teeth.

"Why did the ladies even invite him?" Rafe asked.

Foxstead sighed. "Supposedly, to match him with Isolde Crowder. But I don't think he's interested in her."

He damned well better not be interested in Verity, either.

As soon as the thought came into his head, Rafe winced. He sounded like a jealous fool. Rafe scowled. He was *not* jealous. It wasn't jealousy when he was merely looking out for her welfare. As a friend. A perfectly unbiased friend who happened to know enough of her to see that Quinn was wrong for her in every way. The major had far too strict ideas about behavior for an exotic flower like Verity.

She deserved a man who appreciated her innate wildness, her creative sense . . . her natural seductiveness. A man like Rafe.

He groaned.

Grenwood apparently mistook that for distress. "Don't worry, Wolfford," he said, gazing at where the racing swimmers had turned and were fast approaching. "She's never shown any particular affection for the man."

"I don't know," Foxstead drawled. "She does like chaps in uniform. You should wear your uniform while you're here, Wolfford. Oh, wait, you can't, can you, now that you've resigned your commission?"

Rafe was still reeling from the idea that Verity might actually choose to marry a chap from the house party. That possibility hadn't occurred to him before. And the only thing he could do about it was stand by and watch. Because he had no right to do anything else.

Foxstead turned to watch the racers. "Looks like Chetley's in the lead."

"It does," Grenwood said. "Not surprising, given his massive arms. He probably swims more often than any of us."

Rafe watched Chetley cut through the water like a ship's bow, making Rafe regard him in a new light. The man was fast, strong, and too handsome for Rafe's liking. A rich, attractive American might actually suit Verity.

God, what if she married someone like Chetley and ran off to America? He would never see her again.

The thought made him ill.

Damn, he couldn't take this. It might be best if he left the water before the other men reached them. He'd have trouble being civil right now.

He turned toward the shore, and something out of the

corner of his eye caught his attention . . . a flash of the blue-checked linen some of the ladies' bathing costumes were made of. Shading his eyes with one hand, he scanned the hills above the water. This time he thought he caught sight of a bobbing head of honey-gold hair.

Could that be . . .

Surely not. Even Verity would never be so bold as to spy on half-dressed men, and certainly not in her bathing gown. On the other hand, if it *was* she, and if she *was* spying, he definitely wanted to find out why.

Or whom in particular she was watching.

He stifled a curse. "I think I see someone I know," he told Grenwood. "I'll be back in a moment."

The duke waved him off and went on talking to Foxstead about the race. Rafe grabbed his shoes off the bathing machine porch before darting from the water, not bothering to go inside and snag his shirt. His smallclothes and shoes would have to do. If he didn't hurry, he wouldn't catch her. Assuming it *was* her.

He damned well hoped it was. Because if so, he and she were going to have a frank conversation about the men at the house party. At the very least, he wanted to find out who she was trying to match with whom.

You just want to see her scantily clad, with her hair down.

He tamped down the sudden leap in his pulse.

It had nothing to do with that, damn it. He merely wanted to make sure she wasn't planning on matching *him* with anyone. He was willing to play the game to a certain extent, but not if it meant she was trying to pass him off to one of the other ladies while she waltzed away with some arse like Chetley.

You're definitely jealous.

Fine. Perhaps he was. At least he could learn whom he had to be jealous of.

* * *

Verity couldn't believe it. They'd escaped without being seen. "We must return to the house, ladies," she announced as they trudged up the hill to the road.

"Why can't we go join Lady Foxstead and Mama again?" Lady Harry asked peevishly. "I daresay no one but you even noticed we were gone."

"Actually," Verity said, "Eliza noticed, one of the dippers noticed, and by now even Mrs. Chetley may have noticed. But if you're all eager to explain to your mothers and chaperones why you vanished, we can certainly return to the beach."

It wouldn't reflect well on *any* of them, Verity included. And they apparently knew it, for Miss Chetley cast Lady Harry a panicked look.

"Fortunately," Verity went on, "Eliza is willing to keep your secret. She'll pay off the dippers, no doubt. She said she'd tell anyone who asked that you ladies returned to the house, and she'll probably say I went with you to make sure you remained safe. But if you'd rather provoke more questions—"

"I guess not," Lady Harry grudgingly answered. "It's just not fair we can't walk back with the gentlemen."

Isolde turned scarlet. "I couldn't face them right now, anyway, after seeing, well, you know." She leaned close to Verity. "The major wasn't wearing *anything*. I saw his naked . . . bottom when he was swimming."

"Were they *all* naked?" Verity whispered.

"Just some. A few wore trousers or smallclothes."

Verity wanted to ask specifically about Rafe, but didn't dare.

They'd nearly reached the road, when Isolde said, "You

do realize you're still in your bathing gown. Don't you worry someone will notice at the house?"

Verity halted. "Good heavens." She'd been so intent on getting her ladies out of trouble that she'd forgotten to change.

"We can get to the house ourselves," Isolde said. "I know the way. I'll make sure they both do as they should."

Verity lifted an eyebrow. "I can trust you? Because I wouldn't have expected you, of all people, to go along with them in the first place. You even moved your clothes to their bathing machine without my seeing!"

"I know." Isolde sighed. "I get tired of being the well-behaved one." Then she patted Verity's arm. "But I swear you can rely on me. We'll tell Diana you forgot something and had to return to the beach. Now go change and grab our bathing costumes before someone sees we left them behind. Don't worry. All will be well."

Verity sincerely hoped so. Swiftly, she headed back down the hill, but didn't get far. Just as she was about to pass the fancy bathing machine, she encountered Rafe, wearing only shoes and a tight-fitting pair of smallclothes.

Good Lord in heaven. She'd never seen a man in smalls. Why, they didn't even go down to his knees! And he wore a smile that stopped short of his eyes.

Her breath dried up in her throat. "What are you doing here? This isn't the path from the men's beach."

"And you're not going in the right direction for someone who's already been to the women's beach," he pointed out.

"How do you know I'm not just now arriving?"

He shook his head. "You're in your bathing gown and your hair is wet." His gaze trailed leisurely down her. "Makes me wonder what you've been up to."

"Up to? What do you mean?" Oh, blast, had he *seen* them watching from the hill? "We shouldn't even be conversing, you know, while we're dressed like this. It's quite inappropriate."

"Isn't it, though?" he said in his usual cocky manner. "Almost as inappropriate as a lady spying on half-naked gentlemen."

Lord help her, he *had* seen. "I wasn't . . . It wasn't . . ." Scowling, she turned the conversation back on him. "And you're a bit more than *half*-naked, wouldn't you say?" She gestured vaguely at the smalls that lovingly outlined every inch of muscle and sinew in his thighs and the bulge that surely signified—

As heat flamed her cheeks, she jerked her gaze up. "You're only wearing . . . those."

"And you're only wearing a bathing gown. No corset. No petticoats." He leaned close, eyes gleaming. "No stockings." His expression turned hungry, sending delicious shivers down her spine.

For a moment, she thought he might kiss her. She even hoped he would.

Instead, he surveyed her more closely. "Come to think of it, it's also a very *sandy* bathing gown. Almost as if you'd been lying on the beach for quite a while, observing things no lady should see."

"Not so long as all that." She tipped up her chin. "There was nothing to look at."

When he laughed, clearly not the least put off by the insult, she sniffed and flounced past him, heading toward the other bathing machines on the ladies' beach. "I have to go. If we are seen together here, in this condition . . ."

Taking her by surprise, he pulled her between the fancy bathing machine and the shade tree. "Then let's not get seen." His voice lowered to a throaty murmur as he looked to where her bathing gown, though drier now, still clung to her frame more closely than silk to velvet.

"You still haven't told me why you were spying on us, although I can venture a guess," he went on. "Apparently, the cautious Lady Verity has a weakness for watching men half-naked." Taking her ungloved hand, he laid it on his bare chest. "For . . . admiring the male form."

She should jerk her hand away, but couldn't seem to do so. His body was hard and masculine . . . and as warm as the sun overhead. Dark curls gathered about the two puckered nipples set into his bronzed skin, and her mouth went dry as she stared.

The longer her hand remained, the more his breath grew erratic and his heart began to pound beneath her fingers. That she could have such an effect on him thrilled her beyond anything.

Heavens, she was in deep trouble now. Especially since her own heart was doing little flips in her chest.

There was only one way out of this. "If I tell you why, do you promise to keep it between us?"

He turned wary. "If you also tell me who in particular you were watching, then I promise."

She met his gaze. "I will hold you to that." Swiftly, she explained about discovering the ladies were gone, deducing where, heading after them, and then finding herself trapped temporarily on the hill.

He blinked. "You mean, you were all watching us?"

"No," she said firmly. "*They* were watching you men. *I* was watching over *them* until we could get away." That was almost true, wasn't it? "Then I packed them off home and was heading back to change out of my bathing gown when you encountered me."

"I see." He ran a hand through his hair and peered up the incline as if trying to see the ladies on the road, although the tree blocked both their views.

"You won't tell anyone, will you?" she asked. "If you

do, it's I who will get into trouble for not chaperoning them better."

"For God's sake," he snapped, looking suddenly uncomfortable, "I'm not going to ruin four women's futures simply because they had a perfectly natural, maidenly curiosity about men's bodies."

"*Three* women. Not me. I-I mean, it would ruin my future, too, but it wasn't my idea. So I wasn't the one . . . *I* didn't have the 'maidenly curiosity' . . ."

She trailed off, realizing she should have left well enough alone. His gaze had narrowed on her, and then on her hand where it still lay against his chest and was now apparently *stroking* the broad expanse of glorious masculine flesh.

Oh, Lord.

She tried to yank it away, but he caught it, imprisoning it against him.

"So *you* weren't curious in the least," he drawled. "Then why was your hand caressing my naked chest? Why haven't you slapped me or cut me with your sarcastic remarks or shown in any way you don't wish to be here alone with me?"

She thrust out her chin. "I-I am happy to do all those things if you don't let me pass." A hollow threat, if ever there was one.

He apparently knew it, too. "Well, then, before you go . . ." And *that* was when he finally kissed her.

It wasn't gentle. It was intense and needy and forceful, and she reveled in it, meeting it with all the pent-up desire she'd felt ever since they'd parted over a week ago. As his mouth plundered hers, she drew her hand from beneath his, meaning to push him away. Instead, she returned to exploring his chest with her eager fingers.

Who would ever have thought a man's skin could be so

enjoyable to caress? That his curls could be so silky to the touch? At this very moment, she yearned to have his hands on her, too.

And suddenly, they *were*, one gripping her waist, and the other cupping her breast through her bathing gown.

She tore her lips from his. "You . . . you shouldn't."

"I agree." His eyes darkened, and his voice turned guttural. "But I want to. And you want me to. Tell me I'm wrong."

He knew he wasn't wrong, blast him. His fingers tentatively molded her breast through the linen, and when she didn't stop him, he thumbed her nipple to a hard knot that rose to each caress.

Oh. Good. Heavens.

No wonder people sinned when faced with such exquisite enjoyment. She felt like a coiled spring, tightening more and more by the moment. Perhaps she was still abed and merely dreaming of him so scandalously dressed and conveniently left alone with her, doing *this*. Because the feelings rocking her were indescribable.

"You're so soft," he whispered, touching his forehead to hers. "I ached to do this in the garden last week."

"Why didn't you?"

"Because you asked me not to do anything where it might be seen." He brushed a kiss to her temple. "Right before you fled. And left me wishing I'd filled my hands with your sweet breasts and fondled them until you moaned for more."

With that confession, he lifted his other hand to cup her head and pull her to him so he could cover her mouth with his again.

This time their kiss was a delicious joining of lips and tongues, each of them eager to give more, have more. He smelled of the sea and tasted of spindrift mingled with the coffee they'd drunk earlier. She couldn't seem to get enough of his mouth. His wild, devouring mouth. Heavenly.

And while they kissed, he kneaded her breast the way she'd been imagining every night. So she spread both hands over his chest to explore every inch of muscle and sinew, feeling her way along his ribs.

How could such magical sensations be wrong, when it felt so right to touch him like this, have him touch her like this? Her body gloried in being merely a vessel for these . . . these wild emotions. Amazement thrummed through her nerves, making her want more and more and more.

That was the only reason she didn't stop him when he untied the strings securing the placket of her gown. And when he then drew one shoulder down to free her breast . . .

Heaven save her. Because she wanted him to do whatever he was planning. She was ready to march right along to hell with him.

And he obviously knew it.

Chapter 14

CRafe stared at Verity's pretty breast, as pert as he'd imagined it would be, with such a sweet, rosy nipple. Surely he'd lost his wits to be fondling her like this. Did other people who'd lost their wits know they had? Or did he only know because of years of his uncle telling him not to let desire for a woman addle his brain?

His brain was definitely addled right now. Most pleasurably so.

"I want to taste you," he rasped before she could drag her gown back up to hide her beauty.

She looked bewildered. "You . . . already have been."

With a soft chuckle, he nuzzled her cheek. "Not just your lips, sweetheart. I want to taste this." And before she could react, he bent his head to cover her breast with his mouth.

"Ohhh," she breathed and buried her hands in his hair to hold him closer.

That intensified his arousal tenfold. God save him, he might not survive this. Because he dared not swive her. If he did, he'd have to marry her, and once she found out who he was, what he'd really been up to . . .

She would never forgive him for such a deception. Who could?

All the more reason to take this chance at sipping a bit of

her wine. Filling his other hand with her clothed breast, he sucked and tongued her naked one, exulting when both nipples hardened to pearls beneath his mouth and hand.

Ah, she was a wonder . . . a tart, impetuous wonder that made his blood rush to his head. And the purring sounds she was now making drove him to distraction. So did her soft skin and her delicious scent—seawater with a hint of—

"How can you smell like oranges even after bathing in the ocean?" he murmured against her breast.

A low laugh escaped her. "I barely entered the water, that's how."

He straightened to stare at her. "Makes me wonder where else you smell like oranges." He was just plotting how to find out when a snap sounded near them.

They both froze. Biting back a curse, he turned to see a dog chomping on a bone. Relief coursed through him. "It's no one."

She stared up at him, her expression suddenly guarded. "But someone *will* come along and discover us the longer we stand here."

"Unless we find a more congenial place to play." He circled her to lift her from behind onto the steps of the bathing machine.

By God, she had a shapely bottom, too, which was a lot easier to see when she wore no petticoats. As his mouth went dry, he climbed up behind her and opened the door a fraction, to make sure it was unlocked.

Brushing a kiss to her damp hair, he repeated what he'd said to her in the garden. "How would you like to try some wickedness?"

With a sigh, she leaned back against him, tormenting his hardening prick with her sweet bottom. "How would *you* like to stop reading my thoughts?"

He filled his hands with her breasts. "Is that a yes?"

When she didn't answer right away, he added, "I swear I won't take your innocence, and I'll do my damnedest not to harm your reputation. But neither am I eager to end this yet. Are you?"

"And if I say I am?" she whispered.

He paused in caressing her. "I'll walk away. If that's what you truly want."

She was quiet, obviously trying to decide.

Sensing she might desire the same intimacy he did, he added, "I'm offering a few minutes play, no more. A bit of honest pleasure."

Something for me to dream on when this is over and I'm alone again.

Tensely, he waited, fearing he might have gone too far for her comfort. Then she put her hand on the door handle to pull it open, and he had his answer.

Triumph surged through him so powerfully that he could do no more than help her inside before dragging her back into his arms for a long, heated kiss that had her swaying against him and moaning.

That had *him* stiffening to stone.

She must have felt it—and perhaps even knew what it meant—for when he drew back, her expression held a hint of alarm. "We cannot take more than a few minutes, though, or people will start looking for me."

He tugged one long, curling tress free so he could wind it about his finger and kiss it. "Do you trust me, sweetheart?"

Her lips quivered. "I-I think so."

"Because I swear that when our playing is over, you'll still be as chaste as when we came in here."

She searched his face as if to reassure herself that he meant it. Then her expression cleared and she smiled coyly. "Ah, but will *you*?"

God, the woman certainly knew how to tease. "I stopped being chaste at sixteen, my saucy Venus," he said with a chuckle.

She blinked. "That young?"

He shrugged. "I was going off to war. I thought I might not get another chance." Tipping up her chin, he ran his thumb over her lush lower lip. "But if you'd been my age and anywhere within a mile of Castle Wolfford, I'm not sure I could have resisted you. I can barely resist you now."

Damn. He hadn't meant to admit that.

Still, it seemed to delight her. With a sultry smile, she looped her arms about his neck. "If I had been your age and nearby, I would have set my cap for you. A dashing soldier, about to go off to war? What young lady wouldn't have thrown herself eagerly into his arms?"

"What young gentleman would have withstood all this glorious beauty? Especially if you had your hair down like this." He ran his fingers through her curling, dark blonde locks, which fell in a tangle down her back past her waist. "Do you know how long I've wished to see you with your hair free?" Even when he'd just watched her from afar at Elegant Occasions affairs.

His blood raced as he stroked the satiny length of it. "It's like spun gold, rare and rich and silky." He came to within a breath of her lips. "I dream of it fanning out beneath you as I kiss every inch of you with my mouth, touch every plane of your perfect body with my hands."

"What makes you think it's perfect?" she asked, with an arch of one imperious brow.

"I have eyes, don't I?"

She gave a light laugh. "Your flatteries are improving by leaps and bounds, Mr. Wolfford."

"I aim to please, my lady. And speaking of that . . ." He slid his hands down between them so he could pull her gown up her legs until it cleared her mons. "I promised you a bit of pleasure. And I always keep my promises."

Then bunching the fabric in one hand to hold it up, he cupped her mons with the other.

She gasped, her lovely sea-green eyes going wide. Holding her gaze, he slipped a finger inside her and used his thumb to find and stroke her little button, what he'd heard called the "sweetness of Venus." So fitting for her.

"Do you like that?" he rasped. Judging from how wet she was, she seemed to, but he wanted to see if she'd admit it.

Though she closed her eyes and blushed more deeply than he'd ever seen her do, she also nodded.

"I thought you might," he said, and returned to rubbing her below.

How he wished he could lay her down right here and show her the many roads to enjoyment, but that was impossible. Instead, he'd have to resist his own urges in order to quench hers.

This would be his penance for taking things too far. He would give *her* something to dream on, too, once they had to part, after she learned why he was really here.

And thus, he began the delightful task of satisfying his Venus.

Verity could hardly think, much less breathe. Each time Rafe thumbed her in that one very sensitive spot, she pressed into him, seeking more . . . seeking *all* the pleasures his fingers offered.

"That's it . . . sweetheart," he murmured. "Let yourself enjoy it. I dream of that at night. Of touching you . . ."

"L-Like this?" Something simmered inside her down there, like water on the verge of boiling.

He gave a strangled laugh. "This and more. In my

dreams, I stroke every inch of you. Watch you come apart in my hands."

She wriggled beneath his touch, and Lord, it felt so incredible. But she wanted him feeling it, too. Feeling it alone made her desolate. "In your dreams, do I get to touch every inch of *you*?"

He bent his head to hers. "Oh, God, yes."

"Here, perhaps?" She flattened her hand over the bulge in his smalls and looked at him, afraid to do the wrong thing.

"*Especially* there," he bit out. "But you don't . . . have to . . ."

"I want to." She stroked him lightly through the linen. "But I-I don't know what I'm doing."

"You're . . . doing fine. Just hold it . . . harder, that's all."

Rafe's eyes shone in the dim light, and for a moment she thought she glimpsed something like yearning there. Then he closed them, and she wondered if she'd imagined it.

So she rubbed harder, desperate to make *him* as excited as he was making her.

He slid another finger inside her. "You're so warm and wet, my wanton Venus. If I dared, I'd lay you down and . . . But no, I promised. I promised." He whispered the words again and again like a reminder.

As she thrust against his hand, seeking to reach the boiling point she knew was just *there*, he kissed her hard. Then he released her gown so he could cover her hand where it moved on the rigid flesh through his smalls, and he started guiding her motions.

She would never have used so much pressure. Surely she was hurting him with such fierceness, but his moans of satisfaction said otherwise.

Meanwhile, the strokes of his fingers inside her were frenzied, sending her up on her toes to feel more, have more . . . She gripped his upper arm with her free hand to latch him to her as *his* hand ripped her defenses away with every astonishing caress.

The simmering rose down below, and she knew if she could just . . . hold on for . . . a few minutes more . . . she would . . . she could . . .

Boil. *Over* . . .

"*Rafe,* my God!" she cried as she reached pure bliss. "Oh . . . oh . . . oh . . ."

Never had she known . . . had she imagined . . .

What the devil was *that*? Was that *her* making those sounds low in her throat? But even as the bliss subsided into a steady beat below that felt like vibrations tapering off, Rafe cried out, too, and jerked beneath her hand. Seconds later, a heated fluid dampened his smalls.

Good Lord, could she *actually* have boiled over onto him? That wasn't how things worked, was it?

But then he clutched her to him with an inarticulate cry, his face bearing a rapt expression, and she knew she must have done something right. Then his aroused flesh softened beneath her hand, and he breathed her name as his gasps slowed to deeper breaths.

This time when he kissed her, it was soft and tender, lazy and sweet. He took his hand from between her legs and wiped it on his smalls. Then he clutched her close for several long moments. "I'll have to call you my wanton Venus, now," he whispered as he stroked her hair. "My wanton virgin, Verity Venus."

"That's a mouthful," she murmured, amused by the idea of a wanton virgin.

"I should build a temple to you. That's what the Greeks would have done."

He'd called her wanton, and that gave her pause. She drew back to look at him. "I *am* still chaste, aren't I?"

He pressed a kiss to her forehead. "Yes, you're still a virgin."

She breathed a sigh of relief. She didn't know why, really. She still wasn't sure she even wanted a husband, and if she did ever have one, she didn't want one who put great stock in her innocence, even if most men did.

"Is what I felt how it's *supposed* to feel?" she asked. "Between a husband and wife, I mean?"

Alarm flashed in his eyes before he masked it. "Hell if I know. I've never been married, remember?"

"Of course," she said tightly.

As if realizing he'd been too abrupt, he added, "But I've never had it be like that for me, even with the most wanton of women."

There was that word again. Had doing this made her a wanton? Did she care?

Sadly, she didn't. Because if this was what being a wanton felt like, she'd have to rethink her plan to stay a maid all her life. That meant marriage. She never wanted to be a woman who had to give up her child to the Foundling Hospital.

But neither was she sure she wanted to marry Rafe. Not until she could figure out if he had any connection to her Phantom.

Reluctantly, she left his arms, and he didn't stop her. That told her well enough how he'd regarded this little interlude and whether he wished to marry *her*.

She busied herself by straightening her clothes, making sure no one would guess what they'd just been doing . . . avoiding his gaze. "I . . . um . . . suppose I should leave while I'm *still* chaste."

The change in him was immediate. He straightened and put on what she now realized was a disguise of sorts—the distant, calculating, even cold Rafe. This was the man he showed everyone else—who used a mnemonic device to remember people and gave set-downs to undeserving young ladies.

This was not the one who'd fallen in love with an actress at seven. Nor the one who'd stroked her hair with loving care.

A lump stuck in her throat. This Rafe was always hard to read.

"Yes," he said stiffly. "That would probably be best. You should go first, and I'll stay here long enough to be sure no one has seen us together."

She nodded as tears welled behind her eyes. Best to leave before they leaked out and mortified her.

He said nothing more as she slipped out of the bathing machine. Taking a moment to assess who was around and who might still be near her original bathing machine, she skirted the group of machines until she found hers and could thankfully slip inside without being seen.

But once she did, once she was donning her gown and stuffing her hair back up under her mob cap, she let the tears fall.

She wasn't even sure why. Perhaps it was because no matter what Rafe had said, he'd taken her innocence as surely as if he'd taken her chastity. He'd shown her another world, of sensual pleasures and heady delights, where she could relax her defenses with a man and enjoy his attentions, however briefly.

But now she was alone again. Was she destined to be always alone?

She drew herself up. What a maudlin, silly thought. She'd known from the beginning he would never go beyond flirtation with her. Somehow, she'd sensed that Phantom or no, he hadn't come here in search of a wife. How foolish to think otherwise.

Besides, even if he *was* looking for a wife, he would never let her be part of Elegant Occasions, and she and her sisters had worked too hard to simply let it vanish. Verity was proud of what they'd accomplished. She wasn't ready to throw that all away.

So it didn't matter how Rafe felt about her and marriage. She knew what she must do. She must make sure no one learned of their encounter, and then she must keep away from him. That was the only solution to this situation.

Wiping her eyes, she set about trying to figure out how to cover what she'd been doing. Most people would attribute her red eyes and nose to swimming. But she still had to get past Eliza's notice. And she still had to account for the extra time she'd spent getting back to her sister.

An idea came to her when she spotted a pile of shells in the corner that another of their party had picked up earlier. She stuffed her apron pockets with some, then sauntered onto the machine's little porch over the water to meet Eliza.

As she'd expected, Eliza was none too happy. "Where the devil have you been?" she hissed as she came up close to the machine. "Mrs. Chetley hasn't noticed a thing, but Jimmy is getting tired, and we must leave soon."

"I found the girls, and we were right—they'd gone to spy on the men at the other beach." Verity explained what had happened, exaggerating how long they'd waited for some gentlemen to move away from their hidden spot. "Of course, I still had to change into my clothes, so I had to return here. On the way back, I saw so many unique shells, I kept stopping to pick them up."

Verity patted her apron pockets where the shells made a clattering noise. "I didn't mean to worry you. You know I can't resist a pretty shell. They're tiny works of art. I thought I might use them for a display at one of our meals or something." She was babbling now, which Eliza was sure to notice.

Narrowing her gaze, Eliza crossed her arms over her bosom. "Tiny works of art, hmm? I didn't see you coming back, picking up shells or otherwise."

Verity forced a smile. "How do you think I got here? Swam? You were paying attention to Jimmy. I doubt you noticed where any of us were."

Thankfully, although her sister still looked concerned, she didn't pursue the topic further. "Well, we had better go. I hope the ladies reached the house safely."

"I'm sure they're fine. If you'll have the dippers order the bathing machines towed up on the beach, I'll help you and Molly dress."

With a nod, Eliza turned as if to leave. Then she paused to look back at Verity. "You would tell me if anything untoward happened to you while you were gone, wouldn't you?"

It was all Verity could do not to scream. Instead, she gave a laugh that sounded hollow, even to her. "Untoward! Don't be silly. Unless you consider my frustration at having to deal with three very foolish ladies, I assure you nothing 'untoward' happened."

Eliza sighed. "Very well." Then she left.

Verity walked back into the bathing machine and collapsed on the bench. How she hated lying to her sister. But what choice did she have? Eliza would have heart failure if she knew what they'd been up to earlier.

At least Rafe had kept his promise and hadn't seduced her when he had the chance. She only hoped he was better at keeping secrets than Lord Minton, and wouldn't throw her to the wolves by damaging her reputation. If he did . . .

She would simply have to cross that bridge when she came to it.

Chapter 15

As soon as Verity had left the bathing machine, Rafe had moved to the front to watch her through the window and make sure she entered her own without anyone noticing. Once she had, he'd paced the small room and allowed himself to think about what he'd done.

Gone too far, *that* was what. He hadn't meant to. He'd only wanted to question her about what man she'd been watching. Next thing he knew, he was offering to give her a hint of the joys of the bedchamber, and allowing himself to be so caught up in their "playing" that he'd even asked her to satisfy his own arousal. As if she were some whore. So their encounter had *not* turned out to be the grand sacrifice he'd intended.

For God's sake, he'd barely restrained himself from seducing her. He ought to have known better. Now that he'd tasted her delights, he would want to do it again the next time they kissed, then do more and more until he *did* seduce her.

Bloody hell. They couldn't kiss or caress each other again. Now he must back away. Because he couldn't get her words out of his head. *Is what I felt how it's supposed to feel? Between a husband and wife, I mean?*

If he went further, she'd want marriage, and he wouldn't

blame her. She deserved marriage. But once she learned how he'd deceived her and her family . . . She might resent her father, but that didn't mean she'd want him arrested and possibly hanged. It was better that Rafe not risk her hating him for it.

He looked out just in time to see the horses for her bathing machine and two others being guided to pull the wheeled changing rooms back through the surf and up onto the beach.

Since everyone would be inside those, it was time for him to make his escape. He slipped out, using the cover of shade and trees to reach the road so he could pass over onto the men's beach. Only then did he relax, knowing he wouldn't be caught by ladies outraged over a man in his smalls invading their precious territory.

He'd been gone so long that the other gentlemen in his party had left. Indeed, the attendants to their bathing machine were waiting around for his return. Hastily, he donned the rest of his clothes, since his smalls were now dry, and headed back for the house by the route that led up a street past several shops.

He was just approaching an apothecary shop when he heard an argument from inside spilling out onto the road. Instantly, he recognized one of the voices. Hard to miss the strident tones of the fellow who'd repeatedly tried to outbid him for Verity's dinner.

So when Rafe looked into the shop, he wasn't surprised to find Lord Minton engaged in a dispute with the shopman. Rafe watched unnoticed as the dispute became more heated, Rafe's own temper rising by the moment. Minton's presence in Exmouth couldn't possibly be a coincidence.

"I told you yesterday, sir," the shopman said, "I ain't

allowed to approve credit for nobody. Only the apothecary can, and he's presently in Brighton."

Minton tapped a line on a sheet of paper. "Do you know who this is?"

"I do. Though he could be the King hisself, far as I'm concerned." The shopman put some bottles to the side. "Till the apothecary returns, I can only hold these for you. I can't approve you or yer friend's request for credit."

"Very wise of you, sir," Rafe bit out as he walked inside. "I don't know about his friend's credit, but I assure you Lord Minton's is about as sound as a rowboat in high seas. He owes money to half the merchants in London."

Minton whirled on him, his face flushing bright red as he saw who was accusing him. "That's a lie, Wolfford. I have prospects you know nothing of."

"I gathered as much." And Rafe wouldn't rest until he learned what madman would give money to this arse. Rafe clasped his hands behind his back to keep from clenching them into fists. He didn't like Minton, and he definitely didn't trust him being this close to Verity. "Why are you in Exmouth?"

Minton shrugged. "Not that it's any of your concern, but it's a good watering place for when a gentleman fancies summer entertainment."

Rafe narrowed his gaze on the bastard. "Watering places litter England's coasts, yet you chose the one Lady Verity and her family happen to be visiting?"

"I was unaware Lady Verity is in Exmouth," Minton said coldly.

"You're as bad a liar as you are a suitor." Rafe stepped closer, pleased when Minton took a cautionary step back. "But it matters not. Because if I see you anywhere near her during your stay, I swear it won't be just credit you'll need from the apothecary."

Minton sneered at him. "Afraid I might steal her from you?"

"She well remembers that you threw her away when you had the chance to keep her. I'll make sure you never get another." He edged toward the counter, hoping to glimpse the name of Minton's benefactor. "Take my advice—find another watering place for your 'summer entertainment.'"

"Perhaps *you* should find another lady to torment with your attentions." Minton snatched up the paper on the counter before Rafe could see it. Then, shooting the shopman a baleful look, he thrust it into his coat pocket. "And I will certainly find another apothecary to give my business to."

"As is yer right, sir," the shopman said.

When Minton marched out the door, Rafe was torn between following him to see where his lodgings were and remaining behind to question the shopman. He opted for the latter, since it would be hard to follow Minton in a town as small as Exmouth without the man noticing and taking evasive measures. Besides, there were other ways to get that information.

The shopman cleared his throat. "Something I can help you with, sir?"

"I'd like to buy one of everything Lord Minton just tried to purchase." When the shopman looked reluctant, he withdrew a handful of coins from his pocket. "And I come with cash. My name is Raphael Wolfford. I don't need credit."

The man brightened. "And if you did, I daresay me employer would give it to you. The Wolfford name is well-known hereabouts."

That caught Rafe by surprise. "My home is a long way from here."

"Aye. But the general comes to take the waters for his

leg on occasion and always stops in to chew the cud with me employer."

Rafe wondered if Uncle Constantine had also come this way to investigate Holtbury. That was the problem with not having his uncle's notes. Rafe had never known that the man had been in Exmouth before. Uncle Constantine had clearly never told Sir Lucius. But it did mean Rafe might be on the right track with his theory about Holtbury's smugglers using the River Exe.

"Are you related to the general?"

The shopman's question jerked Rafe back to his surroundings. "He's my uncle."

"Ah. You look a bit like him. But listen to me jawing on, and not gathering yer purchases." The man started wrapping the bottles he'd set aside for Minton. "So, the fellow who was just here. He's got his eye on Lady Verity Harper?"

"He does."

"And you do, too."

Rafe forced a smile. "I'm undoubtedly one of several who do, yes."

The man hesitated a moment, then leaned in. "I'll give you a bit of advice, then, since you're so amiable. You might have trouble ousting Lord Minton as her suitor. The man has her father's ear."

A chill skittered down Rafe's spine. That might very well be who was funding Minton's stay in Exmouth. Just to be sure, he said, "Lord Holtbury provided the baron with his letter of credit, didn't he?"

"I shouldn't say, but aye."

Damn, Holtbury and Minton were in league together. Could Minton's presence here and Holtbury's willingness to help him have anything to do with the spy for the French? Might *Minton* be the spy?

That made no sense. Minton had no known ties to the

French, and if he'd been serving as Holtbury's go-between somehow, surely Rafe would have seen evidence of it sooner. Besides, Minton was a hothead and a fool, hardly sly and clever enough to evade authorities all this time. So securing Verity as his wife must be his only reason for being in town.

Rafe couldn't keep that information to himself. The duke should be informed. And definitely Verity.

The shopman looked concerned now, as if realizing how much he'd revealed to a stranger. "Tell me, Mr. Wolfford, why are *you* in Exmouth?"

"I'm a guest at Grenwood's house party."

"And what do you think of his place?"

Clearly, this was a test. "It seems well-suited for entertaining. He needs to enlarge his carriage house, though. I had to leave my coach out in the weather."

The shopman's expression cleared. "Aye, the place could use more room for carriages." He gazed out the door. "I take it Lord Minton wasn't invited."

Rafe couldn't restrain a grimace. "Definitely not. Lady Verity wants naught to do with him, I assure you."

The shopman bobbed his head. "That says a great deal about the man. She's generally nice to everyone, her and her sisters. And the duke is so obliging whenever he and his wife are in town."

"They bring you a lot of business?"

"The ladies do. Perfume and possets and the usual lady things."

Rafe looked at the vast selection of fancifully decorated bottles. "Does . . . um . . . Lady Verity have a particular scent she prefers?"

"Indeed, she does." The fellow winked at him. "Would you like a bottle?"

He might need a gift to get back into her good graces. Not that he should care. But he couldn't help it—he did care, especially now that Minton had appeared on the scene. "I would."

The chap grinned. "One bottle of honey-and-orange-flower water for Mr. Wolfford. I can even give you the same formulation she uses."

"Thank you." Worse comes to worst, he could always smell it to remind him of her once he was out of her life.

He snorted. As if that would be any substitute for the real thing.

The shopman came back with the scent bottle and added it to the pile. Rafe paid out the price given him, then added several guineas. "These are just for you, sir, payment for all your useful information. But I do have one more question I need answered. Did Lord Minton happen to say where he's lodging in Exmouth?"

The landlord there could tell Rafe if Minton had made regular trips to Exmouth, so Rafe could at least eliminate him as the spy once and for all.

The shopman stared hard at the guineas. Without a word, he scooped them up, wrote down an address, and handed it to Rafe.

"Thank you, sir." Rafe tipped his hat. "A pleasure doing business with you."

Then he was out the door, smiling to himself. Just as Rafe had expected, there'd been no reason to follow Minton after all.

It was nearly time for dinner but instead of mingling with the guests in the drawing room, Verity was closeted with Geoffrey in his study. As Geoffrey sat behind his desk, drawing engineering designs on a sheet of foolscap, she paced the room, unable to contain her agitation.

"Did Mr. Wolfford say nothing about why he wanted to meet with us?" she asked.

"Not a word. Said it was important, though, and it had to be private. Just you and me and him."

So help her, if the man meant to tell Geoffrey what had gone on earlier at the beach, she would pin his ears back, she would.

She stifled a sigh. It didn't seem like something he'd do, though. Assuming she'd judged his character rightly.

Casting her a watchful look, Geoffrey sat back to intertwine his fingers over his stomach. "Is there something you haven't yet told me? Has the man made you an offer?"

"An offer of what?" she asked warily.

Her brother-in-law scowled. "Marriage, of course. Seeing as I'm one of the two male relatives of yours he could seek permission from other than your father, I thought that might be what this is about."

"If Mr. Wolfford made me an offer of marriage, I missed it," she said grimly. "I don't think he's the marrying kind."

"I wouldn't have thought Foxstead was the marrying kind, either, but here he is all the same, happily married to your sister. Some men will surprise you."

"That's certainly true," she grumbled. Rafe surprised her every time she encountered him. She wasn't sure whether that was good or bad.

The door opened, and he walked in, dressed as finely for dinner this night as last. Nathaniel's tailor had certainly done well by him, and quickly, too.

"Thank you so much for meeting with me," he said, not meeting her eyes. "I wanted to keep this to as few people as possible until you two decide who else in the family needs to know."

"Know what?" Verity snapped.

"There's no easy way to say this." He shifted a serious gaze to her. "Lord Minton is in Exmouth."

Geoffrey shot to his feet. "The devil you say!"

With a sickening lurch in her stomach, she went to stare out the window and attempt to gather her thoughts. Why would Lord Minton have followed them here? The blasted devil *knew* she wanted nothing more to do with him.

"Are you sure?" she asked without turning around.

"I encountered him in the apothecary shop on my walk back. We . . . er . . . had words, but it was clear he's in town only to see you if he can."

"Over my dead body," she muttered.

"I don't think murdering you is his purpose," Rafe said dryly. When she whirled to retort, he placed a bottle on Geoffrey's desk. "But this is one of the items he was attempting to buy at the apothecary shop."

Geoffrey picked up the bottle, read the label, then muttered a curse.

"What is it?" she asked, her heart in her throat.

"Laudanum," Geoffrey growled. "Of a very high concentration."

Rafe steadily met her startled gaze. "The kind of concentration one might need to, say, put a person to sleep for a while."

"How could you possibly know that?" she asked.

"My uncle requires that concentration. He has a great deal of pain."

Oh. Right. She'd forgotten his uncle was ill. And the way Rafe said the words, as if he couldn't bear his uncle's suffering, made her feel for him.

"My father did, too, toward the end of his life," Geoffrey added. Coming around in front of his desk, Geoffrey leaned back against it to level his gaze on Rafe. "So, what are you saying? You think he intends to abduct Verity?"

"I'm not sure, honestly. What I do know is he can't afford to be here at all, which is why he couldn't purchase the laudanum. The shopman wouldn't extend him credit. And apparently, he hasn't much ready cash."

"What gives you that idea?" Verity asked.

He sighed. "Before I left London, I asked around about him." Even as she bristled, he added hastily, "I was worried even then that he might follow you here. But I discovered he owed so much money to so many people that I couldn't see how he could afford lodgings in Exmouth, much less travel expenses and food."

She gulped air, trying to remain calm. "Perhaps he's staying with a friend. Perhaps it's just a coincidence that he's here."

Rafe's eyes held pity. "He's taken rooms in Beacon Terrace."

Geoffrey scowled. "That's a costly place to stay."

"Exactly. But I also found out he's not paying for it himself."

Verity blinked. "So, who is?"

He hesitated before saying, "Your father."

She stood there gaping at him, feeling as if he'd pierced her heart. "Papa wouldn't be so . . . he couldn't care that little for me that he would . . ." She shook her head. "No, I can't believe it."

Because if she believed it, then she meant nothing to Papa. And even after all these years, she'd still foolishly nurtured the hope that somewhere in his selfish heart he loved her just a little.

"What is your proof?" she demanded. "Did . . . Did Lord Minton *say* such a thing?"

"Actually, no. According to the apothecary's shopman, Minton had a letter of credit from your father. And I confirmed with the owner of Beacon Place that your father is paying for Minton's rooms."

Dropping into the nearest chair, she stared off into space and fought the nausea rising in her.

"I'm sorry, Lady Verity," Rafe said. "I thought you should know."

She stiffened. "I must admit it sounds like something Papa would do. He's annoyed as the devil that I haven't married. I guess he thinks to force the issue by thrusting Lord Minton on me. Although why he would choose to champion that scoundrel after how the man treated me, I can't imagine."

"Not that I'd ever argue on behalf of my father-in-law," Geoffrey said, "but perhaps he assumes you still want Minton."

A choked laugh escaped her. "He knows better. And even if he did assume that, how could he think I'd find it acceptable to take back a man who shamed me throughout Society? If Papa believes that, then he's gone mad as a hatter."

Geoffrey shook his head. "Oddly enough, I said something much the same to . . . er . . . Nathaniel today."

Rafe scowled at him. "Anyway, under the circumstances, I think you should cancel the tour of A La Ronde tomorrow that's been scheduled for after Lady Rumridge leaves in the morning."

Verity jumped to her feet. "Why?"

"It's too risky," Rafe said. "Your family can control who enters this house, but not who enters a stranger's home. From what I understand, in addition to the house, there are grounds to tour, a chapel, four almshouses, a stables, and even a schoolroom. Minton could lurk anywhere on the property, and you wouldn't know. Given what I've learned, I'd advise against going."

"I'm not canceling that," she retorted.

"Fine," Rafe said. "Then let the others go without you."

"For pity's sake, how do you know he wouldn't try to take me from here?"

Rafe stiffened. "Because I will stay behind, along with all your servants and mine. Beaufort will be here. If a chaperone is needed, I'm sure one of the ladies would prefer not to go. Mrs. Crowder perhaps."

"What? I've been looking forward to this for weeks! I'm not letting that scoundrel scare me into staying home."

"Besides, Wolfford," Geoffrey put in, "we'll all be with her at A La Ronde. We'll just make sure someone stays beside her at all times." He stared at Verity. "And that would be a good practice for anywhere in town, too, my dear. Make sure either I or Nathaniel accompany you outside the house."

"Or me," Rafe said.

"Right." She snorted. "Having a man dogging my steps wouldn't provoke any gossip among our guests at all, would it? Do you mean to follow me everywhere, Geoffrey? To the necessary? Into a bathing machine?"

"Good God, no!"

Her heart thundered in her chest. "I'm finally beginning to regain my reputation, and you lot mean to let Lord Minton strip me of it all over again."

"I don't think—" Rafe began.

"You said Lord Minton couldn't buy the laudanum, so he has none to use at present." Shivering at the very thought of him using laudanum on her, she pulled her shawl more tightly about her shoulders. "And for all you know, he needs it for headaches or a painful attack of bursitis. I shan't stay a prisoner in this house simply because you suspect Lord Minton is lying in wait for me."

"He was lying in wait for you on the terrace at the auction," Rafe said.

"What?" Geoffrey roared, then rounded on her. "Is this true?"

She glowered at Rafe before turning to Geoffrey. "He wanted to talk to me, that's all. Rafe . . . Mr. Wolfford . . . put him in his place, and that was that. He hasn't troubled me since."

"You've mostly been *here* ever since. And he followed you here." Rafe's roughening voice showed his ample concern.

It was touching, though a bit misplaced. "Yes, but to abduct me? It's absurd. And as hateful as Papa can be at times, even if he's behind Lord Minton's appearance here, I doubt he would sanction any behavior that might cause me actual physical harm. Frankly, I also doubt the baron would have the courage to attempt it. He's not a brave man, I assure you, and certainly not in some mission to win my hand, or whatever he hopes to achieve."

"I'm sure he wants money," Geoffrey said. "Your father has probably promised him a dowry for you."

That caught her entirely off guard. She hadn't even considered Papa might do something so awful. The thought of his paying Lord Minton was too painful to contemplate. Not to mention insulting. "Thank you, Geoffrey," she said hoarsely, "for reminding me a man could only be interested in me if I had a fat dowry."

"I-I didn't mean—" Geoffrey began.

"Or perhaps you're right, Lady Verity," Rafe said, with a black look at Geoffrey. "Your father merely wants to see you married and has funded Minton's trip here so he can court you."

That Rafe would offer that sop to her pride was sweet, but . . .

"Your father may have no idea what Minton is actually planning," Rafe went on. "But that wouldn't stop Minton from planning it." His gaze locked with hers. "Some men will do foolish things indeed to gain the women they want."

She stared at him. Was he including himself in that number? Was this his attempt to apologize for the abrupt way he'd left her earlier? To say their encounter this afternoon meant more to him than he'd led her to believe?

"I will testify to the truth of that." Geoffrey smiled faintly. "So will your sister."

"Regardless," she said, "I am going to A La Ronde. Miss Parminter was kind enough to allow us to tour it, even though it's not open to the public. And I wanted to present to her a little gift to show how much we appreciated her donation of her cousin's items at the auction and tell her how much they garnered for the Foundling Hospital. I can't do that if I'm stuck at home."

"Verity," Rafe said softly, "I just wish to keep you safe."

"And I realize that. I do." She thought a moment. "What if I promise to be very careful when I'm outside of this house?"

"What if you promise never to be alone when you're out of this house?" he countered.

"Rafe . . ."

"You don't have to have a gentleman with you," Rafe added. "You've demonstrated that such a requirement would be intolerable. But one of your sisters will do. Either of them could take on any gentleman intending to do you harm. I can just picture Lady Foxstead beating Minton over the head with her harp lute."

"She'd do it, too," Geoffrey said.

"As long as you keep *someone* with you," Rafe said, "I don't think he'll attempt anything. Can you promise me that?"

She looked at the two men, who were only trying to protect her, after all, then sighed. "Of course." She forced lightness into her tone. "I shall go nowhere without a party of sycophants to sit adoringly at my feet."

"Just what we need," Geoffrey muttered. "Sycophants. As if we didn't have enough guests already."

Rafe appeared to be fighting a smile. "They needn't be sycophants. Just someone you trust. I'll leave you two to decide who that should be and how many of the family should know of Minton's appearance. If you're worried about gossip, I would keep the knowledge restricted to only a few."

"Good idea," Geoffrey said.

"That's also why I should probably leave before people start speculating about what's going on in here," Rafe said with a rueful smile.

When he started for the door, Verity called out after him, "Thank you, Rafe. For keeping an eye on Minton."

"Happy to do it." With a bow, he left the room.

"Well then," Geoffrey said with a considering glance in the direction Rafe had gone. "Shall your shadow be Eliza?"

Verity sighed. "Probably. Diana is still recovering from childbirth, and I wouldn't trust any of the other ladies to do it without gossiping."

"Eliza and her harp lute, it is," Geoffrey said.

In that moment, something dawned on her. How could Rafe possibly know Eliza played the harp lute? It was an odd instrument, and her sister hadn't played it since long before Rafe had attended the auction. He couldn't know, unless he'd gone to one of their earlier events.

A chill swept over her. The only way he could have done that was as the Phantom.

Chapter 16

That night after dinner, while everyone played charades, Verity couldn't help watching Rafe, looking for some sign she'd been right about him being the Phantom after all. Should she get him alone and confront him? Try to talk to him again with an eye toward tricking him into admitting who he really was? She could always sneak into his room and go through his things.

A sigh escaped her. She was being absurd. Not about his being the Phantom—she was growing more and more sure she was right about that.

Still, that didn't mean she should act like him. Or Minton. Or them both, skulking about, finding out private information, and following people.

This afternoon's information scratched at her brain like a cat requiring attention. She ignored it. Right now, it was less upsetting to ponder the possibility of Rafe being the Phantom than to dwell on what Minton was up to.

Tonight, she would retire early so she could revisit her notebook about the Phantom, which she hadn't touched in some days. But first, she needed to clarify something. So, when she saw Eliza rise and head for the stairs, she started after her.

"Wait, Lady Verity!" Lady Harry said. "It's your turn to present a charade."

She bit back a tart reply. Fortunately, Eliza had stopped to watch her, so she searched her mind for one she'd heard or read before. Ah, yes, *that* charade would certainly be appropriate. She recited:

> *My first is nothing but a name;*
> *My second still more small:*
> *My whole of so much smaller fame*
> *It has no name at all.*

When she finished, she made sure to catch Rafe's eye, then lifted her eyebrow. His gaze narrowed on her as the others tried to make out the answer. Did that mean he understood? Or that he couldn't figure out what she meant?

"Oh, wait, I know the solution to that one!" Isolde cried. "I read it in one of your charades books."

"How appropriate," Verity quipped. "That's where I got it."

"Not fair!" Lady Harry complained. "Isolde knew it before."

Miss Mudford said, "Oh, hush, child. You've won enough forfeits already to make a veritable nuisance of yourself. Let Miss Crowder have this one."

Isolde looked around as Verity tapped her foot. "Shall I reveal it?"

"Go ahead," Eliza said, apparently noticing Verity's impatience.

So Isolde stood. "The first syllable, of course, is 'name,' since it's 'nothing but a name.' The second syllable is 'more small' so it's 'less.' And together it's—"

"'Nameless'!" Miss Chetley cried triumphantly. When everyone stared at her, she shrank down into her seat.

"Because it has no name at all, yes," Isolde said. "It's 'nameless.'"

As everyone clapped, Verity dared to look at Rafe. He was staring hard at her as if trying to make her out. He couldn't know she'd given him a "name" for all those times she didn't know who he was. But he'd definitely been nameless to her. Might still be, for all she knew. Raphael Wolfford might not even be his actual name. The real Raphael Wolfford might still be fighting on the Peninsula.

How unsettling a thought. She had let him do things to her . . .

"Who's next?" Diana called out.

That was Verity's cue to follow Eliza out to the stairs. To her surprise, Eliza stood at the bottom waiting for her.

"Is this about tomorrow?" Eliza asked. "Geoffrey said you had to discuss something with me regarding our trip to A La Ronde."

Of course, Geoffrey would leave it to *Verity* to explain. He knew Eliza's anger on her sister's behalf might spill over onto him.

Verity detailed everything Rafe had learned, along with why they all thought Eliza would be a suitable companion for her. She purposely quoted exactly what Rafe had said about the harp lute, then waited to see Eliza's reaction.

"I should be flattered that Mr. Wolfford thinks I can best Lord Minton," Eliza said, "but it's not much of a compliment. Lord Minton is a spineless toady, whom Jimmy could probably scare off."

"True."

Eliza paused. "But how odd that Mr. Wolfford mentioned my harp lute. Did you tell him I play it?"

"I did not." Verity watched for when it might dawn on Eliza what that could mean.

"I suppose he heard about it from Mama or Diana or

even Nathaniel." She shrugged. "In any case, I'll be happy to be your constant companion tomorrow, my dear, although I think the men are being a bit dramatic about the whole thing."

So did Verity, but that wasn't the point. In one dismissive remark, Eliza had made her suspicions about Rafe seem absurd. Because he *could* have heard about it in the hours he'd spent with Mama in her carriage. Or the time he'd spent talking to the men while they'd been swimming. Or any number of places.

She sighed. She had half a mind to tell Eliza her suspicions, but something held her back. What if Rafe actually had a good reason for spying on them? Shouldn't she at least give him the chance to explain before she trumpeted his deceptions to her family?

Somehow, she must find out. That meant she must get him alone to talk. But how could she manage that when she'd already put him on his guard around her?

Later that evening, long after everyone else retired, she had just left the kitchen after making some last-minute notes when she heard the night footman speaking to someone. She peeked around the corner to see Rafe coming in the front door and giving his hat and coat to the servant. He was raffishly dressed, especially for him, which was a surprise.

After he'd gone upstairs, she went to the footman. "Was that Mr. Wolfford?"

"Yes, my lady."

"What was he doing out so late?"

"He went to the Lobster Tavern."

A tavern? When he was in a house full of people with liquor and wine available for free? How strange. That was something the Phantom would do, it seemed to her. Unless

Rafe had a problem, like gambling or . . . or soiled doves.
She didn't want to think about that.

"Was he drunk?"

"Not that I could tell. Barely smelled liquor on him,
my lady."

She swallowed hard. "Did you smell . . . perfume?"

He eyed her quizzically. "None of that neither."

With a frown, she turned for the stairs.

"He went to the Lobster Tavern last night, too, my lady,"
he added.

That halted her. "Did he say why?"

"No. Should I ask him why if he goes again?"

She shook her head no. "And don't tell him *I* was asking,
all right?"

"Yes, my lady."

She hurried up the stairs, eager to get to her bedchamber
where she could look at her list of facts about the Phantom.
Tomorrow, she'd have to do her best to get some time alone
with him. This had gone far enough.

The day of the tour at A La Ronde dawned bright and
sunny, but Rafe couldn't enjoy the fine weather. He'd already spent last night tossing and turning, lusting after
Verity's sweet body, worrying about Verity's safety, and
trying to figure out if she'd guessed the truth about him.
Because she'd clearly meant that charade for *him*.

Nameless. He *had* been nameless the past year and a
half. When he'd played a Jack in the Green, he hadn't even
bothered to choose an actual alias. No one ever noticed the
names of such performers, anyway. And whenever he'd
played an aristocrat, he'd avoided saying his name, which
was easy to do when no one knew you, so no one was introducing you to anyone else. As a footman, he'd been "John,"

so common a servant name that virtually every household had one.

Nameless seemed pretty damned appropriate. If she knew, how long had she known? Or was he just making too much of her little rhyme?

He had to be. Besides, Verity wouldn't tell him she suspected him in such a sly fashion. She would accuse him right out. He must have imagined that look she'd given him. And the aptness of her charade. Who unmasked someone by using a party game, for God's sake?

Standing out in front of Grenwood's manor now, smoking a rare cheroot, he wondered if he could get a tête-à-tête ride with Verity to the shell house, as he'd taken to calling it.

Highly doubtful. Young ladies did not ride alone with bachelors in carriages. Which was a shame, since he might be able to kiss her if he got the chance. Although probably not after smoking a cheroot.

He put it out. It had done its job by allowing him a valid reason to get away from the gaggle of people in the drawing room waiting for the guests to finish dressing. The hardest part of this mission had been having to be around so many people in crowded social situations. After a while, the noise and the personal contact got to be too much for him. That was what came of growing up mostly in solitude.

Lady Rumridge had left a short while ago, with many a tearful goodbye to her daughters, who seemed unmoved by her gushing remarks about how she'd miss them. Possibly because she seemed to cry at will, which they must be used to.

And when had he begun to feel sorry for the three women, anyway?

Perhaps when he'd realized that they—and their spouses— were genuinely kind people. They were seducing him into their camp as effectively as Verity was seducing him into her life.

He snorted. Some detached spy *he* was. He'd gone soft, and he couldn't figure out how and when it had happened.

A carriage turned the corner into the lane, and he realized it wasn't any of the others belonging to guests or residents of the house. But before he could wonder whose it was, Verity and Eliza came rushing out to greet it.

"There they are!" Eliza cried. "The three sweetest boys in Devonshire!"

The coach door opened, and three lads ranging in age from five to eight tumbled out and ran to get their hugs and kisses from both women, who were soon joined by their sister.

To his horror, he got a lump in his throat at the sight, especially when Lady Holtbury stepped down, looking genuinely happy to see her stepdaughters and laughingly allowing her sons to pull her this way and that.

It reminded him of when he was ten and watched a family in town disembark from a coach, only to be enveloped by their happy relations. The envy he'd felt in that moment had drowned him, as it would drown him now if he let it.

Throughout his childhood, he'd dreamed of having an aunt or a cousin or one of his mother's relatives show up to join his proud, aloof uncle and make the three of them into a real family.

That was before he'd learned nothing ever came of dreaming. That you had to be born into families like that, and he'd lost his chance after his parents' deaths.

Pen had done her best, but she'd had no family herself, so they'd been two lonely people consoling each other when his uncle wasn't around, which was often. He and Pen and Uncle had been more of a collection of misfits than a family.

Rafe had wanted a family.

He stiffened. But he didn't have one, and that was that. He was letting these self-pitying thoughts keep him from his purpose, which was to find out if Lady Holtbury knew anything about her husband's activities. Time to go to work.

This was his first time to see the woman up close, and he wasn't surprised to find her as pretty in person as she was by reputation. A blonde woman in her early thirties, she had alabaster skin, hazel eyes, and ready smiles. But her timid demeanor had her holding back while her stepdaughters coddled her boys.

Eliza noticed him standing there. "Sarah, may I present one of our guests, Mr. Raphael Wolfford? Mr. Wolfford, this is my stepmother, Lady Holtbury."

The petite lady held out her hand. "I hope you will call me Sarah." She had a soft voice and hesitant delivery. "Everybody does."

With a nod, he took her hand and squeezed it. "You're a brave woman, indeed, to join this crowd in the midst of our heading off to tour a shell house."

"Shell house?" Sarah asked, looking perplexed.

Verity eyed him crossly. "Stop calling it that, for pity's sake. And don't refer to it as such when we're there, either. Miss Parminter will be insulted." She turned to Sarah. "We're leaving soon to tour A La Ronde, a famous sixteen-sided house decorated with shells and craftwork. You needn't go if you're too tired, but if you wish to join us, Diana's nursemaid and Molly will happily look after the boys."

"Truly, I'm fine," Sarah said. "The boys were good on the way here, but the dullness of the journey made them a bit boisterous, so I would enjoy any quiet entertainment. Do I have time to change into more suitable clothing?"

"Of course," Diana said. "Come, I'll show you to your room."

Others joined them in front, chattering about who was riding with whom. Rafe considered inviting Sarah to ride with him, but his conversation with her must be private.

Lady Harry sidled up to him, batting her eyelashes like a siren tempting a man to his doom. "Are you taking your equipage to A La Ronde?"

"I plan to, yes."

"Then I'll ride with you." And with that, she latched onto his arm.

He stifled a sigh. The woman never gave up. She was husband-hunting with a vengeance, and ever since yesterday she seemed to have set her sights on *him.* God help any man who let the chit leg-shackle him. He'd never get any peace.

Looking over to see Miss Mudford standing there, he said, "You're welcome to join us, madam." He hadn't been impressed with the chaperone's control of her charge until now, but every little bit had to help.

He ended up with four extra passengers, including Isolde Crowder, whose mother had chosen not to go, and Lord Harry, who wished to ride on the perch with the coachman. The Chetleys took their own coach, and Grenwood escorted Foxstead and Quinn in his. Foxstead had been told about Minton, too, so since he and Grenwood had already toured the house before, they'd agreed between them to keep watch in front of A La Ronde in case Minton should show up.

Rafe noticed that Sarah and the three Harper sisters rode together in Foxstead's coach, which made sense, although Rafe hoped to separate Sarah from the pack once they arrived at the house.

To that end, as soon as everyone arrived, Rafe positioned himself so he could join Sarah as they entered. He was torn, though. He'd rather stay by Verity the entire time. He still hated that she had come here, where Minton could approach her, but with so many of them around, surely they could head him off. It wasn't as if Minton knew their schedule or that they were doing this tour. Besides, someone would surely notice a stranger come in after them.

But Rafe might not get another chance to interrogate Sarah. Since Eliza was clearly up to the task of keeping close to Verity, he reluctantly offered his arm to Sarah as they entered. Thankfully, she took it.

At first, however, he wasn't even sure he'd get to speak to her alone. As they filed inside, they were greeted by Miss Parminter in the octagon center, around which all the wedge-shaped rooms of the first floor were fitted.

Verity then took her chance to extol the lady's generosity to the charity auction. Amid much applause, Verity revealed how much money Miss Parminter's donations had raised and offered her a gift of shellwork as a thank you.

As Verity came back to stand by Eliza, Miss Parminter explained the history of the house, who'd designed it, and what had inspired it—the octagon-shaped Basilica of San Vitale in Ravenna, Italy. Was the lady intending to take the group through each room explaining things? God, he hoped not.

As if reading his mind, she added, "I will briefly describe what each room holds on each floor, and then you'll be free to wander the house and look at items."

That would work much better for his purposes.

Miss Parminter went through her descriptions, then finished by explaining the unusual organization of rooms. "My cousins and I wanted to be able to follow the sun as it moved around the house, so that we could receive the best light in every room throughout the day."

Eliza, who stood near Rafe, cleared her throat loudly to

gain Miss Parminter's attention. "So, you actually do move from one room to another in a circular fashion throughout the day?"

She nodded. "On the first floor, yes. We do a great deal of handiwork, as you'll be able to tell while wandering the house, and good light is important for that. What's more, the windows are designed in such a fashion as to distribute the most sunlight possible throughout each room."

Someone else asked a question and she began addressing that.

Eliza said in a low voice meant for Verity, "I suppose a person could also move in a reverse circle by seeking out the *darkest* room for the time of day."

"Why would anyone want that?" Verity asked in a whisper.

A mysterious smile graced Eliza's lips. "I can think of a few reasons."

"So could I," Rafe whispered, his gaze on Verity.

Verity regarded them quizzically. He could tell when she understood by her furious blush. "If either of you even hints at such a wicked thing to Miss Parminter," she hissed, "I swear I will serve you gruel for dinner."

Rafe had to squeeze his lips together to keep from laughing.

Then the group began to break up, signaling the end of the presentation.

Taking a deep breath, he turned toward Sarah. "Would you like to join me in viewing the library?"

At last, he could get to work.

Chapter 17

Sarah? Verity scowled. Rafe wished to spend his time with her *married* stepmother?

Perhaps he was trying to emphasize to Verity that yesterday's intimacies were temporary pleasures to him. Perhaps he wished to indicate that she mustn't put too much stock in his attentions or think they might lead to marriage.

If so, a pox on him! He was welcome to Sarah, if he just wanted another woman to . . . to play with. Verity couldn't give a farthing. She wasn't remotely jealous. No, indeed. Why, she'd never been jealous of a man's other conquests in her life, not even of Lord Minton's!

But did Rafe have to pick her stepmother, whom she'd always been envious of? Sarah was a beautiful china doll of perfect proportions. Verity had never had perfect proportions. She was much too thin and tall.

Her mother's voice came to her from her début days: *Slump a little, dear. You don't want to be taller than the men. They don't like that.*

How well she knew.

Sarah also dressed as fashionably as Diana. Verity didn't, unless it was for Elegant Occasions events. Her personal preferences leaned toward unfashionable things—velvets out of season and vibrantly colored gowns. Whereas Sarah only wore the latest fashions.

Most telling was that Sarah was the sort of meek, eager-to-please woman Verity could never be. Never *wanted* to be, truth be told. Still, men did seem to prefer the Sarah type.

But Rafe wasn't that kind of man, was he? Or he hadn't seemed to be. So why was he suddenly determined to spend time with Sarah, whom he'd only just met? Was he being polite? Or was something more going on?

It compelled her to follow them and see what he was up to with Sarah. Not because of any jealousy. It was curiosity, nothing more.

"Where are you going?" Eliza asked as she came along with her.

"To see the . . . er . . . library. You know how I love books."

Eliza raised an eyebrow. "Cookbooks, perhaps. And sketchbooks."

"I like all sorts of books," Verity said defensively.

"If you say so," Eliza said, following her as she neared the library doorway.

When Verity halted just outside so she could listen to Rafe and Sarah talking, Eliza pointed to a glass case across the room. "I'm going over there, to further examine that curious figure of a gentleman sitting at his desk. I thought he was carved, but now I think he might be composed of shells."

"He is," Verity said, straining to listen.

"Thanks for ruining the surprise," Eliza said dryly.

"Shhh," Verity said.

Lifting her eyes heavenward, Eliza headed across the room.

Meanwhile, Rafe and Sarah neared the doorway to

examine something on the bookcase there. Verity shrank back a little, hoping she could still hear them.

"So, have you been to Exmouth before?" he asked Sarah.

Well, *that* certainly sounded like dull, polite conversation. It eased Verity's fears a bit. Only a bit.

"I have, from time to time. My husband enjoys the seaside. As I understand it, he came here often with his previous wife and his girls when they were young."

"That's what Lady Verity told me," he said smoothly. "Then I suppose you've toured this house before."

"On the contrary," Sarah said. "I never even knew it existed. When my husband and I come to Exmouth, we generally go to the beach with the boys or we shop. There aren't many shops in Simonsbath."

The mundane conversation made Verity feel awkward— and foolish—eavesdropping on them. She was about to move away when he spoke again.

"You said your trip from Simonsbath was dull. What road did you take? Or did you perchance come down the River Exe?"

That was an odd question and definitely not flirtatious. Why should he care what route Sarah had gone?

"The River Exe? Oh, dear, no. My boys would surely fall off the boat and drown! They're not used to traveling by water. Besides, no one would take a boat from Simonsbath down to Exmouth. It would take much too long."

Verity struggled not to laugh. As if Sarah would know. She might be reserved and prone to pleasing people, but she wouldn't be caught dead on a riverboat. What would she wear?

"How disappointing," Rafe said. "Some fellows in the tavern last night told me it was navigable."

Which it was.

"They said it made for a pleasant trip," Rafe said. "I was

even considering going by coach to tour Exmoor Forest while I was in this part of the country, and then taking a boat back down the river in a leisurely fashion."

Odd how he'd never said anything about it before.

"You must do as you please, of course," Sarah said gently, "but I would never travel that way myself. The men at the tavern were probably bamming you, you realize. Because you're an outsider."

He chuckled. "That wouldn't surprise me. Nor would it be the first time."

"They've done the same to me up in Simonsbath ever since I married."

Verity had never noticed, but then she didn't live at home anymore, did she? So she wouldn't.

"Why were you in a tavern, anyway?" Sarah lowered her voice. "Did Verity's unusual dishes put you off? Did you go to get a nice beef and kidney pie?"

Just as Verity bristled, Rafe said, "No. I like Lady Verity's dishes. She comes up with things I'd never think to eat. I even ate salad my first night here, and I never eat salad."

He'd eaten *salad*? Hmm. Verity hadn't even noticed.

"So, you went to the tavern for the drink then," Sarah said disapprovingly.

"Actually, I was hoping to learn where to get a bottle of real French brandy. As a gift to Grenwood for inviting me."

That brought Verity up short. The only way one got real French brandy in England these days was if one smuggled it in. He didn't seem the type to buy smuggled brandy, and certainly not from the French, given that he'd been a colonel fighting against them.

"It's . . . it's illegal to purchase French goods, isn't it?" Sarah whispered.

"W-e-l-l, there's illegal, and then there's the sort of illegal that authorities look the other way for. You know what I mean?"

"I-I really don't."

Neither did Verity.

"But I would never buy anything French," Sarah went on. "Why, we're at war with them."

"I realize that," he said, "but it seems to me . . ."

They were moving away from the door now, and Verity could no longer make out their conversation, which she definitely wanted to hear.

She peeked around the edge of the door in time to see them head up the stairs at the far end to the second floor. Glancing back to Eliza, she was annoyed to find that Mrs. Chetley and Miss Mudford had joined her to view the shell man and discuss how it might have been put together.

Blast. Verity didn't want to lose one second of Rafe and Sarah's conversation, and extricating Eliza from the ladies would take more than a few seconds, so Verity stepped quickly into the library and headed for the stairs.

Yes, she'd promised Rafe not to go anywhere alone, but the house was crammed with people, and Lord Minton could hardly abduct her from the second floor, could he? Besides, she was following *Rafe.* So she wasn't truly alone.

As she entered the stairwell, she was relieved to find they couldn't see her, having already gone up well past the landing. Fortunately, the stairwell allowed their voices to drift down to her.

Sarah was speaking. "I don't wish to view the bedrooms— that seems rather personal—but Miss Parminter said the shell grotto on the top floor is lovely."

"Then by all means, let's go up there."

Verity could hear their steps as they climbed.

"You know," Sarah said, "Exmoor Forest is quite beautiful if you do choose to visit it. Then you simply must pay a call on us at Exmoor Court. But you'll have to wait for Osgood to return from London. He's there on business at present."

"Oh? What sort of business?"

"How should I know?" Her dismissive tone came through even from a floor away. "He never tells me that. Do you plan to stay in Devonshire for a while?"

"Haven't decided. I have responsibilities at home, but they can wait."

That was odd, too. Wasn't his uncle ill? Perhaps it was the sort of long-standing illness that didn't require his immediate attention. Still . . .

Verity had reached the second floor, but hesitated there. She couldn't eavesdrop in the one-room grotto, and once they started down, they would encounter her. Perhaps she should dart into a bedroom until they passed by.

Or perhaps she should just leave them alone. She had learned very little, after all, just enough to allay her fear that Rafe was flirting with Sarah, but heighten her suspicion that Rafe was spying on them all. Lord only knew why. And that reinforced her belief he was indeed the Phantom. She might as well go back downstairs before Eliza got frantic over finding her gone.

She sighed. That would be the right thing to do.

Turning for the stairs, she was about to descend when a hand closed over her mouth. Then an arm caught her about the waist and dragged her into a bedroom.

In a panic, she fought, trying to get free, but a familiar voice whispered in her ear, "Peace, Verity, I just want to talk."

Good Lord, it was Minton. She stepped down hard on his foot with her boots, but he was wearing men's boots, and all she got was a grunt for her trouble.

Swinging her around to face him he shoved her hard

against the wall. Then while she had the breath knocked out of her, he grabbed her jaw to hold her still and covered her mouth with his.

She fought him in earnest then, yanking his hair and pushing against his chest. He was stronger than she remembered. So she bit his lower lip.

He jerked his head back, and for a second, fury glittered in his eyes. Then he smoothed his expression. "Verity, my love," he said in a falsely soothing tone. "Why so upset? I want to marry you, for God's sake. Isn't that what you've wanted all this time?"

"You know it isn't!" she hissed, struggling against the bastard, who now held her arms pinned against the wall.

She could scream, but if she brought anyone running, they might misconstrue this, and she'd be ruined. He would surely lie about what had occurred. And she knew what happened to women who ended up in such situations. Society always listened to the man.

Somehow, she managed a smile. "Be reasonable, sir. Do you really want me by force? Can't we discuss this like sensible people? If you'll just release me—"

His eyes narrowed. "I wish I could trust you to behave, but I don't. If you'll only listen to me state my case, however, I can prove we are perfect together. We always were of one mind and one will."

"In your memory, perhaps," she said, "but not in mine. And certainly not after what you did to me."

He winced. "I will admit I made some mistakes by pursuing Bertha, but I've come to my senses now, and I see what I always saw—that you were my one true love. We can be like that again, you know."

Not a chance. She fought to stay calm. "If you will simply let me loose, we can discuss—"

He cut her off with a harder kiss, and she tasted blood—his and hers.

Forget calm. He would surely do her bodily harm if she didn't escape him. But he had her pinned most effectively. She went limp beneath him, hoping to lull him into thinking she'd acquiesced.

To her left was a vase on a table. If she could just bump the table with her hip . . .

To her vast relief, she managed to knock it hard enough so the vase fell off, making a loud noise as it rolled around. But he didn't stop what he was doing, for pity's sake.

Then she realized someone had entered the room, had possibly even seen her bump the table. Lady Harry. Oh, *thank God*.

Except that even as Verity cast her a speaking look, the girl just stood there frozen, eyes wide with horror. Fortunately, Miss Mudford swiftly followed her inside, and gave a shocked exclamation before hurrying over to start hitting Lord Minton on the back with her reticule.

"Stop that, you devil, whoever you are. Lady Verity, make him stop! This is highly inappropriate!"

Lord Minton reacted at last, pushing away from Verity, but he was wearing a smile. "Forgive me, madam," he said to Miss Mudford. "I see that my fiancée and I must take this somewhere more private."

Verity slapped him hard. "I am *not* your fiancée, and you know it!" The audacity of the man to make it seem as if she'd *wanted* his hands on her!

Just as Lord Minton looked as if he would let loose his temper on her, Rafe showed up, and she slumped against the wall.

It was over.

Chapter 18

CRafe took one look at Verity, standing there with a shattered expression, and then at Minton, looking smug, and he said the first thing that popped into his head. "You can't possibly be her fiancé. I am."

Minton blinked at him. "That's a lie."

"It's not a lie," Lady Foxstead said as she entered the room with Sarah by her side. She shot her sister a remorseful look. "Mr. Wolfford and Verity were planning to tell the family today."

Thank God, Lady Foxstead had the good sense to play along.

Miss Mudford snorted. "Then why was Lady Verity just allowing this scoundrel's attentions?"

"I was not *allowing* him anything!" Verity cried.

"For God's sake, Miss Mudford," Rafe snapped, "can't you see the finger marks forming on her cheeks even now?"

Rafe could. And they stoked his blood into a frenzy. Minton had manhandled her. It took every ounce of Rafe's control not to leap on the bastard and beat him to a bloody pulp. Or worse, whip out the knife Rafe kept in his trousers pocket and slit the bastard's throat.

No matter how much he itched to, he could not. Right

now, cooler heads *must* prevail. "Do you think she put those marks there herself?" he went on, fighting for composure.

"He's right," Lady Harry surprised him by saying. "I saw it happening. Lady Verity is the one who kicked the table to make the vase fall." She shot Verity a downcast look. "I-I'm so sorry. I didn't know what to do."

Wrapping her arms about her waist, Verity gave a tight nod.

Foxstead and Grenwood then burst into the room. Earlier, Lady Foxstead had summoned them to look for Verity.

"Get him out of here," Rafe ordered the pair, falling into the role of colonel. "Take him downstairs and make him stay put until I can deal with him."

They didn't question his authority. Instead, they grabbed Minton and forcibly walked him out of the room and down the stairs even as the scoundrel protested.

"Well, this is all very irregular," Miss Mudford said with a sniff. Why the hell had Miss Mudford chosen now, of all times, to behave like a proper chaperone? When Rafe glared at her, she added, "But if I have made an error in judgment, Lady Verity, I apologize."

"And you will keep quiet about it, won't you, Miss Mudford?" Lady Foxstead said in a steely voice.

"I-I . . . of course. Many felicitations to you on your engagement, Lady Verity," Miss Mudford mumbled. "Come, Harriet. We should let the family deal with this."

Verity offered another of her scarily stiff nods. As soon as they were gone, however, she turned to her sister and stepmother. "I should like to speak to my . . . er . . . fiancé alone right now, if you don't mind."

Lady Foxstead glanced warily at Rafe. "Are you sure you want to—"

"Yes," Verity said with a thin smile. "I'll be along shortly.

Perhaps you and Sarah could go let Diana know what has happened."

"Certainly," Lady Foxstead said, though she cast Rafe a speaking look that was impossible to interpret.

Damn. What he'd done was beginning to sink in. But he couldn't take back his offer. He wouldn't.

As soon as everyone left, Verity edged closer to the door. "Perhaps we should go outside for this discussion and not remain in a bedroom, further fueling gossip."

The fact that she wouldn't look at him gave him pause. "I agree." He led her down the stairs and out a small back door he'd noticed earlier, which thankfully put them right out into the meadow that ran alongside the house.

After scanning to make sure no one was around to hear them, she halted to face him. "You don't have to sacrifice yourself to marriage for me, you know. I've been through scandals before. I know how . . . to manage the gossips."

That little catch in her throat twisted something inside him. The thought of standing by and watching as rumor-mongers and high-in-the-instep types dragged Verity through the mud *again* was more than he could bear.

He chose his words carefully. "It's not as if I haven't considered marrying you, especially after yesterday at the beach. I should have offered marriage then." *I should have kept my hands off you.* Yet he couldn't regret that he hadn't. "I just . . . I needed to . . ."

"You aren't ready for it." She met his gaze steadily. "It's fine."

It wasn't the least fine. And it was too late to worry about whether she might hate him once she learned why he'd been spying on her family. Or even how she'd react if Rafe turned out to be illegitimate. He would simply have to deal with all that when it happened, and pray to God she didn't leave him.

She went on in a throttled tone. "I'll explain to everyone I turned down your very kind offer because of what happened, and you won't suffer any reprisals."

"Suffer any—" Frustration welled up in him. "For God's sake, what kind of man do you take me for, to let a woman I care about go through . . ." He raked his hand through his hair, feeling all at sea about how to handle this. "Surely you realize that despite our hasty betrothal and what we tell people about Minton, unless we marry everyone will assume something happened. Nor will Minton stop trying to compromise you. Next time, he might even use laudanum."

When she paled, he added, "You don't wish to marry him, do you?"

"Lord, no!" she said fiercely. "And I won't." She hugged her waist. "But what happened just now is what I deserve for underestimating him. You told me to cancel this house tour and I didn't listen, so now I'm not about to make you suffer for what was my fault in the first place."

"*Your* fault!" He walked up to pull her rigid body into his arms. "It was Minton's fault, sweetheart, and no one else's. More likely it was *my* fault because I knew how dangerous he was. I should have stuck to your side like a barnacle on a ship instead of leaving you to your sister."

She shook her head helplessly and drew away from him with a look back at all the windows in the house.

"I'm not abandoning you to endure this alone," he growled. "And that's that."

"I will not be the wife you choose out of pity!" she burst out.

Now Rafe could see the tears glimmering in her eyes, and they reduced him to ashes. She was far more upset than he'd realized.

"I would rather endure the gossip," she whispered. "At least I know what to expect."

Apparently, she wasn't sure what to expect of marriage to *him*. Not that he blamed her. "I'm certain you could endure the gossip on your own behalf. But what about for Elegant Occasions? For the charities you support, for the women you help? That would all end. Once Miss Mudford starts talking about today's events—and if we don't marry, she will—there's no more Elegant Occasions."

She stared at him, her eyes huge in her face. "There's no more Elegant Occasions, anyway. You know perfectly well that the wife of a viscount's heir cannot run a business full-time."

He thought about that and realized their roles in Society would indeed be somewhat circumscribed by his rank—assuming he still had one. And after they had children . . . "True, I suppose. Although your sisters do it."

"Not so blatantly, though. Diana keeps her hand in, but Rosy is rapidly taking over that role. Eliza has been training me to do more of the business part, and as long as no one sees the inner workings of how it's run, it seems more of an amateur operation. But the minute I marry—and presumably don't need the money from it—everyone will expect the business to end. Including you."

"It doesn't have to. Nor must it be done for money. You and your sisters could take a more advisory role. Then you could help whomever you choose. The expenses, of course, would still need to be paid, but your clients pay for those directly half the time anyway, don't they?"

She appeared to consider that. "They do. But that's not my only concern."

A bitterness welled up in him so powerfully that he couldn't keep it from spilling over into his voice. It was just as he'd thought—one only got a family one was born into. "You don't *want* to marry me. That's it, isn't it?"

Apparently, the bitterness got her attention, for her

gaze on him softened. "Honestly, I wouldn't be opposed to marrying you under any other circumstances."

The relief that coursed through him over that answer unsettled him. He didn't like feeling dependent on someone else for his future. For his happiness.

Yes, his happiness. He wanted her that badly . . . which made her even more dangerous to him. She could still scuttle all his plans if she so chose.

Not that he could do anything about that right now. He sighed. "Look, both of us would prefer not to marry under these circumstances. But this is the situation we've been handed, and no amount of conjecture or assigning blame will change that. So we must simply make the best of it."

"What a romantic notion," she said sarcastically, a sign that her usual tart nature was reasserting itself.

Thank God. He ventured a smile. "To be truthful, you never struck me as the romantic type."

"I'm not," she said, tipping up her chin. "But I would still not prefer the sort of formal and disastrous marriage my parents had. Or Eliza's hasty first marriage."

"It wouldn't be that. We could make of it what we wish. You must admit we're attracted to each other. And we are friends of a sort, aren't we?"

She dragged in a heavy breath, as if weighing some decision. "How can I consider us friends when I don't even really know who you are?"

His blood ran cold. "What do you mean?"

She cast him a hard look. "I thought I knew the Mr. Wolfford who's been acting as a gentleman and a soldier around me. But you are not that man. And I don't know the man who's been spying on my family for over a year. Is your name even Raphael?"

He gaped at her. Over a year? Oh, God. Had she uncovered the truth? Surely not. She must be guessing. Or perhaps Minton had found out somehow and told her. But how? From her father?

No chance. If her father had guessed who Rafe was—or rather, what he was doing—the man would have come after Uncle Constantine at Castle Wolfford by now.

"First of all, of course my name is Raphael." He gave a hollow laugh. "And I already told you, I've been in England a little more than a month."

"I already told *you* I never forget a face." She reached up to stroke his hair. "I suppose you wore a blond wig for that ball at Lady Sinclair's last year."

She'd *recognized* him at the second event he'd attended incognito? Bloody hell.

When he didn't respond, she said, "I suspect that's why Eliza doesn't remember you now even though she saw you face-to-face that night."

And Eliza knew about him, too? Damn.

His alarm must have shown in his expression, for she added, "Oh, don't worry. I haven't told her it's you. I haven't told anyone, actually, just in case I was wrong. They've laughed at me too often over my sightings of the Phantom."

"The *Phantom*?" he echoed, a sick feeling settling into his stomach.

God help him, all the times she'd said things he'd taken for knowledge of his mission and then dismissed . . . He should have considered them more seriously.

But perhaps it wasn't as bad as he feared. "So, you've decided I'm this Phantom character."

Anger flashed in her eyes. "For pity's sake, don't bother to deny it. And I invented the name. What else was I to call you? You seemed to come and go at will without anyone noticing but me. I would ask a servant who you were, and by the time they turned to look, you were gone. I did point you out to Geoffrey at Rosy's ball once, and he actually saw you, but again, you vanished. It happened so often, I took to calling you the Phantom."

"Yet none of your family noticed but you."

A bitter look passed over her features. "Sadly, no. By the next time you appeared, they had dismissed it as my imagining that two gentlemen who looked vaguely alike were actually one man. Or I was seeing things that didn't exist. Or it was just a coincidental series of unusual men at our affairs."

He just stared at her, not sure what to say that wouldn't contribute to her seemingly extensive knowledge of what he'd been up to. He didn't know how long he could hold this deadpan expression.

She thrust out her chin. "The Jack in the Green was a nice touch, though. Unfortunately for you, I had hired the other fellow myself, and I *knew* I hadn't hired two of you. Besides, your bush was yew and his was box, a fact that I confirmed when Geoffrey and I found your costume stuffed behind a garden wall."

Wonderful. Now Grenwood knew her suspicions, too.

He wanted to laugh hysterically. Verity had actually seen through his Jack in the Green costume. And he'd given himself away by using a yew bush instead of a box bush? Good God, how the mighty had fallen. Sir Lucius was going to laugh himself silly over that one.

He sobered. Sir Lucius was going to send him packing. His mission had failed, undone by a wily woman.

"I've already promised to marry you, Verity," he said in a last-ditch effort to throw her off the track. "You needn't make up some story about me being a spy in some foolish attempt to . . . to blackmail this Phantom fellow."

"Blackmail you?" She shook her head. "As if I could ever do that. Which is precisely why I *won't* marry you.

Clearly, you don't know me well enough to trust me. Even now, you're refusing to tell me the truth about whoever you are and whatever you're doing."

"I'm not doing—"

"Although I've already figured out it has something to do with my family because it's always Elegant Occasions events that you attend. And after your sudden interest in Sarah and the odd questions you asked her today—"

"You were listening?" His stomach roiled. "Oh, God, that's why you were upstairs, isn't it? Why you got separated from Eliza." He groaned. "I'm even more to blame for what happened with Minton than I realized."

"Don't be silly. I'm the one who should have known better than to skulk about the house alone." She turned away. "Sadly, I don't have your obvious skill at doing it incognito."

She wasn't going to let this go, was she? She might tell her family, ruin everything, and all because he refused to trust her. For the first time in his career, he was torn between doing his duty and doing what he wanted. Which was to trust Verity with part of his secret. To *marry* Verity, absurd as it seemed.

He laid his hand on her shoulder. "Listen to me, sweetheart."

"Don't call me that when you don't mean a word of it!" She whirled on him, her face ashen. "Oh, Lord, is that why you've been . . . flattering me and trying to seduce me and lying to me? Because of some scheme?"

"No!"

The expectant look in her eyes drove a stake through his heart.

He took a deep breath. "Well . . . yes." When she looked stricken and started to back away, he added hastily, "At first, that is. I mean, I never really suspected you of doing anything wrong yourself, but . . ."

"Doing anything wrong with what? About what?"

He paused, considering how to proceed. He had to keep his plans intact, but he couldn't do that without her agreement to keep his secrets. He wasn't used to relying on anyone else. Spies were lone operators, and he'd especially been so. But now he must navigate these unknown waters with her, because if he didn't . . .

"The truth is . . ." He sighed. "I can't tell you the truth. Not yet." How much did he dare say? "All I can reveal is that I'm secretly still in the army."

"And you're the man I've been calling the Phantom."

He gritted his teeth. "Yes. And yes, you've been right all along to suspect me of spying on your family." When she beamed at him, he added, "But what I'm doing is for England. It's more important work than you can possibly know."

She blinked. "Or than you can tell me, I take it."

"You take it correctly. It's precisely *because* it's so important that it puts anyone you tell, anyone I tell, in possible danger just for knowing it. You cannot talk about it to your family or anyone else."

He caught her by the arms. "And only after you marry me do I dare reveal more than I have. Because then your safety will depend on me, and mine on you. Your life will be mine, and mine yours."

"If we have a real marriage, you mean," she choked out.

"I don't know about you, but I want a real marriage," he said fiercely.

Looking surprised, she searched his face. "While you continue to keep secrets?"

He sucked in a heavy breath. "Not for long. This is my last mission, and since it now somewhat involves you, I'll tell you as much as I can once we marry. If I accomplish my mission, you'll learn everything anyway. Until that day comes, you'll simply have to trust me not to harm you."

"But which you am I trusting? The Phantom or Rafe Wolfford?"

Gazing down into her eyes, which seemed to see all sometimes, he took her hand. "I swear to you that the man you call the Phantom in his many guises is merely a role I, Colonel Rafe Wolfford, have been playing for the last year and a half. But I've been Rafe my whole life, and certainly since we met."

He held her hand against his heart. "Surely by now, you know me as Rafe well enough to trust me a little. The question is, is that enough for you?"

Chapter 19

Verity stared at him, wondering if she should tell him the truth. But at this point, she might as well. "It's not entirely you I don't trust. It's me. Because I have truly deplorable taste in men—Minton being a case in point."

He squeezed her hand tightly. "That's just another way of saying you don't trust me." When she frowned, he added, "Not that I blame you. I always hoped you'd never find out any of this."

"You mean, you intended to break my heart in the end."

He stiffened. "I never thought your heart was engaged."

Lord, she hadn't meant to give away so much of those feelings just now. "It wasn't," she lied with attempted nonchalance. "But you didn't know that."

He glanced away. "True."

"And you never anticipated this situation, either." That was what hurt more than anything—that his courtship had only been a ruse all along. She'd feared it might have been, but some part of her had hoped she was wrong.

I intend for us to have a real marriage.

Had he told the truth? "What did you mean when you said we would 'have a real marriage'?"

Judging from the furrow between his brows, the question perplexed him. "Just what I said. Unless you'd prefer otherwise, we would live together as man and wife, have children, and in every way behave as a married couple."

"Except for being in love."

He hesitated. "Except for that."

Well, at least he was being truthful now. But she was already half in love with him. How was she to go on in a marriage, knowing he didn't love her? Might never love her?

Then again, she'd fancied herself in love with Lord Minton, and look how that had turned out. Perhaps it was time to set aside her girlish dreams of love. They had gained her nothing but heartache.

"What did you mean by 'unless I'd prefer otherwise'?"

A harsh laugh escaped him. "You're really trying to nail this down, aren't you?"

"It's better to do it beforehand, don't you think?"

He sighed. "Of course. I meant that if you want a contractual marriage, where we live separate lives except for coming together to . . . er . . . breed, you can have that, too."

"You'd do that for me," she said incredulously. "Set up something formal and cold when you could marry anyone else and have an actual marriage?"

A muscle flexed in his jaw. "If that's what you want."

Lord Minton would *never* have agreed to such a thing. No man would. So the fact that Rafe would do so was humbling. And a little disturbing. "Do *you* want a real marriage?"

He'd become stiffer by the moment. "I'd prefer it, yes." When she continued to be silent, he said hoarsely, "I do *want* to marry you, sweetheart."

"You'll regret it later." *As Papa had regretted marrying Mama.*

"I won't."

"You'll feel trapped." *As Mama had.*

"Not that, either."

She sighed. "Even though you're marrying a woman you didn't choose?"

"While I'll admit I initially didn't plan on marrying you, it doesn't change the fact that I want to marry you now." Rafe looked down his nose at her and said in a snooty tone, "Besides, like any man with a title, I must have an heir."

She arched an eyebrow. "You don't have a title yet."

"But I will and probably soon." He stared off across the meadow, his throat working convulsively. "My uncle is dying."

If she hadn't seen his reaction, she might have fought harder against marrying him. But with such clear evidence that the man who could fool anyone with countless masquerades could feel true emotion, could actually love *someone* . . .

That went a long way toward convincing her that everything might turn out all right in the end.

Then the thought of the orphan child Rafe who'd kissed Mary Robinson's picture until it faded away leapt into her head, and she knew there was a heart in there somewhere, too. A very bruised one, but a heart nonetheless.

"I'm sorry about your uncle," she said softly. "I know he's been like a father to you, and it must hurt just as much to watch him languishing."

His gaze swung back to her, fraught with emotion. "For a tart-tongued woman who pretends to be invulnerable and cynical, you can be impossibly kind sometimes."

So could he. He'd taken her side against Lord Minton without even hinting that she might have welcomed the scoundrel's advances. He'd offered her marriage when it apparently ran counter to his plans. He hadn't breathed a word to anyone about what they'd done in the bathing machine.

It was a better foundation for a marriage than she'd ever had with Lord Minton.

She dragged in a calming breath. "Do you swear to tell me everything you can about your 'mission' once we are married?"

As if sensing she was weakening, he flashed her a crooked smile. "If you swear to tell me how you figured out it was me beneath all my disguises." When she opened her mouth, he added, "And not just that you never forget a face."

"It's the only answer I have for you, I'm afraid."

"I'm skeptical, but all right, I'll accept that. For now." He caught her other hand in his. "Anything else you wish me to swear to?"

She considered whether to mention one more thing, but it was too important to leave out. "Do you swear never to lie to me again?"

"Will you take, 'I can't tell you,' as a sufficient answer?"

She narrowed her gaze on him. "It depends. If you start an affair with an actress as beautiful as Mary Robinson, I will not accept 'I can't tell you' as an answer to my concerns about it. And I might also box your ears."

He smiled faintly before his expression turned solemn. "I swear I will never lie to you or commit adultery. I will never kiss the maids behind your back or swive an actress or go to a brothel or break my marriage vows in any way. All of those I can absolutely swear to."

A long breath escaped her. "Then I can absolutely swear the same to you."

"Good. Because I might lose my mind imagining you swiving an actress as beautiful as Mary Robinson."

When he followed that with a laugh, she rolled her eyes. "Very funny. If I had my reticule, I'd smack you with it the way Miss Mudford smacked Lord Minton."

Those words sobered them both.

She swallowed. "What will you do about Lord Minton?"

"You needn't worry about that," he said in a chilling

voice. "I'll see to it he never bothers you again." Then he paused. "I do have one thing I need *you* to swear to. You once told me you could keep secrets that were important. Well, the secret of my other life is extremely important. You must swear not to reveal it to anyone until I say you can. Not to your sisters or your brothers-in-law or your parents. The Phantom must vanish again until this is over."

Pressing his hand against her heart, she nodded. "I swear. I won't tell a soul until this is done." Although it might just kill her not being able to say to her family, *I told you so.*

He threaded his fingers with hers. "This does mean you've agreed to wed me, doesn't it?"

"It would seem so, yes."

When he broke into one of his brilliant smiles, she realized he'd meant it when he'd said he *wanted* to marry her. What was more, she truly wanted to marry *him,* Phantom or no.

But she sincerely hoped neither of them ended up ruing the day.

While Verity went to tell her sisters what they'd decided, Rafe sought out Grenwood and Foxstead. As he found them at the back of the first floor, Grenwood lifted his eyebrow in question.

"Looks like I will soon be a married man," Rafe told them, then broke into a grin. He couldn't help it. Though he might regret it later, for now, he was ridiculously pleased to be marrying Verity.

"Thank God." Foxstead pointed below them to the ground floor. "We locked him in the strong room at Miss Parminter's suggestion. We had to—he was shouting and fighting us.

Honestly, Minton would never stop his nonsense if she weren't marrying you."

"That's one point I made in convincing her to say yes."

"Very wise of you to use logic," Grenwood said. "She's no fool, our Verity."

Grenwood had no idea how little of a fool she was.

The Phantom. Rafe couldn't believe it. Only Verity would give him such a fanciful name. Although he supposed it wasn't much different from Chameleon.

With any luck, he soon wouldn't have to be either to anyone. Once he married Verity, he intended to use his status as a member of the family to find out every last bit about Holtbury's smuggling operation. He hadn't learned nearly enough from Sarah in their short conversation. Nor had she appeared to know anything substantive.

"What do you intend to do with the scoundrel?" Foxstead asked.

"I'd prefer to carve him up into little pieces," Rafe said grimly, "but the law apparently forbids murdering men who try to force women into marriage."

"And you can't really prove in a court that he did so, although we all know the truth," Grenwood said. "According to Eliza, Miss Mudford was a bit of a prig about it, and can't be relied on for unbiased testimony."

"Eliza is right. But although there's not much I can do about Miss Mudford, I've got a few tricks up my sleeve for Minton. He won't be bothering *my fiancée* again, I assure you."

His fiancée. Rafe rather liked the sound of that, and that worried him a bit. So had her comment about love. He'd never experienced the sort of love her siblings had for their spouses or even each other. What if *she* couldn't love *him* like that? Especially if he had to put one of her family members in prison?

He mustn't let himself be seduced into feeling that deeply for her. Because if he found himself in a marriage where he loved his wife, and she couldn't reciprocate, it might very well destroy him.

He shook off that thought. He could handle anything as long as he accomplished his mission. He could.

But for now, protecting her must take precedence. After Grenwood gave him the key to the strong room door, he marched down there and opened it to find an irate Minton stomping about.

"I will see you hang for this," Minton cried. "I will go straight to the magistrate here, and make sure that—"

"You will do nothing of the kind." Rafe shoved a chair at Minton. "Sit down, and I will tell you how this is going to go."

Pulling his knife from inside his coat, Rafe calmly began to clean his fingernails with it, and Minton got the message. Keeping his wide eyes on the knife, the fool sat down in the chair.

"Verity is marrying me," Rafe continued, "and swiftly, if I have anything to say about it. You would be wise to accept that. Because I have more friends in high places than you and Holtbury put together."

When Minton's eyes widened, Rafe added, "Yes, I know he's behind your sudden new interest in her. I don't know exactly what he promised you if you married her, but if you attempt to do so by force again, I will call you out."

He stalked up to the chair and drove his knife into it, squarely between Minton's slightly spread legs. Minton gulped.

"*Then* you will die. Because as you might imagine given my background, I am more skilled in every weapon that exists than you are. I'll kill you in a duel of honor, get my friends in high places to hush the matter up, and that will be that."

"But Holtbury—"

"Let me worry about Holtbury. Besides, I mean to go straightaway to marry Verity. She will not be out of my sight until it's done, so you have no future with her." He tugged the knife free of the chair. "Do you understand?"

Minton nodded.

"Good." He jerked his head toward the strong room door. "Now go. Before I'm tempted to change my mind and call you out anyway."

The man ran out of there like a rat with a cat at its heels.

When Rafe strolled out of the strong room, he found Verity waiting beside the door. Apparently, Minton had run out so fast he hadn't even noticed her there. Rafe wondered when she had sneaked downstairs. It bothered him a bit that she'd seen him in his element.

"That was an impressive display of force, Colonel Wolford." She cocked her head, her expression as inscrutable as ever as she watched him sheathe his knife. "But would you really have called him out?"

"In a heartbeat. I would have killed him, too."

"No doubt."

He couldn't tell what she was feeling. "Does it scare you off?" Because he wouldn't want that.

"It depends. If you routinely challenge men to duels—"

"*Threaten* to challenge a man to a duel," he corrected her.

She searched his face. "How many duels have you fought in your life?"

"None thus far."

"Oh." A smile tugged at her lips. "Then I'm not scared off." She turned serious. "But I would hate for you to die defending my honor or some such."

He pulled her close. "I'll do my best not to duel with

anyone. Honestly, I think duels are absurd posturing that accomplishes nothing. I've seen enough men die on the battlefield without picking a fight with one. But I'd still call Minton out if I had to in order to keep you safe."

She slid her arms about his waist. "I wish I could have seen his face when you threatened him."

"Too late. If I'd known you were there, I would have made sure you had a good view. Next time, announce yourself." He gazed earnestly into her face. "Though I'd rather not have a next time."

"Me, either." She kissed him lightly on the lips. "Thank you for slaying my . . ." She thought a moment. "Dragon isn't really the word. Worm? Dung beetle? Perhaps—"

He kissed her back, needing to be sure she really was fine with marrying him. When she opened her mouth for him to deepen the kiss and tightened her hold on him, he hoped she was.

But before he could do more than get a taste of her, Grenwood called down from upstairs. "Minton is off the premises, and your friends await. So, unless you two wish to foment more gossip, I suggest you come upstairs."

Rafe drew back from her with a sigh. "I cannot wait until we can be truly alone." He couldn't wait until he could have her in his bed.

She laughed, then released him. "I feel the same. Because now we have to field everyone's questions and convince them we've been engaged for days. And I'm not as good at lying as you are."

The word "lying" cut deep, even though it was true. He eyed her closely. "I should point out that *you* spent the past two weeks pretending you'd just met me, that you'd had *no* idea I wasn't who I said I was. You fooled *me,* and I am hard to fool. So, we've both been . . . untruthful until now.

We've both been playing roles. If it helps, think of this as your acting début."

"Hmm. I'll try. I just hope the role of secretly engaged bride will be both my début and my final role before settling into a married life where we keep no secrets from each other."

For her sake, so did he.

Chapter 20

After their announcement, which of course precipitated having everyone return to the Grenwood beach house, things moved so quickly, it made Verity dizzy. Now she, her sisters, their husbands, and her fiancé—mmm, *fiancé*—had gathered in Geoffrey's study, having sent their guests off to play cards before dinner.

She and Rafe sat in chairs beside each other, which was good since she still wasn't sure about this. The legalities of a wedding were never something she'd handled for Elegant Occasions or her sisters' weddings, so the cumbersome rules came as a surprise. Fortunately, as Rafe had told Minton earlier, he did have friends in high places. So Rafe said he was sure he could get a special license.

"It will take two hard days of travel each way," he told Verity as he took her hand, "but at least when I return, we'll be able to marry right then rather than waiting seven days for a regular license. And while you await my return, you can pack for Castle Wolfford. I'd like to introduce you to my uncle once we've wed."

"Or . . ." Verity said, holding on to his hand for strength, "perhaps you and I could travel to London together." She wanted this wedding business done, so they could begin their life. So she could find out about Rafe's secret life, and how it might affect hers. "Once we're wed, we can go straight to your home. We'll gain two days that way."

"But if we do that," he said with a furtive glance at her sisters, "your family can't attend the wedding. It's not as if the duke and duchess can leave their guests here to run off to London."

"No, but *I* can," Eliza put in. "You can't travel without a chaperone, anyway."

"I can, too." Nathaniel took Eliza's hand. "You're not going without me, love. Besides, they'll require two witnesses."

"We'd have to leave Jimmy and Molly with Diana since we can't take them on a whirlwind trip like that." Eliza looked at their sister. "Do you mind?"

Diana sighed. "Well, it's not as if we could all go, and Sarah can help me, too. Besides, it won't be much of a wedding with all that rushing around. Even if Verity waited for Rafe here, we'd barely have time to set up a wedding breakfast."

Her family had started calling him Rafe the minute Verity had announced their betrothal. He seemed to like it.

Diana brightened. "I have an idea! When the house party ends and we're all about to head to our homes, we'll have a wedding *dinner* instead of a breakfast." Gazing at Verity, she added, "You can both come here from Castle Wolfford for a few days. The celebration won't be timely, I'll grant you, but it will give us some chance to plan."

"Ooh, if I'm going to London," Eliza said, "then I can fetch whatever we might need for the dinner."

Verity perked up. "And I can tell Mr. Norris what to pack for me in London that I can take to my new home. That way I'll only need a few things from here, so the coach won't be overladen and slow us down. Plus, I have the perfect dress for the wedding at Eliza's house. I haven't even worn it yet."

"You should save it for the dinner," Diana said. "Hardly anyone will see it at the wedding."

"Rafe will," Verity protested, squeezing his hand. "I should think he's the most important one."

"And I will, too," Eliza said in mock outrage. "Besides, Verity can wear it both places, since 'hardly anyone will see it.'"

"I won't remember it in a week or two, anyway," Nathaniel put in. "If Eliza's not wearing it, it doesn't exist."

The men laughed. The women shook their heads.

Diana turned to Verity. "Monsieur Beaufort will be here until the end of the house party, won't he?"

Verity gaped at Diana. "Oh, no! I haven't told Monsieur Beaufort I'm engaged. I must tell him at once. He'll be upset to hear it from anyone else." She jumped to her feet. "I'll be back shortly."

Rafe rose. "I'll go with you. We can tell him together."

"Sorry, Rafe, but no. This is between him and me. I won't be long."

A strange alarm crossed Rafe's features, which she ignored. Monsieur Beaufort would be spoiling for an argument, and she didn't want Rafe to hear it. Besides, she still thought her friend had known Rafe from before. Now was the time to find out how, since she wasn't at all certain Rafe would say.

"Before you go, tell me one thing," he said. "Shall I ask your father for your hand?"

"Absolutely not," she said. "I shall do exactly as my sisters, and leave him out of it."

"But you need a marriage settlement," Rafe said earnestly. "It's important, and it protects you in the future."

"He's right," Eliza said. "I did my own settlement, with some advice from Geoffrey."

"I wouldn't know where to begin," Verity said.

"I can negotiate that for you," Geoffrey said. "If you wish."

"Very well." Verity leaned up to kiss Rafe's cheek. "Stay here and talk to Geoffrey about my marriage settlement. I will join you soon." Then she left.

She found Monsieur Beaufort in the kitchen, growling at the staff, cursing to himself, tossing pans about, and in general, showing himself to be in high dudgeon.

"Monsieur Beaufort, may I have a word with you outside in the garden?"

He scowled. "You may, mademoiselle," he snapped and stalked out, leaving her to follow after.

She sighed. Apparently, he already knew about her impending wedding. He confirmed that when he hissed, "So, you shall marry Wolfford, eh? You have no idea what you are doing."

"Then tell me," she said.

That took him aback. He looked as if he were struggling with his conscience, but finally said, "He is a *spy, merde tout*!"

She blinked. "For the French?"

"What? Of course not. For your countrymen."

"Oh." Relief coursed through her. "How do you know?"

He dragged in a heavy breath. "Because I have spied for him a time or two."

She gaped at him. "On us?" That would be quite the betrayal.

"No! I would never do that."

"Then on whom?"

Monsieur Beaufort avoided her gaze. "You will have to ask him. I promised not to say."

"You promised a stranger that you'd keep his secrets." She cocked her head. "Admit it—you didn't just meet Rafe last week. You knew him before."

Avoiding her gaze, he sighed. "*Oui*. The first place I worked when I fled France for England was Castle Wolfford."

That stunned her. "*What*? Why didn't you tell me from the beginning? And how long did you work there?"

"Four years." He gave a Gallic shrug. "Rafe asked me not to reveal it."

She wrapped her arms about her waist. All this time Rafe and Monsieur Beaufort had known each other, and neither had let her see the full extent of their friendship. Or whatever it was. "And you agreed to keep quiet, just like that."

A look of resignation crossed his face. "I have known him since he was nine and ate mussels and onions in my kitchen." He shook his head. "I felt sorry for that child. No playmates, and an uncle who spent his time fighting battles. When he was home, General Wolfford trained Rafe like a miniature ensign. And Rafe lapped up everything he was taught. Because he admired his uncle and had nothing else to do but read and drill."

Drill? At nine? Poor Rafe. "General Wolfford was a hero, from what I understand."

Monsieur Beaufort flashed her a thin smile. "Yes. But sometimes heroes make the worst parents, *non*?"

"Perhaps. But villains do, too, as I can attest."

He patted her back. "I know, *mon amie*, I know. So, which is Rafe these days? Hero? Or villain?"

"To me? A hero. He saved me from having to marry Lord Minton."

That brought him up short. "Minton? What does that *bâtard* have to do with this?"

Briefly, she explained what had happened that afternoon.

Monsieur Beaufort released a string of colorful French curses. "That is why you are marrying Rafe?"

She shrugged. "I had to choose between Rafe, Lord

Minton, and more scandal. Of those three, Rafe is by far the best choice. And I certainly like him better than Minton."

Her friend scowled. "So you *want* to marry Rafe, then."

"Yes. I do."

Judging from the relief on his face, that changed the Frenchman's feelings on the subject. "Rafe should have called Minton out," he grumbled.

"That would have ruined my reputation as surely as if he'd let Lord Minton's behavior stand. He did the only thing he could think of and offered for me. I don't think he felt he had a choice."

Monsieur Beaufort snorted. "Raphael Wolfford always has choices. So if he chose to marry you, it is because he wished to. I have never seen a man more sure of what he wants. And more determined to get it."

"I haven't, either, but you must admit I'm a bit like that myself," she said with a little laugh.

"The two of you together . . . *Mon Dieu.* I am glad I will not be at Castle Wolfford to see you butting your heads." He gazed at her with concern. "You will be careful around him, I hope. When he is on a mission, he is *tres* single-minded."

"I gathered as much." She smiled. "I'd love to hear more of your trenchant observations concerning my fiancé's character, but I can't right now. I must pack. We leave for London early. We're to marry by special license."

"Will I see you after the wedding?"

A lump caught in her throat. "Not for a while. We're heading straight to his home from London. But Diana wants to throw us a wedding dinner, and we'll certainly come back here for that."

"I see." He lifted her hand and kissed it. "*Bonne chance*, then, to you both. If anything goes wrong, send for me. Remember, I am always your friend."

"And his, too?"

"His, too." He held her hand between both of his. "Though if he breaks your heart, I will teach the upstart a thing or two."

"If he breaks my heart, I will cheer while you do so." She dragged in a deep breath. "I hope he won't, though. I really like him."

"I can see it in your eyes." With a shake of his head, he released her hand. "All young people wear their love on their faces. Only later in life do they learn to hide it."

"What I feel is not love," she said stoutly, hoping she meant it.

"Good. Love has the power to stab you through the chest. Better to hide from it and be safe."

Forcing a smile, she left.

But the words resonated as she went in search of Rafe. So far, love had never worked in her favor. Monsieur Beaufort was right—better to be safe and not embrace such a fickle emotion. If she could.

She found Rafe sitting alone in Geoffrey's study, writing letters.

"I thought you and Geoffrey were discussing my settlement," she said, coming around to the back of the desk to look over his shoulder.

"Actually, we decided Eliza and Foxstead could do it in the carriage on the way, so you can be there and Eliza can explain anything you don't know."

"Hmm," she said. "Marriage by committee. Perfect."

Flinching, he took her hand. "If you wish to wait until you can have a proper wedding—"

"No, sorry. I'm just a bit anxious. This happened very quickly, and I honestly never expected to marry."

"I don't know why." Tugging off her glove, he kissed her

hand. "Dusty old divorce scandal or not, you're a beautiful, witty woman. Anyone would be glad to marry you."

"Except you," she murmured, wondering if what Monsieur Beaufort had said about the marriage being Rafe's choice was true.

"*Including* me," Rafe said firmly. "Unlike you, I *did* expect to marry, but after this was all over. If you would have had me then, I would have courted you as vigorously as Minton."

That was the most reassuring thing he'd said to her yet. She smiled. "But without the laudanum, I hope."

He laughed. "Yes, without the laudanum. Which Minton never got to use, thank God."

She stared down at his letter. "To whom are you writing?"

He tapped the sheet on top. "This one's to the house-keeper at Castle Wolfford, telling her we'll arrive in three or four days. The second is to my attorney since we'll need to make the settlement legal once we arrive in London. That way, he can be waiting to meet me at a moment's notice."

"Good thinking."

"Actually, it was Eliza's idea." He sorted the sheets into three piles. "The last is to Sir Lucius, informing him of our betrothal and asking him to use his influence for that special license. All three should reach London before us since I'm sending them express. With any luck, we'll be able to finish up the settlement, acquire the license, and marry a day or two after we arrive."

"How efficient! And I should have known your friend in high places was Sir Lucius. I suppose he can manage to get just about anything he wants."

He folded both letters and addressed them. "We can only hope."

Chapter 21

Verity packed most of what she needed, then headed down to dinner, which went fairly well, with only one fly in the ointment. Lady Robina had been unable to coax her brother and his wife into attending, even though Mama had left. Lady Robina had sent a woeful message to that effect, which had arrived in the middle of dinner. That was a disappointment to the gentlemen, some of whom—particularly Lord Harry—had fancied courting Lady Robina—but not so much to the ladies, who were glad to have less competition.

Lady Harry was subdued, a surprise to everyone except those who had witnessed Minton's attempt to force Verity into marriage. Verity suspected that for the first time in her life, Lady Harry had realized how easily a woman could have her future upended by a man. It was a good lesson for the reckless young woman.

After dinner, the gentlemen agreed they should join the ladies rather than drink port, since four of their party were leaving early in the morning. Rafe excused himself entirely, saying he had to finish packing. After an hour, Verity and Eliza went upstairs—Eliza to tuck Jimmy in and explain that they would return in a few days, and Verity to add a few more items to her bag.

It didn't take Verity long to finish. Then she remembered Rafe had been writing to his housekeeper, and she wondered if she should bring gifts to his servants and how many. Would Verity have a lady's maid? Should she bring hers from London? She should have asked earlier, but if he was merely packing, she could go knock on his door and ask him now.

But no one answered her knock. She peeked inside to find the room empty. Could he have gone downstairs to join the others? His bag appeared almost packed. Good Lord, surely he hadn't headed back to that tavern.

Then again, if he truly was seeking brandy as a gift for Geoffrey, this would be the time to purchase it. That thought brought up some unsettling ones about why he would do something illegal if he was still in the army, or if he'd been making that up for Sarah's benefit, and was simply going to the tavern for wine, women, and song. It was, after all, one of his last nights of freedom.

Grimacing, she closed the door and headed downstairs by a route where she shouldn't encounter any guests. Fortunately, the same footman was on duty tonight as had been last night. When he saw her coming, he seemed to get very nervous.

That only heightened her suspicions. "Did Mr. Wolfford leave again to go to the tavern?"

The footman tugged at his collar. "H-He didn't tell me where he was headed, but he did go out about half an hour ago. Said he wouldn't return until late."

Hmm. She hoped this tavern visiting wouldn't continue once they were married. "Thank you for informing me. And when he comes back, please don't reveal that I asked."

She was reserving *that* right for herself.

"May I just say, my lady, that we servants are very happy

about your engagement and wish to congratulate you on your impending nuptials."

"How kind of you," she said, barely mustering a smile.

Turning on her heel, she headed upstairs. At first, she went to her room, but she couldn't sleep even after she'd donned her nightgown and wrapper. Instead, she paced the room, her agitation growing. What if he didn't return from the tavern? What if he hadn't even gone there and had fled or something?

No matter how much she told herself she was being silly and illogical, and no matter how much she reminded herself that his packed bag was still in his room, she knew she wouldn't sleep a wink until she knew what he was up to.

After a while, she gave up and ventured into the hallway and down a circuitous route to his room. She knocked softly, but there was no answer. He was *still* gone, blast him. It was nearly midnight!

After glancing at both ends of the hall, she opened the door and slipped inside. The fire was going, but it was languishing, so she added a log.

Then she settled down in a chair to wait.

Rafe hurried toward the house, cursing how late he was. At least he'd finally found out what he needed to know and could include it in the report he'd be giving Sir Lucius once they reached London.

The footman acted a bit strange when Rafe entered the house—avoided Rafe's gaze completely—but it probably had something to do with the betrothal that every servant above and below stairs was talking about.

A self-satisfied smile crossed Rafe's lips. In two nights, he would finally have Verity in his bed. At the moment, that future event seemed like more than enough to make up for any inconvenience she would give him in his spying life.

He'd barely had that thought, when he opened his door to find the fetching vixen looking coolly vexed as she waited for him in the chair by the fireplace.

All right, perhaps not *any* inconvenience.

"Please tell me you've come to get the wedding night out of the way," Rafe said as she rose and he realized she was wearing only a nightdress and a wrapper.

Good God. It was even more tempting than the bathing gown. The firelight shone right through it to reveal a very erotic silhouette. He could already feel his prick rising.

She seemed oblivious. "Originally," she said primly, "I came to ask you a few questions about what I might need at Castle Wolfford. But that was before I found out you went to the Lobster Tavern for the third night in a row."

That caught him off guard. Again. "How did you know I was at the Lobster Tavern?" He thought a moment. "I realize you overheard me talking to Sarah, but I didn't mention the name of the place."

"I saw you come in late last night. So I asked the footman why, and he told me where you'd gone."

"Ah," he quipped, "no privacy for the wicked at a house party, I see." He removed his cravat and threw it over a chair, then sat down to remove his boots. "And here I'd been planning to give your footman another guinea when I left."

"Another? No wonder he was willing to look the other way while you ran off to meet smugglers." She pulled her wrapper more tightly about herself. "Do you mind telling me why you were really there? Clearly, it wasn't to get illegal French brandy for Geoffrey, since at present you're empty-handed."

"I suppose you heard me tell Sarah about the brandy,"

he muttered, trying to buy time while he figured out what to say. He rose to remove his coat.

She scowled. "Are you going to tell me why you really went to the tavern?"

"Are you going to be this nosy once we're married?"

"Are you going to be this secretive?" She crossed her arms over her chest. "I can play this game all night, you know."

He stalked toward her. "I can think of better games to play all night." And taking her head in his hands, he kissed her. Possessively. Thoroughly. Savoring the softening of her mouth and quickening of her breaths.

She drew back a fraction to regard him with a glittering gaze. "You can't kiss the questions out of me."

"Oh, but I think I can if you'll just give me the chance," he said as he tugged her into his arms.

She pressed her finger to his lips. "I didn't come here to do that."

"I see." He drew back just enough to gaze down at her skimpy attire. "So you always wear your night clothes when interrogating a suspect."

"What?" She pushed away from him. "No! I didn't . . . I wasn't trying to . . . I couldn't sleep, all right? Not after I discovered you'd gone back to the tavern."

With a sigh, he returned to undressing.

"Stop that," she said in a loud whisper.

"See here," he grumbled. "I have just spent three hours in a smoky public house with a lot of bad-smelling fishermen who probably break the law and men's jaws regularly, merely so I could learn whether the River Exe is navigable."

She sniffed. "Of course it is. I could have answered that if you'd asked."

He narrowed his gaze on her. "And how do you know?"

She shrugged. "Because Papa used it for a while to transport planks from our sawmill at Exmoor Court down to Exeter and beyond."

"There's a sawmill at Exmoor Court?" He'd never known that. "How did he get the planks from Exmoor Court to the Exe?"

"On the River Barle. It goes right through our property. Then it joins up with the Exe lower down."

"Well, I'll be damned." He hadn't even considered the possibility that the smugglers could come down straight from Exmoor Court itself without having to be seen on roads. No one had ever mentioned the River Barle in his discussions, and the maps didn't show it. "Then why did Sarah say the Exe wasn't navigable?"

"The sawmill failed long before Sarah even met Papa. Don't get me wrong, I adore Sarah because she's a dedicated mother who will do anything for her boys. Plus, she's always nice to us. But she doesn't know a thing about boats and rivers. She's a city girl."

Breaking into a grin, he walked over to pull her into his arms again. "You, my lady, are clearly my good luck charm."

She eyed him as if he were daft. "Why?"

"Never mind. I'll explain later. I'll explain everything later, I swear. But for now . . ." He kissed her soundly, then more intimately.

For a moment, he thought she was relenting. Then she tore her mouth free to whisper, "We cannot—"

"Have our wedding night early?" He cupped her breast, thumbing the nipple with the delicate touch it required. "I don't see why not."

"If anyone discovered us—"

"They'd force us to marry?" He chuckled. "I think we've passed that point already, sweetheart."

She blinked. "Oh. Excellent observation."

"I thought so." This time when he returned to kissing her, she not only participated enthusiastically, but unbuttoned his waistcoat and shoved it off.

So he removed her wrapper with great haste. But the ties of her nightgown were knotted. "Take this off," he ground out against her lips. "I can't manage it."

With a light laugh, she simply drew the gossamer thing up and over her head. "You're very high-handed, I see."

He barely heard her. He'd stepped back and was too busy drinking in every inch of her naked body, wishing he could see her in the full light of day. "And you're the very picture of Venus, sweetheart." He circled her, noticing everything. Her fine, high breasts. Her dimpled belly. Her slender arms.

How her hair poured down between her shoulder blades like a golden river to curl sweetly at the top of her gently curved bottom. He filled his hands with her firm bottom. *His.* Or she would be soon. "You're a work of art." He leaned forward to whisper. "A very clever work of art."

Wearing a minxish smile, she faced him. But before she could speak, the firelight illuminated the bruises bracketing her mouth. Minton's work.

Anger rose in him again. "I should never have let that bastard leave here." He brushed the dark smudges on her jaw with a bleak sense of helplessness he'd never before experienced. "I should have challenged Minton just for these." He'd failed to protect her. That must never happen again. "Do they hurt?"

She swallowed. "Not really. He hurt my pride more than anything. Although if Lady Harry and Miss Mudford hadn't come along when they did . . ."

"Yes, thank God for that," he said hoarsely. "I only wish it had been me."

"I don't. You might have killed him, and then you couldn't have stayed around to marry me."

"There is that." He gently kissed each bruise, wishing mere kisses could wipe them from her skin . . . and her memory. "Still, no man who would do this to a woman deserves to live."

"Can we not talk about Lord Minton? Or what happened?" Her tone grew determinedly cheerful. "Let's talk about the fact that *you* are still wearing far too many clothes."

He let her change the subject, knowing she probably abhorred being seen as a victim. But privately, he vowed to punish Minton somehow for what he'd done.

She unbuttoned the placket of his shirt and pulled his shirttails from inside his trousers. "Take this off," she demanded with a saucy look. "I can't manage it."

"Tit for tat, is it?" he said as he did her bidding. "I do like that game. Now it's my turn. Get on the bed."

Damn. That was not the way to go about seducing a woman, especially one who'd just been assaulted.

But she simply ignored him, flashing him an amused look. "You enjoy giving orders, don't you, Colonel?"

"Forgive me. It's all I know." He kissed the tip of her pretty nose. "Although I suspect it's all you know, too. More than once, I've heard you in that kitchen ordering people about."

Her eyes widened. "At the Crowders' May Day affair. You really *were* in the kitchen that night! Eliza was sure you had been, but I never glimpsed you."

He scowled. "If I can agree not to talk about Minton, you can agree not to talk about the Phantom." He walked her backward to the bed. "There's only one person I want to discuss at the moment."

"Oh? And who is that, Colonel?"

"You." He pushed gently on her shoulders. "Sit, Verity. Because I mean to show you how a man is supposed to treat a woman." Even if holding himself back took all of his strength.

One way or the other, he'd make sure she didn't regret agreeing to marry him.

Chapter 22

Verity folded her arms over her breasts. It was one thing to be nude when Rafe was right there caressing and kissing her, but quite another when he was looking her over while still partially clothed.

"Am I making you nervous, my Venus?" he asked.

"I feel . . . rather awkward, but I'd feel less so if you'd undress."

"Your wish is my command."

In a matter of moments, he'd shed his trousers, smalls, and stockings, leaving him entirely naked. His "thing" was thrust out in the air as bold as brass and took her by surprise. It looked unnatural, nothing like ones she'd seen in drawings of statues.

She gestured vaguely in its direction. "Is it swollen or something? Did you injure it?"

He laughed. "No, sweetheart. It always looks like this when I'm aroused."

"Every man's . . . er . . ."

"Penis? Prick? Member? Cock? Take your pick. There are hundreds of words for it, most of them absurd."

None that she knew. "What do you call yours?"

"My prick."

"Every man's . . . um . . . *prick* looks like that when it's aroused? And has hair around it?"

"To varying degrees."

She eyed him skeptically. "The ones on Greek statues don't."

"Greek statues depict men who aren't aroused." He came nearer. "I suspect it's difficult to sculpt a man in full arousal. No man could sustain that for very long. And I have no idea why artists never sculpt the hair around privates. They don't do it for women, either, if you'll notice."

"That's true." She stared at his rigid flesh, fascinated by the color and the way it bobbed. "Why wasn't your . . . like that at the beach?"

"It was constrained by my smalls." He lifted it up against him to demonstrate, and his ballocks hung down underneath, covered with hair, too.

"Oh! It's flexible. It can move around."

He choked out a laugh. "Somewhat, yes. Are you done interrogating me about my privates? Because I really want to be inside you, but I have something else I want to do first."

"What?" she asked warily.

He knelt in front of her. "Remember how I put my fingers inside of you?"

"Yes."

"Did you like it?"

"As if you need to ask." She'd loved it, wished it would never end until it did, and then she'd wished he'd do it again. "Of course I liked it."

"Well . . . it's possible to do that with one's tongue, too."

As he carefully opened her legs to his gaze, she gaped at him. He was going to put his tongue . . .

That sounded odd.

"You know how you keep talking about my 'special

meal'?" he said. "*This* is the only 'special meal' I care about."
Then he placed his mouth right on her mons.

Good *Lord*, that was so much better than his fingers. His
tongue darted inside her, first stroking, then caressing.
Rousing her as he had before. Closing her eyes, she surren-
dered to the sensations as he used tongue, lips, and teeth to
seduce. It felt *wonderful*. Like the way a powerful orches-
tra's playing vibrated through her, making her body hum.

"Rafe . . . *Rafe* . . ."

He chuckled. "You like that, do you?"

"It's . . . amazing." Eliza had never mentioned *this*, to be
sure.

Verity gripped the bedclothes as she widened her thighs.

"Sweetheart," he murmured against her, then smoothed
his hands along her legs. "You're so soft, I could stay here
forever. And so wet, I could drink you up."

He was making her wetter with every word, every
caress. Her heart pounded in her ears as she gave her body
up to his ministrations. He sucked a certain spot, and she
nearly came off the bed. "Oh . . . oh . . . *yes*. Like that!"

That's when he started pleasuring her in earnest as if
he'd just been waiting to see what she liked. She liked
this. The rhythm of his tongue, the heat of his mouth, the
intensity of his attentions . . . oh, all of it! She reached for
his head to hold him there, reveling in the silky strands
of his raven hair. *Hers*. Soon he would be hers entirely.
Tonight was but the first of many.

Then she stopped thinking, swept up in the beating of
her pulse, like a drum carrying her forward, playing through
her louder and faster, until she joined the music as it thundered to its crescendo and landed her squarely in . . . in . . .

Ah! Heaven!

As her body shook, she roared into heaven. He'd carried
her there himself. Her heart filled up and her blood sang . . .

Good Lord!

"Rafe . . ." she said as she fell back on the bed, her release rocking her. "Oh, yes, *Rafe* . . ."

Even as she was still quaking, he kissed each of her thighs. "Nothing like a meal of Verity Venus to arouse a man," he whispered as he wiped his mouth on the sheet. Then he rose to gather her up in his arms and lay her out on the bed so he could lie down beside her.

Rafe knew he should give her a chance to rest, to enjoy her climax. But the taste of her, the sight of her experiencing release had so aroused him that he couldn't stand it.

"Sweetheart," he said hoarsely as he propped himself up on one arm, "will you let me in?"

Her unfocused gaze met his. "Let you . . ." She flashed him a brilliant smile. "Right. Tit for tat."

"If you're ready," he whispered.

He'd never seen her look more Venus-like as she took his hand and pulled it to her breast with the accomplished air of a born seductress. "I am definitely ready for your . . . prick, sir."

Just the sound of the dirty word on her ladylike lips sent his prick impossibly harder. "You, my dear, are a wanton in the making," he said as he moved over her, using his knee to open her for him.

"But only with you," she whispered as her eyes met his. "I . . . I hope you believe that."

Remembering suddenly the rumors about her, he brushed a reassuring kiss to her lips. "Of course. Trust me, every man wants a wanton wife in his bed. As long as she stays in his alone."

Breaking into a smile, she looped her arms about his

neck. "How appropriate, since every woman wants a rakehell in her bed. As long as he doesn't go into another's."

He felt for the opening of her honeypot, then paused. "You . . . know how this works, right?"

She bobbed her head. "I know it hurts sometimes and doesn't other times."

"I will make it as comfortable as I can." He eased his prick in slowly, watching for any grimace.

"It's . . . fine," she said, though her stiff expression gave her away. "A bit tight is all."

God knows she felt tight to him, like a velvet glove milking his cock. "That's to be expected. It will get better." *I hope.* He didn't know for sure. He'd never deflowered a woman. "I will do my best to make it better."

Her throat moved convulsively. "I know you will." Her soft smile hit him hard in the heart. "I trust you."

And he meant to be worthy of that trust if it killed him. Which it very well might, since she felt like heaven, and all he wanted was to take her hard and fast. "Ah, sweetheart, you are a wonder," he said.

Then he set about trying to make it better for her— arousing her with one finger below, then pulling her knees up for a better position. That must have worked, because she gave a happy sigh and shifted beneath him in such a way that he sank even further into her.

He increased his motions, almost without realizing it. It felt so damned good to be inside her, to see the surprise and sudden pleasure on her face.

"God . . . help . . . me," he muttered. "You'll be . . . the death of me . . . yet, my Venus."

Using one hand to knead her sweet breast, he thrust into her, chasing his climax, seeking to cause hers again. Her eyes slid shut and she began moaning.

"Better?" he choked out.

"Much," she answered. "Ohhh . . . my dearest . . . That is . . . oh . . . yes . . . I'm yours . . . I'm yours . . . yours . . ."

The fierce words sent him right to the edge. But the feel of her inner muscles tightening around him as she reached her release pushed him over the cliff into a thunderous climax like none he'd ever experienced. She was *his*. Forever. She'd called him *dearest*.

He would fight for her . . . and win. Because he meant to keep her, whatever it took.

As he spilled his seed inside her, he prayed he'd sired a child. And that fervent wish surprised him.

After he collapsed atop her, he whispered, "I'm yours, too. Never forget it."

A look of pure contentment crossed her face that warmed him to his soul.

It took some time for him to regain his senses, to settle his fragmented thoughts enough to roll off her, but when he did, he found her lying there exactly as he'd imagined—with her long curls fanning about her like a golden nimbus.

"That was . . ." he began.

"Unexpected."

"You thought I'd be bad at this part of marriage?"

"No!" She shifted onto her side to gaze warmly at him. "I just never dreamed it would be *that* enjoyable, not from how my sister described the . . . er . . . mechanics of it. Did you take lessons or something?"

"I refuse to answer that on the grounds that it may incriminate me." The minute the flippant words left his lips, he wanted to kick himself.

Fortunately, she laughed. "Well, whoever gave you such lessons was obviously very talented."

He winced. "Forget what I said. Sometimes I have no idea how to answer you. You ask the most interesting, most unpredictable questions." And her figuring out that all his disguises were him had completely altered how he regarded her. That she could see through them all to the him that lay beneath . . .

She snuggled up next to him. "That's why you're marrying me."

"I'm marrying you to keep you safe," he said.

She blinked, and the light left her face. Then she rose and left the bed. "Of course. I keep forgetting that. Thank you for the reminder." She found her nightdress and shimmied into it, using some alchemy only women seemed to know. "And now that I've lost my innocence, you're marrying me for that, too."

"No, I'm . . ." Damn it, he never knew what to say to her. Perhaps Sir Lucius was right—he wasn't great with women.

He slid off the bed and dragged on his smalls, then caught up with her as she put her wrapper on over her nightdress. Grabbing her hand, he kissed it while she stared at him, her gorgeous eyes solemn and uncertain.

"I'm marrying you because I like you. I feel comfortable with you." *You make me happy.*

God, he couldn't say that. It wasn't true. Was it?

A faint smile crossed her lips. "I like you, too. And I feel comfortable with you." She arched one eyebrow. "Although when you were slipping in and out of all of our events, I feared you might be a villain."

"You know I'm not," he said irritably.

She tipped up her chin with a hint of defiance. "Monsieur Beaufort says you're a spy for England."

Rafe cursed his friend roundly. "What else did he say?"

"That he cooked for you and your uncle for four years. Is that true?"

He sighed. "Yes."

"So, you *are* a spy."

Rafe hesitated, but he'd already told her he was working

for the government, so it wasn't much of a leap from there to spying. "Spy. Soldier. What's the difference?"

She secured her wrapper with its tie. "The first means you're paid to deceive people. The second means you're paid to fight. Which is it?"

"Both. But I'm not deceiving you now. I'm just not . . . telling you everything until after we marry. And that is absolutely all I can say for now."

Releasing a long breath, she turned for the door. "I must go. Dawn still comes early this time of year."

"Sleep well," he said as he followed her. "I'll see you in the morning."

"I hope so," she murmured.

He hurried to stop her before she could leave. "What does that mean?"

"Nothing."

He cupped her cheek. "Not nothing, I think."

She wouldn't meet his gaze. "If all you wanted was to take my innocence, then you've had what you want of me, haven't you?"

"Had what I want of you," he echoed, incredulous. "You have no idea what I want of you, how badly I want it, and what I'd do to get it."

"Even marry me?"

"Especially marry you." He drew her close for a long, heated kiss. "If I had my way, we'd leave this room together in the morning and get on the coach for London. But since I know that my way would rouse gossip, I will try to be content until we marry. So yes, you'll see me in the morning. You can count on that."

That must have reassured her, for she smiled. "Good night, fiancé."

"You've got a few days before you lose your freedom,

Lady Verity Harper. You'd best make them count. Because after that, you'll never be rid of me."

She leaned up to kiss his cheek. Then she was gone, leaving him feeling bereft.

That *really* worried him. Because if she had that effect on him before they wed, how would he feel afterward, knowing that their marriage was built on her assumption that he wouldn't harm her family? Knowing he might be illegitimate, and if that ever came out, she'd be thrown into yet another scandal?

It didn't matter. He would make her his and hold her close and hope he could keep her from regretting it later on. Right now, he could do naught else.

Chapter 23

Rafe rose at four AM the next morning to make sure his carriage was ready for the trip, and that they were able to leave on time. Thank God he had, because just the tumult of the family alone was more than he was used to. From Diana's tearful goodbyes to the children's running about to Lady Holtbury's gentle admonitions that they be careful on the road, the scene was pure chaos.

And pure love, too. It was like that scene he'd witnessed as a boy, but in reverse—an affectionate leave-taking. He was part of the family now, but not really. Because when they learned the truth . . .

He wouldn't think about that. He mustn't.

Eventually, even the chaos sorted itself out, probably because two soldiers like he and Foxstead were old hands at rousting troops for marches. Still, he didn't relax until the carriage pulled away as the sun rose over the hills.

"Remind me of this the next time I wish to go on a trip with my husband that requires our leaving early," Eliza grumbled to her sister.

Foxstead nudged Rafe. "My wife isn't fond of early rising."

"To put it mildly," Verity said. "I was barely five when

I realized my sister would never welcome being tugged out of bed for an adventure at six AM."

"You're an early riser?" Rafe asked. "Frankly, that surprises me."

"Why?" she said. "Because I didn't skip down the stairs when a certain man sent my maid up to rouse me at four-thirty AM? What did you expect? I stayed up late packing my trunk. You could hardly assume I'd be ready at a moment's notice this morning."

Not after the night we had. He could practically see her thinking it. "I'm not surprised, given the size of that trunk. I thought you said you meant to pack light."

Eliza snorted. "That *is* packing light for Verity. She doesn't go anywhere with less."

"That's not true," Verity protested. "I once went to stay with Papa carrying only a valise."

"Because you had a closet full of clothes at his town house already." Eliza shot Rafe a long look. "Prepare yourself, sir. Verity squirrels away shells, stones, bits of ribbon . . . anything she thinks she can use for displays at our events. For your sake, I hope Castle Wolfford is huge."

Rafe chuckled. "Huge enough to suit your sister's whims, I assure you." He looked at Foxstead. "Speaking of my property, we should probably discuss Verity's settlement."

"It's a good thing I've had three cups of coffee this morning," Eliza said as she drew out a portable writing desk. "Otherwise, this would not go well."

Thus began their long discussion about jointures, dower, and life interest, among other things. Thank God Foxstead was familiar with all of it, because Rafe definitely was not.

But it soon became evident it was no different from the will his uncle had insisted on making for him or the agreements Rafe managed with his tenants. So he was relieved when, after Eliza had made copious notes and explained several things to her sister, Foxstead pointed out they should wait to finish until Rafe's attorney could join them.

After that, the trip was more enjoyable. The weather was fine, so they made such great time that they reached an inn halfway to London on the first day. Rafe had hoped to slip into Verity's room that night for another course of love-making, but Eliza's insistence that her sister sleep in a room adjoining theirs dashed his hopes. So Rafe had to be content with a full night's sleep.

They left early the next morning, and as a result of a hearty breakfast at the inn, reached Foxstead's house in London in time for dinner. They'd already decided to make the Foxstead town house their base of operations for the short time they were in London. Since everyone was exhausted, they planned on retiring early to get an early start the next morning.

But first, Rafe had to send notes to his attorney and Sir Lucius asking them to come in the morning. Rafe was still writing the missives when an unexpected visitor arrived at Foxstead's town house.

It was Holtbury himself, demanding to see Verity. Fortunately, the servants knew better than to bother Lady Verity for the likes of her father, so they showed him into Foxstead's study instead, where Rafe was finishing up his note to Sir Lucius.

As Rafe rose, Holtbury glared at him. "My wife sent me an express from Exmouth, informing me that you intend to marry my daughter. How dare you attempt such a thing without consulting her family?"

"I did consult her family. Your other two daughters and their husbands were more than happy to approve the match. We've all agreed to a settlement, and I'm merely awaiting my attorney's arrival tomorrow so we can make it final."

"How dare you?" Holtbury hissed. "I will have you—"

"What's going on?" Verity asked from the doorway. Then she saw her father. "Papa! What are you doing here?"

Holtbury barely looked at her. "I came to talk to Mr. Wolfford. It is none of your concern, girl."

Oho, even Rafe knew that wasn't the way to Verity's heart.

If Holtbury *had* bothered to look at her, he would have seen her eyes flashing. "I'm no longer a girl, Papa, and haven't been for some years." Then Verity walked up to Rafe. "Dearest, Nathaniel wanted me to ask if you'd like him to arrange for his attorney to meet us here tomorrow at eleven AM."

"That's perfect. I'll just amend the note to my attorney to reflect those arrangements."

"Should we meet in here?" she asked, as if her father were invisible. "Or do we want to gather in the drawing room? I could have Cook prepare some cakes and such if you wish."

Rafe rather enjoyed watching her play lady of the house, since he'd never seen her in that role, and it fit her surprisingly well. Besides, she had Holtbury pacing like a toothless old tiger, seething in his cage.

"The drawing room would be best. More room. And food is always welcome, especially yours, since it's so tasty." *And you, old man, will never get to taste it again, if I know Verity.*

"One more item of business," she said, "Eliza and I want to talk to you about servants, and if I should bring any with me to Castle Wolfford."

"Certainly. I can discuss that with you both now." He turned to Holtbury. "Excuse me, sir, but even at this hour we are very busy. I'll have someone show you out."

"No one is showing me out, damn you. My attorney

should be the one doing this settlement. I deserve to have a say in this wedding!"

"I don't see why," Verity said. "You took back my dowry. So I'm free to strike whatever agreement I wish with whatever man I wish to marry. And I wish to strike an agreement with Mr. Wolfford. To *marry* Mr. Wolfford."

Now Rafe could hear the hurt beneath the defiance in her voice. Her father clearly had no idea how badly he'd wounded her by championing Minton.

"I've already chosen a husband for you," Holtbury said.

She laughed coldly. "Lord Minton, you mean."

Holtbury crossed his arms. "As a matter of fact, yes. He regrets he took so long to see the advantages of the match and has already asked my permission to court you."

That sent Rafe over the edge. He marched up to Holtbury, his hands curling into fists. "Did you also give him permission to attempt *abducting* my fiancée? To try forcing her into marrying him by assaulting her?"

Holtbury paled. "What are you talking about?"

"Lord Minton tried to carry me off against my will, Papa," Verity said, coming up behind Rafe to take his hand. "And *you* were the one who paid him to go to Exmouth so he could attempt it."

"I didn't pay him for *that*!" her father spat. "I paid him to . . . to . . ." He trailed off as he realized what he'd revealed. "He said he wanted to court you. Honorably. But he had no money, so I paid his expenses."

"Why would you do that, knowing how he publicly humiliated me?" Verity cried. "How could you think I'd ever accept him as a suitor again?"

When Holtbury stiffened but said nothing, the truth hit Rafe all at once. "You struck a deal with Minton, because he was a weasel you figured you could always keep under your thumb. Which you assumed meant you could always keep *her* under your thumb."

"So you want her under *your* thumb instead," the earl said with a sneer.

Rafe held up their joined hands. "I want her hand in mine. Nobody under anybody's thumbs. That's what *I* want."

Holtbury gaped at him. Apparently, Rafe had stymied the arse, who couldn't seem to imagine a world where his daughters got to live their own lives as they pleased with the men they chose.

"There's something you don't appear to understand about your daughter," Rafe said. "She knows what she wants, and she'll never accept anything less. So your scheme wouldn't work. Neither you nor Minton could *keep* her under your thumbs. She would sooner kill Minton than marry him."

Verity stared at her father with a glittering gaze. "You see, Papa? That's why I'm marrying *him*. Because he knows me so well."

"And now, sir, you really must leave," Rafe said. "We have other matters to attend to." Releasing Verity's hand, he walked up to grab Holtbury's arm and urge him toward the door.

"You'll regret this," Holtbury ground out.

"I doubt it."

"I will ruin you in Society!" Holtbury said.

That one made Rafe laugh. "I seriously doubt *that*."

They cleared the door to find Eliza and Nathaniel just outside, having apparently heard that Holtbury was there. Eliza was waiting patiently, but Nathaniel paced the hall.

"Ah, Nathaniel," Rafe said, "would you mind helping Lord Holtbury find his way to his carriage? I have matters to discuss with your wife and my intended."

Nathaniel smiled at Rafe. "I would relish the chance to throw my cursed father-in-law out of my home, thank you."

"I don't need help," Holtbury snapped, snatching his arm

from Rafe just in time to find Nathaniel's wrapped about his like a manacle. "You cannot treat me this way!"

"Watch me," Nathaniel growled, and propelled him down the hall.

With a smug smile, Rafe swept his hand toward the study door. "Shall we, Eliza?"

She shook her head. "You and my husband are enjoying this immensely, aren't you?"

"As am I," Verity quipped as they entered.

"I'm sorry about your father, sweetheart. I now see why your mother ran off with another man. Who could endure his machinations for an entire lifetime?"

"Not any of us, to be sure," Eliza said. "Starting Elegant Occasions was the best thing we ever did. In one fell swoop, we escaped Papa and found a way to use our vast store of knowledge in doing what we love—helping people succeed, in Society and out."

Verity added, "But I'm sorry he didn't offer you my dowry. You deserve to have it."

"The price he would have expected me—expected *us*— to pay for it would have been far too high, anyway."

But Rafe would make sure Holtbury paid a price for his own sins, and not just for spying for the French, if he was the one doing it. No, Rafe would make him suffer for wounding his daughter and nearly getting her raped. Because the bastard clearly deserved whatever Rafe could dish out.

The next morning, Rafe was already settled in to handle any other business affairs related to the marriage itself before the ladies rose to join them with the attorneys. He knew they planned to spend the rest of the day unpacking and repacking what Verity would need for Castle

Wolfford and choosing her wedding clothes and other female fripperies.

For now, he commandeered a table in the drawing room, not only for the meeting, but also so he could look over certain other business matters involving the marriage.

Then a footman came in to announce Sir Lucius.

Rafe rose and went to meet his superior. "Come in, sir. We will have privacy enough in here."

As soon as Rafe closed the door, Sir Lucius turned on him. "I heard that Holtbury was here yesterday."

"Yes. He came to demand that I not marry Verity. I told him to hike off. I'll tell you the same if you try to stop me from it."

Sir Lucius's gaze narrowed. "Before this began, you promised *not* to marry her."

"I didn't promise." Rafe groaned. "Please tell me you got the special license all the same. That you vouched for me in the allegations. That I can legally marry Verity as planned."

"You can. I did as you asked, since I couldn't risk neglecting something necessary to your plans. But—"

"This has nothing to do with my spying," Rafe snapped. "I didn't have time to put everything in the letter. It all had to be done very quickly after Lord Minton compromised her."

Rafe rarely succeeded in shocking his superior, but judging from the sudden lack of color in Sir Lucius's expression, he'd managed to do it this time. "Minton compromised Lady Verity? Was it in connection to your work?"

"I don't think so." Quickly, he summarized what had happened, then went to the table to pull a sheaf of papers out of his satchel. "I put everything in my reports. Suffice it to say, after what happened with Uncle Constantine, I wanted to make sure you were fully informed."

When Sir Lucius regarded him consideringly, he added,

"I couldn't let her be ruined or subjected to scandal, you understand." He steadied his shoulders. "Or worse, be forced to marry Holtbury's lackey, Minton. I had no choice."

"How surprisingly gallant of you," Sir Lucius said as he took the papers from Rafe. "I suppose I approve. I just pray *she* will approve once this is all over, and she learns what you've been doing and why."

Rafe raked his fingers through his hair. "You and me both."

"Have you told her anything about your actual activities and purpose?"

"I didn't need to, thank God. She was willing to marry me under the circumstances." It was the truth. What she knew, she'd figured out on her own, and he wasn't about to admit that mortifying fact to Sir Lucius unless he had to. "Had you any trouble obtaining the license?"

"Of course not. I told the archbishop it was a matter of national security. He didn't blink an eye." Sir Lucius searched his face. "Do you mean to *stay* married to her? Because I won't help you get a divorce. Even if I could manage it."

"Of course I'm staying married to her." *Especially since we've already consummated the marriage.* No, Rafe would never embarrass her by revealing that to anyone. "I mean for us to have a real marriage."

Sir Lucius smiled for the first time since he'd entered. "That should be interesting."

"Trust me, I know all too well."

"Do you want me to attend the ceremony?" the spy-master asked.

"If you wish. Now that we have the license in hand, I'll suggest we marry here first thing tomorrow so we can head on to Castle Wolfford right away. She'll be safer there than anywhere else while I'm gone. I know enough now, I think, to pursue this to the end, but it may take me some time of following various avenues. I vow I *will* catch him eventually."

"Good. Somebody needs to." Sir Lucius headed for the door. "Send a note to let me know what time the ceremony is, and I'll be there."

That had gone better than expected, thank God. Now Rafe could only pray he could make good on his vows. The one to Sir Lucius. *And* the one to Verity.

Chapter 24

Eliza and Verity awoke to find Rafe already settled in to handle any business affairs related to the marriage itself. After the meeting about the settlement, they were free to unpack and repack what Verity would need and to choose her wedding clothes and make other swift wedding plans.

The next morning, as Verity and her family awaited Rafe in the drawing room, she tried not to be nervous. She'd never thought her wedding day would come, and under the circumstances, she wasn't sure whether to be happy about it.

Especially since Rafe had been busy at his lodgings at the Albany since dawn, doing Lord knows what. Could he have cold feet? Might he even now be racing off on horseback to avoid going through with it?

Stop being an anxious ninny. He wouldn't do that.

Lord, she hoped not.

She smoothed out her satin gown of light sage green, which shimmered in the morning light. She had fallen in love with this dress the moment she'd first seen the design and had it made, never dreaming it would soon serve as her wedding gown.

She prayed she didn't look as tired as she felt. Three nights of little sleep had taken its toll, and no amount of pinching her cheeks had given them color. She hoped he didn't take one look at her wan countenance and run the other way.

But at least Eliza had done her hair very prettily, weaving orange blossoms in a lovely bandeau about her veil made of layers of lace. Nervously, she patted it to make sure it stayed in place.

As if Eliza could read Verity's agitation, she leaned over from her chair to squeeze Verity's hand. "You look lovely. And he'll be here. Have faith in him."

"I do." Mostly. Though she wouldn't be completely satisfied until she heard his explanations about why he'd been spying on her family.

At least Sir Lucius had arrived and was making small talk with Nathaniel. That did reassure her. She was fairly certain the man was Rafe's employer. Twice, Rafe had dropped everything to speak to Sir Lucius, and the man *was* with the War Office. Given that Rafe was spying for the government . . .

The drawing room door banged open and Rafe rushed in. "Forgive me for being late." As Verity rose, he hurried over to offer her a box. "I was looking for this." He opened it to reveal a gold filigree ring with a red stone at its center. "According to my uncle, it was my mother's. He gave it to me years ago, and I couldn't remember where I had stored it after moving into the Albany, so I had to hunt for it."

His mother's ring? Swallowing past the lump in her throat, she beamed at him. "It's beautiful."

He scanned her from bandeau to ballroom slippers with an appreciative gaze. "*You're* beautiful."

The bishop who was to marry them cleared his throat. With a last smile for her, Rafe nodded to show that the clergyman should begin the service.

The ceremony went on rather long. Verity tried not to wince when the bishop began her part of the vows with,

"Wilt thou obey him, and serve him . . ." The rest of his words faded as the gravity of the situation hit her all at once. She'd hoped to marry for love—if she ever did marry—and clearly this was not that. In exchange for avoiding scandal, she was handing over her freedom.

What if she regretted it? What if she found herself in one of those horrible marriages where the man was faithful but cruel, demanding obedience and servitude? What if . . .

Suddenly, she realized that the bishop and Rafe were staring at her expectantly, awaiting her answer. At that moment, when she gazed into Rafe's face, she saw something flicker in his eyes that she'd seen before at odd times—something that looked suspiciously like yearning.

It was enough. "I will," she said.

She repeated the rest of the vows mechanically until the bishop began the ring part of the ceremony, and Rafe said, in his lovely baritone, "With this ring I thee wed, with my body I thee worship . . ." He paused briefly to give her the faintest knowing lift of his brow.

She should have blushed like a proper bride. Instead, she had to stifle a laugh. There was *that* part of marriage, after all. He was very good at worshipping her body . . . and at making her laugh. Tonight, he would likely do both again. She could hardly wait.

The remainder of the very long service passed in a blur, until at last they'd taken communion and were finished. Or rather, almost finished. They still had to go to her parish church to sign the registry.

But Rafe had said he wanted to leave for Castle Wolford as soon as possible after that, so, armed with fond farewells from Eliza and Nathaniel, a buss on the cheek from Sir Lucius, a friendly handshake from the bishop, and champagne toasts all around, they left the Foxstead town house for the parish church.

Signing the registry took only a few moments, though she did notice that Rafe signed his full name, which she was laughing about as they were leaving.

"What?" he asked.

"Raphael *Gabriel* Wolfford? I can't believe you have not one, but two archangel's names. Yet you still manage to be wicked."

"Only occasionally." He grinned. "And mostly only with you."

"Mostly?" she said.

He merely laughed.

Once they were on the road, she realized it was the first time they'd been alone without it being considered improper. Hard to believe he was legally her husband now.

"So, should I assume you would prefer to be styled as Lady Verity Wolfford until I inherit?" Rafe asked. "Given that I'm merely a mister until then?"

"Since I'm allowed to choose, I'd rather be Mrs. Wolfford. In deference to the man who saved me from the awful Lord Minton."

The pleased smile that crossed his lips made her glad of that decision.

"So, what would my new missus like to do now that we're alone?" He tugged off his gloves, then leaned forward to remove hers, too.

Though she let him, she eyed him askance. "Not what you're thinking, I suspect."

He stared at her hard, as if trying to make her out. Then he sighed. "You want me to start telling you all the things I promised to reveal."

"How clever of you to guess that." She gave him her best insolent smile. "And how clever of me to have married such an astute man."

With a lift of his eyebrow, he sat back to cross his arms

over his chest. "As someone I know once said, 'Flattery begets vanity, a vice I'd rather not acquire.'" He raked her with a decidedly lascivious gaze. "Are you sure you wouldn't rather consummate our marriage? I am more than ready to 'worship you' with my body."

"And you shall. But first—"

"All right. But you must promise not to unleash your temper on me until I can say the whole thing."

"Temper?" She drew herself up, rather insulted. "I don't have a temper."

"As I reminded you before, I *saw* you in the kitchen whenever things weren't going your way."

He did have a point. She could be a very exacting taskmaster in the kitchen. "Speaking of that," she said, "how many of our events did you attend exactly? And which ones?"

"*That's* what you want to know first?"

"Why not? Ever since you as much as admitted the truth about spying on us, I've been trying to figure it out." She drew her notebook from where she'd stowed it under the seat, then began flipping through it. "By my count, you were at . . . fifteen, perhaps? I listed all the ones I could remember."

"Let me see that," he growled, and snatched her notebook from her before she could stop him. He flipped through the pages, looking more incredulous by the moment. "What is this?"

"A list of the events I thought you'd attended, what elements you'd used in each disguise for each event, where I encountered you, any other notes I had concerning your behavior. Oh, if you go to the end, you'll also find my theories about why you were spying."

"Good God." He shook it at her. "You must promise not to show this to Sir Lucius. I'd never live down the shame."

"What shame?" she grumbled. "I was the only one who

noticed you, and I often doubted myself about it. Why do you suppose I started my notebook? To stop me from thinking I was losing my mind."

He drew himself up, clearly irate. "You're missing the point. Do you know what my fellow soldiers called me on the Peninsula? The Chameleon, because I could take on any character without being unmasked."

"The Chameleon? Ooh, that's a better name than the Phantom! Give me my book—I have to write that down."

"You cannot— Damn it, Verity, we're talking about my life and, presently, my career! You must swear not to write down anything I relate to you now, or I won't tell you a damned thing."

"Oh, all right," she muttered.

"Indeed, as soon as we arrive at my estate, I will burn this."

"Must you?" she complained. "I want to keep it as a remembrance of how we met. What if I promise to lock it away somewhere until the war is over?"

That seemed to pull him up short, for he narrowed his gaze on her. "What makes you think this is about the war?"

She shrugged. "Well, it has to be. You did say you're still a colonel, and you're working for the government. Colonels generally don't handle domestic matters unless their regiment or militia is doing so."

Clearly frustrated, he scrubbed his face with his hands. "Sir Lucius should have just hired *you* for this mission. You would have rounded up the criminals in a lot less time."

While he was distracted, she snatched the book back to read her notes. "By my calculations, that would have been almost eighteen months ago, yes?"

He sighed. "Thereabouts."

"Now, answer the question. How many events? How close to the right number was I?"

"Do you promise to take this seriously, and not talk about

it to anyone? Because if word got out that I was the Chameleon or even your Phantom—"

"I promise. I generally do take it seriously, you know. Indeed, at first, I was outraged that some fellow kept sneaking in. But I guess after the past few days, I'm tired of taking things seriously." And laughing at things made her feel as if she had some control over matters . . . like the fact that her father had conspired with Minton to have her forced into marriage.

Understanding showed in his features. "It *has* been a rough few days for you, hasn't it?"

She nodded.

"But it wasn't too rough a couple of nights ago in my room, was it?"

She couldn't resist teasing him. "That was tolerable, I suppose."

"Tolerable!" he protested.

With a laugh, she said, "I'm joking, my husband. Not that I want to enlarge your big head, but in all actuality, it was . . . how do I put this . . ."

"Verity—"

"Wonderful," she said softly. "Absolutely heavenly."

"Thank God." He drew in a heavy breath. "All right, then. Regarding the Phantom, your calculation was fairly close to the mark. I attended sixteen events." He held out his hand. "Give me the book, and I'll tell you which ones you had right. Have you a pencil?"

"Always." She dug it out of her reticule. "Here."

He went through marking things, muttering to himself, then adding things in the margin. "You can read all of it right before I burn it."

She grabbed for it, but he stuck it behind his back. She sighed. "You did say your mission was important. So, how important is it? And what is your mission, exactly? Does it have anything to do with smuggling?"

A wary expression crossed his face. "Why do you ask about smuggling?"

"Because you told Sarah you were at the tavern trying to get French brandy, and the only way one can do that is to purchase it from smugglers."

"God help me." He scratched his eyebrow. "Promise me you won't tell Sir Lucius any of this, or he'll try to recruit you. And that's the last thing I need."

"I have no desire to spy on people."

"No, just to record the spy spying on *you*," he said testily.

"Can you blame me?"

"I suppose not." Placing his hands on his knees, he added, "And it does have to do with smuggling. But I'm getting ahead of myself." He settled into his seat, obviously preparing for a long tale. "Two years ago, Sir Lucius noticed that the French always seemed to anticipate our troop movements. I was still on the Peninsula, and my . . . er . . . corps had confiscated and deciphered occasional coded reports from the enemy to their officers."

"Coded messages and everything," she said dryly. "How very mysterious."

He scowled at her. "It didn't take the French long to figure out we could read their messages, so they changed to a more complex cipher after that, but not before we figured out we had a spy somewhere in England, either high up in our own government or connected to someone in our government, who was feeding them information."

"Oh, dear."

"There are spies all over England, mind you, but we generally catch them when they attempt to get information *to* the Continent through the mails. These didn't seem to be going through the mails." When she opened her mouth, he added, "And don't ask me how we know that. I can't tell you."

272 *Sabrina Jeffries*

She closed her mouth. She could see that being married to a spy was going to be enormously frustrating.

"Anyway, Sir Lucius tasked my retired uncle with finding out how the information was reaching the French. Uncle Constantine was a good choice because who'd suspect an old man with a bad leg of being with the government?"

"True."

"Using an alias, he managed in six months to find out . . . er . . . some crucial bits, including the fact that there was a connection to your family." When she tensed, he went on hastily. "He kept records and did reports, but probably not as frequently as he should have because he was trying to be cautious." Rafe paused to gaze out the window. "All we know is he had narrowed down his suspects and had found who he thought would be a useful source within the Holtbury household."

Verity caught her breath. Lord, she feared she knew where this was heading.

"He planned to meet with the individual. But if he wrote down who it is, we don't know where that information is. Before we could learn the results of the meeting, he was . . ." Rafe let out a ragged breath. "He was shot outside a tavern in Minehead."

Her mouth dropped open. "Your uncle is *dead*? And you think someone in my family did it? Oh, damn."

He didn't even blink at her bad language. "Let me finish. My uncle isn't dead. He survived the pistol shot, but only because someone found him wandering witlessly outside the tavern and brought him to a doctor. His alias was intact, but unfortunately, that meant no one knew who his family was."

"Good Lord."

"Thankfully, our coachman, who'd driven Uncle Constantine to Minehead for his meeting, went looking for him when he didn't return the next morning. He heard about the wounded stranger, tracked him down, then got Uncle Constantine moved to Castle Wolfford. He also wrote Sir Lucius to send word to me on the Peninsula about what had happened. And I came home."

He met her gaze steadily. "But my uncle isn't the same man he was before. We think the shooter was inexperienced at using a pistol, so the bullet didn't hit Uncle full-on and lacked the force to penetrate the skull. It did receive a glancing blow, however, and he ended up . . . unable to tell any of us what had happened and who had done it." Rafe swallowed convulsively. "All he can do is babble nonsense. Some of it might make sense, but we haven't figured it out so far."

She was torn between outrage that Rafe had suspected her family in this horrible tragedy, and sympathy for what Rafe must have gone through in nearly losing the man most like a father to him. The latter won out. "Oh, Rafe, I am *so* sorry. It must have been awful for you."

Looking embarrassed by her sympathy, he cleared his throat. "Anyway, my uncle has been in that state for eighteen months. I retraced his steps and followed the clues he left behind, hoping to learn who the culprit was. But he hid his full records somewhere secret. And going to your events incognito, following people, and listening in on conversations, only got me so far."

Her stomach knotted. "So you thought courting me would get you further."

"Precisely." He smiled faintly. "But it didn't go as planned."

"Because you had to marry me?" She folded her arms over her stomach.

"Because I ended up liking all of you too much." He leaned forward to seize her hands, and she reluctantly let him hold them. He rubbed them as he continued. "In the months I watched you and your family from afar, I could stay impartial. I eliminated your servants, friends, and distant family members as suspects." His gaze met hers. "But I had to determine if the rest of you were involved."

When she tried to tug her hands free, he gripped them tightly.

"So, what did you decide?" she asked with a defiant air. "When did you eliminate *me* as a suspect?"

"Before I started courting you."

That was hardly reassuring. "You're saying I was just a means to an end, a way to get closer to my family."

"Yes," he admitted. "Then you became a friend, and I don't have many of those. Then a lover. Then my wife." He kissed her hands. "I don't regret what I did—it seemed the best tactic at the time. But I do regret upending your life in the process. You didn't deserve that."

"I certainly did not." She stared down at their joined hands, choosing her words carefully. "Do you suspect my sisters or brothers-in-law? Because if so, that's absurd, and—"

"I think it's your father."

That brought her up short. It made a frightening sort of sense. But it was also appalling. "Look, I know he can be awful, but he would never sell secrets to our enemies."

"I don't believe he's doing that, exactly. I believe he's allowing the spy to send information through his smuggling network."

"You think Papa has a smuggling network," she said, incredulous.

He searched her face. "You didn't know? I figured none of you did, but I wasn't sure until you told me about the River Exe. You wouldn't have done that if you'd been trying to hide his activities. Now I just have to prove I'm right. What you told me was a big help. I now know how his smugglers are reaching the Devon coast from Exmoor

Court without anyone seeing them on the roads. You cleared that up."

"But you don't know for certain Papa has anything to do with that."

"I do, actually. Right before the auction, we intercepted a communication from one of the smugglers to him that made it clear he was in charge of them. But we still didn't know if he was the one providing them with troop information or where the information could be coming from. Hell, the only thing we could prove was he has dealings with the smugglers."

He stiffened. "And the community is so wary of strangers, especially after my uncle asked questions and then got shot and mysteriously disappeared, that it has taken months for me to uncover *that* much. So, if we arrest the smugglers, the spy will merely find someone else to send his missives through. We need to unmask the spy himself. Or herself, although it doesn't seem like the work of a woman to me."

She drew her hands from his. "Because a woman would never be clever enough to be a spy," she said acidly.

He chuckled. "Because a woman wouldn't have access to information about troop movements. Although I did briefly consider your mother a suspect, possibly passing on things she learned from her new husband."

"Are you daft? Mama could never be a spy—she'd have to care about politics and the war and such. None of that would ever interest her."

"After speaking to her, I drew the same conclusion."

She folded her hands primly in her lap. "Oh. Well . . . that was clever of you. Although she can be very manipulative when she wants, especially when it comes to attractive gentlemen." She considered that a moment, then shook her head. "Still, I can't see it. Not Mama."

"Neither can I. I've also considered Major Quinn, since

he keeps taking suspicious leaves of absence. Sir Lucius is looking into that. But no matter who the spy is, your father's smugglers are the ones carrying the information to France."

She gazed out the window, her mind whirling as she tried to take in this new information. "What about Monsieur Beaufort? You don't suspect *him,* do you?"

"No. I would trust him with my life." He grinned. "And he does make the best syllabub I've ever tasted."

"Not to mention, apparently, mussels and onion soup." Releasing a breath, she smiled. "I, too, would trust him with my life."

"And, once again, he has no access to information about troop movements. Although I suppose he could have connections to someone who did. But I know he hates Napoleon. My uncle would never have helped him escape France otherwise."

"Your uncle helped him . . . Good Lord, no wonder you two are such good friends."

"For many, many years."

A heavy silence fell between them. After a few moments, Verity asked, "So what now? Do you have plans for catching Papa?"

"I can't tell you about that, you know," he said, with a troubled expression. "I won't risk your being part of it and thus put you in danger from his compatriots. That's why we're headed to Castle Wolfford. I'll stay long enough to get you settled in and make sure you're comfortable with the staff, but then I must pursue the new avenues you gave me, and that means leaving you."

Her breath caught in her throat. "For how long?"

"I'm not sure. Hopefully, not more than a couple of weeks. I made certain no one except a couple of trusted servants knew my uncle had been shot. I told the others he took a fall and now is ill. My uncle's alias has kept him from harm thus far, so you should be safe at the estate."

"What about you?" she asked anxiously. "What will keep *you* safe?"

"So far, no one has realized I'm doing an investigation. You still haven't told anyone that you suspected me of being your Phantom, have you?"

"No. But . . . but what if they guess? I guessed."

"You didn't guess—you made a series of good deductions. Besides, you're an exception to every rule, sweetheart. No one else will figure it out."

"I hope you're right. I may not like the way you deceived us all, but I don't want you to . . . to . . ." *Die.*

She didn't have to say the word. He clearly knew what she meant. With a ghost of a smile, he grabbed her hand and tugged. "Come over here, my Venus."

She did so, letting him enfold her in his arms.

He brushed a kiss to her head, the top of which was still covered with lace. "You're not angry with me, are you? I wouldn't blame you if you were."

"I'm not sure what I feel. I don't know how to separate what was real between us and what was false."

"I tried to speak the truth whenever I could. But lest you think that was for some noble reason, I confess it was mostly because of my uncle's training. He taught me that the more truth you could put into your lies, the easier it would be to remember them. People always remember the truth. Or at least the truth as they saw it. Memory is faulty."

"So . . . what parts were the truth? Were the compliments and flatteries you always spouted—"

"Truth," he said firmly. "I never lied to you about your attractions. I noticed them before we even met officially."

Something awful occurred to her. She drew back to gaze

at him. "You didn't spy on me while I was sleeping or bathing or anything private like that, did you?"

He laughed. "No. I couldn't have ventured close enough to do *that* without being noticed. Thank God, since your eagle eye would have caught me at once. Besides, I wouldn't have done such a dishonorable thing. Although I'm glad I have the right to do it now."

She lifted an eyebrow. "Just remember, I too have that right."

"Of course. Spy on me asleep all you wish—you will find me a very dull sleeper." He kissed her forehead. "But if you spy on me bathing, you'd best be prepared to join me in the bath."

"Duly noted." She glanced away, not yet ready to consummate their union. She had more questions. "You mentioned your uncle's training. Was everything you said about your regiments and parents and childhood the truth?"

He hesitated. "Yes. I may have left some things out, though—like the fact that Beaufort and I had known each other for years. Couldn't have you plaguing him for information about my profession, you know."

"That makes sense."

She wanted to ask about that day in the bathing machine, whether there had been some spying strategy behind his giving her pleasure. She just wasn't sure she was ready for the answer. It was painful enough to know he'd courted her only to get close to her family.

"Did you really spend all your time as a child reading and wandering the estate alone?" she asked, snuggling up against him.

"I did. As well as learning languages and training to be a soldier."

"And a spy. I assume your uncle did *that* training. Was he a spy, too?"

"I'm honestly not sure. He spent most of his time abroad at various postings. But when he was home, he'd teach me useful things that weren't skills the average person would know—like how to make invisible ink."

"You have to show me that!"

He chuckled. "You were born to be inquisitive, weren't you? Like me."

"Perhaps that's why we get along."

"I prefer to think it's due to my consummate ability as a lover, but—"

"Oh, dear, I see I've already swelled your head."

"Both of them," he said. When she looked at him quizzically, he added with a chuckle, "Anyway, I didn't realize my uncle was training me for the army during my childhood until years later, when he made me his aide-de-camp after I turned sixteen."

"What sorts of things did he have you doing as a child?"

He began to detail a variety of soldierly activities, and before long she was nodding off, lulled into a dreamless sleep by his rumbling voice and the warmth of his body against hers.

Chapter 25

After Verity had been breathing slowly for several minutes, Rafe realized she was asleep. It was probably just as well. He'd seen in her face how exhausted she was, and given what might be awaiting them at home, she needed as much rest as she could get.

He waited until she was truly slumbering, then reached behind his back for her notebook. It rattled him that she'd recognized him so early on in his investigation. He would be more worried if anyone else had, but from what she'd said, nobody noticed a thing except when prodded by her.

Inquisitive wasn't the only word for Verity. Intuitive. Sharp-witted. Observant. Those described her to perfection.

Making sure she was sleeping soundly, he flipped open her notebook and examined what she'd written, hoping to glean information that might help with his investigation. But he found nothing. Damn it to hell. She'd focused entirely on trying to uncover who he was, writing nothing pertinent to his scrutiny of her family.

Still, perhaps Verity's method of recording all her ideas about the Phantom might help him make sense out of Uncle's babbling, too. Uncle's rants about people who sounded like characters from an opera had to be important, or he wouldn't keep repeating them. Rafe should try doing what she had. After all, by ignoring the lack of logic in what she'd observed, she'd come closer than anyone ever had to unmasking Rafe's alter ego. So, he must ignore the lack of logic in his uncle's rants if he wanted to unravel the meaning. Because he didn't have weeks to find the culprit. He needed a shortcut to the truth.

Careful not to wake her, he slid his arm out from around her shoulders. He retrieved her pencil from the floor and found some empty pages in her notebook. Then he wrote down every absurd phrase he could remember his uncle saying.

It took him an hour to bleed his memory dry of them all, then two more hours poring over them. He made acrostics of them, reversed their order, tried them as riddles, anything to hint at what was going on inside his uncle's mind.

They had just pulled away from a coaching inn where they'd changed horses again when Verity asked, "What are you doing?"

He jumped, so absorbed in his work that he hadn't even noticed she'd awakened. She looked adorably confused by her surroundings and eminently luscious. But he wasn't so unthinking a husband as to pounce on her when she'd just roused.

"I'm trying your tactics on my uncle's rants." As she wiped sleep from her eyes, he handed her the notebook. "Sorry. I've made a hash of your tidy observations. I ran out of room and had to write in the margins and such."

Interest sparked in her pleasingly flushed features. "Has it helped you figure out anything?"

"That I'm bad at riddles? Or my uncle is stark-raving mad?" He buried his head in his hands. "Or perhaps *I* am mad for thinking he means anything useful in what he's saying."

"Do you mind if I have a try?" she asked. "I'm generally good at charades."

"Yes, I know," he said acidly. "Your 'nameless' bit was very clever."

She chuckled. "Sorry about that. I didn't even make it up—I stole it. So I shouldn't take credit for it." She glanced down at his scribblings, then looked at him apologetically. "I hate to ask this, but did I see Cook put a basket in the carriage before we left? Because I always think better after eating."

"Of course." He fished out the basket. "Apparently, I'm also bad at feeding my new wife."

"Nonsense. You're simply absorbed in continuing your mission. I'm sure you didn't expect to have to haul a spouse along while you did."

"A spouse I find very entertaining, I might add. I'm delighted to haul you anywhere, my dear." He peered into the basket. "Looks like we've got some nice cheddar sandwiches here, pickles in a crock, a couple of boiled eggs, some pears, a few parkin cakes. And wine."

"I'll take a sandwich and a parkin cake. I like treacle."

"Who doesn't? I'll take the same, along with a boiled egg. And some wine."

As she munched her food, she read through the ranted phrases slowly and methodically. "'Honeybee is honey'? Is that what your uncle actually said or a notation of yours?"

"A notation. He speaks in a sort of odd code. He uses words to mean other words. Honeybee is what he says when he wants honey in his tea. I don't think everything he says stands for other things, just the words that are representing his needs or wants. The people he mentions are like characters from an Italian opera—the old bitch, the boy who's locked up. And he talks about keys most urgently."

"Keys to the room the boy is locked up in?"

"Or the cage? Or a castle or who knows? I can never get him to say what, when, where, who, or how." He ate his

parkin cake first, savoring the treacle and oat mixture. Then
he started on the sandwich.

"These characters don't sound like opera ones to me.
The old bitch could be a witch, don't you think? Those two
words are very similar."

"And similar in meaning, too. Bitch, witch," Rafe said,
waving his sandwich. "It's a cranky old woman. What's the
difference?"

"No, I think he might mean an actual, magical witch,
you know, like in children's stories of fairies and giants and
ogres. He shows such glee in thwarting 'the old bitch' that
she seems larger than life. Especially to the boy."

Rafe frowned as that tickled something in his memory.
"A witch who locked up a boy. A *magical* witch. She has
keys to a . . . to a . . . Oh, God, it's a cage. And I'm a complete idiot."

"What? Why?"

He snatched the notebook from her, thumbing through
until he found what he was searching for. "My uncle said
the clouds 'should be black.' When they're bright, Uncle is
not happy." He stared at her. "I know what he's talking
about. I *know* now!" Grabbing her head, he kissed her
soundly. "You did it!"

"I don't know what I did," she said uncertainly.

"You were right—he's not referencing an opera, but a
fairy tale. I can't remember the title but it involves a brother
and sister."

"Lots of fairy tales do."

"Yes, but this one had hand-painted illustrations. When I
was a boy, my uncle bought a handwritten fairy-tale collection from some elderly woman in Hesse and brought it back
for me. I learned German just to read it."

Her eyes widened. "You learned German just to—"

"That's not the point. If I remember right, there's a

picture of a boy being locked in a cage by a witch holding keys in her hand. They're outside, and overhead are storm clouds—black, not bright. When the clouds are bright, it doesn't fit the picture in the book, so my uncle gets upset by that."

He thought a moment. "The only thing that doesn't fit is the keys. Uncle Constantine always says the *boy* has the keys, not the 'old bitch.'" His pulse quickened. "It's a code. The boy has the keys to Uncle's reports. Uncle Constantine must have put a code in the illustration before he left that night for Minehead. He probably didn't want to risk writing everything down in case he was followed home, and he chose a book he thought only I would think of if he didn't return. We have to get the book."

Verity nodded. "So, where is it?"

"At Castle Wolfford." Scowling, he sat back to eat a bite of his sandwich. "I can't believe I searched every book in Uncle's library, thinking that's where he might have hidden his reports or a code to find them, but it never occurred to me he was talking about a fairy tale. *That* book is kept in the nursery, not the library."

"So, as soon as we arrive, you can look at the book, and you'll know the answer!" She appeared as excited as he felt.

With a grin, he rubbed her arms. "It's as I told you the other night—you're my good luck charm."

"I'd rather be your wife, mundane as that is—less magical, more practical."

"That just means I'll have a practical wife who is also magical, *capisci*?"

She eyed him with suspicion. "I don't know that word."

"It's Italian slang for 'Do you understand?'"

"I understand you're showing off now," she said, obviously fighting a smile.

"I have to," he said with a wink. "Can't have my wife

showing me up, doing all my spy work, you know. It's embarrassing. Especially after she figured out what no one ever has—my true identity."

"I should probably admit that despite all my suspicions, up until the day before we went to A La Ronde, I was confused about whether I had it right."

"What happened at A La Ronde to change that?"

"Not there. In Geoffrey's study the day before. You gave yourself away when you spoke of Eliza playing the harp lute."

"But she does." He stared at her and suddenly realized the huge blunder he'd made. "Bloody hell. She hasn't played in public since I supposedly appeared in Society. Right." How had he managed that mammoth misstep? "To be fair, I was more worried about your safety at that point than I was about my mission."

"I know." She kissed his cheek. "And I'm glad you chose my safety over your mission. Even if it did give you away."

"To you only? Or to you and the rest of your family?"

"Just me. I mentioned the harp lute thing to Eliza, and she said you must have heard about it from one of us. I couldn't argue with that. But I knew you hadn't. I could just tell from the way you said it."

"So, I sort of kept my identity secret almost to the end."

"Exactly!" She patted his hand. "Now, don't you feel better? You're still secretly the Chameleon and the Phantom to everyone."

"Everyone but you."

"I'd never betray your secrets," she said solemnly.

"I know. Especially now that we're married."

She frowned. "That's not why. I didn't set my family straight about you precisely because I wanted to know your game first. I didn't want to mess things up in case what you were doing was important. I still won't say a word to them about the Phantom. Not because you married me, but because I care about you. Because I trust you to do what's right." She seized his hands in hers. "Because . . . because I *love* you, Rafe."

His breath caught in his throat, and for one moment, he felt pure joy. This woman who was more amazing than any woman he'd ever met, *loved* him. No one, not even his uncle, had ever said those words to him.

They thrilled him. And terrified him. Because what if it turned out he was illegitimate and couldn't inherit? Would she stop loving him then? For a woman who seemed deathly afraid of scandal . . .

"You barely know me," he blurted out. "How can you love me?"

"I *do* know you." She kissed his cheek. "I saw your character the night of the auction when you spent so much money for our charity. Then when we talked and later when we kissed. Even when we shared a bed two nights ago." She kissed his other cheek. "And just now, too, when you showed me how much you cared about your uncle and his problems."

Casting him a hesitant smile, she gazed up into his eyes. "How could I not love the man who risked so much to make sure I didn't end up in Lord Minton's hands? The man who—"

He grabbed her head and kissed her hard. He couldn't hear any more of this, or he'd tell her his fears, and she'd learn the truth about him and then she'd hate him for not telling her before they married. Surely, she would.

So, he showed her with his kisses how much it meant to him that she would say such a thing, even if he couldn't quite believe it. He drew her into his arms and took her mouth and tried to convey how much he cared about her.

Then he exulted when she slipped her arms about his waist and gave herself up fully to his kisses.

They kissed a long time, lover to lover, husband to wife, and wife to husband. He'd expected it to seem old hat by now, but it was far from that.

He tore his mouth free to whisper, "I want you, sweetheart. I need you more than you can know, and I've never needed anyone before. Not like this." He reached around to unbutton her gown. "I think it's time we consummate our wedding, don't you?"

She cast a furtive glance to the window. "Aren't you worried someone on the road will see? Or the coachman will hear?"

He choked back a laugh. "First of all, he's not going to hear anything above the thundering of those hooves. And we had a change of horses just before you woke up, so we have a good hour ahead of us before the next one. Fortunately, carriages these days have these things they call 'curtains.'" He drew all of them closed. "Very handy for giving one privacy, I understand."

"You're going to be *that* sort of husband, are you?" she said with a tip of her chin. "A little smug and a lot sarcastic?"

"Don't forget, I'm also good at giving you pleasure." When she softened a fraction, he added, "Make love to me, Verity Venus."

"Doesn't it go the other way around?" she teased.

"It doesn't have to." He unfastened his breeches and smalls, then rose from the seat just enough to pull them down. "Here. I'll show you."

Chapter 26

Verity didn't know what to think when her new husband lifted her skirts to her waist, then pulled her over to straddle him. She'd just bared her heart to him, admitting to being in love with him, and he could only say he *wanted* her.

Then again, her proud, arrogant husband had unbent far enough to say he *needed* her, too. That was a step forward, wasn't it?

She shifted on his thighs, trying to figure out what to do. "This is . . . odd."

"We're merely doing what we did before, but in reverse positions."

"If you say so." Still, straddling him pressed her naked privates against his bare thighs, an action that aroused her inordinately. And him, too, judging from the stiffening of his . . . er . . . prick.

He dragged her gown down and off her arms to expose her undergarments to his piercing gaze, then tugged on the taut ribbons of her corset. "How difficult would it be to get this off?"

"Difficult in a carriage. More importantly, it's hard to get back on. I refuse to arrive at your home looking like a hoyden." When he appeared disappointed, she added, "Fortunately for you, the cups can just be pulled down like this."

And with one quick motion, she unveiled her breasts, covered only by her chemise.

His eyes gleamed at her. "That's much better." He bent to cover one breast with his mouth, sucking hard enough through the linen to send rivulets of pleasure coursing to her nether regions.

As if he could feel that, he widened his legs, and she said, "Rafe, what are you up to?"

"I daresay I'm up to this," he said as he reached down between her thighs. "And rising further up to it by the moment."

"I can see that," she said, hardly able to tear her gaze from his growing prick. She gasped as he fingered her most effectively. "You, sir, are wicked."

"I do try." He kneaded her breast with his other hand. "I love your breasts. They're so pretty and soft."

"And rather small. I-I know men prefer—"

"Men prefer different things, dearest. I happen to like your breasts as they are. Some men like big, some men like small. And some men like breasts of any size. I'll like whatever you have, because they're yours." He tweaked her nipple through the linen, and she gasped. "Now, they're mine, too."

She'd never thought she would enjoy having a man be possessive of her, but his pronouncements were making her burn. She caught his prick in her hand. "And are *you* mine? Is this mine?"

He uttered a shaky breath. "God, yes, always." He moved his hands to her thighs. "Please, sweetheart, rise up on your knees to come down on my prick. Or I swear I will lose my mind with wanting you."

"Come down on . . ." She stared at him. "Oh! How very interesting. Lovemaking in reverse." Kneeling on either side of him, she rose up high enough to move fully over his erect flesh.

"That's it, dearest." He broke out in a sweat. "Now, please, help me in."

"All right," she said warily. "I don't want to hurt you."

A guttural laugh escaped him. "You won't. Just hold on to me, and everything will be fine." He thrust up toward her. "If you'll just take me into you, I'll . . . make it worth your while. I beg you, Verity . . . don't leave me aching for you."

She rather liked the begging and aching. It made her feel like a goddess holding power over a mere mortal. As she inched down on top of him, she relished his "ahh" of satisfaction.

Closing his eyes, he thumbed her nipples and caressed her breasts. "You have to move . . . the way I moved in you."

"Right." Ah, in this position she could control what happened. She held complete sway over his release—and hers—which she liked a *lot*. It served him right after how he'd controlled their courtship to do his spying. "How's this?" she asked as she moved slowly up and down.

"Too . . . slow . . ."

"Did you say you need it slower?" She managed to undulate even slower.

He groaned. "You're going to torture me endlessly . . . aren't you?"

"Endlessly," she said, and grinned.

His eyes slid open to reveal a man in the grip of great need. "Two can use that strategy, minx." He rubbed her with his finger right where they were joined.

"Good Lord," she whispered as she squirmed for more.

"Faster, my sweet temptress . . . and I'll give you . . . anything you want."

"If you insist . . ." she said on a sigh.

It took only moments to find their rhythm, one that stoked his fire while also rousing hers.

"Damn, woman," he muttered, "you really . . . are a goddess. Take me, Venus. Do with me as you will. Ride me to . . . the very end."

"My pleasure," she gasped, then rode him in earnest, feeling like a queen, a siren, and, yes, a goddess. For once, she was in control, and she liked it. She could grow very used to this. To doing this with *him*. Her husband.

"Ah, yes . . . like that, yes . . ." His face lit up with pleasure. "Promise me something, sweetheart?"

"Anything," she breathed.

"Never . . . leave me. No matter . . . what happens."

She was too far gone to question that, her body straining toward release, her heart filling with her need for him. "I would never . . ."

"Promise," he rasped. "Please. Promise."

"I promise. But why on earth would I—"

He cut her off with a kiss that felt more like the acceptance of a vow. So she gave it back to him a hundredfold, showed her love in the way she held him and took him and kept him close in her arms.

She felt him reach his release, which plummeted her into hers, and they quaked together, tangled up in their promises and vows, each needing reassurance and finding it in each other.

Her husband. Hers. She would forever keep him in her heart. Perhaps one day he would keep her in his. Until then, she would give their marriage all she had. Even if in the end, he might break her heart.

Afterward, she lay atop him, treasuring the closeness of being able to make love without worrying that they'd be caught. How lovely to be his wife. To have him be her husband.

Rafe nuzzled her cheek. "You're a born seductress, do you realize that?"

"My husband taught me everything I know about such things," she said with a smile of pure satisfaction. "I am always willing to learn."

"Oh, the things I will teach you . . ." he murmured, and kissed her softly.

It dawned on her why he might have asked her not to leave him. "Are you afraid I'm like Mama? That I'd leave you if . . ."

"No. Not that. I just . . . Forget what I said."

How could she? But this wasn't the time to press him on it, she suspected. "For now, I should probably get off your lap."

He chuckled. "Probably." He pulled the curtains aside to look out. "Definitely. We're about twenty minutes from Castle Wolfford."

"Rafe!" she cried, grabbing for her bodice. "You should have told me sooner. Oh, Lord, I'll never have time to make myself presentable. They'll all guess what we've been doing!"

"I should hope so. We just got married." When she scowled at him for that response, he added hastily, "I'll help you with your clothes."

"Oh, no, you will not." She scooted off him. "You've done quite enough already."

"Not nearly enough," he said teasingly.

She poked him in the chest. "If your staff looks down their noses at me because I resemble a strumpet when we arrive, I will never forgive you."

He caught her hand and kissed it. "They will like you as much as I do or more. Pen has wanted me to get married forever, and you're just the sort of woman she would have picked for me."

"Who's Pen?" she asked warily.

"Mrs. Pennyfeather, my housekeeper and former nursemaid. The nearest thing to a mother I had growing up."

That only prompted her to moan and hurry her movements. "Thank heaven, I didn't let you talk me into removing my corset."

"Thank heaven, indeed," he said. "Because now I can remove it tonight and enjoy the experience all the more."

"So, you're staying with me tonight?" she asked.

Apparently, that reminded him of what they'd been doing *before* they'd made love, for he grew sober. "Yes. My coachman needs a rest, and I do, too. But I'll be leaving in the morning, assuming I can decipher Uncle's code and find his records."

"Then I don't think you'll be removing my corset tonight," she said with a sigh. "You'll be too busy."

"Probably."

To avoid thinking of that, she straightened her gown. "Do I look presentable, at least?"

"You look beautiful. But you *smell* like you've been having intimate relations with your husband."

"Rafe! Do I really?" she said, horrified.

"Fortunately, I got you this as a present." He carefully pulled out a box from beneath the seat. "Don't turn it sideways. It's sealed, but—"

She looked inside to see what appeared to be a bottle held upright by crumpled paper. When she pulled it out, she recognized the shape from ones she'd had before. Unsealing it, she sniffed, and her heart swelled in her chest.

"How did you know?"

He looked a bit sheepish, as if caught doing something naughty. "After I confronted Minton at the apothecary and he ran off, I asked the shopman if your family shopped there, and if you had a favorite scent. He sold me this."

"Oh, Rafe." She dabbed some on her wrists and neck. "You don't know what this means to me."

The tips of his ears turned red. "It means I can deduce what my wife might like," he said gruffly. "I *am* an investigator."

"I know." But it meant to *her* that he'd been thinking of her romantically even before she'd been compromised. That their bathing machine encounter hadn't been just about having his desires satisfied. And neither was their marriage.

He opened the curtains. "Look, we're coming up on Castle Wolfford."

She gazed out, then caught her breath. If a fairy-tale castle ever existed, it was the one before her.

Like the sugar paste castles Monsieur Beaufort excelled at creating for their events, this was dazzling white, with turrets and cupolas and crenellated parapets of the purest Gothic style. The pointed arches of the latticed windows added to the effect.

"That is the most beautiful building I've ever seen," she whispered. "Oh, Rafe, you must love living there."

"I do," he said, a hint of pride in his voice. "But it needs a great deal of work, I'm afraid, to make it comfortable for a family. Uncle Constantine didn't live in it for many years, so it's taking me time to restore it to its original beauty from the 1750s."

"Once you uncover the spy for the French, you'll have more time to give to it. And I can help." She sat up straight. "We should have the wedding dinner here!"

"You'd better wait until you see the state of the kitchen before you contemplate that," he said with a rueful laugh. "We haven't cooked for a crowd in decades."

"Still . . . Monsieur Beaufort cooked here, so he'll know if it's possible, wouldn't he?"

"I suppose he would."

They rode through a gatehouse—a gatehouse, of all things—and into a large courtyard paved with stones. She was taking in everything, delighted by the house's picturesque quality. Then she spotted a tall, thin, middle-aged woman standing there waiting for them.

"That's Pen." Then he frowned. "Why aren't the rest of the staff out here to greet the new mistress of the manor?"

"Perhaps they simply aren't as pleased as you thought they'd be to hear you're married."

"That's not it. Something's wrong." Almost before the carriage stopped, he opened the door and leapt out, pausing only to help her out, too. After the hastiest of introductions, he asked Mrs. Pennyfeather, "What's happened?"

"Oh, sir, I'm sorry to tell you, but it's your uncle. He's sicker than usual. Dr. Leith says he has pneumonia. He doesn't expect him to survive it."

Verity grabbed Rafe's hand, which he squeezed so tightly it broke her heart.

"Why didn't you send me a letter?" he said hoarsely. "I would have come sooner."

"I did. But your letter about the trip to London crossed it in the post, so I knew mine didn't have a hope of reaching you in time."

He nodded. "Take us to him. Is he still in the master bedchamber?"

"No, we moved him downstairs so we could hear him better and keep him warmer." She paused to curtsey to Verity. "I'm so sorry, my lady, that you had to arrive here in the middle of this."

"Nonsense, Mrs. Pennyfeather. I—"

"Call me Pen. Everyone does."

Verity reached out to press the servant's hand. "I wouldn't want to be anywhere but here with my husband right now." Especially since he wore a look of such devastation, she didn't know how he could bear this alone.

Pen escorted them into a drawing room where the staff had brought a bed from somewhere and set it up against one wall. The man lying there looked older and more withered than she'd expected. Even in sleep, he wheezed so horribly that she wanted to gather him up in her arms. She could only imagine how Rafe felt.

Careful not to awaken him, Rafe tugged the covers up that his uncle had fitfully thrown off. "Has he asked for me?" Rafe said.

The housekeeper winced. "I'm sorry, Colonel, but no. When he does rouse, it's only to speak of the boy and the old bitch. He struggles so even to talk that he barely says much of that."

When Rafe stiffened, Verity said softly, "Go. Find the book. You can do little for him here, and I'll sit with him."

"Forgive me, my lady," Pen said, "but I'm sure you would like to refresh yourself and change clothes, so first let your husband show you to the master bedchamber where you'll both be sleeping. It's all been prepared for your arrival. I can sit with the general until you return."

"Since I'm still in my wedding gown," Verity said, "I must admit that would be lovely, thank you."

As they climbed the stairs, Verity took in everything about her new home—the stained glass window in the staircase, the intricately carved balustrade, and the Gothic-style hall furniture on the second floor.

"I've never slept in the master bedchamber," Rafe said. "It feels wrong somehow. But I suppose, with him more comfortable downstairs . . ."

"It was kind of Pen to think of it."

When they entered, their bags had already been deposited there. "If you don't mind," Rafe said, brushing a kiss to Verity's forehead, "I'd like to go—"

"Of course. Pen can always direct me to the nursery if I need you."

"You can trust her. Explain to her about the book." Then he disappeared through the door before she could clarify exactly how much to explain.

Thankfully, she could change gowns herself, so she'd finished everything and was back downstairs in half an hour.

As soon as she entered the drawing room, Pen asked, "What book is your husband looking for?"

"The one that contains the boy and the old bitch. On the journey here, we figured out what General Wolfford has been trying to say."

The housekeeper's face lit up. "That's wonderful! The colonel has been desperate to understand. I hope he's finally got it right."

While Rafe was gone, Verity and Pen talked, with Verity trying to explain how she and Rafe ended up together without also revealing the spying connection. Rafe might trust the woman, but without being sure how much he'd told her, Verity thought it best not to say too much.

Instead, she asked Pen about Rafe as a boy. The stories the good lady told her reinforced the few things Rafe and Monsieur Beaufort had said concerning Rafe's boyhood. Some of them made Verity wish she could have been that mythical girl on the estate who would have set her cap for a sixteen-year-old Rafe. Because he sounded as if he'd been very lonely.

At some point, she heard a commotion in the hall, but when she went out to see what it was, she caught only a glimpse of Rafe's back as he ran up the stairs.

Hours passed and Verity's stomach growled. So Pen insisted on going to cook dinner for her and Rafe, and Verity let her. But she was growing impatient. Had Rafe found the records? Was it who he'd thought? If it had been Papa who'd shot Rafe's uncle, she couldn't bear it.

No, she wouldn't think of that right now.

A short while later, Rafe entered the room, looking triumphant.

"Did you find the information?" she asked.

"I did. Written in invisible ink in the boy's cage were instructions for finding Uncle's reports. The instructions were in code so I had to decipher them, and then find the place where Uncle had hidden the reports—inside the baluster of the nursery stairs. I don't think I would ever have found them on my own. As it was, I had to use my blade to get into the baluster. Then I had to skim the reports."

"Did he say whom he suspected?"

"He did. And I think he's right."

"Who is it?"

Frowning, Rafe seized her hands. "You know I can't tell you, sweetheart."

"Because you don't trust me," she said in a small voice.

"Not true. I merely think that the less you know, the safer you'll be. No one could force you to reveal it if you don't know."

Verity didn't quite believe him. "You're worried I'll warn whoever it is. Because it's someone in my family."

"It's not actually a relative of yours." He kissed her lightly. "You can put your mind to rest on that score."

So, not Papa or Mama or Sarah, thank God. She already knew it wasn't one of her sisters or their spouses. But who did that leave? Perhaps Lord Minton? It wouldn't surprise her. Then again, Rafe could simply be lying to her. She sighed. The stubborn arse refused to trust her that little bit.

Then she noticed he'd changed clothes, too. Now he wore all black, not even a white cravat, as if he expected to be in the dark where he didn't want to be seen.

"You're going after whoever it is right now, aren't you?" she said, her heart dropping into her stomach.

"It will take me time to get there, but yes, I'm leaving now. The moment I found Uncle's reports and realized I would soon know who it was, I sent an express to Sir Lucius to meet me with men to apprehend the suspect. But it will take time for him to receive the express and reach our meeting place. In the meantime, I don't want our quarry to get wind of anything and flee, so I must arrive there as early as possible to keep an eye out in case they try something."

She nodded, unable to trust herself to speak.

He kissed the top of her head. "Don't worry about me. I went to hell and back on the Peninsula and emerged without serious injury."

"There's always a first time," she said. "It's nearly night, a dangerous time to travel. If anything happened to you—"

"Nothing will happen." He chucked her under the chin. "Have a little faith in me, sweetheart. I've done this nearly my whole life. I know what I'm about."

"Take me with you," she whispered. "I could help . . . I could be a lookout or . . . or something."

"As interesting as that sounds, if I had to worry about you, I wouldn't be able to do my work." He nodded toward his uncle. "Besides, I need you here, looking after *him*." He dragged in a harsh breath. "Do what you must to keep him alive until my return, will you? I don't want him dying without knowing he finished his mission."

"I will. I promise."

"Thank you. I'm sorry, but I must go. Until I return, admit no one except the doctor. I've given the men at the gatehouse the same instructions. I'll send you a message when it's done, so you won't worry about me."

She grabbed him by the arms. "Before you leave, you listen to me, Raphael Gabriel Wolfford. You'd better come back to me alive. Because I swear I will follow you into hell to bring you back if you don't."

He smiled faintly. "Leave it to my goddess of a wife to threaten such a Persephone-like strategy," he said, and drew her close for a long, intimate kiss.

Moments later, he was gone.

Soon, Pen came in bearing a tray of food that Verity feared she had little stomach for, although it smelled delicious.

"Where's the colonel?" the woman asked.

"He's gone to . . . to . . . I don't know where." She fought back tears. "He wouldn't tell me, but I know he'll be away a few days."

"He left without eating?" Pen said, incredulous.

Verity nodded. And without saying he loved her, either. But then, she hadn't expected him to. She still wasn't sure he even knew what love was. "Pen, why don't you get some sleep while I sit up with Rafe's uncle? You must be exhausted from doing it alone these past few days."

"Oh, my lady, I could not let you—"

"I promised my husband I'd stay by his uncle's side." She managed a smile. "Please let me keep my promise."

Pen nodded reluctantly. "If you need anything, ring the bell. My room isn't far. I'll hear it. Oh, and try to get him to drink some broth. He needs sustenance."

"I will. And thank you, not just for welcoming me so kindly, but for taking care of Rafe and his uncle all these years. Rafe says you're the closest thing he ever had to a mother."

Pen burst into tears, then blotted her eyes just as quickly.

"Thank you for saying so, my lady. That boy is the closest thing *I* ever had to a son."

"Please go get some sleep," Verity said. "I'll see you in the morning."

With a nod, Pen walked out, leaving Verity with an invalid, a meal, and a pile of worry she wouldn't soon be rid of.

Chapter 27

While reading one of Rafe's many books, Verity dozed off in the comfy chair across from the general. A while later, a sound awakened her and she bolted upright. It wasn't the general—his rhythmical, slow wheezing showed he was still asleep. Perhaps Pen had arisen and was puttering around in the hall?

A glance at the case clock showed it was after eleven p.m., so that was unlikely. Pen had retired only a few hours ago. Besides, she would have come into the drawing room first before going anywhere else.

Verity headed for the hallway and whispered into it, "Pen?"

"Oh, Verity, thank God you're here!" came an entirely unexpected voice, making Verity jump.

It was her stepmother's. But how could Sarah be in Wiltshire?

Verity grew instantly suspicious. "What are you doing here? Why are you creeping about Castle Wolfford at this hour?"

Sarah looked apologetic. "I didn't want to wake anyone. When I told the gatekeepers I was your stepmother, one of them let me in through the gatehouse and then into the house."

That alone didn't sound right, given what Rafe had told her.

Sarah looked furtively around. "My coach is waiting just outside for us."

"For us?" Verity squeaked, her mind racing through possibilities. Rafe had said the spy wasn't her relative. But perhaps he wouldn't have considered Sarah a relative, since she'd married Papa long after Verity left home. "Why, for pity's sake?"

"I hate to tell you this, but your father has had an apoplexy." Sarah dabbed at her eyes with a handkerchief. "The doctor says he'll die very soon, so we must go now if you are to see him before he does. I've come to fetch you home."

A chill ran down Verity's spine. "I saw Papa in London the day before yesterday, and he looked the very picture of health." Certainly, well enough to rant at her and Rafe.

"That may be so, but he came home to Exmoor Court late yesterday in a rage over your impending wedding, which I had written to him about. The doctor thinks that learning of it—and his posting all night from London to get home—is what caused his apoplexy."

"So why did you come fetch *me*? Why leave him?"

"He keeps asking for you. I'm . . . I'm hoping that your presence will convince him to fight to live."

All of that sounded plausible. Papa *had* been in a rage, but would he really ask for *her* if he were dying? And Rafe had said not to let *anyone* in. He'd even instructed the gate-keepers not to do so.

Verity tried to read Sarah's expression to see if she was lying, but the anxiety in her voice and features was exactly what Verity would expect of a woman frantic about her husband's ill health. Sarah *had* already been widowed once, after all. What if Papa really was near death from apoplexy?

"Is Mr. Wolfford here?" Sarah peered into the room behind Verity. "He might wish to come, too."

That gave Verity pause. Sarah wouldn't have asked for Rafe if she'd meant to cause them harm. Rafe could overpower her easily.

Still, Verity decided to be careful. "He went to fetch the doctor."

"For his ill uncle, I suppose. I heard all about the man from your sisters." Before Verity could react, she stepped into the drawing room. Her eyes widened, and she lowered her voice. "Oh, dear, is that General Wolfford? He *sounds* ill."

"He has pneumonia."

"The poor thing." Sarah was being her usual self, yet something seemed off. "I hate to tear you away from him and your new husband, but your father needs you."

"Rafe should be back soon," Verity said hastily. "I can fetch you some tea while we wait—"

"We can't wait. We must leave now. Every moment we delay might be your father's last."

"Very well, then let me go rouse our housekeeper so I can tell her—"

"No, no," Sarah said, "don't wake her. We don't have a minute to lose. Just leave a note. That will suffice."

Sarah's insistence that Verity leave without actually talking to anyone sparked Verity's alarm. Sarah was the one. She was almost certain.

If that were true, then Sarah might also have been the one to shoot General Wolfford. Which meant she might want to finish what she'd started. Verity couldn't even tell if she was armed beneath the voluminous cloak she wore.

What if Verity called out for Pen, and Sarah shot Verity? Or Pen when she came in? Or worse, the general?

Do what you must to keep him alive until my return, will you? I don't want him dying without knowing he finished his mission.

"Fine," she said swiftly. "A note is a good idea." Whatever happened, she had to get Sarah out of here and away from the general and others. Better not to have her do something out of desperation.

Unfortunately, Sarah watched her write it, so she had to repeat Sarah's lie. And after leaving the note on the salver, she had to pretend not to notice that Sarah came after her when they left and simply stole the note.

"We should hurry," Sarah said, practically pushing her out the door. "Your father will be waiting for you."

Until she could find out what was really going on, Verity had to pretend that being rousted out of her new home in the middle of the night was perfectly normal. She needed to figure out what Sarah actually intended, and how she meant to use Verity to get what she wanted. Then Verity would do whatever she could to put a stop to it, at least until Rafe could find her.

It turned out Verity didn't have to pretend for long. When she reached the carriage, there was a burly fellow with cold eyes waiting to help her in. That was most alarming.

"I forgot something," Verity said and turned for the house, but the man didn't let her do more than pivot before he was on her, clapping a beefy hand over her mouth and dragging her to the carriage, where he tossed her unceremoniously inside. Then he jumped in to grab and subdue her while covering her mouth again as Sarah climbed in and they set off.

Verity struggled against him, but it was like kicking and elbowing a sack of iron. Lord Minton's actions had been nothing compared to *this* fellow's manhandling. And who *was* the wretch, anyway? Why had she never seen him among Papa's servants?

As they rode through the gatehouse, she glanced over to see both gatekeepers gagged and bound on the ground. At least that explained how Sarah had managed to get past them. Verity prayed someone found them soon.

They went a mile with the big ox restraining Verity. Then Sarah told him to release her.

"If she yells, no one will hear. This road seems pretty desolate." Fixing her gaze on Verity, Sarah removed her gloves. "When next we stop to change horses, my dear, we'll have to bind and gag you, but otherwise, you might as well be comfortable. After that, we'll only keep the bindings on and just gag you before we stop."

The ox released her, and Verity vaulted across the coach to sit opposite them. She fought to calm herself, to breathe evenly, to not panic. Then she glanced out the window, but Sarah was right. No one would hear her cries here. "What is going on, Sarah? Is Papa well or not?" she asked, playing dumb.

"I regret to tell you, my dear, but as far as I know he's fine and as heartless as usual."

"So . . . so where are we going? And why?"

"I merely need something from your new husband, and once I get it, I'll be out of your hair and his. So you see, there's no point in struggling. Or asking questions."

"If you'd wanted something from *Rafe*," Verity said snidely, "you should have waited for him to return with the doctor."

Sarah narrowed her gaze on her. "If your husband told you he was fetching the doctor, he lied. I've been watching the house since before you two arrived earlier, so I know he's been gone for hours. Fortunately, when I saw him leave, suspiciously dressed in black, I had my other man follow him. I assume he's halfway to Simonsbath or Exmouth by now. No matter where your husband ends up, my man will deliver my message to him anonymously as instructed, then join me at our appointed spot."

Verity struggled not to show her alarm. If a scoundrel like the man across from her was following Rafe . . . "I don't understand," Verity said, determined to keep Sarah talking. "What message? Why would you watch our house or carry me off by force? Why have my husband followed?"

"Your husband is meddling in things he shouldn't."

Verity folded her arms over her stomach and continued to play dumb. "What sort of things?"

"Are you always this nosy?"

Remembering Rafe asking her the same question, she nearly smiled. But the thought of Rafe being followed by a villain prevented that. "Surely you know the answer to that. I am rather famously nosy."

"So am I, actually, when I'm not around your family." Sarah looked her over. "Tell me this. Is your husband as wealthy as I've heard?"

The conversation was starting to irritate her. "Why? Are you planning to rob him? Is that why your blackguard is following him?"

Sarah's eyes narrowed. "Just answer the question."

"I'm not telling you anything until you tell me why you've carried me off by force. Clearly, you're up to no good, although I wouldn't have expected it of you."

"Yes, I know. Everyone assumes I'm under your father's thumb. In a way, I am. Fortunately, I've found a path out from under it."

By selling secrets to the French. "Do tell," Verity said acidly.

Sarah sighed. "I might as well, since you'll know it soon

enough. Your husband is going to give me a fortune to get you back, so I can flee England with my boys."

That wasn't the answer Verity had expected. "You're asking Rafe to pay a ransom for me, so you can run away from Papa?"

Sarah gave a bitter laugh. "And . . . others. If anybody deserves being forced to give me the money, it's your husband."

"Why? What did he do to you?"

"Nothing yet. But it's only a matter of time before he ruins my life."

"You're talking in riddles," Verity said, hoping Sarah might elaborate. Verity wanted to know how much her step-mother knew of Rafe's investigation. If she'd figured out what Rafe knew about *her*.

Verity had several questions she dared not ask for fear Sarah would decide just to kill her and have her man kill Rafe. How had Sarah figured out that the general was the same man who'd been shot in Minehead? What had sent her to Castle Wolfford? Why was she spying for the French? She was English, for pity's sake! Didn't she care about her country? Wasn't she worried about what would happen to her boys if she got caught?

When Sarah continued to sit in silence, Verity added, "You'll hang for kidnapping me when they catch you."

"*If* they catch me." Sarah shrugged. "First, they'd have to know I was the one who did it. And they won't. You'll be kept so deep in Exmoor Park that by the time they follow my instructions to find you, I'll be long gone with my boys and the money."

Well, at least that told Verity two things. Sarah didn't realize that Rafe would instantly guess who'd taken his wife. And Sarah intended to let her live, which was quite a relief. "Where will you go?"

"Far away from here," Sarah said. "You should sleep while you have the chance. We've still got hours before we reach Simonsbath or wherever your husband is headed."

"Good idea." Verity should at least rest, so she'd be prepared for whatever might come—a chance to escape, a threat to her life, more explanations from Sarah. But she doubted she could actually nod off.

She laid her head against the bolster and closed her eyes. That's when something awful occurred to her. *Instructions to find you* could also mean *instructions to find your body*.

Verity gulped. She'd just have to hope Rafe went looking for her *before* he gave Sarah the ransom.

Rafe was being followed. He was almost sure of it now.

Still hours from Simonsbath, he glimpsed again, in the gray light of pre-dawn, the same man he'd noticed in the shadows of three previous coaching inns where Rafe's carriage had stopped to change horses. And when Rafe's coach had driven off from the last inn, he'd noticed the man had mounted his own horse, too.

Of course, the roads had been so dry of late that there was no way to see anything behind them while the carriage was moving, kicking up dust. And anyway, with all the woods they were traveling through, the man was surely keeping to the trees.

But Rafe had a plan to be sure the fellow didn't just happen to be traveling the same road as Rafe. After all, it was possible—this was the most direct route from London to Simonsbath. Fortunately, Rafe knew every inch of it, having traveled it more times than he could count. This route had a particular combination of elements at a spot coming up after the next posting inn that would be perfect for Rafe's uses.

When they halted to change horses, Rafe spoke to his coachman and footmen to explain what he wanted. Then they set off again. Up ahead lay a sharp turn, followed by a smaller road that diverged from the main one to meander through the woods.

As soon as they passed the turn, his coachman slowed the carriage so Rafe could get out. Then the man turned onto the smaller road and traveled just far enough to be hidden from view of the main road. Now, all they had to do was wait. Rafe stood behind a tree, watching the turn until his quarry came around it and halted.

The man clearly couldn't decide whether to head down the small road or continue on the main road. He dismounted to peer up the small road, then knelt to examine the ruts themselves as if hoping something would tell him whether the coach had passed that way.

So he was entirely caught by surprise when Rafe pounced, shoving him onto the ground and holding a blade to the fellow's throat.

Rafe searched the man's pockets and relieved him of a dagger, which he tossed onto the road ahead. "Now, then, sir, why don't you tell me why you've been following me?"

The man's eyes widened. "I-I don't know what you mean, sir."

By that time, Rafe's servants had returned on foot to surround them. One of them picked up the dagger. Fortunately, Rafe and his uncle had always trained their servants like soldiers. They could all at least use a blade, if not a pistol.

"Check his saddlebags," Rafe ordered. "See what you can find."

His coachman dug through them. "He's well-armed, to be sure. Two pistols. Another knife. A flask. Oh, and he's got a letter of some kind in here, judging by the wax seal. No address or stamp, though, and the seal is blank."

"Open it and see what it says," Rafe ordered.

"You can't do that!" the fellow protested, to no avail.

The coachman scanned the letter, then muttered, "Bloody hell. This looks like a note demanding a ransom of *you*, sir."

"What?" Rafe said, dread settling in his chest. "For whom?"

"Lady Verity."

Rafe saw red. He dug his blade into the man's neck just enough to draw blood, then growled, "Tell me who wrote the note and what you were to do with it! You'd better say when and how they're planning to take my wife, or I swear I'll cut your tongue out!"

"I-I ain't saying a word. You'll have to kill me first."

Right. The arse foolishly assumed a gentleman like Rafe wouldn't do so. Little did he know. "I wouldn't be tempting me if I were you," he growled. "Templeford is but a few miles away and the constable is a friend of mine. So you are headed to jail, one way or the other."

The man thrust his chin up belligerently. "You'll hear not a word from me."

Abruptly, Rafe pushed himself to a stand. "Tie him up and we'll haul him to Templeford jail," he told his men. "We have the note he's carrying, so it follows he's in league with the kidnappers, probably just waiting for a chance to leave it in my coach in stealth while they abduct my wife." He looked at his coachman. "What's the sentence for kidnapping, again?"

"I believe it's hanging, sir," the coachman said.

"I believe you're right." Rafe started to walk away as his men lifted the fellow bodily.

"Wait!" the man cried. "Wait! Don't be accusing me of no kidnapping. I only did what I was told, which was just to follow you, and as soon as you settled somewhere, to leave the note without being seen and then go join the others."

"Who gave the orders?" Rafe asked, although there was only one person it could be.

Sarah Harper, the Countess of Holtbury. According to Uncle's coded message, she was who his uncle had been going to meet in Minehead. And she, Rafe was sure, was who'd shot Uncle Constantine.

The man looked frantic. "If I tell you, she'll have me killed."

"If you don't tell me, you'll hang." He stepped up to press the point of his blade to the man's throat. "That's assuming I don't slit your throat right here."

Now the fellow believed him, for he trembled in the footmen's grip. "It was Lord Holtbury's wife."

Rafe's own men were shocked, because Rafe hadn't told even them his suspicions, but Rafe was only surprised she had a lackey as low as this to command. "You're a servant of hers?"

"I do a bit o' work for her husband time to time."

"You're a smuggler."

The man's eyes went wide with alarm. "Didn't say *that*, sir."

"You didn't have to." Rafe considered what the man had just said, and something leapt out at him. "Why would she want you to 'wait until I settled' to give me the note? And why send you out with it before she does the kidnapping?"

Then it dawned on him, and his heart sank. "She's already got Verity. Sarah's behind us on this road, and she doesn't want me to know." As rage slammed into him, he glowered at Sarah's lackey. "I'm right, aren't I?" When the fellow blanched, Rafe repeated, "*Aren't I?*"

"Yes, sir. I was to follow you while she and the other fellow lay in wait until it was safe to take your wife."

Verity had fallen into the hands of a woman who'd shot Uncle in cold blood, and Rafe hadn't been there to protect her. Oh, God! Worse yet, this was his fault. He could have kept her from harm if he'd just told her what he knew. Or had taken her with him.

Rafe tried to reassure himself that the men at the gatehouse would have stopped the villains, but if Sarah had come in the middle of the night and talked her way in, with a scoundrel at her disposal? She could easily have won the encounter, especially if she'd crept inside by stealth. Just the thought of Verity at the mercy of a woman that ruthless made him so sick he wanted to roar his rage to the skies! It took all his will not to slit the throat of Sarah's lackey.

But he couldn't. He mustn't. He had to keep his wits about him, or he wouldn't be able to help her. To get her back alive.

He had to get her back alive. How would he live without Verity?

"Give me a moment," he said, and began pacing. "I have to think."

Somehow Sarah must have figured out that Rafe's uncle was the stranger she'd shot. But why had that made her kidnap Verity? What would that gain her other than temporary funds? She had to know he wouldn't stop hunting her even after he retrieved his wife. And if Sarah was fool enough to kill Verity, he would move heaven and earth to find her. So why—

A grim smile crossed his lips. Sarah still didn't realize that Rafe knew who she was. And he was fairly certain Verity would have the presence of mind not to tell her.

Of course, if she'd gone inside Castle Wolfford . . .

Oh, God, his uncle was surely dead now. Sarah wouldn't have let him live. Rafe just had to pray she let *Verity* live. That was by no means certain. Sarah had to escape with the money, and that meant she had to make sure he never found out she'd been the one to abduct Verity. If her man managed to sneak in without being seen, he could have taken her without her even knowing who her kidnappers were.

Or they might be planning to kill her once they had the money. Damn her to hell. His grief over the loss of his uncle was bad enough, but if he lost Verity . . .

Rafe wouldn't survive *that*. She was as essential to him as air and sun and water. He had to save her, whatever it took.

He turned to his coachman. "Read the ransom letter in full."

The man nodded. "It says, 'Bring two thousand in guineas to the old sawmill on the River Barle. Leave them with the man there, and he'll give you instructions on where to find your wife in Exmoor.'"

Exmoor? Good God, the royal forest covered over 22,000 acres. That was how Sarah meant to gain time to escape. She'd keep him traversing Exmoor in search of Verity while she took a boat down the Barle and the Exe to the coast and then to France on one of those smuggling boats she used for her letters.

Still, why would Sarah pick Exmoor Court's property, where she lived, as the place for him to pay the ransom?

Because she was probably setting up her husband. She would escape and Rafe would go after Holtbury for the kidnapping.

But that meant she must have figured out that Rafe's uncle was the man she'd shot, and thus Rafe was the one hunting for the culprit. He wasn't sure how—no one had known the true nature of his uncle's illness but Rafe, Pen, his coachman, and the doctor, and he'd sworn them to silence—but that didn't matter at present. Because she and Verity were, at most, a few hours behind them, so he had to lay a trap for her. *Now.*

He scowled at his captive. "Much as I would rather see

you hang, you have my word that if you're open and honest with me now—and my wife remains unharmed, you'll suffer transportation at worst and possibly a lesser punishment, depending on what the government decides. Is that agreeable to you?"

"Ain't like I got a choice, is it?" the man grumbled.

"No choice in hell," Rafe said. "Will you help me?"

"S'pose so."

"Good. Where were you to join your friends?"

The fellow swallowed. "At a place we know in Simonsbath."

"Is this the road Sarah planned to take back to Simonsbath?"

"Aye."

Better and better. Not only were they all now traveling the same road, but Sir Lucius should be receiving Rafe's express about now, which had directed him to Simonsbath. Depending on how fast the man traveled and how far ahead of him Sarah was, he and his men might reach Templeford in time for the arrest. Or shortly after.

So all Rafe had to do was set his trap with the help of his constable friend and Rafe's own men, then wait for Sarah to fall into it.

He addressed his men. "Would any of you recognize Sarah's coachman if you saw him? I remember the carriage she came in for the house party, but in case she took a different one, we're better off watching for the coachman or footmen."

"I remember the coachman well," one of his footmen said.

"Well enough to point him out in a carriage courtyard?"

"Oh, most assuredly, sir. We chatted quite a bit about the war. He asked about the general, and I told him how your uncle had been wounded in the war. How his bad leg made it hard for him to ride, but he managed it all the same."

Rafe groaned. "I suppose you told him he walked with a cane."

"Aye. We had a long conversation about the general, and how proud we all are of his army record."

And now Rafe knew how Sarah had deduced that Uncle was the man she'd shot. His own footman had painted the picture for her. Coupled with Rafe's questions about the Exe, that might have been all she'd needed to figure out what Rafe was up to. Perhaps, if Rafe had trusted his *servants*, too, they wouldn't have unwittingly led Sarah to Castle Wolfford.

To Verity. God, he only hoped that Verity could hold on until he got to her.

Until he could tell her how he felt about her. Because he'd been foolish not to tell her before. He loved her. He could see that now, in the face of possibly losing her. Her constant, unflagging concern for him had already begun to nourish and sustain him. All the rest—his fears that she'd leave him, his worries that she'd be upset if he turned out to be illegitimate—were just so much noise, keeping them apart. He was tired of holding her at arm's length to protect his heart.

She *was* his heart. And he couldn't live without that.

Chapter 28

When Verity woke up, it was broad daylight. Why were her wrists and ankles bound, and why was she sitting up in a carriage across from—

Oh.

Everything came back to her, and she groaned. This time yesterday, she'd been getting married. Now she might be about to die.

"I see you're awake," Sarah said, her usual placid expression intact.

Ever since Verity had met Sarah, she had assumed that her stepmother's expression meant Sarah was peaceful and calming. Now Verity knew it reflected an emptiness within. Sarah simply had no soul.

"How long was I asleep?" Verity asked.

"Hours," Sarah said. "I gather you were tired."

Verity must have been if she was able to sleep amidst all this. Then again, it had taken her more than one stop to manage to drift off.

"Once I fall asleep, I sleep heavily," Verity said. "Where are we?"

"We're coming up on Templeford. Do you know it?"

"Not really. I take it we're still headed for Simonsbath?"

"That's where my children are. And I'm not going anywhere without them."

That was Sarah's one saving grace—her love for her children. If it came down to whether Sarah would kill her, Verity would just have to appeal to the mother in her, which held the only remnants of Sarah's soul.

"When we reach Templeford, can I use the necessary?" Verity asked.

"You must think me an utter fool. No, you can't." She pulled something out from under the seat. "Here's a carriage pot. Use that. Or else wait until we're out of town, and you can relieve yourself on the side of the road."

"Fine," Verity grumbled. "What about food? Is there any?"

"Tell me what you want, and I'll have my man here get it for you. I don't need you passing out from hunger before I can get my ransom. Besides, I could use something to eat myself." Sarah straightened her fichu. "You see, my dear? I'm not a cruel woman. I just need to take measures to protect myself, and I intend for your husband to help me with that."

"By taking all his money," Verity said. "So I can starve."

"Do not be absurd. Wolfford is rich. And he would never let you starve, anyway. He's mad for you. If you can't see that, you're less observant than I gave you credit for."

Was he mad for her? Oh, she certainly hoped so. Or at least mad enough to give her children and a home forever and all the love she wanted to give to him.

Tears stung her eyes. He'd better find her. She would never forgive him if he didn't!

"We're approaching the town," Sarah said. "Pardon me, dear, but you'll have to endure the gag again. Don't make a fuss. It's getting tiresome."

So, she didn't. What was the point? The big ox just

manacled her with his arms while Sarah pulled the gag up. They always kept the curtains closed, and no one could hear her muted struggles over the noise and bustle of a regular coaching inn, anyway.

Only this town's inn seemed rather quiet. Almost eerie. Sarah didn't seem to notice, too intent on telling the big ox what food she wanted him to order for them both. But Verity did. Hope rose in her chest.

The ox left the carriage. Apparently, Sarah had finally noticed the quiet, for she reached for the curtain to look out. Verity just reacted, trying to push her own curtain aside with her head just in case someone was doing something in the innyard.

She glimpsed the big ox fighting Rafe and two equally ox-like men when Sarah cried, "Stop that!" and tried to pull her away from the curtain.

Verity just kept struggling, determined to distract Sarah from what was going on outside, kicking at her with her bound legs, wriggling to make more trouble.

But that didn't go as planned when Sarah pulled out a small pistol and aimed it at her. "Be still!" she ordered, though her hand shook.

At that moment, the door swung open, and Rafe appeared. It took him only an instant to assess the situation. Though the blood drained from his face, he spoke calmly. "Lady Holtbury, give me the pistol. The innyard is crawling with armed men waiting for my command. If you shoot my wife, you will hang. Surely, that's not what you want."

Since Verity was gagged, all she could do was cast her stepmother an imploring look.

Sarah looked past Rafe to the men she could apparently now see ranged beyond him. Then, with a shaky breath, she nodded and let Rafe take her weapon from her. He gave it to someone Verity couldn't see, and then grabbed Sarah and hauled her out. Handing her off to two strong fellows, Rafe leaped into the carriage and took Verity in his arms.

In a matter of moments, he had the bindings and gag off her and was examining her with an anguished gaze. "Are you all right? Did she hurt you?"

"No" was all Verity managed to say as she buried her face in his shoulder, so happy to see him that she thought her heart might burst.

"God, I was terrified she would already have . . ."

"I knew you'd come," Verity whispered. "I knew you'd find me somehow."

"I love you," he said, taking her by surprise. "I would have gone to the ends of the earth to find you."

She could only gape at him.

"I know I should have said how I felt about you sooner. I should have done a lot of things, like tell you Sarah was the culprit once I found out and not leave you the moment I learned the truth. I've made many mistakes—I only hope you can forgive them. Because without you, my life would be just one dreary day after the next trying to make it make sense. *You* make everything make sense. And I want you to know—"

She kissed him because *he* made her everything make sense, and she was better at showing it than saying it.

They were still kissing when someone outside the carriage cleared his throat.

Rafe drew back. "I'm sorry, my love, but I have to go to work now."

"Can I come?" she asked.

He broke into a grin. "If you're up to it, I'd like nothing more."

Together they left the carriage.

The throat-clearer turned out to be a constable friend. "We've put the lady and her compatriot in separate, guarded rooms at the jail," he said. "Do you want to wait for Sir Lucius to arrive to question them?"

"Yes. I just received word he's only ten miles behind us, so he should be here within the hour."

After the constable left, she said, "I'm surprised you don't want to go straight home to see your uncle."

Rafe stared at her. "He's still alive? Sarah didn't kill him right there?"

"I think she might have if she hadn't been trying to coax me out the door." She explained how Sarah had tried to trick her, and she hadn't wanted to risk his uncle's life.

"Oh, sweetheart," he said, "I never wanted you to sacrifice yourself for him. Don't misunderstand me—I love him, but he is dying regardless. I would have mourned him, but I wouldn't have survived losing *you*."

That earned him another kiss, this one so public that the people in the innyard who knew what was going on cheered.

Rafe colored to the roots of his hair, which she found vastly amusing.

"I think we need a bit more privacy," he said. "I already arranged for us to have a private dining room, just in case, so you could eat and rest if you wanted."

"That sounds lovely," she said, and let him lead her inside to a small, but neat room equipped with a table and chairs.

After ordering food, Rafe said, "While we're waiting for Sir Lucius, there's something I need to tell you."

The sudden grave tone in his voice alarmed her. "Must you?"

"I don't want to keep it from you any longer. I don't want to keep anything from you ever again." He sighed. "You see, I've been trying to figure out who my mother was. Uncle Constantine was always vague about it, but when I was younger, I just accepted that as his way. Then something peculiar happened while I was working on the Peninsula."

He dragged in a heavy breath. "I recently learned I had a wet nurse who spoke Portuguese and whom Uncle brought back from Brazil. Uncle also spoke very bad Portuguese to me, but she was the one I learned some of it from, apparently, though she died when I was a few years old, so I didn't remember her."

He gripped her hand. "The thing is, on the Peninsula, I learned that Portuguese isn't the same in Portugal as in Brazil. The words my uncle used, the words I vaguely remembered from probably hearing them in childhood from my wet nurse, were Portuguese from Portugal. So, my father couldn't have been in South America when he learned it. He had to have been in Portugal. Which means my mother probably wasn't Brazilian."

Her mind started working through that, considering possibilities.

"That means Uncle lied about it," he went on. "And the only reason I can think of for that is my father must have had a mistress in Portugal before moving to Brazil and having the accident. That means I'm illegitimate. I could never inherit his title if it's found out."

It meant something else entirely to *her*. "Hmm. Is the accident in Brazil documented?"

"Yes. I've seen the death certificate. But only for my father. I can't find one in Uncle's files for my mother."

And Rafe had probably had plenty of time to look during those months he'd been searching for his uncle's reports. But it reinforced her suspicions.

"Rafe," she said softly. "Think. The likelihood of your supposed father changing continents and then dying, shortly after you were born, is slim to none. What's more probable is you are *your supposed uncle's* illegitimate son."

He blinked at her, clearly having never considered that possibility. "But that would mean he lied to me about all of it. That he chose not to claim me."

"Of course he didn't. You would have inherited nothing, possibly not even his property, depending upon how the patent and will are written. The only way he could be sure you'd inherit was to create a fiction where you were legitimate."

Rafe stared past her. "He never even said he loved me. I always wanted him to say it, but—"

"He was probably afraid people would guess the truth." She covered his hand with hers. "But any man who brought a hand-illustrated, handwritten book all the way back from Germany for his young son was showing he loved him." And Rafe learning German just to read it probably showed the general that Rafe loved *him*.

Rafe swallowed convulsively. "There's no way to prove your theory, though. And if the College of Arms researches my lineage and can't prove I'm legitimate—"

"Does it matter that much to you?"

"To me? No." He gazed into her eyes. "But it would drag us both through a scandal, and you have already suffered enough from one. That's why I was . . . too much a coward to tell you before you married me. I was afraid it might matter to *you*. That you would balk at wedding me if you knew."

"Good Lord," she said, squeezing his hand. "I shall try not to be insulted that you would think so little of me. But you are not getting rid of me that easily, sir. Even if you turn out to be an urchin from the far reaches of the earth without a penny to your name, I will still love you."

Sabrina Jeffries

This time when he kissed her, it was long and slow and deep, the kind of kiss that hinted at good things to come.

Then she drew back to look at him. "There is *one* person whom your uncle might have entrusted with the truth."

"Pen?"

"Sir Lucius."

Rafe stiffened. "I can't ask him about it. Once I do, I can't put the genie back in the lamp."

"Do you trust the man so little? Hasn't he held your life and future in his hand for years?"

"Yes, but—"

A knock came at the door. "Think about it," she said swiftly as he rose to answer. "That's all I ask."

It was Sir Lucius, of course. When he tried to draw Rafe from the room and away from her, Rafe merely said, "She's just been kidnapped for this mission, for God's sake. Besides, she knows it all. I trust her with my life and with the safety of my country. So, she stays."

To her surprise, Sir Lucius accepted that. And she didn't think it was wise to point out that she still hadn't had anything to eat.

The two men planned how to question Sarah and agreed that her lackey was inconsequential unless she wouldn't speak to them. Then they drew off a ways to discuss something else in terse whispers.

Apparently, Sir Lucius had another card up his sleeve. "What do you think, Lady Verity? Should we give Lady Holtbury a choice between hanging for treason or serving her country? We could use a spy feeding false information to the French. Do we dare let her continue her activities under my supervision and promise to allow her to go on with her life as she has been? Can we trust her not to go behind our backs?"

"I only know this," Verity said. "She will do anything to

keep her children safe and under her protection. That's the most important thing to her."

"Ah. Motherly love." Sir Lucius smiled. "I can work with that."

When the three of them entered the small room in the jail next door, where Sarah was being kept, the woman gave a start. "Who the devil is *this* fellow?"

Gritting his teeth against the urge to snap at her, Rafe answered, "Your new employer. If you're lucky."

Sarah didn't seem to know what to make of Rafe's reply. She would know soon enough. Rafe had approved Sir Lucius's proposal. He didn't really have a choice, though he didn't like it one bit. The woman had threatened Verity. He wished he could see her hang for that alone.

But he grudgingly admitted it would be better to use her. After all, the mechanics of sharing information with the French were already in place. The War Office might benefit more from *not* hanging her.

"It appears, madam," Sir Lucius said, "that you've been transporting messages to the French through your husband's smuggling network. What the Crown is willing to do is ignore your prior crimes if you will simply start transporting messages written by *us* to the French in the same fashion."

Sarah's eyes widened. "I could keep my children and continue as Osgood's wife?"

"Yes, you could do the former, and you would be *required* to do the latter since the smugglers are the ones facilitating the intelligence-sharing." He leaned forward over the table. "But you'd also be required to reveal who's giving you the information about troops, who your contact in France is, and what information you've provided to them so far, to the extent that you can remember."

"And I want to know how you came to shoot my uncle," Rafe added.

"That, also," Sir Lucius agreed. "You would be sworn to secrecy, too. Even your husband can't know you're working for us."

"That's no problem," Sarah said. "He doesn't know I'm working for the French, either."

That shocked Rafe. "He's not helping you with this?"

She scoffed. "For him, the smuggling is only business— bringing in French brandy and silks to sell or émigrés escaping the war who are willing to pay his price. Then sending out gold guineas and English newspapers, along with the occasional escaped French soldier, for the same high price. He makes money coming and going. He only cares about the money."

"Money that nonetheless feeds our enemies," Rafe pointed out. "So, how do you fit in?"

Sarah shot Rafe a resentful look. "All I did was agree to send letters by Osgood's smugglers. Just . . . occasionally, when my London contact had something important to send. I told the men they were letters to my grandmother in France, and they were happy to take them without Osgood knowing . . . as long as I met their price, which my London contact was more than happy to do."

Sir Lucius was making notes. "And who is your London contact?"

Sarah glanced over at Verity. "Are they really going to let me return to my family?"

"Yes," Verity said grimly. "As long as you deal truthfully with them, and do as they ask."

Then Sarah looked at Sir Lucius. "And if my London contact learns of it somehow, the government will protect me and my children?"

"I swear on my honor as a gentleman," Sir Lucius said. "Assuming you aren't the one to give it away."

"It's better than you deserve," Rafe bit out. "You were going to abandon my wife in the wilderness. Or kill her outright."

"I would never have done that, I swear," Sarah protested. "I meant Verity no harm. I just had to get away before my contact found out. Or you."

Rafe wasn't entirely sure he believed her, but he could never prove her intentions.

"And the name of your contact is?" Sir Lucius prodded her.

Sarah sighed. "Comte de Grignan."

Rafe and Sir Lucius exchanged surprised glances.

"What?" Verity was bold enough to ask.

"No one's ever suspected him of spying," Sir Lucius said. "He's supposedly a royalist. As an aristocrat, he fled the French Revolution. And he's friendly with a number of British officers."

Sarah shrugged. "All I know is that my late husband, the father of my children and a very bad gambler, owed him a fortune in gaming debts. When Osgood started sniffing around me, the Comte told me he would forgive the debt if I would accept Osgood's offer of marriage, so I could use his smugglers to send out a letter or two."

Staring off through the window, she added, "I had no choice. If I didn't do as he said, he said he would have me sent to debtors' prison." She looked at Verity. "I couldn't let the boys grow up in debtors' prison. Surely, you can see that."

Verity nodded, although Rafe suspected that after being Sarah's prisoner for nearly a day, she felt less sympathetic than she looked. But he did know that children died in droves in debtors' prison—her desperation was somewhat understandable.

Somewhat.

"After Osgood and I married," Sarah went on, "I did try to get him to pay the debt to keep me from having to do anything for the Comte, but no matter how I begged, Osgood wouldn't, even though he could afford it." Sarah grimaced. "As the war continued, one letter became two, and two became five, and soon I was regularly ferrying mail for the Comte. It made me terribly uneasy, even though it wasn't hard to do. Until . . ."

"My uncle came along," Rafe said coldly.

Sarah's gaze snapped to him. "I didn't mean to hurt him. When my meeting in the tavern with him turned sour and I realized he suspected *me* of being involved with the spying, I panicked. I walked out, hoping to escape him and go into hiding somewhere. But he caught up to me as I was mounting my horse and grabbed my reins to stop me from leaving. So, I just fired blindly in his direction. To get him away, you see. Instead—"

"You caused an injury that will soon kill him," Verity said.

"Yes." Sarah drew herself up. "I had to protect myself, after all. And my children."

Rafe suspected there was far more to it than Sarah was saying, but he doubted she would ever tell him the full truth about the shooting. Not as long as there was any possibility she could hang for it.

Verity gazed at her. "You never suspected Rafe's uncle of being connected to Rafe?"

"Not until my coachman described the man to me a few days ago." She looked at Rafe. "You'd only been in England a few weeks by then. I assume that's why it took you so long to act upon your uncle's knowledge about Osgood's smugglers."

"Exactly," Rafe said with heavy irony.

When Verity flashed him a long, meaningful look, he stifled a smile. So, his clever wife was still the only one who'd recognized him from disguise to disguise.

"Why didn't Grignan just offer to pay Holtbury to send the letters?" Sir Lucius asked.

"He did," she said with a sniff. "But Osgood drew the line at sending intelligence to our enemies. You'd be surprised how many smugglers refuse to cross that line, especially for a Frenchman."

"Good to know that Papa draws the line at committing treason," Verity said sarcastically. "Apparently smuggling, which is almost as bad, is perfectly fine to his mind, along with refusing to pay his wife's debts."

Rafe fought a laugh.

"And God forbid that Holtbury report Grignan to someone," Sir Lucius added.

"That would have drawn attention to his smugglers and cut off his revenue," Rafe drawled. "We'll have to decide what to do about Holtbury."

At that moment, Verity's stomach growled, and she blushed.

Sir Lucius stood. "We will, indeed. But I think it's long past time you get your wife home and check in on your uncle. I'll join you at Castle Wolfford to retrieve his reports and further discuss how to handle this business." He glanced back at Sarah. "Is your husband expecting you soon?"

"He's actually still in London. So, no."

"Then I will see Rafe and Lady Verity out," Sir Lucius said, "and when I return, we will work out the details of our agreement."

Sarah nodded.

Once they were in the hall, which was deserted, probably at Sir Lucius's order, Sir Lucius held out his hand to Rafe. "Good work, Colonel. I thank you, and your country thanks you. If you ever need anything—"

"Actually, I do." Rafe looked over at his wonderful wife, whose face showed purest love and encouragement, and realized he had to ask about his parents. He would never be satisfied with not knowing.

After drawing them down the hall a little way, he decided the direct approach was best. "Who is my father, really? The man I know as my uncle? Or his younger brother?"

Sir Lucius stared at him a long while, then seemed to come to a decision. "Constantine, of course. His younger brother died alone in Brazil."

Rafe froze. Although he'd thought he was prepared for the answer, he wasn't in the least. His world felt upside down and all akilter.

Then Verity slid her hand in his, and everything righted itself.

"How long have you known?" Rafe asked.

"A few years, ever since you started spying for Wellington. Your uncle—your *father*—came to me and explained that he'd long ago fathered a son by his mistress who'd then died. He agreed to go back to working for the War Office if I would do one thing for him. He wanted legal documents to say his son was his nephew. His legitimate nephew."

Rafe blinked back sudden tears. That his uncle . . . his *father* had gone so far to ensure Rafe's legitimacy meant Constantine had cared far more for Rafe than Rafe had realized, just as Verity had said. The very thought staggered him.

"He'd always said you were," Sir Lucius continued, "but I think he'd begun to realize that the lack of documents would create problems eventually. From what he told me, the wet nurse he'd brought to England from Portugal around the same time his brother died had actually been your mother, who was already dying of consumption. But he'd wanted his son in his life—and her, for as long as she lived, which, sadly, wasn't long."

Sir Lucius smiled faintly. "Your . . . father is a canny fellow, you see. He knew you had become an invaluable asset to the Crown—and that he could still be one—so that was his request. And I arranged it. My superiors agreed to it. Of course, if you ever reveal this to anyone, we will all disavow it, but I can't see why you would."

"I told you he loved you," Verity said softly. "He just couldn't tell you."

Sir Lucius smiled at her. "You have a very perceptive wife, Colonel."

"Trust me, I know," Rafe said, the lump in his throat throttling his words.

"Your father fairly burst with pride every time he spoke of your exploits," Sir Lucius went on. "I'm only sorry I couldn't do more for him."

"What you've done is give *me*—and his heirs—the world," Rafe said. "I think he would appreciate that."

Sir Lucius nodded. "I believe he would. Later, I'll bring the documents we have that 'prove' your lineage. From there, you'll be on your own." He clapped Rafe on the back. "Now, go home and see if you can't spend his last moments with him. As soon as I can get there, I will, but if I don't make it, tell him I'm proud to have been his friend."

"I will," Rafe choked out.

He and Verity walked downstairs in companionable silence. His heart was so full he could hardly speak, anyway.

Just as they were about to leave the jail, the innkeeper from next door came running over with a basket. "The food you ordered, sir!" he cried. "You already paid for it. We tried to keep it warm for you and the missus."

"Thank you," Verity said. "I'll take that, if you please."

As they headed for the carriage, Rafe quipped, "I can see I will always be having to feed you."

"Food is my life," she said blithely. "And you, of course."

"I do hope the last one becomes first in priority one day."

"It already is." She flashed him a minxish smile. "Well, most of the time. At the moment, they're neck and neck."

He laughed all the way to the carriage.

Even though they arrived at the castle exhausted, Verity had never been so happy to see a place in her life. She prayed that Rafe's father was still hanging on.

Pen met them at the door. "Come quickly! The doctor says it may be any time now."

Rafe asked that the doctor give them some privacy, and the man retreated to the dining room where Pen was already laying out food.

Then Rafe went to his father's side. "I'm here," he said softly. "It's Rafe."

"Raphael?" His father opened his rheumy eyes and grabbed Rafe's hand. "Did you . . ." He struggled to breathe. "Did you . . . let the boy out?"

Verity couldn't help it—she started to cry. She barely knew the man, and yet she felt like she knew his soul.

Meanwhile, Rafe looked ashen. "Yes. The boy is out. I found his keys and the old bitch. The sky is black with clouds." He choked up at that point. "And Lady Holtbury is in custody. Sir Lucius is proud to be your friend, he says. You did well . . . Father. I love you. I only wish I'd been there to save you."

His father smiled at him. "You saved me . . . when you were born." And still smiling, he died.

They sat there a long time, grieving and holding each

other. After a while, Rafe went to tell Pen that he'd gone, while Verity continued to sit there with Rafe's father.

She smoothed the hair from his brow, thinking how much he looked like Rafe. "Thank you for all you did for him. It's my turn to look after him now. And I promise I'm up to the task."

"I know you are," Rafe said from the door. "And I hope you'll let me look after you, too, from time to time."

She smiled at him. "Always." Then she rose to go stand at his side.

"I wish he'd had a chance to know you," he said. "He would have liked you a great deal. He always did like irreverent ladies."

"Like father, like son," she murmured, and kissed Rafe's cheek. "I wish I could have told him about the Phantom. He would have been very proud."

Rafe shook his head. "No self-respecting spy is supposed to be unmasked by a lady, you know. He would have been horrified you found me out."

"I don't think so. I believe I've figured out exactly why I found you out."

"Oh?"

"Because the first time I saw you, something inside me knew you were my true love. My soul cried out for you even when I didn't realize it. So, I didn't stop seeing you places until I had you for my own."

With a smile, he drew her into his arms. "I like *that* explanation best of all."

Epilogue

Castle Wolfford
July 1813

Nearly a year after his wedding, Rafe sat in his study, relishing the calm before the chaos of tonight's big dinner as he held his sleeping newborn in his arms. Constantine Lucius Wolfford's eyes were gray like his father's, and his hair was golden and curly like his mother's, but the decidedly pugnacious chin belonged to his grandfather. Pure Constantine.

"He's so adorable when he's asleep," Verity said softly as she entered the room.

"I still can't believe he's ours," Rafe said. "I was terrified you wouldn't survive labor. Your cries—"

"Were normal, according to my sisters."

"If that's normal, I hate to hear what's not."

She chuckled. "You might get another chance, as often as you and I keep—"

"My lord," one of his new footmen said from the doorway. "There's a Sir Lucius Fitzgerald here to see you."

That caught Rafe off guard, but he wasn't about to refuse entrance to his former superior, especially after the man had traveled so far. "Send him in." Rafe looked up at Verity. "Did you invite him?"

"No. Was I supposed to?"

"It's a family gathering, so I wouldn't have expected you to." Rafe had become surprisingly protective of time spent with Verity and the rest. No Phantom would ever invade his domain, not if he had anything to say about it.

Rafe was looking forward to entertaining the whole boisterous crowd at Castle Wolfford for Constantine's christening. In the past year, he'd come to enjoy their company more than expected. They'd swept him up into their messy nonsense, and to his surprise, he had fit right in.

Of course, under the circumstances, Lord and Lady Holtbury were never included in those family activities.

Sir Lucius appeared in the doorway. "I hope I'm not intruding."

"Not at all," Rafe said.

"I'll carry Constantine up to the nursery," Verity told Rafe, and took the lad from him.

"You will not," Sir Lucius said as she started to pass him. "I want to see my namesake." He spent a few moments admiring their son, which gratified Rafe and made Verity beam with pride.

Then he added, "Besides, Lady Wolfford, this news concerns you, too."

His solemn air made Rafe leap up to give her his seat. She took it, concern showing in her pretty face as she cradled their still-napping son. Rafe laid his hand on her shoulder reassuringly. They would face this as they'd faced everything else. Together.

Sir Lucius cleared his throat. "The government has authorized me to tell you both that it intends to bestow on Rafe the title of Earl of Exmoor. Once the war is over, of course. We can't do so as long as the Exploring Officers are still . . . er . . . exploring. It might draw attention to them."

As Rafe and Verity stared at him stunned, he added, "I'm sure you've heard by now about Wellington's enormous victory at the Battle of Vitoria, which could not have happened if Sarah had continued giving intelligence to our enemies. Instead, her false intelligence was most timely in securing victory. Wellington's success has rallied the Prussians, the Russians, and the Austrians to renew their fight against Napoleon. So, the Crown wishes to reward you, Colonel, and this seems the best way to do it."

His wife recognized at once what the offer of a title meant. "Now Rafe doesn't have to fear anyone finding out that he's illegitimate." She reached up to cover his hand. "Because even if the title of Viscount Wolfford is snatched from him, he'll have the earldom as his own, received on his own merits."

Rafe looked down at their son, tears stinging his eyes. His children wouldn't have to worry about the sort of scandal that had tarnished his wife's life and reputation. They could hold their heads high even if it leaked out that Uncle Constantine hadn't been Rafe's uncle but his father.

"We, of course, would prefer that the title of Viscount Wolfford not be snatched from him," Sir Lucius said, "and it goes without saying that we'll have to cite Rafe's service under Wellington as being the thing that gained him the earldom, but . . . yes . . . it will insulate him against harm to the degree my superiors are able to do so."

"Thank you," Rafe choked out, overcome with the knowledge that so many were looking out for him in his father's stead. "My father would have been proud."

Verity rose to shake Sir Lucius's hand with her free hand. "We are so very grateful, sir. I know this means the world to my husband. And our son."

Sir Lucius looked a bit embarrassed. "Thank you, Lady Wolfford. You are too kind."

"You must join us for dinner," Verity went on. "Tonight's meal shall be most memorable."

"I'd be honored," he said. "Though please do remember that you cannot reveal—"

"I know," she said testily at the same time as Rafe said, "She knows."

Sir Lucius laughed. "I see the two of you are of one mind as usual."

"Always." Rafe smiled down at her. "Please, Sir Lucius, do go join the rest of the family in the drawing room. We'll be with you in a moment."

Sir Lucius plucked little Constantine right from Verity's hands. "I shall take this little chap with me to buy my way into everyone's good graces."

Verity stiffened and held out her hands. "Watch how you hold his . . . Take care you don't—"

"I may be a bachelor, dear lady," Sir Lucius said, "but I do have nieces and nephews. Your heir is safe with me, I assure you."

"He'd better be," Rafe drawled, "or you will face the wrath of Venus."

Sir Lucius merely laughed and walked out the door.

"Our son will be fine." Rafe tugged Verity's tense body into his arms. "Sir Lucius merely has to make it down the hall to the drawing room, and four mothers will instantly vie for who gets to take his place."

"A pity that this isn't an Elegant Occasions event," Verity said. "Or there'd be plenty of ladies in there vying with Constantine for Sir Lucius's attention. The man needs a wife, you know."

"He does. Perhaps Elegant Occasions should offer

to find him one. It does seem more popular than ever these days."

"That's partly because of your brilliant suggestion about us taking on only clients we choose. I enjoyed what I did before, but I like it even better now that I'm working with people who need to be helped, and not worrying over how much they can pay."

"When you get the chance to work with anyone, that is." He squeezed her waist. "I appreciate you being willing to miss that last month of the Season because of your confinement. I'm sure our son appreciates it, too."

"I warn you that I'll be making up for it at Diana's Exmouth house party. We have big plans for this one. I think it may even become an annual Elegant Occasions activity, although I'm glad Mama will be too busy to attend this year."

"I'll be there for certain. For one thing, I look forward to seeing you in a bathing costume."

She laughed. "You always like seeing me in a bathing costume. And in my nightdress and pretty much any low-cut evening gown . . ."

"And as naked as Venus. Don't forget that one."

"How could I? These days I can almost tell when that is in your mind."

"Like now, perhaps?" Rafe gave her a lengthy kiss that she eagerly returned. After a few moments, he drew back and sighed. "But at present we should probably join our guests."

"I suppose." Verity brushed lint off his black coat. "Before we do, however, I need to tell you something."

"Oh?" he asked suspiciously. "Does it have anything to do with why tonight will be 'memorable'?"

"It does, actually." She cast him a teasing smile. "Because tonight you get to have your special meal at last."

Thinking of the last time he'd had one, his eyes lit up.

"For pity's sake, not that kind of special meal," Verity

said, blushing. "You'll get that kind later tonight. This is the one you should have received nearly a year ago after bidding so much at the auction. Every dish is designed with you in mind, and that menu is the same for everyone else."

"Then I suppose it's a good thing it's not the other sort of special meal."

With a shake of her head, she pulled free of him to head for the door.

He followed after her. "There won't be any mulligatawny, will there?"

"Good Lord, no. I hate lentils. No husband of mine will ever be served lentils. Besides, according to Monsieur Beaufort, you hate them, too."

Rafe grinned. "He's here already? The christening isn't for three more days."

"He had to cook your meal, of course. Though I had to tear him away from his godson this morning to get him down to the kitchen. He already loves that boy as if he were his own. He swears that Constantine smiled at him, even though the child hasn't even smiled at me yet. I daresay those two will be thick as thieves when our son is older."

"Excellent," Rafe said as they headed down the hall. "Perhaps young Constantine can wheedle out of the man the secret recipe for his delicious Duke's Trifle."

"Don't you trust your wife to do that?"

"It's not in those old recipes of his you found in the kitchen, so, no." He slipped his arm about her waist. "Please tell me it's part of my 'special meal' tonight, the one with actual food, I mean."

"Duke's Trifle is part of both," she said slyly.

Rafe pretended to stagger. "Good God, you're going to stop my heart, woman. Will the one for dinner have extra syllabub on top? He used to put extra on it just for me."

"I know. That's why it's part of both special meals."

He eyed her closely. "You do read minds."

"Only yours, my darling."

It was true. She had an uncanny way of knowing what he was thinking. Meanwhile, she still never ceased to surprise him.

They'd reached the drawing room, but he held her back a moment to stand with him in the doorway, taking in the scene. Constantine was now settled contentedly in Eliza's arms as she sang a soft lullaby to him. Nathaniel was bombarding Sir Lucius with questions about the war, and Diana was showing her mother how to wear some new fichu thing properly.

Geoffrey was dandling Suzette on his knee while Jimmy tried to talk to the babbling one-year-old and Geoffrey's mother tried to instruct him on the proper way to raise a daughter. Meanwhile, Rosie and her husband were examining the drawing room bell pull from the new system Rafe recently had installed throughout Castle Wolfford.

Amidst the mayhem, little Constantine slept on.

Rafe caught his breath to realize that Constantine would never know precisely how lucky he was. He wouldn't have to envy anyone for having a family. He would never wonder if he was loved, or follow a path he did not choose because he was told it was his duty. He would take all of this affection and warmth and support as his due, the fortunate boy.

But Rafe would know. And he would always be aware that he and his son had those precious things because the woman standing beside him had refused to give up on having him for her own. Thanks to her, Rafe had a family at last.

That wasn't even the best part of it. Thanks to Verity, Rafe had a love to last for generations to come.

What more could a man want?

The real question is:
can a man who hates the *ton* ever fall for
a woman whose life revolves around it?

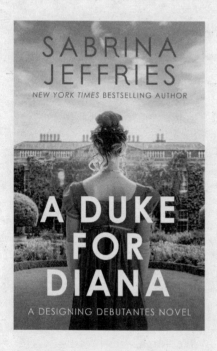

'Synonymous with smart, sexy historical romance'
Booklist

Available now from